BROWSING COLLECTION
14-DAY CHECKOUT
No Holds • No Renewals

KING OF THE
ARMADILLOS

ALSO BY WENDY CHIN-TANNER

POETRY

Anyone Will Tell You

Turn

KING OF THE ARMADILLOS

—

WENDY CHIN-TANNER

FLATIRON
BOOKS
NEW YORK

KING OF THE ARMADILLOS. Copyright © 2023 by Wendy Chin-Tanner. All rights reserved.
Printed in the United States of America. For information, address Flatiron Books,
120 Broadway, New York, NY 10271.

www.flatironbooks.com

Library of Congress Cataloging-in-Publication Data

Names: Chin-Tanner, Wendy, author.
Title: King of the armadillos / Wendy Chin-Tanner.
Description: First edition. | New York : Flatiron Books, 2023.
Identifiers: LCCN 2023003952 | ISBN 9781250843005 (hardcover) |
    ISBN 9781250843012 (ebook)
Subjects: LCGFT: Novels.
Classification: LCC PS3603.H5677 K56 2023 | DDC 813/.6—dc23/eng/20230222
LC record available at https://lccn.loc.gov/2023003952

Our books may be purchased in bulk for promotional, educational, or business use. Please
contact your local bookseller or the Macmillan Corporate and Premium Sales Department at
1-800-221-7945, extension 5442, or by email at MacmillanSpecialMarkets@macmillan.com.

First Edition: 2023

10 9 8 7 6 5 4 3 2 1

For my dad and for Carville,
for without them, I would not be here

AUTHOR'S NOTE

Set in the 1950s, *King of the Armadillos* takes place, in part, at Carville National Leprosarium, a federal institution established as the Louisiana Leper Home, known later as US Marine Hospital #66 and known now as the Gillis W. Long Hansen's Disease Center, which, from 1894 to 1999, was the only inpatient hospital in the continental United States for the treatment of Hansen's disease.

There is perhaps no other disease on earth that carries greater symbolic meaning than leprosy, to the extent that the word has become a universal metaphor for stigma. "Hansen's disease" is the preferred designation for the illness historically known as leprosy, which, along with the word "leper," is considered a slur by Hansen's patients at Carville and beyond. The mission of *The STAR*, the internationally circulated magazine founded and run by Carville patients, was to shine a light on the disease in order to humanize and restore dignity to its sufferers. One of its goals was to disassociate the words "leprosy" and "leper," and, more importantly, their incumbent stigma, stereotypes, and misinformation, from Hansen's disease and Hansen's patients.

While the mission of this book is most certainly in line with that of *The STAR*, readers will find that the words "leper" and "leprosy" nonetheless appear in its pages. This language was chosen mindfully in instances where it is contextually appropriate in a cultural and historical sense, to convey the fear, stigma, and deep emotional charge around the disease. As the daughter of a former Hansen's patient, I have made this choice with the deepest respect for the tenet that words matter and with the intention of carrying on the legacy of illuminating the struggles and triumphs of Carville's remarkable community.

KING OF THE
ARMADILLOS

ONE

At the ticket booth, Victor watched the nurse count out several bills from a crisp white envelope. Pushing them through a slot, she received in return two tickets with the destination, New Orleans, Louisiana, printed in black ink on yellow card stock. She slid them both, along with the remaining cash, into her pocketbook "for safekeeping," she said, and clicked the brass clasp shut.

It was six days after Victor officially became a leper. He stood, rubbing sleep from his eyes under a smoke-smudged mural of the constellations—a crab, a lion, a scorpion, a bull, and a man with his arm raised, ready to club it. A silent ambulance had whisked him uptown through the dark Manhattan streets from Bellevue to Grand Central Terminal so early that the city was still half asleep.

Already standing ramrod straight, Ba drew himself up a millimeter more. His jaw tightened, and Victor could tell his father was bothered by the nurse implying that he couldn't be trusted with the tickets. What did she think he was going to do—run off with them and go to Louisiana himself?

"Let's go," said Ba. He took the lead through the warren of underground tunnels to the departure platform, walking so fast that Victor could barely keep up.

Ducking his head, he pulled down the bill of his Dodgers cap as people rushed past, hoping they wouldn't be able to tell that something was wrong with him. The nurse boarded an empty passenger car marked "Restricted Area: Authorized Personnel Only." Hanging halfway out the door, she gestured for him to hurry, but Victor stayed rooted to the spot, trying to memorize his father's face, the sharp edges of his cheekbones, the sternness of his jaw, as if looking at him for the last time. The doctors said his condition was curable, but who knew if that was true?

"Don't make trouble. I'll send some money soon," Ba said in Toisanese.

"You don't have to," said Victor. They didn't have much to spare, not with the hospital bills they already had to pay, but Ba waved him off.

"Go," he said, "before the train leaves without you."

Victor looked down at his faded tennis shoes before lifting his eyes to see Ba tap his forefinger against the brim of his best gray trilby. In response, Victor stood at attention, chin up, chest out, shoulders back, and stomach in, just like Ba had taught him, and gave a full military salute, noting the twitch of a smile at the corner of Ba's mouth.

"At ease," said Ba in English.

This was an old routine they'd begun on the journey from China to New York when Victor and his brother, Henry, had pretended they were soldiers and Ba was their commanding officer. It seemed to Victor now that the ritual was as much for Ba's sake as it was for his own, not in spite of the fact but because they were both terrified, and they couldn't afford to feel it.

Victor's eyes began to blur. He bit his lip and held back his tears, knowing how much it would disappoint Ba if he cried. He was sure his father wished he were tough and strong like Henry, like boys were supposed to be. He wished he were like that, too.

Turning to the train, he hesitated, wanting suddenly to fling his arms around his father and cling to him, but as passengers jostled one another on the platform, streaming into nearby cars, he trudged up the steps. The nurse was struggling with their bags at the luggage rack. Behind him, the click of a dead bolt made him jump when a porter locked them in from the outside. The train spluttered and puffed, the whistle sang its high, clear note, and by the time Victor and the nurse had settled on seats across from each other at the window, they were moving. Victor pressed his nose against the glass, straining to see the fast-fading platform in case Ba was still standing there waving. But all that was left of him was the back of a man in a gray suit getting smaller and smaller, walking away.

The tunnel swallowed the train as it slid underground, deep beneath the Hudson River, where the dark turned the window into a mirror. In it, staring back at Victor, was a face he didn't quite recognize, with puffy cheeks and eyelids to match. The fingers that touched it looked like sausages whose skins were about to burst. The swelling was always worse in the mornings. At the station, he'd felt monstrous, afraid people would take one look at him and know what he had— what he was—but here with the nurse in their private car, he could relax, even though the door wasn't locked for his comfort, but to keep the public safe from him.

Earlier that summer, when Ba's girlfriend, Ruth, pointed out a small rosy lesion on his chest at the pool, he'd thought it was just a rash, but when it didn't go away, she got worried. Ba agreed to let her take him to a doctor, not their regular one in Chinatown, but a skin specialist in the Bronx. The doctor didn't seem too concerned until more lesions popped up. From the way he peered at those new sores, first through his glasses and then more closely without them, Victor knew something was very wrong. A biopsy was sent off to a lab, and a few days later, Victor was sent to Bellevue, where the doctors gave him the terrible news: he had leprosy. Because he would need aggressive drug treatment and an operation on his nerves, one of the doctors, who'd been a medical officer at Carville, urged Ba to send him to the institution. Ma, who was still in China, had always said he had the hands of a scholar, long-fingered and delicate as birds. What would she say if she saw them now? He could hardly believe these throbbing mitts belonged to him.

It wasn't just the lesions. There were other changes, too. He was getting fevers from out of nowhere, bursts of heat followed by chills. Waves of nausea and fatigue would overcome him when he'd been fine the moment before. And even though his asthma never flared up in the summer, he was having trouble breathing. Things got even stranger when he started to lose the feeling in his arms.

One day, on a delivery run for Ba's laundry, a pin poking through a package of shirts had scraped his skin, and it was only when he saw the blood on his wrist that he knew he was hurt. But he hadn't worried too much about it until his fingers swelled up not long after that, when he woke up one morning to find them tender to the touch, as if they were full of fluid. Rooting around in Ba's sewing kit for a fine-tipped needle, he thought he could relieve the pressure like he did when he popped a pimple or lanced a blister. But when the needle pricked his thumb, a searing sensation tore through his hand.

His body had gone haywire; the contradiction of feeling nothing on his arms while lightning bolts of pain were striking his hands made no sense. How could anyone feel too little and too much at the same time? It made him think he was imagining it. Or that he was going crazy.

As horrified as he was to have leprosy, a part of him was relieved to at least get an explanation for what was happening to him, though as soon as the lab results came in, people began to treat him differently. Ba and Henry got quiet on their visits, their faces solemn and still, while Ruth hovered over him, filling the silence with a constant stream of talk. Even though the doctors told them the disease was rarely contagious, the nurses started to wear gloves in his room, and a couple of times, he caught a group of young men in white coats peeking at him through the glass panel of the door. Inside, he was the same as he'd always been, but with a single test, he'd become something else. A creature so scary and dangerous that he had to be banished from New York to live with other outcasts like him.

The Bible said leprosy came from sin. In China, he once saw a beggar whose face had been covered in a grotesque mask of sores. When he asked Ma about it, she said the gods must have been punishing the man for sleeping with prostitutes or dead people. Victor hadn't slept with anyone, of course, dead or alive. And what kind of sin could he have committed to deserve such a punishment unless it was for not being a Christian? But there were tons of non-Christians in the world and they didn't all have leprosy. The doctors said ninety-five percent of the population was immune and he was just one of the unlucky five percent.

The bathroom door swung open, slamming against the wall. A sewer smell crept up the aisle. Victor wrinkled his nose and watched the nurse get up to shut it, holding on to the seats to steady herself as the train hit a curve. A part of him still couldn't believe he was going to Louisiana to live in a federal institution. He didn't want to leave New York, just like he hadn't wanted to leave China, but after the argument in the hospital a few days ago, it became clear that he didn't have much of a choice.

In his room at Bellevue, Victor had watched Ba sift through the papers and pamphlets in the file the doctor had given them.

"If we take him to the place on Staten Island, he could still live at home. The doctor called it an out . . ." Ba stumbled, groping for the word.

"Outpatient facility," finished Ruth, peering over his shoulder and pointing. "It says here it's for checkups and services after discharge. And for mild cases. You heard the doctor. His case isn't mild. He would have to go to the clinic every day. That's what? Two, three hours on the subway? Plus, he needs an operation."

Victor didn't want to think about surgery, but with the pain in his hands and the numbness in his arms getting worse every day, he knew he'd have to have it one way or another, either here or at Carville. The doctors kept talking to Ruth about Victor's case instead of Ba, who stood close by with his arms folded. And when she wasn't there, they spoke slower and louder, as if they thought he wouldn't be able to understand them otherwise. Victor was about to ask Ruth to explain his treatment plan again when he started to cough.

A glass of water stood sweating on his bedside table. He made an awkward grasp at it and fumbled as pain shot through his fingers, the skin there tight and burning. Rushing over to help, Ruth squeezed past Henry, whose whole body seemed to tense up when her full skirt brushed against his leg. She put the glass in Victor's hand and watched him gulp down the water before wiping his brow with the wet washcloth the nurse had left. Though the window was open, the hot, humid air of New York City in late summer did nothing to cool down the room.

"If he gets the operation here," Ruth continued, tucking a loose, dark curl behind her ear, "you'll have to pay for it yourself. But Carville is run by the government, so everything there is free."

Ba's eyebrows rose at the word "free." He nodded, fanning himself with the file. "I *was* thinking about taking out a loan, but the interest is very high. And we have to be careful or people will find out."

Victor frowned. He didn't know how much everything would cost, but the other day, he'd overheard Ba whispering to Ruth about his hospital bills. If Ba was already having trouble with those, how would he be able to send Ma and Grandmother their monthly stipend in China with the added expense of the surgery?

"What people?" Ruth pursed her lips. "Who cares what they think?"

"Ridiculous," muttered Henry in Toisanese. His eyes narrowed like a hawk's, putting Victor on edge.

"English," warned Ba. His nearly identical features echoed his elder son's.

"Maybe your mistress should learn to speak Chinese." Henry cut his eyes at Ruth and switched to English. "If people find out, we'll all pay for it, not just Victor."

"This kind of sickness makes people afraid," agreed Ba. "If they know he has it, they will blame the whole family, maybe say all the Chinese have it."

"He'll have to leave school," said Henry.

"Not if he goes to Carville. There's a school for patients," Ruth said, plucking one of the pamphlets out of the stack and showing him a picture of a small group of surprisingly healthy-looking teenagers smiling in a classroom. "See? Plenty of kids his age, too."

"What's the point if they're locking him up for the rest of high school anyway?" said Henry.

Victor shot Ruth a worried look. That wasn't what the doctors had said.

"That's not going to happen," she snapped at Henry before catching Victor's eye. "You're going to be cured. The doctors said some people get well in just a few months. If you go to Carville, they'll fix you right up and you'll be home before you know it." She tossed the pamphlet on the pile of papers Ba was still holding and, turning back to Henry, she enunciated every word: "Do not scare your brother like that."

Henry's chest puffed up like a rooster's, but before he could speak, Ba jumped in. "If people find out about that place, he will never get a job, never get married, even if they let him come home. And we will have problems, too."

By reflex, Victor's fingers grasped the rough cotton sheet covering his legs and immediately let go from the sting. Henry made it sound like his future depended on keeping his illness a secret. Was leprosy really so horrible that it would ruin his life whether or not he got well? And what would it do to his family?

"Come on, Sam," Ruth scoffed. "It's 1954, not 1354."

"You don't understand. Customers would stop coming to the laundry. We could lose everything."

Ruth shook her head. "I think you're making too much of this."

"Then why are they shipping him off to a leper colony?" Henry interrupted.

"Wait a second," Victor began, but no one was listening to him.

"It's a residential facility," Ruth corrected Henry. "An institution for Hansen's disease. The best in the country."

"Who cares what they call it?" said Henry. "None of this would have happened if it weren't for you."

"Excuse me?" Ruth's voice went loud and high as beads of sweat popped out all along her hairline. Her eyes darted over to Ba and widened.

"Henry," said Ba, but Henry was on a roll.

"You wouldn't let Victor see our own doctor. You took him to some jerk who just sent him to the hospital. And now the government wants to lock him up someplace we've never heard of. It's a thousand miles away, in the South, where they hate us even more than they do here. You say it's so great, but how do you know?" Henry cocked his head to the side.

"Listen," she said, "this isn't a cough or a sprained ankle. Chinese herbs can't cure leprosy. And Dr. Wu doesn't even have a medical license. Believe me, I checked."

"This isn't your family," Henry barked. Tiny specks of spit flew through the air. "Why don't you mind your own business?"

The color drained from Ruth's face, her bloodred lipstick making it look extra pale. She brought her hand to her throat as if to protect herself, but she didn't seem to know how to respond. None of them did. Henry's feelings about Ruth were no secret, but Victor had never heard him talk to her like this.

A car honked, followed by the whooshing sound of traffic, and Victor, who hadn't been able to get a word in edgewise, was fed up. None of this would've been happening if it weren't for him, but nobody would admit it.

"Doesn't anyone care what I think?" Victor said, his skin hot and tight on his face. They all turned to him now, looking down at him in the bed.

"You're just a kid," said Henry.

"I'm almost sixteen. And it's my life."

"Of course we care," said Ruth.

"You shouldn't even be here," Henry snapped. "You're not our mother."

"Enough," said Ba, silencing Henry. He turned to Victor. "What do you want to do?"

Ba had never asked him that question before. All he'd ever done was give him orders and expect him to obey. Victor was eight when Ba had taken him and Henry from China, leaving Ma and Grandmother behind, and it hadn't exactly been easy for him to settle in. Now that New York finally felt like home, he was about to get uprooted again, and this time, he wouldn't have any family with him. At Carville, he would be alone.

Victor tried to imagine what it would be like in the Bronx if he couldn't go to school or make deliveries for the laundry, and could only go back and forth to the clinic on Staten Island. He pictured himself watching other people living their lives through the windows of subways and buses while he, the family secret, would be kept in hiding. If he stayed, Ba would have to find a way to pay his medical bills and figure out how to get him to his appointments. Plus, the family's business and reputation would be in danger. The problem wasn't just that he was sick with something hard to treat like cancer or even something contagious like polio or TB. People would have felt sorry for him if he had any of those things, but once they knew he had leprosy, even Henry and Ba seemed to flinch whenever they saw him. The very idea of it disgusted people so much that it made Victor feel like he was disgusting, too. In a way, the shame of that was worse than what the disease was doing to his body, especially since he'd become such a burden.

"I'll go," Victor said.

Ba nodded once, his lips compressed in what looked to Victor like relief.

Now, with his family's words swirling in his head as the train burst into the open air of New Jersey, Victor was beginning to wonder if he'd made a terrible mistake. He gripped the armrest hard, sending a bright surge of pain through his hands. At Carville, his operation and treatment would be free, but he wasn't convinced they would work. Maybe they'd slice him open and he'd lose his hands anyway, or maybe he'd die on the operating table. Even if he lived, he might not get well—and then what kind of life would he have? He'd be locked up in that place until he died. In the half-light of early dawn, Victor watched the telephone poles and tenements whiz by. The sheets flapping on the clotheslines like handkerchiefs waved goodbye.

Pylons and factory chimneys gave way to creeks and streams. The soil approaching the Virginias grew redder and redder with clay. At every stop, passengers got off and on, walking past Victor's window. He noticed the same sequence of expressions move across their faces as soon as they read the "Restricted Area" sign on his door. Their eyebrows would go down, then up, then knit together before they picked up their pace. No one could have prepared him for these reactions before he left the hospital, just like no one in China could have prepared him for the kids in the Bronx who made slant eyes at him. It was one thing to be told that people might hate him for where his family came from, but it was another thing to feel it.

With a swollen forefinger, he tapped on the stainless steel ashtray—

Morse code, SOS—releasing the odor of stale smoke into his nose. He sneezed, and the nurse looked up from her book, *Murder on the Orient Express*.

"Bless you," she said and went right back to reading.

She wasn't much of a talker, or at least she wasn't interested in talking to him. He had a bunch of questions, like whether she'd taken patients to Carville before and if she knew what it was like, but since she didn't ask him much besides how he felt and what he wanted to eat from the dining car, he kept his thoughts to himself. He wished he could walk around, maybe see if the train had an observation car like the one he'd taken from San Francisco to New York when he first got to America. For days, he'd gazed up at the sky, the novelty distracting him from missing Ma as the black steam engine chugged through desert mesas, flat green plains, and circular tunnels cut out of mountains. Ba had pointed out these tunnels were made by Chinese workers almost a hundred years before. Victor tapped on the ashtray again, harder this time, mimicking the rhythm of the wheels on the tracks. The resulting sting in his finger made him stop thinking, at least for a moment, about anything else.

By the time the main lights were lowered, the nurse was asleep, snoring lightly, with her mouth open and her temple trembling against the windowpane. Victor tried reading the Lash LaRue comic Ruth had bought him for the trip, but holding the book hurt. Underneath the single overhead light, the letters in the word balloons kept blurring. He stuffed the comic book in his backpack, turned off the light, and stared out into the twinkling dark, letting himself be lulled by the gentle patterns of the night. With a yawn, he stretched the bony length of his body along the seats and ignored the dull throbbing in his hands.

The train traveled south through the night and into the following day until the conductor hollered, "Last stop, Union Station, New Orleans!" as the wheels screeched to a halt. Victor's stomach lurched. The taste of the roast beef sandwich he'd eaten for lunch rose up his throat. Just then, the porter unbolted the door, sending a flood of adrenaline through his body.

"Quickly, now. Don't be nervous," said the nurse.

"I'm not," Victor muttered, lying.

Of course he was nervous, but he wasn't about to admit that to her. With a shaky hand, he tugged down his cap, gritted his teeth against the pain as he grabbed his backpack and suitcase, and lumbered down the steps. On the outdoor platform, he breathed in the warmth and moisture of the air, the nutty smell of coffee from the station café.

"Shouldn't we go inside?"

"Of course not." The nurse gave him a cockeyed look as if he ought to know better. "Quarantine is strict in Louisiana. Someone's going to meet us here." She dropped her bag on the concrete and Victor did the same.

After a moment, a lanky, dark-skinned man dressed in a chauffeur's uniform came striding toward them with a clipboard.

"Afternoon. You the folks from Bellevue?"

"We certainly are," said the nurse as the man handed her a pen.

Victor bent to grab his own suitcase, but she held up her hand.

"Let the boy take the bags," she said. The chauffeur looked at least thirty.

He cast his eyes down, tucked the clipboard under his arm, and plucked their luggage from the ground with ease. Leading them to a pale green station wagon, he slid the bags in the trunk and opened the passenger-side door painted with the words "United States Public Health Service Hospital, Carville, Louisiana." Victor climbed into the backseat and lowered the window, taking in the scent of fried dough and flowers as they drove past streetcars, pastel-colored houses, and balconies overflowing with plants on their way out of the city.

After the suburbs, they turned onto a smaller road dotted with tin-roofed shacks and rusted pickup trucks. In an open field, a boy with no shoes rode bareback on a scrawny, piebald horse. A gas station attendant leaned against a pump, smoking a cigarette. Staring out at the low, unfamiliar country, Victor thought of his mother and realized that, for the first time in his life, she had no idea where he was.

Shortly before he set sail for America, when she'd found him crying in the garden shed, she'd gathered him in her arms and soothed him with a promise. She would be with him, she'd said, for every mile of the thousands he would travel because she knew where he was going.

When he wanted to be with her, all he had to do was picture her at home, and in this way, they could be together, each holding one end of the thread connecting them through their imaginations. Her words had made him feel, if not entirely safe, then loved through the sorrow and seasickness of his journey, and the homesickness that came after. Later, in the letters they wrote to each other, Ma would always ask him to describe his surroundings—the laundry, the apartment, his school, their neighborhood, the city—and though the sharpness of missing her had dulled over time, the ritual still comforted him.

But how could he tell her where he was going now that Henry had forbidden him? It would kill her to know, Henry had said, cornering him at the hospital and making him promise to pretend that he was perfectly fine in New York when he wrote to Ma. Of course he'd kept secrets from her before—the biggest one being Ba's relationship with Ruth—but lying about his illness and where he was seemed different. It didn't feel right, but if he defied Henry and something bad happened to Ma, he'd never forgive himself. So he'd agreed. But now he couldn't shake the thought, childish as it was, that she wouldn't be able to watch over him anymore. She wouldn't be with him at Carville to keep him safe through whatever came next because the thread between them had been cut with lies.

Thinking about this, Victor's whole body seemed to flush. A fresh layer of sweat bathed his skin. Even with the window open, he felt like he wasn't getting enough air. He glanced at the nurse, who'd nodded off, her head drooping like a tulip and bobbing as the car drove over the uneven surface of the dirt road. Bits of gravel pinged the underside of the station wagon, but still, she didn't wake up. He searched his pockets for his inhaler and realized he'd left it in his backpack, buried in the trunk under his suitcase and the nurse's bag. If he could just calm down, maybe he wouldn't need it.

Sticking his face out the window, Victor tried not to breathe in the road dust. To his right was a high metal fence topped with a loose braid of barbed wire. On the left, a low, hilly area with overgrown shrubs and trees. They were going slow enough now that if he wanted to, he could jump out of the car and run. Given his condition, though, the driver would probably catch him before he got too far. And even if he didn't get caught, where would he go? They'd only passed one little town.

"Almost there," said the driver, glancing at him in the rearview mirror. "You all right?"

Victor nodded, his throat too tight and dry to talk. He turned to the window again.

"The Mississippi's on the other side of that levee," the driver added.

The slight summer fetidness of the water hit Victor's nostrils along with a spicy, evergreen smell. His breath dropped down to his belly, slowed.

Above the tree line, a pair of birds scanned the river for fish, tracing slow circles in the air, black against bright blue. He'd forgotten that the sky could be like this, so broad and bare, unbroken by buildings or telephone poles. He hadn't seen anything like it since he left China, when, crossing the ocean, there'd been nothing but air above water as far as his eyes could see. It hadn't occurred to him until just now that he could miss such a thing. With a light, experimental touch, he traced the metal of the door handle, his skin registering heat.

The nurse shook herself awake as they arrived at a set of iron gates. A guard scurried to open them and the station wagon drove toward a big white mansion. Columns like the ones in front of the courthouse in Manhattan studded the upstairs balcony, where metal railings bent in swoops and curlicues. Neatly mown lawns and flowering bushes surrounded the mansion, and just like in the brochure they'd given him at Bellevue, Victor could see an avenue of trees, old and twisted and draped with moss, leading to a broad white building that looked like a hospital. It had columns, too, but was simple, more modern than the mansion in the front. He spotted some smaller buildings in the distance. Maybe those were the dorms. Looking out at the grounds in that direction, he saw so much green that he could barely make out the fence he'd seen from the road.

"The administration building's right there," said the nurse, pointing out the window. "They call it the Big House. Used to be a plantation. They should have all your records. I'll send your father a telegram to let him know you're here."

"Thanks," Victor said, taking a deep breath.

The chauffeur opened the car door for him.

"Good luck," he said.

Victor met his eye and nodded as he set his feet on the ground. His body still felt the motion of the station wagon. He unclenched his jaw.

Waiting in the shade on the front porch was a nun with a kind, delicately lined face. Her dark blue robe had a heavy-looking skirt that reached the ground and a white collar over her chest. Instead of the simple black-and-white headdress Victor was used to seeing on the nuns in New York, she was wearing a stiff white headpiece folded around her face in two big arcs like a seagull's outstretched wings.

"Welcome to our home," she said, consulting the folder in her hand. "You must be Victor."

"Yes, ma'am." He wondered how she could stand the heat covered in all that fabric.

"You may call me Sister Laura. What name will you be taking?"

"What?"

"Don't say 'what,' say 'pardon,'" she corrected. "It's more polite. Some of our patients choose to go by different names here, on account of their families, but it's up to you."

Victor frowned. He didn't want to cause any more trouble, but New York was far enough away that he didn't think it would matter.

"I'd like to keep my own name," he said.

"As you wish." Sister Laura placed a warm, dry hand on his shoulder, surprising him. She was the first person outside his family to touch him without gloves since he was diagnosed.

"This way," she said, and gestured for him to follow her. She seemed to glide as if she were on wheels, her skirt so long that he couldn't see her feet.

"Are you taking me to my room?" After the long trip, he was a bit light-headed and his whole body ached.

"In time, when you're up to it. But first you'll need to be admitted, and I expect you'll stay at the infirmary for a spell."

Victor wasn't familiar with the term "infirmary," but since "infirm" meant sick, he figured it was what they called the hospital.

"Look, Ma, no fingers!" a raspy voice bellowed. An old Chinese-looking man rounded the corner in a wheelchair, cranking furiously with a pair of oddly crooked hands on pedals attached to the wheels with bicycle chains. With one eye almost entirely fused shut and a single leg, he was like a real-life Long John Silver barreling toward them so fast that they had to leap apart to get out of his way.

"Mr. Wang, honestly!" Sister Laura called after him as he pedaled off, laughing, and to Victor, she said, "Don't mind him. That's just his idea of a joke."

"But what's wrong with him?" Victor said, unable to keep the horror out of his voice.

"Nothing you have to worry about. He went without treatment for so long that some of his nerves were destroyed. Doesn't stop him from getting around, though, as you can see."

Victor managed a small, polite smile as they continued to walk, but in his pockets, he balled his hands into fists. Even though it hurt to close them all the way, he clenched and unclenched them while he still could.

TWO

Sam stared at the curls of cream swirling in his coffee cup while Ruth, wild-haired in her blue satin robe, prepared toast in the tiny kitchen of his studio apartment behind the laundry. It was the morning after Victor's departure, the first time they'd spent the whole night together at his place since the boys arrived from China, but neither of them had slept well.

"I wonder when he'll get there," Ruth said, setting butter and orange marmalade on the table.

Sam shrugged without looking up, imagining his son arriving at that strange place alone. He'd wanted to take him there himself, to make sure he was safe and that the institution was, at the very least, as the doctors had described it. Ruth had wanted to go, too, but Carville's director allowed only hospital-appointed escorts to travel with patients from out of state. No family. What kind of rule was that? He should have taken it as a bad sign.

"How was he at the station?" Ruth persisted.

Sam shrugged again as she sat down with the toast, knowing his silence would annoy her but not caring.

"Did he seem scared? Nervous?"

"I don't know," he said, finally. "And I don't know how he is now either."

Ruth gave him a quizzical look. "What are you going to tell Mei Wan?"

"I don't know yet," said Sam, though he had no intention of telling her anything. He'd overheard Henry warning Victor to keep his diagnosis a secret from their mother, and he hadn't put a stop to it. If Mei Wan knew what was going on, she would probably blame him.

"Well, I'm sure they're taking good care of him." Ruth spread a pat of butter on a slice of toast.

So she didn't want to fight. But what if he did? It had started to sink in while he lay awake in the night that Victor had never been without him or his mother before, and he had no idea what lay ahead for his child. The doctors said the surgery had to be soon, but they didn't give a prognosis, and they were vague about how long the treatment would take. Maybe a few months, they said, or maybe more. How much more, they didn't say.

"It was a mistake to let him go," he said. He took a sip of coffee and grimaced. Ruth always made it too strong.

"Come on." She put down her toast. "You sound like Henry."

"Maybe he's right," Sam said, watching Ruth narrow her eyes. "You know what governments do to people."

"Not in America."

"Depends on who you are. He is a Chinese boy with leprosy. You think they care about him? Best care, all free, they said. I should have known it was a trick. And you took their side."

"Yeah, I get it," she said, her voice dripping with sarcasm. "You don't trust the hospital. You don't trust the government. Everybody's against you. Even me, right?"

"You always think you know best. You never think, even for one moment, that you could be wrong. And now I don't know when I will see my son again."

Sam expected Ruth to yell or at least contradict him, but she didn't. Without a word, she plucked her napkin off her lap, folded it into quarters, and laid it beside her plate. The chair squealed as she stood up, her eyes filling with tears. She turned on her heel and stalked through the curtain separating the living area from the shop floor.

"What are you doing?" he said, following her.

"Leaving."

"Like that?" He pointed at her nightclothes.

"Why not?" She crossed her arms and glared at him. "You've been horrible to me all morning. Isn't this what you want?"

Sam stood perfectly still, breathing slowly through his nose, attempting to control his contradictory emotions. Seeing her with her cheeks flushed, the morning light setting off sparks of amber in her eyes, he felt his anger start to melt. She was so proud and unselfconscious, with so much fire in her belly. Though she wouldn't have been considered a beauty in China or Hollywood, her very bones spoke to the marrow in his, and as it so often happened, he felt himself being pulled to her with a bewildering force.

This was how it was between them, even after all these years. When they were alone together, his fingers sought her touch, her skin so pale it seemed to create its own light in the dim behind the drawn curtains. They were the same age, thirty-nine now, and Sam teased her gently about it, tracing the fine webbing of lines beginning to appear around her eyes, especially when she smiled. Crow's-feet, she said they were called, tapping them with the tips of her red, manicured nails. An apt name since her thick black brows arched up and out like a pair of crow's wings taking flight. Her figure was neat and trim, and in the high-heeled shoes she wore to her job as a secretary at a Manhattan accounting firm, she reached his height, five foot six exactly.

The sight of Ruth dressed up in her work clothes never failed to arouse him—her tidy pencil-skirted suits in a variety of plaids, blue, gray, brown, and green; her smart little hats in an array of complementary colors; her nylon stockings with seams he couldn't help but follow with his eyes, imagining where her garters held them taut at the tops of her thighs. In fact, it was on account of her clothes that they'd met eight years ago—when she moved into the six-story apartment building across the street and came in to do her laundry.

The shop bell had rung on a slow Tuesday afternoon while Sam was organizing the laundry tickets behind the counter with his back to the door.

"One moment, please," he said.

"Sure," said a woman whose voice he didn't recognize. That was unusual—he didn't get a lot of new customers.

The radio was playing Ella Fitzgerald, and the woman began to sing along, not entirely in tune.

"I love this song," she said, "don't you?"

"Yes, it is very nice."

Sam turned around to face a petite, dark-haired figure in a navy blue swing coat, struggling with an enormous pile of suits. When he reached out to take it from her, his hand grazed her wrist and a shock of static electricity stung them both. They laughed, and he noticed with pleasure how generous her laughter was, how her whole face seemed to open up with it, showing small white teeth whose incisors were charmingly crooked.

"Shocking," he said in what he hoped was a droll voice. He was rewarded with another full-throated laugh.

"I know this is a lot, but I just moved and . . ." She gestured at her suits.

"No problem at all, Mrs. . . ." Sam let the word hang in the air and began to sort through her clothes as the scent of a perfume he remembered from France wafted up from the fabric.

"It's Miss, actually. Miroshnik, but you can call me Ruth. And you are?" She extended a hand whose fine, dark blue glove looked almost black in the weak winter light.

"Sam Chin. I am very pleased to make your acquaintance, Miss Ruth Miroshnik," he said, taking care to pronounce the many consonants of her name correctly.

"You speak English so well, Mr. Sam Chin." She had a smile in her voice and held on to his hand for a touch longer than mere politeness required. "Where did you study?"

"Here." He gestured around his small but extremely tidy shop before producing a well-worn copy of *Great Expectations* from behind the counter. He might not have had a formal education, but nothing stopped him from reading, not just novels but history and science books, too.

"Oh . . ." Her voice trailed off and, blushing, she began to babble. "You must think I'm crazy, cleaning so many clothes at once, but I'm just terrified of moths. They were Public Enemy Number One at my uncle's fabric store."

"It's fine," Sam said. He rubbed the wool of a winter weight jacket between his fingers.

The song on the radio changed to "I'll Be Seeing You" by Billie Holiday. As he concentrated on counting her items, Ruth hummed along.

"Everything will be ready on Friday," he said, handing her a ticket.

"Wonderful. I'm looking forward to coming here, to getting my laundry, I mean." She blushed and laughed at herself again.

On Friday, Sam's heart leaped like a golden retriever every time the shop bell rang. How unseemly for a man like him to behave that way. After all, he was married, and though, with his wife so far away, he'd allowed himself a few dalliances, this felt like something else. Something dangerous. But he couldn't help himself.

It wasn't until five minutes past closing time that Ruth finally arrived, flustered and harried.

"I'm so sorry." She let the door slam behind her. "I missed my train and I can't seem to find my ticket." She opened her pocketbook and rummaged around in it.

"Not to worry. I remember your order."

"But the rules." She pointed at the sign saying, "No ticket, no laundry," but Sam dismissed it with a wave of his hand.

"Well, you're very kind. I'm late because I went to renew this book at the library." Ruth presented him with a copy of *Mansfield Park*. "Since you like Dickens, I thought you might like Austen, too."

Sam ran his fingertips over the title. "How thoughtful. Thank you," he said.

"Just let me know when you're finished and I'll return it for you. I'm right across the street." She indicated the row of mock-Tudor buildings facing the laundry.

He nodded and put the book beneath the counter. When he looked up, Ruth was staring at him with her chestnut-colored eyes, and his heart started knocking against his rib cage as if a bird were trapped in his chest.

"I will get your laundry now," he said, unable to break away from her gaze. "One moment. It's in the back."

"Can I come?" She raised the flip-top on the counter and started fiddling with the latch behind the swing door.

He undid it for her, and when their fingers touched, he guided her through the opening, past a heap of unsorted laundry, rolls of brown wrapping paper, and the curtain he'd hung in the partition in place of a door. He didn't let go until they reached the meager back room where he lived.

"It's not much."

"It's fine," she said, peeling off her gloves.

Ruth had surprised him then, and she surprised him now, standing there staring daggers at him in almost the same spot where he'd first laid eyes on her. On the street, the milkman set down a bottle by the door, the loud clink of the glass making Sam glance out the shop window, hoping they hadn't been seen. Still half naked, he was beginning to feel as foolish as he looked—as they both looked, facing each other like a couple of gunslingers in a Western. Ruth was vibrating, waiting, perhaps, for him to tell her not to go, but he didn't make a sound or a move.

Suddenly, she advanced until they were only inches apart, and he had no idea what she was going to do next. She might just as easily kiss him as yell, but she did neither. Instead, quick as an adder, she pinched him on the arm.

"If you don't want me to leave, then maybe that's what you want," she said with a slight, sarcastic edge to her voice.

Caught off guard, he shrugged.

"How about that?" She pinched him again, even harder, on the other arm. "Is this what you want?" She reached out again.

This time, he grabbed her by the wrist to stop her, but she twisted in his grip and dug her fingernails into his hand. He growled with pain, though he didn't let go. Instead, he closed the space between them and caught her in a bear hug, pinning her arms to her sides. Then, in a single swift motion, he picked her up and deposited her on the counter.

From the look in Ruth's eye, Sam could see he had succeeded in shocking her. He could feel her holding her breath, but she didn't stop him when he parted her robe, nor when he pushed her nightgown up around her hips and went down on his knees.

"Shh," he quieted her, his mouth pressed against her inner thigh. He sank his teeth into her flesh, holding her still as she squirmed.

"Is this what you want?" he said in a low voice. "How about that?"

She closed her eyes as he applied the slow, feather-light pressure he knew she liked. After a few moments, he felt the bowstring tightness of her body relax. When finally, straining and shuddering, Ruth cried out with her hands cupping his head, Sam thought he must have been forgiven.

Afterward, lying in bed with her head resting uncomfortably on his arm, he passed her his cigarette and considered broaching the subject of Victor's illness again. He'd been too upset to explain things properly before, and he wasn't used to having to. Over the years, Ruth had learned how to read him, or so he'd thought, and she did seem to know what he was feeling most of the time. What she didn't know didn't concern her and could remain unspoken. This, however, was one of the rare times that they weren't on the same page.

"Old Mr. Chin's father . . ." he began.

"Your grandfather?" said Ruth.

"No, the father of the man who adopted me. He was a carpenter in San Francisco. There was a man, he said, in the old days, a labor leader from Ireland, not even born here himself, but he thought the Chinese did not belong in America. First, he said we were taking white men's jobs, we work for too cheap, we sell opium, but that was not enough to make the politicians listen. So then he said we all have leprosy and spread disease." Sam paused, watching Ruth wince and nod.

"He found a sick Chinese man with sores on his face and marched him through the streets, saying, 'See? This will happen to you if we do not kick out the heathen Chinese.' And it worked. People got scared. Then the government passed the Exclusion Act."

"Horrible," said Ruth, shaking her head, "but that was what, seventy years ago? Don't you think things have changed? After all, China was our ally in the war."

"Sure, but not in Korea. Things do change all the time, just like that." Sam snapped his fingers. "Back and forth, but not for the better. Not for us. Bad enough to be Chinese in America, but to have leprosy, too? Don't you see? People will think just like that Irishman. They will shut down the laundry or, even worse, send me and the boys back to China."

"How can they?" said Ruth. "You're a veteran."

Sam let out a small, scornful laugh. "Remember those articles in the paper? They said Chinese laundrymen spit water on the clothes before ironing and spread leprosy that way. This is why we cannot let anyone know about Victor."

"All right." Ruth turned to him, propping her head on her fist. "So it's safer for him to be at Carville. And for us, too. You did the right thing."

Sam made an affirmative sound and looked up at the ceiling, letting her words lift the weight of his guilt a little bit. He'd been blaming himself for not insisting that Victor stay, for not taking out a loan to pay for his surgery and not being able to figure out a way to take him to the clinic every day. But even if he'd worked it all out, with all the comings and goings, how could he have kept Victor's condition a secret?

"What if someone asks where he is?"

Ruth took a drag of the cigarette and thought for a moment. "Maybe we can say he has TB and went to a sanatorium."

"Good idea," he said, taking the cigarette back. Lying would be easier if they stayed close to the truth. "I should send him some more money."

"I can do it. I'm mailing his care package anyway."

"You spoil him," Sam said. Ruth rolled her eyes.

Now that their argument had blown over, he wondered if he should apologize. Not knowing who or what to blame for Victor's diagnosis, he'd lashed out and hurt her. The doctors said the cause was unknown, but it was impossible for him not to speculate. He'd read the medical reports, and beyond the science—exposure, an indeterminately long incubation period, and now a Hansen's infection of the lepromatous type, attacking Victor's skin and nervous system—he found himself ruminating over how and why this had happened. Had Victor caught it on the ship from China or at Immigration in San Francisco when the boys were detained? If Victor hadn't come to the States, maybe he wouldn't have gotten sick, but then again, if he'd caught it in China, he would have been worse off than he was here. What kind of treatment did they have in their village when there was barely enough to eat?

Wherever Sam had been in the world, people had their superstitions. Most Americans seemed to believe that leprosy was a punishment from their god, but at least there was some hope for a cure. In China, they said it was a curse for necrophilia or fornication with prostitutes, and people were too afraid to seek treatment, even in the cities. Both here and in China, leprosy was shrouded in shame, and he couldn't help but feel it. Wasn't he, after all, fornicating with Ruth? She wasn't a prostitute, but she wasn't his wife either, and ever since Victor's diagnosis, Sam could hear a little voice in his head whispering that this was all his fault.

He didn't usually think of his relationship with Ruth that way. On his first trip back to China after emigrating to America, he'd married Mei Wan in a hasty arrangement that didn't seem to suit either of them, and they'd lived together for only a few months before he went back to New York, leaving her behind, pregnant with Henry. Five years passed before he saw her again, then another seven, and now, though they'd been married for over twenty years, he hadn't seen her since he brought the boys to America. He and Mei Wan barely knew each other, but in the eyes of the law, she was still his wife, and as she was the mother of his children, he sent her money every month. Even if there was no love between them, there was gratitude and family. This was how it was for many of the men he knew in America, and it wasn't unusual for them to have mistresses, too, though they were kept in the shadows.

Sam couldn't do that to Ruth. She was the woman of his life despite the fact that in most people's eyes, loving her so openly was wrong. If leprosy was a shameful disease, then maybe the shame was his, and his son was being punished for it.

The mattress creaked as he rolled to his side, pressing his nose against her shoulder. He inhaled the warm, sweet smell of her skin. None of this was her fault and she'd only been doing her best to help. She was closer to him than anyone in the world, so close that, in spite of himself, he'd come to need her, and sometimes he resented how vulnerable it made him. Maybe he did blame her, after all, not for what happened to Victor but for making him love her.

How could he tell Ruth any of this? His thoughts were such a jumbled mess, so ugly and raw, he could barely make sense of them in his own mind, much less explain them to her in English. If he tried, he might lose her and, perhaps, himself. A man like him couldn't afford to be led by his feelings.

Since childhood, a necessary coldness had kept the private core of him alive. Like ice on the surface of a winter pond. The ice allowed him to brush it off, for instance, when customers mocked his English or when, on the street, passersby made ching-chong noises and told him to go back to China.

Recently, a customer whose boorishness had always put him on edge came in with an ink-stained shirt. Sam told him he might not be able to get it all out, but he promised to try. When he was done, only a faint tinge of ink was visible, but when the man saw it, his face contorted into a malicious half smile.

"You poured ink on my shirt, you Jap bastard!" he shouted, his thick neck bulging over his collar.

The two other customers in the shop stepped back and kept quiet. Though they were regulars, Sam didn't expect them to intervene. It was barely noon, but even from across the counter, he could smell the beer on the man's breath.

The next day, Sam put a sign in the window saying, "Chinese Business. Owner is United States Army Veteran. God Bless America. No Japs," and to avoid a lawsuit he was sure to lose, he agreed to give the man twenty dollars even though the laundry only grossed twenty-five a week.

Sam's self-control, or sangfroid, as the French put it, had served him well over the years. It kept him from being crushed by the myriad pains of his life—his childhood begging on the streets of Toisan City before his destitute parents sold him into adoption; his awkward, early marriage; his Army days, which, despite the photograph he kept of himself in uniform, were marked by countless humiliations at the hands of his so-called buddies.

It wasn't until he met Ruth that the ice began to thaw. When they first fell in love, he'd often wondered how she could understand him so well. Instead of being put off by his coldness, she absorbed and mirrored it back. And for the first time in his life, he didn't feel so alone.

What had she been through to make her this way? He'd been curious but hadn't pried. He'd figured if she wanted to tell him about herself, she would. And sometimes she had. Little stories here and there about her childhood. A tenement on the Lower East Side. An uncle with a fabric store who spoke English with an accent and laughed like a jellyfish, jiggling his whole soft body. An aunt who was quiet and sad, and always afraid. Her mother was dead, her father gone, and her grandparents, aunts, uncles, and cousins had been systematically extinguished in the death camps of Europe. Ruth had told these stories matter-of-factly, as if they didn't hold within them vast caverns of grief.

There must have been more. Ruth was fond of children, but if it upset her to have none of her own, she didn't say. She'd never married, and to this day, Sam didn't know why or if she'd been in love before. Just as he didn't press her about her past, she didn't ask too many questions about his life before her either, about his marriage or other lovers. He was glad he didn't have to explain the bonds of blood and obligation he and Mei Wan shared. She was, after all, a good mother to his children and a dutiful daughter-in-law to his adopted mother. Whenever he thought of the hardships she'd endured during the Japanese invasion and its aftermath, he felt a terrible pang of guilt.

Most of the time, Sam was convinced that the discretion he and Ruth maintained wasn't just a mark of mutual respect but a pact protecting what existed between them, allowing their love to grow in spite of the constraints the rest of the world put on them. He imagined it as a sturdy little shelter from the problems that could ruin them—the fact that he was married, the fact that they weren't the same race—and inside of it, they could dare to be happy.

But other times, especially after fights like today's, he wondered if he'd been kidding himself all along. What if the cold light of reality revealed their shelter to have no walls at all, just curtains so paper-thin that the shadows they'd evaded would finally become visible, looming right outside? If jealousy, betrayal, and resentment were the price of what they'd refused to see, then he didn't want to pay it. But with Victor's illness forcing the issue, how could he not?

Sam watched the plume of smoke rise from Ruth's lips to the ceiling. He opened his mouth to speak, but shut it again. It wasn't as simple as saying he was sorry or asking how she wanted things to change. Maybe she'd want to move in together now that Victor was gone. Maybe they could. Why not? There was nothing stopping them anymore. But what if she expected something else, something more than he could give? After years of avoiding conversations about the future, the future was suddenly here.

"What is it?" Ruth asked.

"Nothing," he said. "Everything is fine."

He plucked the cigarette from her fingers and inhaled, feeling the calm of the tobacco move into his bloodstream. If he wasn't careful, his heart might grow so ripe, it would fall and smash to the ground.

In the early days, before the boys came, he and Ruth had had a running joke that they were so in sync, they could read each other's minds.

"What card am I thinking of?" Ruth would demand out of nowhere.

"Queen of hearts," he'd reply.

"Right! Now what am I thinking of?"

"Ace of spades?"

"Right again!"

Sam had believed it then, but now he knew this to have been the folly of new love. Folie à deux, as they'd said during the war, when some young, Midwestern private would fall for a French whore and insist on playing house with her, pretending they were a regular American family. Pretending until the day they couldn't pretend anymore.

THREE

Victor was right. The big building at the end of the avenue of trees
was the infirmary. He could see a small crowd of people gathered by the front steps, and when he and Sister Laura got closer, he
realized they were patients, all staring at him, sizing him up from
head to toe. They were an unusual mix of people—men and women,
old and young, brown and white and everything in between. A few
looked so healthy that Victor would never have known they were
sick, while others had canes and bandages on various limbs, and telltale pink splotches on their skin. A young woman with a bun of tight
black curls pinned high on her head studied him with a look of frank
appraisal, the skirt of her peach-colored dress spread out across the
seat of her wheelchair. Behind her, a man whose forehead was dotted
with angry wine-red spots, his brow bumpy with ropelike nodules,
openly gawked. Seeing past the mask of the disease, Victor could tell
he wasn't much older than Henry, and he wondered how long he'd
been here and why he was in such a bad way if the treatments were
supposed to work. The man stared Victor down until he looked away.

"Don't you folks have anywhere to be?" Sister Laura said, the
wings of her headdress tilting along with her head.

The crowd murmured and started breaking up in twos and threes,
whispering to one another, but no one spoke to Victor.

"How did they know I was here?"

"News travels fast," Sister Laura said, opening the door. "We don't get new arrivals every day."

The bitter tang of antiseptic shot up Victor's nose as soon as he stepped inside, where the halls, echoing with voices and the squeaks of wheels and shoes, were painted in the same shade of green as the ones at Bellevue. He followed Sister Laura as she strode ahead, noticing how everyone, even the doctors, nodded or said hello to her with respect in their eyes.

"We've got sixty-eight beds on two open wards," she said, gesturing toward a flight of stairs, "and screened porches so you'll get plenty of fresh air. I know you're tired, but we just need to get your interview done and run a few tests. Everything's right here in the infirmary, though. This way."

She led him around a corner where, at the end of the hallway, a woman was staring down at a piece of paper. Victor couldn't see her face, but she was slender, with black hair pulled back into a bun, and the sight of her struck an old chord in him. Though his mind knew she was a stranger, his heart leaped in reflex, thinking she could be Ma.

There was a time when he saw her everywhere in New York—on a subway platform through the window of the train just as the doors were closing, on a distant street corner underneath an umbrella on a rainy day. Echoes of her in the tilt of a woman's head or the curve of a back reminding him of how Ma bent to her gardening, the delicate bumps of her spine showing through her shirt. In Chinatown, it was even worse. The pain of those ghostly glimpses intensified with the familiar smells and sounds, but it hadn't happened in a long time, not for years. So why now? Why here? The illusion of Ma was shattered as soon as the woman looked up to reveal a mass of lumps and bumps on her face, a craggy, flattened nose, and lips cracked in deep fissures. Victor's heart fell, and he was relieved when she went into the bandaging clinic.

As they continued on, Sister Laura pointed out the eye clinic, the laboratory, the pharmacy, the X-ray room, the dental clinic, and the medical photography studio.

"Physical therapy is up the hall, along with the surgical wing. And here's the record room." She stopped and opened the door. "This is where we keep all our patients' clinical histories."

Victor took in all the folders lining the shelves from the ceiling to the floor. At least a thousand, maybe more. Sister Laura sat down at the desk, motioning for him to sit across from her. From a pitcher by her side, she offered him a glass of water. It was lukewarm and smelled odd, like a puddle the day after it had rained, but he drank it anyway, holding his breath, letting the moisture wet his parched lips. Sister Laura took out a pad and pencil from the desk drawer, and Victor watched her write the date, his name, and a number at the top of the page.

"What's 2276?" he asked, reading upside down.

"Your case number."

Victor frowned. In movies, inmates were given numbers when they got to prison.

"It's only for organizing your records," Sister Laura added.

She asked Victor to describe his symptoms, when he first noticed each one, and how he was diagnosed. She asked him, too, about his family history, and when and how he came to the States. The last time he was questioned like this was when he'd been interrogated by Immigration in San Francisco. There, he'd learned that the more he said, the more potential there was for trouble, so he kept his answers straightforward now and tried to make his family sound as wholesome and normal as possible. At least by American standards.

"My brother and I lived with my mother and grandmother in China before my father brought us to America," he said, watching the cryptic strokes of Sister Laura's pencil as she wrote everything down in shorthand.

"When was that?" she said.

"1947."

"Your father was already living in the United States?"

"Yes, in New York. He owns a laundry business. And during the war, he served in Europe. He's an Army man."

Sister Laura gave a slight nod of approval, and Victor knew he'd been right to mention that. There were so many things he had to be careful not to say, like the fact that Jackie, a boy from their village, had traveled with them illegally as Ba's Paper Son, so he and Henry had been coached to pretend that the three of them were brothers. He glossed over leaving Ma and Grandmother behind, too, in case it sounded strange, but even though he didn't want to bring her up, he couldn't explain how he was diagnosed without mentioning Ruth. She was the one, after all, who'd discovered his first lesion when they went swimming earlier that summer.

The Crotona Pool was Olympic-sized, Ruth had said, holding the bag of bathing suits and towels she'd already packed. He hadn't known what this meant exactly, but recognized from her tone that it was supposed to impress, so he'd nodded and left it to her to convince Ba to let him go.

"Why don't you close up and come with us?" Ruth suggested. "Just this once?"

Ba's face went blank. "Close? For swimming?"

On Saturdays, shirts were delivered from the wet-and-dry factory where they normally pressed, folded, and packaged them, but Ba could make more money if he just got them wrung dry and did the rest himself. It was a lot of extra work with a handheld iron, and on a hot day like this, the shirts had to be done fast before they mildewed, so he relied on Victor to at least mind the storefront.

"It'll be fun," said Ruth.

Ba made an incredulous face, but before any more could be said, the shop bell rang. "Customer," he announced with a finger raised in the air and turned his attention to the man walking in. "How can I help you?"

Taking advantage of the distraction, Ruth grabbed Victor by the arm and said, "C'mon, let's make a break for it," between her teeth like James Cagney in *Public Enemy*.

"See you later," she called, pulling the door shut behind her.

Moments later, through the dirty window of the elevated train barreling toward Crotona Avenue, Victor peered out over the streets. His guilt at leaving Ba with all that work dissolved. From up there, he couldn't see the filth, the rats, or the water bugs. Just the hot breath of summer rising up from the manholes and the burning asphalt below.

At the pool, the strong, bleachy smell and the intensity of the heat hit Victor immediately. The sun made a blinding plane of the water's

surface, broken here and there by bobbing heads and furious splashing. He'd never been to a swimming pool; he'd never seen so many
uncovered bodies at once.

An army of teenage girls were sunning themselves, all knock
knees, thin arms, and cone-shaped breasts, the sweet scent of baby oil
wafting up from their shiny, roasting skin. In China, everyone wanted
to be pale because it was a sign of wealth. Grandmother said only
servants and farmhands were brown from having to work outdoors.
Since she was a proud Gold Mountain wife, she was never without
a hat in the garden or an umbrella at the market, and scolded Ma
whenever she forgot hers.

Small gangs of teenage boys formed clusters, circling around the
girls, stealing glances at them. The tiles amplified everything: the slap
and splash of the water, the music from a transistor radio, the chatter
and whoops of the teens, the laughter and screams of the children.
Watching them all were groups of mothers in modest floral bathing
suits with canvas bags by their sides. The absence of grown men reminded Victor of China, where nearly everyone's father was somewhere
overseas.

"Know how to swim?" asked Ruth.

"Yeah, Henry taught me," said Victor, "back home."

"Good! Know how to dive?"

"No."

"Well, I'll teach you," she said.

Ruth ran over to the ladder and scrambled up to the high diving
board. Shouting for Victor to watch, she raised her arms, expanded her
chest, and rocked up and down on her arches like a dancer on the edge.
When she dove, the arc of her razor-thin body knifed into the blue,
leaving barely a splash. Swimming underwater across the expanse of
the pool, she popped up on the other side, dark hair plastered to her
head.

"Your turn!" she called out to him with a wave.

For the next couple of hours, they went back and forth like this,
with Ruth tirelessly demonstrating and coaching. Studying her movements in such close detail—the exact placement of her feet, how she
held her arms and head just so—he couldn't help but compare her

body to his mother's. Ma was broad of hip, unlike most Chinese women, even during famine time, and she was tall, taller than many men, including Ba.

At lunchtime, when the sun had reached the center of the sky, Ruth bought them each a hot dog from the street vendor whose cart was parked just outside the gate, the works—sauerkraut, relish, ketchup, and mustard—for herself and just mustard for him. They ate together sitting cross-legged, sharing a single abandoned deck chair.

"Did you hurt yourself?" Ruth pointed at a flat, pink, amoeba-shaped blotch the size of a quarter on Victor's chest.

"I don't think so." He pressed on it, but couldn't feel anything there at all.

"Probably just a rash." Ruth shrugged and wiped a smudge of mustard off Victor's chin with her own paper napkin.

"I'm Walking Behind You," an Eddie Fisher song the disc jockeys wouldn't stop playing that summer, drifted over from someone's transistor radio. Victor found it sappy and annoying, but impossible not to sing along to.

"My goodness," said Ruth after he'd sung a couple of bars, "you sound just like him. I didn't realize how much your voice had dropped."

Victor smiled and ducked his head to hide it. In chorus last term, the teacher had said he was a tenor now and complimented the quality of his voice, too.

"When you were little, you used to sing to yourself all the time," said Ruth. "What were those songs?"

"I don't remember," Victor said, though he did. They were nursery rhymes Ma had taught him.

Later, on the way home, Victor was sunbaked and drowsy, his muscles pleasantly exhausted. His skin smelled like the pool.

"Victor's kind of an unusual name, huh?" Ruth said out of nowhere.

"Yeah, I guess." He stifled a yawn. "Ba liked it because it means winner. And he named Henry after Henry Pu-Yi, you know, the emperor. He thought it would be easier for us if we had American names."

"He's probably right about that. So what's your Chinese name?"

"Vee Kun. It means Powerful One."

"Very manly," said Ruth, prodding him in the ribs. "I'll tell you a secret. Ruth's not my given name either. It's Rufa. Isn't that awful?"

Victor shrugged. "It's not so bad."

"Not bad if you live in a shtetl," she said in the funny voice she sometimes used when she was telling a joke.

"What's a shtetl?"

"A little village where Jewish people lived in Europe, you know, before Hitler. Anyway, the kids at school never let me hear the end of it. 'Ruff, ruff, like a dog,' they said. And then, in sixth grade, they started calling me Babe Ruth."

"How come?"

"Believe it or not, I was a fat kid. But look at me now," she sang, waggling her hands.

Victor laughed. "Your parents let you change your name?"

"They had no say in it. My mother died from the Spanish flu when I was a baby, and then my father left me with my aunt and uncle."

"Oh, I'm sorry," said Victor in a quiet voice. "But why would you want that name if kids said it to be mean?"

"I liked the sound of it. Ruth," she said, drawing out the *U* like a fancy lady in a play. "Suits me, don't you think? Why should I let a bunch of nudniks spoil a perfectly elegant name?"

After that day, they went to the pool a few more times, taking care not to go on Saturdays so as not to press Ba's buttons too hard. A couple of weeks later, Ruth noticed that the rash was still there and mentioned it to Ba when they got back to the laundry.

"I think he ought to see someone," Victor heard Ruth say from the back room where he was changing.

At first, the doctor had thought it was only a stubborn case of eczema and prescribed an ointment. Even though Victor put it on every day, it got worse, darkening from pink to red. When new lesions showed up along with pain and numbness, the doctor sent him to Bellevue, where he was diagnosed.

Victor blinked and the memory vanished. As he finished answering Sister Laura's questions, a longing for home—and Ruth—welled up inside him before he could push the feeling away. He swallowed, trying to keep his face and voice neutral, and his details to a minimum.

"So your stepmother is responsible for your medical care?" Sister Laura shuffled through the paperwork Bellevue had sent. "She didn't sign your consent form."

Victor's face burned red and he started to sweat. It wasn't that he was ashamed of Ruth exactly. To him, she and Ba were just a fact of life, and things were just how they were, normal and ordinary. Henry would disagree, of course, but people in their neighborhood seemed to accept them, or were at least used to them enough to mind their own business. At the hospital, though, Victor had seen the looks people gave them, some curious, others disapproving, as they tried to figure out why there was a white woman with a Chinese family. Now, when the question of how he was related to Ruth came up, he worried not only about how she might be judged, but about how he and his family might be, too. He didn't know what to say. "Stepmother" was better than "my father's girlfriend," which implied worse things like "mistress" and "other woman," so he didn't correct Sister Laura. "No, my father is."

"All right," she said, putting the pad and pencil down, "if you've got nothing else to add, let's get to your next appointment."

She led him down the hall to the medical photography studio, where a tall, sturdy nun covered head to toe in white linen was standing with her back to the door, arranging equipment on a table. Against one wall was a stand with a big roll of paper pulled down to the floor, and in front of it was a box-shaped camera on a tripod.

The nun, who'd introduced herself as Sister Helen, picked up a cone-shaped lamp before turning around and blinking at him. Her owlish blue eyes were magnified by a pair of round, wire-rimmed glasses. With her smooth, square face and thin, stern lips, she looked younger than Sister Laura, but not by much, and she didn't seem nearly as patient.

"They only sent us two headshots," she said in a no-nonsense voice, "but we have to document all your lesions to keep track of your progress. Now, remove your clothes behind the screen and leave them on the chair. Shoes and socks as well, but keep your underthings on." Without waiting for him to reply, she turned away again and started attaching the light to a stand.

Victor froze. The shame of exposing his body was magnified by the thought of the camera capturing every last detail of how the disease had marked it. "The camera never lies," people said. It was one thing for doctors and nurses to examine his lesions, but another thing for pictures to make a permanent record of them as if each one were a crime.

Sister Laura glanced over at him and her face softened. "You'd be surprised at how many gentlemen think it's funny to get stark naked in front of a nun," she said, "as if they've got anything we haven't seen before."

Sister Helen gave a short chuckle, and catching Victor's eye, Sister Laura nodded once in an encouraging way. He managed to flash her a weak smile before she walked out of the room.

Behind the screen, he crumpled in the metal chair and stared out the window. A young couple was strolling arm in arm between rows of palm trees and bushes with big purple flowers yawning wide in the late-summer sun. Laughing and chatting, they didn't look sick to him.

Victor bent to take off his shoes, untying the laces gingerly. A light breeze dried his sweat and raised goose bumps all over his skin. One of the worst things about having fevers all the time was the unbearable cold after his clothes got drenched. Not to mention the smell. Shivering, he sniffed his armpits and wrinkled his nose with disgust. After a night on the train, the fabric reeked of ammonia, and he was almost glad to take off his shirt and pants.

Out in the studio, Sister Helen had pulled down the blinds and was adjusting a set of lights in front of the roll of paper. Victor knew the unforgiving glare would show her not only his lesions but also everything else that was wrong with him, from his unkempt hair to his bony ribs and chicken legs. Stepping forward, he braced himself, but she wasn't even looking at him. She was bent over the black box of the camera, twisting the dials and knobs, and when she lifted her head, the reflection of the lights in her glasses made it impossible for him to see her eyes.

"Stand there, please," she said, pointing at an X of masking tape on the floor, and Victor wished he could run back behind the screen. He hunched over a bit, shrinking into himself as he squinted against the bright lights.

Sister Helen slid a film holder into the back of the camera, pushed the door shut, and flipped the piece of black fabric over her headdress, making a mountainous lump above the lens.

"On three."

"Excuse me," said Victor, suddenly realizing that he'd lost track of his bags. "When will I get my things back?"

"You won't need them until you're discharged to the colony," said Sister Helen. Victor's stomach dropped.

When they were arguing about it at the hospital, Henry had called Carville a leper colony, conjuring up images of a terrifying place where sick people were left to rot, out of sight, out of mind, and away from society for the rest of their miserable lives. Afterward, when they were alone, Ruth had made a point of explaining that while those places might exist in other countries and even in America long ago, Carville wasn't one of them. With words the doctors and the pamphlets used, like "state-of-the-art treatment center," "federal institution," and "community," she'd reassured him. Hansen's was curable now; his stay at Carville would be temporary.

"'Colony'?" he repeated.

"It's what we call the dorms where the patients live." Sister Helen pulled out the film holder, flipped it, and slid it back into place. "Now, turn to the left, please."

The term "leper colony" didn't even make sense to him. From what he'd learned in school, colonies were created when people left their homes to take over someplace else. How could people with leprosy colonize anything when they were the ones being locked up? And since bacteria lived by taking over people's bodies, weren't they the real colonizers here?

Then there were penal colonies, too, like the one in *Great Expectations*. He'd seen the movie with Henry years ago, before he spoke much English, though he'd understood enough to know that the convict got rich after he was sent away. As far as Victor could tell, there was no way to get rich here. If Carville was a leper colony, then it was probably worse than a prison.

After Sister Helen finished with Victor's face, she repositioned him, turning him this way and that, pointing the camera at each of the lesions on his body in turn. Standing there in his underwear, he wasn't any more naked than he was a moment ago, but he felt far more exposed. He wanted to escape, to be anywhere but here, and his mind began to drift away, making the shutter's rhythmic clicks and the blinding white of the lights fade. Now it was as if the pictures weren't really of him anymore. They were neutral, clinical, just a collection of parts. Arms, legs, chest, back.

He didn't return to his body until the photographs were done and, as if waking from a trance, he found himself fully dressed, walking into the X-ray room. Now another nun was telling him to take off his shirt so she could get pictures of his insides. This one was young and short, with a pale, heart-shaped face and soft brown eyes. She didn't bother to introduce herself, or if she did, Victor didn't hear her name. When he was undressed, she put on a heavy apron before pressing the glass plate of the machine against his chest. At Bellevue, when his first set of X-rays was taken, the technician had worn the same kind of apron and had told him it was made of lead to protect him from the radiation. If the machine was so dangerous, Victor wondered, why didn't they give him an apron, too? Was it because he was already so sick that cancer wouldn't matter?

"Take a deep breath and hold it until I say," said the nun.

He inhaled and immediately started to cough. "Sorry," he said, taking another breath, and this time, the nun switched on the machine.

Every second felt like twenty. A tickle in his throat threatened to erupt into more coughing. Finally, she said, "Okay," and he was able to let go.

The nun adjusted the machine, her movements quick and efficient. She didn't speak beyond giving him directions, and before he knew it, she was telling him to put his shirt back on. They were walking down the hall to his last appointment in the surgery when, after just a few steps, a buzzing sensation overtook his body. His vision went fuzzy around the edges, tunneled, and blurred before his knees crumpled beneath him. By instinct, he threw out an arm to catch himself, wincing as he smacked the wall hard.

"Are you all right?" said the nun. "Do you need a wheelchair?"

"I'm fine," said Victor through his teeth, with his eyes shut against the burning in his hand.

The pain had a bracing effect, steadying his legs. He opened his eyes and straightened up. When he started walking again, the nun put her hand under his arm, meaning to help.

"No, thank you," he said, and she let go. The surgery was only a few feet away and he was determined to make it there himself.

Inside, it looked like a regular doctor's office with glass containers on the shelves, anatomy posters on the walls, a cart with a tray of medical instruments, a stool, and an examination table.

The nun handed him a fresh hospital gown. "Put this on and wait here. The doctor will be with you shortly."

When she left, Victor undressed again, pulled on the gown, and stacked his clothes in a small, neat pile. He lay on the table, staring bleary-eyed at the spot where the white popcorn ceiling met the green wall.

"Some shortness of breath, but asthma's also in his chart," Victor heard the nun say in the hall.

"We won't know if there are nodules until the films come back," said a man's voice. "Thank you, Sister."

The doorknob turned, and a burly man wearing a white coat and stethoscope lumbered in, opening the folder he was carrying.

"Victor," he said slowly, in a loud Southern voice that was different from how he'd just spoken to the sister-nurse in the hall. "I'm Dr. Behr. On a scale of one to ten, how bad is the pain?"

For a moment, Victor thought it was because of his accent that the doctor was talking that way, but then he realized it was exactly how the doctors at Bellevue had spoken to Ba.

"Eight, maybe nine," Victor said. The paper covering the examination table crinkled as he sat up. "Hard to say when it keeps getting worse. My five now would've been a ten before."

Dr. Behr's bushy eyebrows shot up over his glasses and fell. His tone shifted. "How about swelling?"

"Seven or eight, but mostly in the morning." Victor hid a smirk as the doctor jotted that down in his chart. "My face is puffy when I wake up, too, but it gets better during the day."

Dr. Behr nodded. "Lie back, please." He checked his watch, snapped on a pair of rubber gloves, and popped a thermometer in Victor's mouth.

Victor concentrated on the cold glass under his tongue, trying to ignore the doctor lifting his gown, exposing him again as he checked the lesions on his body. When he got to his face, Victor could see sparks of the individual silver hairs in his otherwise black brows. Not once did Dr. Behr look him in the eyes.

"The meds ought to clear those up." The doctor plucked out the thermometer. "One hundred point five. They should take care of the fevers, too."

"I thought leprosy was a skin disease."

"Hansen's," Dr. Behr corrected, "is the cause of a wide range of symptoms." He checked Victor's chart again. "Fevers, fatigue, nausea, nerve pain. All common."

Victor nodded. The doctors at Bellevue might have already said some of that, something about inflammation and his immune system, but he hadn't been able to take it all in. Even if he had, medical talk couldn't tell him what it was like to have Hansen's, just like a map of a place couldn't show him what it was like to walk across it.

"Let's have a look at those nerves." Dr. Behr touched his right arm, starting at the wrist and moving up his forearm, pressing lightly and then harder and harder. Now he was finally looking him in the eye, watching his reactions. When he got to his elbow, Victor winced and bit his lip so he wouldn't cry out.

"Tender? The ulnar nerve is severely enlarged." Dr. Behr started to touch his left arm at the same spot, and this time, Victor couldn't stop himself from whimpering. "This one's even worse."

"Are my hands going to fall off?" Victor kept his voice quiet so it wouldn't shake. He'd been too afraid to ask anyone before, though it was the first thought that popped into his head when he found out he had leprosy. No one had said that would happen, but no one had said it wouldn't either.

"Of course not!" scoffed the doctor. "Didn't they tell you that at Bellevue?"

"No." Victor tried to read his expression, but the light over the examination table hurt his eyes and he looked away. "So the medicine will fix them?"

Dr. Behr sighed. "Not exactly. You need surgery as soon as possible. Did they at least tell you that?"

Victor nodded.

"Well, you've come to the right place. Once I transplant the nerve from here"—Dr. Behr pressed on the swollen area near his wrist—"to here," he continued, touching an area on his outer arm, "it'll be like you never had Hansen's at all, give or take a few scars."

That sounded a bit too good to be true. "What if I don't get the surgery?" said Victor. It wasn't that he didn't want to. It was just that he hadn't been given a choice and wanted to know what would happen.

"Well," said Dr. Behr, in a tight voice, "the pain and numbness would get worse, and you'd probably wind up with clawed hands. But the consent forms you and your father signed agree to any treatments we deem necessary."

Victor frowned. Did that mean he had no say over what they did to him? He didn't remember reading that in the forms.

With his arms folded, the doctor continued talking about good attitudes and medical advice, but Victor had stopped listening. A wasp flew in through the open window, its black and yellow stripes catching his eye. He tracked its movements as it landed on the tray of instruments and crawled toward Dr. Behr's elbow, imagining what would happen if it decided to sting him.

"The Carville jail has seen more inmates since Dr. Morton's been in charge," said the doctor, snapping Victor back to attention.

All his muscles tensed. He thought about his so-called case number, 2276, and wished he'd been listening, because now he wasn't sure what was going on. Would they put him in jail if he didn't obey the doctors? And this was the second time someone had mentioned Dr. Morton. His rules were the reason Ba and Ruth hadn't been allowed to drop him off at Carville.

"Will you put me to sleep during the operation?" he asked. He figured he'd better act cooperative.

"Don't worry, you won't feel a thing." Dr. Behr's friendly tone returned, though he didn't answer Victor's question. "Let's take care of these biopsies and get you in the operating room tomorrow."

Victor's tongue felt dry, too big for his mouth. It must have been pretty bad, maybe worse than they were saying, if they had to do it so soon.

Dr. Behr soaked a cotton ball in alcohol and swabbed the lesion on his arm. He reached for a syringe from a tray filled with silver tools arranged in a neat line.

"What is that?" said Victor, his voice coming out embarrassingly high.

"Something for the pain."

Victor braced for the impact of the needle, but he barely registered it going in. When Dr. Behr pushed down the plunger, he felt a cold pressure and, after a beat, nothing. He heard the clink of glass on metal and watched the doctor pick up something that looked like a mechanical pencil without any lead.

"A little pinch," Dr. Behr said before pressing its sharp edge into Victor's skin, extracting a small circle of flesh from the center of his lesion.

Seeing a piece of himself cut from his body made him suddenly queasy. He closed his eyes and willed himself to hold still while the doctor sewed up the hole.

"Just a few more. We won't do these very often."

At Bellevue, to diagnose him, they'd taken only a single biopsy from his chest, but now the process was repeated on each of his lesions, on his arms, torso, and legs. By the time Dr. Behr got to the last one, Victor could only manage quick, shallow breaths. He was afraid he was going to have an asthma attack.

"There." Dr. Behr snipped the last bit of thread and looked at him. "You all right?"

Victor sat up, thinking it might help, but he couldn't answer. A sick, icy sweat was bursting from his pores. His heart was rabbiting against his breastbone. His throat went tight. He clapped his hand over his mouth, trying to swallow. Then, all at once, he doubled over and threw up what was left of the sandwich he'd eaten on the train, narrowly missing the doctor's shiny black shoes.

"I'm sorry," he gasped, eyeing the mess on the floor. The sight and stench made him want to heave again.

"Happens all the time." Dr. Behr handed him a tissue and called down the hall, "Wheelchair, please, and tell the janitor we need a cleanup in the surgery."

After a moment, a young man with brown skin and green eyes appeared in a white uniform, pushing a wheelchair. Victor saw his nose wrinkle at the smell, and heat crept up his neck to his cheeks.

"Tony will take you to your room now." Dr. Behr peeled off his gloves and dropped them on the tray of used instruments.

Throwing up had made Victor feel a bit better, though his mouth tasted bitter and his throat was sore. He turned to the chair where the small pile of his shoes and clothes was sitting, topped with his Dodgers cap like a sad, melted replica of himself. He reached for it, but Dr. Behr stopped him.

"Don't worry about your things. Tony will get them later."

Victor glanced up at the young man and caught him pursing his lips for a split second behind Dr. Behr's back.

With a light touch to his shoulder and a final nod, the doctor skirted around the puddle of vomit and walked down the hall, where Victor heard him say, "Sister, book the OR for 2276 at 13:00 tomorrow and get me 798's chart."

There was that case number again. He knew he was supposed to go with Tony, but he couldn't seem to make himself get up from the examination table.

"Boy, you look like you got the gris-gris on you," Tony said in an unfamiliar accent, Southern with a tinge of something foreign. And what was that word he'd used? Was it even English?

Victor eyed the wheelchair with suspicion, thinking of Mr. Wang and the young woman who'd stared at him out front.

Tony caught his look and said, "First day's always the same. You think it's all over, but you'll be back to your old self in no time." Victor bet he said that to all the new patients, and his face must have betrayed his thought because Tony went on, "I've seen it all. And my father worked here before me. You're young. If you follow the rules and let the doctors do their job, ca va, cher. You'll do just fine."

There was that language again. This time, it sounded French, except Tony didn't look it. The only people Victor had seen with his skin tone and eyes were Puerto Rican, like the girl on his block with tight black curls and pale blue eyes, whose bubble-gum-flavored lips he'd once kissed beneath the slide at the school playground. But Tony didn't seem to be speaking Spanish. In any case, whether it was what he said or how he said it, Victor let himself relax and got in the wheelchair.

Pushing him down the long corridor, Tony greeted everyone they passed—from the janitor heading to the surgery with a bag of sawdust, to patients, doctors, sister-nurses, and other orderlies along the way. Victor felt their eyes boring into him, curious, sympathetic, wary. He wished he hadn't left his Dodgers cap behind so he could at least hide his face. Sitting there in his hospital gown was like a waking version of the nightmare where he showed up naked at school. He imagined how, with his scrawny, stitched-up arms and legs exposed, he must look like a cricket someone had stepped on. Two women stood in front of the dental clinic, their heads almost touching in close conversation, stopping only to give him the once-over as he passed.

"Another young one," he heard the woman on crutches say to the woman carrying a cane.

So he wasn't the only new patient his age.

Farther down the hall, Tony stopped and reversed, wheels squeaking, into Room 33, where tall, open windows filled it with light and the sweet smell of freshly mown grass. There, waiting in a patch of sun, was a middle-aged man with a cane laid across the armrests of his wheelchair. Unlike the plain metal one the woman in the hall was using, this cane was made of polished wood, with a silver handle in the shape of a lion's head.

"Anton," the man said in a stage actor's voice, "who do we have here?"

"New boy, Mr. Klein. Victor Chin. Fresh from New York City. Sorry for the wait, sir." Then he said to Victor, "You sit tight."

Mr. Klein grunted as Tony helped him up from the wheelchair and over to one of the beds where he lay still for a moment, seeming winded, his eyes invisible behind a pair of dark glasses. From the way the fingertips of his clawed hands roved over the sheets, Victor could tell he was blind.

"Herb Klein. Pleased to make your acquaintance," he said as Tony fussed over him, grabbing an extra pillow and plumping it up so he could sit more comfortably.

Who was this man? Was that his real name? Victor wondered if the disease had made him go blind or if it was just a coincidence, but he couldn't think of a way to ask without sounding rude.

"Hi," he said, and got out of his wheelchair. Following the sound of a bird calling in a series of sweet, clear whistles, he wandered over to the window. He couldn't find it, but looking straight ahead, he saw the twin lines of mossy oaks he and Sister Laura had passed, and all the way to the left, he thought he could make out the road he'd driven in on. Next to it was the levee, as the driver had said, but he still couldn't see the river through the trees, the Mississippi he'd read about at school last year, in *Huckleberry Finn*.

"I'll get you some ginger ale," said Tony as he turned down Victor's bed. "Dinner will be ready soon."

"But it's only 4:15." Victor frowned at the clock on the wall.

"We eat at 4:45 here. Extra dessert, Mr. Klein? Bread pudding today."

"Yes, please," said Herb. "And extra for my friend here, too."

On his way out, Tony put a large manila envelope on the bedside table. "Welcome packet," he said.

Victor opened it and pulled out a card. At the top was an illustration of a smiling cartoon doctor, with the heading "Your Treatment" written in bold.

"Medical care should be your primary concern," it said. "Your first few days will be busy ones with examinations and laboratory studies being made to help us determine the type and stage of your infection and the status of your general health. In a short time, your treatment will be started and it will be changing from time to time to suit your particular needs. You are welcome to discuss your treatment and progress with your doctor at any time."

Victor shoved the card back into the envelope and tossed it aside.

When Tony brought the ginger ale, he sipped at it, feeling the sugar perk him up and the spiciness settle his sour stomach.

"I know how you must be feeling," said Herb, trying to make conversation again.

Victor rolled his eyes. "I doubt it."

"Rotten inside and out, am I right? Pun intended." Herb paused for dramatic effect and Victor smiled in spite of himself. "You're mad as hell and you think you're the only person in the world this could be happening to. But the thing is, we're all in the same boat."

"How long have you been here?" Victor asked.

"Since 1931."

Over twenty years.

"But you're not cured?"

"Strictly speaking, no. I've been in remission a couple of times and was out for a while in the '40s, but it didn't stick." Herb shrugged. "I ended up back here, but I don't mind it much. This is my home now and the people are like my family."

Victor was quiet for a moment. "So some people never get to leave."

"Nah. Just a few of us old Carville vets who got Hansen's before they discovered the cure. There was a seven-year-old kid who came the same year as I did and he's still here, too. But some folks who got here even earlier have been discharged. It's the luck of the draw. Some get no more than a couple of sores, and others wind up looking like me."

Victor eyed the healed lesions on Herb's face, his dark glasses, his clawed hands. He looked down at his own hands, swollen but unmarked, and a bead of anxious sweat trickled from the nape of his neck down his spine. He might not have any sores on his face, but he had more than a couple on his body.

"You don't have to worry about any of that," Herb added. "It won't be the same for you."

"I'm supposed to have an operation tomorrow. Nerve transplant in my arms."

"Ah, Behr's very proud of that. The old operation relieved the pressure, but you still lost a lot of sensation. His new method gets rid of the pain and numbness, and gives you full use of your hands, too. Way better, don't you think?"

"But if I have to do it right away, doesn't that mean it's really bad?"

Herb flipped up one of his palms. "The sooner it's done, the sooner you'll get out of the infirmary, and the sooner you'll get to go home."

"Everyone keeps saying that," Victor said.

"That's because it's true. If I'd had a chance like yours when I got here, you'd better believe I'd have grabbed it. With both hands." Herb wiggled them for emphasis, and the gold pinky ring on his left hand glinted in the afternoon sun.

"Dr. Behr said something about how Dr. Morton puts people in jail if they don't do what the doctors say."

Herb made a dismissive sound in his throat. "Morton's a blowhard. More of a military man than a doctor, if you ask me. The jail's full of bikes they confiscate from patients who ride them near the blind dorms. As for human inmates, it's mostly drunks and people who break quarantine and run off. You're not planning to do that, are you?"

"No." Victor laughed.

"He hasn't been here long. The old director, Dr. Albrechtson, retired last year."

"Isn't Albrechtson the name of the lake?" Victor remembered that from the brochure.

Herb nodded. "Dr. Al had it built specially for the patients. Morton's got some big shoes to fill."

"So things were better before."

"Sure, but the quality of our lives shouldn't depend on the temperament of the man in charge."

Victor thought about this, how some people had power over others while other people had none, and he realized that Hansen's had turned him into someone who didn't even have power over himself. From the moment he'd agreed to leave New York, he was subject to Dr. Morton's rules, from having to travel to Carville alone to being forced to accept all the medical treatments Dr. Behr advised. He'd never even met the man, but like a president or a king, Dr. Morton made decisions that could change Victor's life—and all the other patients' lives—for better or worse.

Regular doctors had that kind of power over their patients, too, and in a way, it was even more immediate. Dr. Behr could either cure him or not, and tomorrow, on the operating table, he'd be holding Victor's life in his hands. As for the rest of what Herb said, Victor wasn't sure if it meant they were prisoners or not, and he didn't know what rights they should be fighting for, but he certainly didn't like the sound of Carville being his home. The whole point of coming here was to leave as soon as he could.

Victor hadn't eaten a thing since the few bites of sandwich he'd thrown up. He should have been starving, but when Tony came in with a shiny metal cart loaded with chicken potpies, vegetable soup, milk, and the promised bread pudding, he didn't feel hungry at all. Holding the utensils hurt, and with every movement, the stitches from his biopsies tugged and stung. The anesthetic had worn off. Still, he prodded the crust of the potpie with his fork and lifted its lid to uncover a gluey white sauce with bits of meat and mushy vegetables. He'd seen it on the lunch menu at his old school before but had never tried it, finding it unappetizing, even after seven years in America, to eat creamy foods that were savory. Now he didn't have a choice. Herb, who'd tucked his napkin into the collar of his hospital gown, seemed to be digging in, so he stabbed a small piece of chicken and touched it to his tongue. The thick sauce coated his mouth. If he'd been alone, he would have spat it out, but Ruth had taught him that spitting was impolite. Instead, since Herb couldn't see him do it, he wiped his tongue with his napkin and drank some water to wash the taste away.

Ba often complained about how picky he was for a boy who'd come from war-torn China, blaming Ma and Grandmother for spoiling him. It was true that since he was born with asthma, they'd treated him with unusual care. But hunger and its lack weren't things his body could control any more than fear or sickness. He couldn't help how his stomach heaved when it was confronted with strange new foods. The first time Ba served him a breakfast of cold milk and cereal, it had seemed like bits of tree bark floating in a pool of phlegm. He'd managed to choke down half the bowl before turning his head from the table and depositing it undigested on the floor.

"Such a waste," Ba had hissed, glaring at him with disgust as he threw him a rag to clean it up.

Knowing he had to eat something now even if he had no appetite, Victor drank the soup. His brain vibrated with thoughts about tomorrow's surgery. Would he be in much pain afterward? What if Dr. Behr made a mistake or something went wrong? Could he die on the table? And if he did, how would Ba and Henry tell Ma?

"Victor Chin." Herb's voice interrupted his thoughts. "Is that your Carville name?"

"No," said Victor, taken aback. "Is Herb Klein yours?"

"Sure. Most people my age have Carville names, but I guess it's a dying tradition." He paused, as if waiting for Victor to laugh at his dark joke, and when he didn't, he went on, "Were you born in New York?"

"I moved there from China when I was eight," he said, with a flash of pride. He was pleased that his English was good enough for Herb to think he might be American-born. He took a sip of milk and considered asking what Herb's real name was, but guessed, since he didn't volunteer it, that he didn't want anyone to know.

"You must be a fast learner. That'll help you now. I know a thing or two about surviving tough times myself, and I'm not just talking about this package." Herb gestured to the parts of his body affected by Hansen's. "I come from the only Jewish family in Gonzales, Texas, and I can tell you, that was no walk in the park."

Victor thought about the things Ruth had told him about being Jewish. How her people had been driven out of every country they'd ever lived in, and during the war, the one Ba had fought in, they'd been locked up in concentration camps and murdered. Maybe Herb did understand how he never felt like he belonged. How he had to always be careful. How his passport said he was American, but nobody treated him like he was.

When Tony came back to collect the dinner trays, he cocked an eyebrow at Victor's barely touched meal and made a note in his chart, but didn't say anything about it. Instead, he took a miniature cup of white liquid from the cart and tried to give it to Victor, but the swelling in his hands made it too hard to hold.

"Here," said Tony. And before Victor knew it, Tony was tipping the chalky goop into his mouth. He could barely get it down without choking.

"What was that?" he said when he could speak again.

Tony hesitated and then said quietly in Victor's ear, "Milk of magnesia, so you can give us a stool sample in the morning. Nobody can just go on command." But he hadn't been quiet enough.

"Nothing to be ashamed of," Herb piped up from the other bed.

"Guess there's no such thing as privacy around here," Victor quipped, trying to cover up his discomfort.

Herb gave a little laugh. "Not really."

For the next few hours, Victor lay in bed, drowsy and feverish but unable to sleep. Everything hurt or prickled or itched, and his blood felt so hot that he imagined it burning the insides of his veins. Dr. Behr had said the medicine would help. Victor wondered how long it would take to start working, but he was too tired to ask Herb about it, or even to read. All he could do was watch the sunlight tiptoe backward out of the room as the sky dimmed and night rose along with the volume of the crickets' song. It was a sound he hadn't heard in seven years of living in New York, though he'd never noticed its absence until now.

At nine, a bell rang.

"Bread and milk!" a voice called from the hall.

"From our own dairy and bakery," said Herb. "You should have some. The watchmen bring it around every night."

Soon the man who'd opened the front gate came in pushing a cart with a beat-up metal pitcher and loaves of sliced bread. From the fragrant, yeasty smell in the air, Victor could tell it was freshly baked, and for the first time since he'd arrived, he felt a twinge of real hunger.

"Any takers?" said the watchman. "Mr. Klein? How about you, kid?"

Victor nodded. The man poured milk from the spout into the water glasses on the bedside tables and handed out the bread. Closing his eyes, Victor sank his teeth into a still-warm slice. Crusty on the outside, with a springy chew on the inside, it tasted a bit like the Italian bread from the deli on Allerton Avenue, only better. He swallowed, taking a sip of the cold, sweet milk that smelled faintly of grass, and waited. Once he was confident that his stomach wouldn't rebel, he wolfed down the rest.

Later, in the hush after lights-out, after Herb began to snore, Victor shifted from side to side in the dark, trying to find a position where the throbbing in his hands would dull enough to let him sleep. But it was no use. He couldn't escape his body or his thoughts. Would tonight be the last time he would feel this pain? What would happen if they opened up his arms and discovered that his nerves were even worse than they'd thought? Dr. Behr had sounded so confident about his technique, but if it was new, did that mean he hadn't done it much before? This was the kind of thing Henry would worry about. Ruth said he was paranoid, and maybe he was, but he usually had a point.

Victor wondered what Henry, Ba, and Ruth were doing right now. It wasn't that late. Henry was probably in his rented room, smoking and listening to the radio after a dinner eaten alone in Chinatown or at the diner on Allerton Avenue. In the apartment behind the laundry, Ba was probably reading a novel while Ruth sat beside him writing a letter. She'd promised Victor that she'd send him mail right away, and with a pang of guilt, he realized he should have written to her earlier. He wouldn't be able to for a while after the operation. Were they worried about him? They must be. The nurse who'd brought him from Bellevue said she'd send a telegram to let Ba know he was here, but who would tell him about the operation?

The fever continued to roll through him in surges of liquid heat as the night pulsed around him. It was too quiet without the soothing hum of the traffic sounds he was used to at home. He tried taking off his socks, sticking one foot out of the blanket, then both, but it wasn't enough. Bathed in sweat, he threw off his blanket completely. After a brief moment of relief, the air drifting over his clammy gown made him shiver with cold. He should have been used to this nighttime cycle by now, but he wasn't, and he couldn't stand it anymore.

Out in the hall, Victor thought he heard something, footsteps, maybe whispers. He couldn't make out what they were saying and he didn't much care. A bone-deep tiredness had finally overcome him. And nothing, not fear or pain, could stop his body from switching off like a light.

FOUR

The next morning, Victor woke up swollen and achy, his skin clammy, as usual. He started to sit up until he remembered that he had surgery today. Dread knocked him back down. As he lay there, the weight of it sat like a boulder on his chest, heavy enough to push him through the mattress and the floor, all the way to the basement. Ruth would have told him to be positive, to look forward to getting well. He told himself to imagine how much better he'd feel when it was over, but he couldn't, no matter how hard he tried.

After Tony took his urine and stool samples to the lab and a sister-nurse came to draw his blood, Victor was instructed to shower.

"Make sure you put it all over your arms," said Tony, handing him a small bottle of liquid soap. "It's to kill the germs on your skin before the surgery, but don't use any on your head or face. And careful not to catch your stitches on the towel. Pat yourself dry, don't rub."

Victor nodded, glad to finally be able to wash away two days' worth of sweat and grime, and to have a moment to himself. Ever since he got here, he'd been poked and prodded and watched. His stitches burned as if he'd been bitten by fire ants, and his hands felt especially tender. Under the gentle spray, the water felt so good on his skin that he didn't mind the strong antiseptic smell of the soap or the sting of it on his wounds. He stayed under the water, making it as hot as he could bear, until he heard a loud knock on the door. It was time.

Releasing a cloud of steam as he stepped into the room, he saw that instead of a wheelchair, Tony had brought a gurney.

"Hop on," Tony said, lowering the bars.

"Good luck," said Herb.

Victor gave him a nervous smile, but remembering that he couldn't see it, murmured, "Thanks," as he climbed up on the gurney. "Do I have to lie down?" he asked Tony.

"Not if you don't want to." Tony pushed him out of the room.

In the hall, Victor's eyes skittered from left to right, from the posters to the bulletin boards, as he avoided the eyes of the people they passed. His heart was flopping around like a hooked fish. Sweat dampened his fresh gown.

When they reached the operating room, a sister-nurse met them at the door wearing white linens over her robes. A surgical mask covered her nose and mouth.

"Wait here," she said.

Was there something wrong? Victor's eyes flicked over to Tony.

"Ca va, cher," he said. "They won't be long."

Victor turned to the window, where his eye caught something—someone—in the distance. A girl, dead center, in the avenue of oaks. Behind her, the sun lit the top of her brown hair like a crown as she walked toward the infirmary in a white blouse and a pair of cuffed dungarees. She turned her head, and her face became clear. Heart-shaped, with strong, even features. A wide mouth, a pointed chin. Catching the light through the leaves, her silver barrette flashed like a signal lamp, and Victor felt sure she was the most beautiful girl he'd ever seen. She must have been a patient on her way to an appointment or to get her meds, and she looked about his age. Would she be in his class when school started, that is if he was alive and well enough to go?

After a moment, the operating room door opened again and the sister-nurse came out.

"I'll be here when it's over," Tony said, holding the door so she could push him through.

Inside, the light over the table was bright enough to make Victor see spots. It reflected off the metal instruments—scalpels, clamps, tweezers, syringes. The two sister-nurses and Dr. Behr, whose broad back was turned to him, looked otherworldly in their white uniforms, like angels.

"Ready?" said Dr. Behr, turning around. Above his mask, his eyes were the color of blueberries.

This is it. This might be the last thing I see, Victor thought. His rib cage clamped down on his lungs like an iron corset. A sister-nurse swabbed his arm with alcohol and handed the doctor a syringe.

"Just a quick little shot." Dr. Behr jabbed in the needle and slowly pushed down the plunger. "Now count backward from twenty for me."

"Twenty, nineteen, eighteen . . ." Victor counted until he couldn't count anymore.

A MOSQUITO WHINED in Victor's ear. His eyelids fluttered open, but he couldn't see anything distinct. Only dense, black shapes in a softer dark that must have been empty space. Was it night? He'd been sleeping since the operation, turning his head this way and that in search of a cool spot on his pillow. The chirping of the crickets seemed distorted, eerie. But underneath that sound was an old, forgotten quiet from his early childhood in the countryside. Not silence, but the static of wind and plants, and the small movements of living things.

His mouth felt cottony, his throat parched. He caught the glint of the glass on the table beside his bed, but he couldn't move his arms. They were propped up on pillows on either side of him, bandaged with bulky dressings from his wrists to his elbows, and they were beginning to register a sharp pain. It was different from the dull ache he was used to. So this new pain was good, or at least better, since it meant he wasn't numb.

"New boy," Victor heard a man say out in the hall.

"From China?" said a woman.

"No, New York City."

They were talking about him. Victor cleared his throat and was about to call out to them for water, but the soft snores from the bed beyond the curtain told him Herb was asleep. He decided to wait until morning.

Asthmatic since infancy, Victor had taught himself long ago how to wait out panic, the horror of suffocation, of drowning in his own lungs. The asthma came without warning, in clusters of attacks that were particularly scary during the war. In Toisan Province, with so many of the men in America or Canada or the West Indies, when the Japanese invaded, there was nothing anyone in his village could do but run to the hills and hide. Victor had been born smack in the middle of war and famine. Like the floods that turned the ground floor of his house into a pond every monsoon season, his asthma became just another fact of life, another difficulty to endure. Nobody was afraid of asthma or what it meant to have it, and nothing about it made people recoil in horror. He'd learned to live with it, but Hansen's, or "this package," as Herb called it, had already taken away the life he'd known.

In the morning, when the sun slipped through the drapes, it was the purity of the light that told him he wasn't at home in the Bronx. At the laundry, no matter how much they cleaned, fabric dust was always floating around, sparkling in the few hours of sunlight that made it through the windows, through the buildings and the smog. When he was younger, before he knew it made his asthma worse, the riot of tiny sparks had seemed magical, as if America had been called Gold Mountain because even the air glittered.

He turned his head to the wall, where beads of liquid were trickling down. Was he hallucinating? He felt the prickle of sweat deep beneath his bandages and knew that in a moment it would cause a terrible itch he couldn't possibly scratch. To distract himself, he turned his attention outside, to the clickety-clack of ladies' heels.

"I swear, I've already used up a whole can of Aqua Net this week," a woman said, "and look at me. My hair's still as limp as wet noodles."

Another woman laughed.

No, he wasn't hallucinating. The air vibrated with heat, and after the footsteps faded away, the quiet had a texture. Victor yawned.

"Congratulations," said Herb. "I heard you sailed through with flying colors."

"Doesn't seem that way to me," Victor croaked, his throat hoarse.

"It takes a while for the drugs to leave your system. How are you feeling?"

"Seasick. And it hurts," Victor said, but he didn't want to think about it. "Why are you in the infirmary, anyway?"

"Just a reaction to my meds. I should be back in my cottage soon." Cottages weren't mentioned in the brochure, only dormitories. "You missed breakfast. Tony can bring you something if you're hungry. And something for the pain."

"No, thanks." A wave of nausea rolled through Victor's body, followed by a wave of drowsiness. "Maybe later. I just want to sleep."

For the rest of that day, he drifted in and out of consciousness, missing lunch, dinner, and the bread-and-milk cart before lights-out. Sweat-slicked, dreaming furiously, he swam over and over to the surface of waking, only to sink back into sleep. In one dream, he was in his neighborhood, watching a jumble of scenes from *I Love Lucy* and *The Lone Ranger* through the window of Sal's Appliance Shop.

In another dream, he was at the corner candy store, watching an egg cream being made—the fast, practiced movements of the soda jerk's hands, the ribbons of chocolate syrup, the splashing of milk, the clinks of the long silver spoon stirring white into brown, the jet-spray fizz of seltzer filling the glass with foam.

Victor opened his eyes, disoriented, and tried to take a deep, slow breath. From outside, the honey-sweet scent of magnolias—Ma's favorite flowers—drifted in on a breeze. At the window, the pale white wings of a moth fluttered, tangled in the curtain, ghostly and delicate as flower petals or a woman's nightgown.

"Ma," he whispered. And shaken, he tried to push the thought of her away.

He didn't want to bring her here, not like this, not without her knowing where he was so she could meet him in her imagination. He felt his throat close, the pain choking him like it had when he'd first left her. Henry had told him the feeling would go away, but it never actually did. It just appeared less frequently. Now he was afraid the clench of emotion would seize his heart, too, and kill him right then and there. He tried to control it, to think of something else, but his mind wouldn't listen.

"Stem of my heart," she called him. She'd let him sleep in her bed long after he'd grown out of it, smoothing his brow with the coolness of her work-worn hands.

A RAY OF morning light shone on Victor's face, reddening the insides of his eyelids. Wanting more sleep, he tried to get away from it by rolling onto his side. Pain shot down the length of his arm. He flopped onto his back again, whimpering, and watched the blades of the ceiling fan turn. He counted their slow revolutions until the agony in his right arm dulled to a bone-deep ache that matched the one in his left.

"You okay?" said Herb.

"Yeah," said Victor, embarrassed. Henry wouldn't have made noises like that. He would have been stoic no matter how much it hurt.

Victor could hear the sounds of the infirmary waking up around them—footsteps, wheels, metallic clangs, the opening and closing of doors. His head was clear enough now for him to feel the emptiness of his stomach, and when Tony came in with the meal cart, the smell of bacon, eggs, toast, and coffee made it growl. His sheets were twisted and damp with sweat. He felt bad that Tony would have to change them.

After giving Herb his breakfast, Tony helped Victor sit up, stacking a couple more pillows under his forearms before arranging his tray in front of him. To his disappointment, it had only a bowl of broth, a mug of tea, and a little paper cup of pills.

"You've got to start slow," said Tony. "We'll see how you get on with this, and maybe at lunch, you can have something solid."

When he was little, Ma would make him jook when he wasn't feeling well. The thin rice porridge settled his stomach with just the right amount of blandness and starch. When he was sick at home in the Bronx, Ba would make it, too, or tell Henry to bring some from Chinatown. Victor longed for jook now. He sniffed at the broth. It smelled like chicken, vegetables, and herbs. He reached for the spoon and paused, wondering if he'd be able to hold it.

"Go ahead," said Tony. "It's good to use your hands right away. Helps with the stiffness and swelling. The pills are for the pain. You can take them once you've got a little something in your stomach."

Victor's hand shook, but he managed to get a spoonful of broth in his mouth without spilling it down his front. He lifted the mug of dark, fragrant tea to his lips and was surprised by the taste of lemon and honey, unfamiliar but soothing. When his bowl and mug were empty, he swallowed the pills with some water. He imagined the network of nerves the doctor had cut deep inside him, then moved and stuck back together.

Waiting for the pills to kick in, he gazed out the window and let his eyes roam to the trees where he'd seen that girl yesterday. To the left of them, the plantation house stood like a guard by the gate, to the right was an expanse of green, and wherever he looked, the barbed wire fence loomed, though he couldn't see any of the other things the brochure had mentioned. Not the school, the recreation center, or the mall of patient-run shops. Not the golf course, the softball field, the tennis court, or the lake. He couldn't see any of the dorms either, or the cottages where Herb said he lived. There were supposed to be five hundred patients here, enough to populate a small town, and Victor wondered how many besides the girl were his age.

His head felt a bit floaty now. Moving his fingers, he watched them wave in slow motion below his bandages like seaweed on a calm day. They looked the same as they did before, when he was struggling with his breakfast, but the pain was somehow muffled, as if its volume had been dialed down. The throbbing in his arms was less intense, too. He couldn't feel his heartbeat in them anymore, and the pull and burn of his sutures had dulled. Even the heat of his fever seemed bearable, almost pleasant, and the urge to scratch the poky stitches from his biopsies had faded.

Victor sat, relaxing into the growing relief when, with a start, he realized he'd forgotten to ask someone to tell his father about the operation. He groaned.

"Pills not working yet?" said Herb.

"No. It's just that my family doesn't know I had the surgery."

"That's no problem. Tony can send a telegram, or better yet, why don't you give them a call?"

Victor had only ever used the pay phone at the drugstore because they didn't have a phone at the laundry, but he'd called Henry once or twice at the print shop where he worked and he remembered the number.

"I guess I could call my brother," he said, "but it's long distance and I don't have any money."

"Wouldn't do you any good if you did. The canteen's got the only phone for patients, but there are a few in the infirmary. Sister Helen has one in her lab."

"Oh," said Victor, remembering how he'd felt under the gaze of her camera and sharp blue eyes. "I don't think she likes me."

"I don't know about that, but she likes *me*," Herb said. "I've got an appointment for a new set of beauty shots in a little while. I can ask her for you."

When Herb got back from the medical photography clinic, he said Sister Helen had agreed as long as Tony could bring him to the lab right away. Victor had thought she was just a photographer, and when he said so in the hall, Tony told him she was a pharmacist and ran the lab, too. She'd been studying how Hansen's progressed and responded to different drugs and doses for years when, in 1941, she helped discover Promin, otherwise known as the Miracle of Carville.

"Most folks remember Dr. Faget as the hero," he said, "but Sister Helen and the other sister-nurses did a lot of the work, too."

"That doesn't seem fair," said Victor.

"No, but I guess it's not godly to complain."

The research lab was tucked in a nook of the infirmary. When they got there, Sister Helen was perched on a high stool, squinting into a microscope with Bunsen burners, beakers, and bottles all around her. She removed the glass slide she was looking at, put it in a box, and wrote something down in the notebook by her side before turning her owl-like stare on Victor.

"Mr. Klein tells me you'd like to call your family in New York." She raised her right eyebrow. "Patients don't have phone privileges in the infirmary, but I'm prepared to make an exception this time, on account of your surgery."

"Thank you," said Victor, unsure of what to make of her tone. He couldn't tell if she was doing him a kindness or doing Herb a favor.

"Well," she said, with a hint of impatience, "what's your number?"

"We don't have a phone, but my brother has one at work. Henry Chin at Lee's Print Shop, Canal-6–2260."

Sister Helen scribbled on a pad beside a big black telephone and put the receiver to where her ear must have been beneath her cornette. Victor watched her dial 1–1–0, which he knew was for long-distance calls.

"Hello, operator, I'd like to place a person-to-person call from Victor Chin to Henry Chin in New York City at Lee's Print Shop, Canal-6–2260. My number is Carville-1605." She paused, then said, "Thank you. Yes, I'll hold," and, stretching the cord over to the wheelchair, she handed the receiver to Victor.

He reached for it and fumbled, wincing at its weight as he tried to wrap his stiff fingers around the handset. Worried that it might put too much pressure on his stitches, he glanced at Tony to see if it was okay. When Tony nodded, he raised the receiver to his ear, cradling it on his shoulder just in case.

"Five minutes," said Sister Helen as she and Tony left the room, keeping the door open.

"Hello?" said Victor. There was silence on the other end, and for a moment, he was afraid he'd been disconnected.

But the operator said, "I have Henry Chin on the line."

There was a crackling noise, and after a beat, Henry said, "So, you're alive."

The sound of his voice, with its usual wry tone, was both familiar and strange through all those miles of telephone wire, and hearing it, Victor was surprised by the tears prickling his eyes over such an ordinary thing. He'd only seen Henry a few days ago, but it felt like they'd been apart for much longer. Before he left New York, he'd never been more than a few miles from his brother in his entire life.

"Didn't Ba get the telegram?"

"Yeah," said Henry. "That was just a joke."

"Ha," Victor said in a deadpan voice. "It was so funny, I forgot to laugh." Henry laughed at that like he always did, and as always, Victor felt a little glow of pride. "Can you talk?"

"Sure, I'm on my break." Victor could hear the sound of a match being struck followed by a sharp intake of breath.

In the background, over the gentle noise of the machines, someone was shouting in Hong Kong–style Cantonese, "One hundred invitations for the Liu wedding!" and he could picture his brother standing there next to the letterpress, with the earpiece in one hand and a cigarette in the other, stooping a bit to speak into the receiver.

Victor had always envied how Mr. Lee's shop was filled with all sorts of interesting objects, making it seem so much better than the laundry—sheets of gold and silver leaf, sheaves of paper in different colors and thicknesses, trays of letters and characters made of lead. Whenever he'd visited, it was busy with the squeak and hum of the printing machines, the sound of the paper running through them like soft applause. Even the air smelled good there, like ink and oil and tobacco smoke, like the kind of work that made beautiful things.

"So, how are you?" said Henry.

"I got the operation."

"Are you serious? They're supposed to clear that with Ba first."

"He signed a consent form, so I guess they did," said Victor, fudging the truth.

Henry made a grudging sound. "Does it hurt?"

"Yeah, but not too bad. The pain pills help. They said it would take a while for my arms to heal and the medicine to work, but I haven't started it yet."

"What's the holdup?"

Victor tried to explain that the doctors had to do more tests and that, according to the forms Ba had signed, he had to stay until they said he could go. He could hear Henry's skepticism in his silence. To lighten the tension, he told him how Dr. Behr had used a new, improved technique that would make his hands the same as they were before he got sick.

"So they didn't give you the operation you were supposed to get?" Henry sounded almost happy to have caught him out. "They're experimenting on you. The Japanese did that to POWs, you know, and the Nazis did it, too."

"What are you talking about?" Victor snapped. "The doctor said it was better than the one they do at Bellevue."

"Don't be such a chump. If they can't force you, they'll trick you. Bet you a million dollars they're going to keep saying you're sick. They'll lock you up and throw away the key."

Victor thought of how Herb had been here since 1931 and would probably stay for the rest of his life. But he also said people got discharged all the time.

"I don't think that's true," said Victor, trying to sound sure of himself. "The guy I'm sharing a room with says plenty of people get sent home."

"Is he Chinese?"

"What's that got to do with it?"

"Don't you know the papers say that Chinese people spread leprosy?"

"So?" he said, starting to get lost in the twists and turns of Henry's logic. "The papers don't run Carville, the government does," and as soon as he said it, he knew he'd made a mistake.

Henry launched into a speech Victor had heard a million times about how the Chinese came to America to work for nothing, doing things other people didn't want to do, only to be accused of stealing jobs and driving up wages. And the government was just itching for an excuse to get rid of them.

"Yeah, I know." Victor rolled his eyes. "Last I checked, I was in Louisiana, not China."

"Believe me, they'd send you back if they could. But keeping you there is the next best thing. Just like they put Japanese people in those camps. Even kids who were born here. If the government can do that to them because of the war, why can't they do that to you because you're sick?"

"I don't know," Victor said, and went quiet, thinking. Were those camps really like Carville? Henry talked as if the comparison were obvious, but he wasn't sure if it added up. There were patients here from all over, and as far as Victor could tell, a lot of them were white. On the other hand, there was the barbed wire fence.

Henry seemed to take his silence as a win and changed the subject. "What's it like there, anyway?"

"I haven't gone around much yet," said Victor, relieved that Henry had quit badgering him, "but the nurses are nuns with these huge white hats and the place is really pretty. I think it was a plantation once."

"That means it had slaves, you know. They kidnapped Africans and forced them to work there until they died."

Victor thought of the fields outside, so innocent-looking and green, and pictured them as they must have been back then, filled with suffering. He didn't know what to say. Taking the receiver away from his ear, he realized it was covered in sweat. He wiped it on his chest and wedged it between his other ear and shoulder, shifting uncomfortably in his wheelchair. The backs of his legs were sweaty, too, and slippery on the leather seat. His temperature was shooting up again. Even though the pills were taking the edge off his pain, they made his head feel like he was underwater. Sister Helen came back in with Tony trailing behind her.

"Look," said Victor in a low voice, "I don't want to fight."

Henry sighed. "All I'm saying is, if you want to come home, I'll help. We can figure out the forms later, okay?"

"I have to go. Tell Dad I called."

"'Dad'?" Henry repeated.

Sister Helen tapped the face of her watch.

"Bye," Victor said, and hung up fast, dropping the heavy handset with a thunk.

VICTOR WAS QUIET on the way back to Room 33, staring into space, barely registering Sister Laura waving in the hall as his brother's words echoed in his head. Fatigue weighed him down like a rain-soaked blanket. Lying back on the pillows, he grimaced with his eyes closed, nostrils pinching and flaring along with his breath. He knew Herb would want to talk about the call, and he prepared himself to get some answers.

"He's not happy about me being here," Victor said when Herb asked how Henry was. "He thinks it's a prison where the doctors experiment on us and I'll never get to go home."

"I see," said Herb. "And what do *you* think?"

"I don't know about the experiments, but there do seem to be a lot of rules. And why aren't we allowed to leave?" There were the case numbers and guards, and the fence, too, but Victor wanted to hear what Herb would tell him on his own without too much prompting.

"Tell you the truth, it used to be like a prison, but that was a long time ago. Of course we're still under federal quarantine, but life's pretty good here now. You'll see once you move to the dorms and start going to school."

"But what about the fence?"

Herb paused for a moment, readjusting the pillows behind his back before explaining that the fence kept the public out as much as it kept the patients in. Outsiders were afraid, he said, not so much of the disease itself, but of what it represented, because the stigma of leprosy was more contagious than Hansen's could ever be. When Dr. Al was in charge, for instance, the staff would turn a blind eye if patients snuck out for a bit of fun, or to get married, as long as they came back. If they didn't, the police would have to go after them, and even if they didn't get caught, they'd usually wind up back at Carville when their symptoms got bad again. Then they'd have to do their thirty days in jail.

"What about now?" Victor was getting the impression that Herb was trying to make things sound better than they were and he wanted the truth.

"Morton's stricter," Herb said, waving his hand in a vague sort of way. "As for experimenting on people, this is a research hospital. Without experiments, we wouldn't have a cure, but nothing happens against our will. I was in the clinical trial for Promin, so I guess you could say I volunteered to be a guinea pig."

That sounded reasonable enough, but a drug wasn't the same as an operation where you weren't even awake to see what they were doing to you. "My brother said my surgery was an experiment and they shouldn't have done it."

"Science is based on trial and error," said Herb. When doctors got a new idea, he explained, they'd run a study like the one they did on Promin, where patients would agree to try something on the chance that it might make them feel better. The doctors would see what got the best results and scrap the treatments that didn't work, which was most of them. When Herb first got to Carville, they were testing out chaulmoogra oil.

"Still makes me sick to my stomach thinking about it." He made a disgusted face, remembering. "Before that, they tried plenty of other stuff, like trypan blue dye, the smallpox vaccine, diphtheria toxoid. All failed experiments."

Victor was willing to believe that Herb was telling the truth about the fence and the drug trials, but he hadn't really addressed Henry's concern about the operation. What would his brother think if he were here right now? Herb was white, he'd probably say, so things were bound to be different for him. Judging by the way Tony and Sister Helen acted around Herb, he did seem to get special treatment. Victor thought of Mr. Wang and some of the other non-white patients he'd seen, people who couldn't walk or use their hands, people whose skin was rough and leathery, whose faces seemed somehow smudged, as if they'd been in an accident or a fire.

"Why do some people have deformities?" Victor asked without thinking. He tried to read Herb's face to see if he was offended, but his dark glasses hid too much.

"Bad luck. We were sick for too long before they found the cure," said Herb in a normal voice before it got quiet. "A couple of the guys I knew back then lost hope and committed suicide."

Victor frowned. He was lucky, he supposed, to be at Carville now, just like he was lucky to have gone to America when he did. In Ba's time, instead of the few days his sons had spent at Immigration in San Francisco, Chinese newcomers were detained at Angel Island, a prison of a place where they could keep you indefinitely, regardless of your passport or visa, and people sometimes killed themselves while waiting. Victor had never understood before why anyone would do that, but now he could see how it might have been a relief for them to die.

DR. BEHR SNIPPED through the gauze and removed the bulky surgical dressing. Victor closed his eyes when his skin met the air. For the past few days, he'd only been allowed sponge baths, which he couldn't even give himself. He couldn't risk getting his bandages wet, though they were yellow and grimy around the edges. The salty-sour smell of old sweat hit him as the gauze was lifted away, and he opened his eyes to see his incisions for the first time. Running along his inner arms from an inch below his elbows to the middle of his triceps, they were perfectly straight, as if drawn with a marker, and sewn shut with tiny black sutures. Fields of bruises surrounded them in vivid purples and deep blues that would have been beautiful if they weren't on a human body. But they were. Victor could hardly recognize his arms as his own.

"Bruising is normal," said Dr. Behr, pressing on the flesh surrounding one neat row of stitches after the other. "No weeping, no sign of infection. We can start you on Promin today."

Victor was expecting pills, but a young nurse with a small, doll-like face handed the doctor a syringe and a glass ampoule, and he realized he was about to get a shot. He listened as Dr. Behr told the nurse in a patient voice what the dosage was supposed to be—one per day for six days, one day off, then another six in a row until he was discharged from the infirmary. After that, they'd transition him to Diasone tablets before the start of the school year.

"We administer Promin intravenously." Dr. Behr gave the nurse a little pat on the arm before turning to Victor. "You're going to hold still for me, right?"

Victor nodded.

Dr. Behr turned over his hand and tapped on one of the veins. "We can use your other hand tomorrow. Makes it easier to alternate."

"No," said Victor more loudly than he'd meant to, remembering how excruciating it had been to poke his own finger with a sewing needle. "I mean, can't you do it somewhere else?"

Dr. Behr sighed. "I guess I could try here." He pointed to the spot on Victor's inner elbow where he'd gotten his blood drawn the other day. "It'll be a lot less comfortable, but suit yourself."

Victor braced himself as the needle pierced his skin, but it didn't hurt very much, though maybe that wasn't a good sign. Not if it meant he'd lost more sensation. He shuddered when the medicine went in, the cold of it spreading slowly, traveling up and down his arm, into his wrist and hand. Staring at the poster of the man with his insides exposed, he tried to imagine the Promin flowing into the larger network of his veins, winnowing like water through the roots of a tree to kill the bacteria invading his cells and repair what had been damaged from the inside out. But his mind wandered to other things, taking him out of his body, to Coney Island, to the beach and the rides, to a root beer float at the corner drugstore, the way the foam spilled over the lip of the glass when a scoop of ice cream was dropped in it. Then he thought of the girl he'd seen on his way to surgery, wondering what she might be doing right now and when he would see her again. Would he run into her in the infirmary? What would he say if he dared to speak? She was the type of girl who wouldn't have given him the time of day in the Bronx, but here, maybe it would be different.

Later, in his room, when Victor was done retching into a bedpan, he sat back against the pillows, wiping his mouth on the shoulder of his gown. He hoped he wouldn't have to go through this every day. He didn't know if he could bear it.

IN THE INFIRMARY, Victor's mornings began at 7:15 with a breakfast tray. At 8:00, Tony came back to take it away. Lunch was from 11:15 to noon, and if there was any mail, Tony would bring it then.

Herb seemed to receive something every day—letters, magazines, newspapers—along with proofs of articles for *The STAR*, the magazine he'd founded with some other patients three months after his arrival. Not only had Hansen's taken Herb's sight, but the loss of sensation in his hands meant he couldn't read braille either, so he needed everything read to him out loud. Usually, a group of volunteers would do it, but since the infirmary restricted visitors, he asked Victor to help him instead. Victor didn't mind at all. He found most of what he read interesting, especially the stuff in the magazine about regular life at Carville. In one article, a patient wrote about the annual golf tournament and another complained about how some businesses—even local ones that ought to know better—wouldn't deliver to the institution because they were afraid to touch "leper money."

Since his arrival, Ruth had sent Victor a care package he shared with Herb and Tony, and some letters, cheerful, chatty, and full of questions he didn't know how to answer. Was he settling in? Was he making any friends? Was it really like a country club, like the doctor at Bellevue said? Ba didn't write on his own, but added a line or two when Ruth was done, just practical things like how much money he was depositing in his Carville account. Henry hadn't written at all and Victor wasn't disappointed, not just because he was sick of his rants, but because a letter from him would mean one from Ma. The thought of writing back to her now, from this place, filled him with dread.

The afternoons passed quickly, especially since dinner was so early. Sometimes, at home, they wouldn't eat until nine, but here, lights-out was at ten.

In between meals, when Victor wasn't in his room, he was at one of his many appointments. His dressings had to be changed every day at the bandaging clinic, where he quickly discovered which of the sister-nurses had gentle hands, which one was impatient, and which one liked to ask questions without listening to the answers. Unlike the nurses at Bellevue, none of the sisters wore gloves here. The warmth of their touch soothed him, both because the human contact felt good and because it meant they weren't afraid.

But that didn't make it any less uncomfortable. If the gauze got stuck on a suture, the sister would have to tug it free, and whenever that happened, he couldn't keep the hurt from coming out of his mouth. The feeling of his skin pulling apart at the seams was worse than the ache inside his wounds. The best part was the relief he got from the ointment when they swabbed it on his itchy, healing incisions. They were still pink and raw, and crusted around their edges, but the bruises were fading and the swelling had gone down a bit in his hands.

After the bandaging came the Promin injections and the tests. Blood work in case the Promin was causing anemia. Urinalysis to make sure his kidneys were working okay. Soon he was ready for physical therapy. Three times a week, Miss Abigail, a public health nurse sent by the government, taught him exercises for his nerves. He'd begin by extending his arms with his palms up, as if he were holding a pizza, and curling his fingers inward one by one. Then, with his elbows bent, he'd touch his shoulders with his fists and repeat the exercise five times. On his first try, his arms shook so badly, he couldn't even curl his middle fingers before he gave up, slumping in his chair.

"It'll get easier," said Miss Abigail, sitting down next to him. "You'll see."

"Not if my hands fall off," Victor muttered.

"That's a myth. And a very unhelpful one."

He shrugged and she explained how lack of treatment caused symptoms often mistaken for loss of limbs. Numbness from nerve damage, for instance, made patients unable to feel anything when they got hurt, and if their wounds got infected, the doctors would sometimes have to amputate.

"What about people whose hands look like this?" Victor tried to crook his fingers in the shape of Mr. Wang's.

"Mains-en-griffes." She nodded. "That happens when the Hansen's bacteria attack the bones and the fingers start to retract. If you leave it untreated, they grow shorter and shorter, and full of tiny holes."

Did Miss Abigail say "man in grief"? It seemed like an appropriate name. If that was what had happened to Mr. Wang, then maybe it was for the best that he was numb.

The surgery made moving less painful, as Dr. Behr had promised, but Victor was shocked by how much effort it took to get his hands to do even the simplest things. Sending a message from his brain to his finger, telling it to bend or flex, reminded him of his futile childhood attempts to make rocks levitate. And though they were better than they'd been when he first got here, his hands were still so stiff and swollen that it was hard to imagine they'd ever be anything like normal again.

"Your nerves are learning, just like you," Miss Abigail said.

At their next session, though he couldn't curl them all the way, Victor was able to will each of his ten fingers to move at least a little bit.

One by one, as his hands became less inflamed, he added exercises to his daily routine, squeezing tennis balls and waving his arms like semaphore signals. The therapy went at a snail's pace and made him ache for hours afterward, but each day, he was getting stronger.

He was well enough now to get around the infirmary by himself. After appointments, he'd wander a bit, peeking into different rooms, careful not to get in trouble. When he was younger, after finishing his deliveries in an apartment building, he'd often go down to the basement and poke around in the junk people left there, treasure troves of unwanted things—old magazines and comics, bicycle parts, lampshades, broken clocks, and dressmakers' dummies. But here in the infirmary, at the bottom of the stairs, the basement door had a sign that said "Morgue." As soon as he saw it, he did an abrupt about-face and never went down there again.

Upstairs, Victor was strolling around the men's ward one day, whistling a tune from *Peter and the Wolf*. Ruth owned that album and had let him listen to it on her record player as much as he wanted. "Peter's theme" had always given him a bittersweet feeling, reminding him of summer days, or, more accurately, the days of his last summer in China, when he was eight and the war was over. When nobody was hungry or in danger, and his father hadn't written yet to say he was taking him away from Ma. That summer, he'd finally been old enough to hold his own with Henry and his friends when they went frog hunting, fishing, and swimming. He'd been so innocent and naive, just like that little tune. Like Peter before he knew the wolf was coming.

On the other side of the hall, Victor saw two brown-skinned patients, one old and one young, resting in their beds. Their room was the same as the one he shared with Herb except for the view. Instead of facing front toward the river, it overlooked the covered walkway and the buildings behind it, making it far less bright. That didn't surprise him. He knew he was getting special treatment only because of Herb, and not just for little things like extra dessert. If it weren't for him, he never would have been able to call Henry after his surgery. It reminded him of how Ruth helped his family with things that were harder for them because they were Chinese, and though it hurt Ba's pride, Victor knew they'd be worse off if she didn't do it. What surprised him was that he'd been put in Herb's room in the first place.

Another time, venturing to the third floor, he found a patio with a row of rocking chairs. Walking its perimeter, he could see all of the grounds, including the lake and beyond the fence, to the levee and, finally, the river. With no one else around, he sat down and rocked back and forth under the canopy, facing the Mississippi. The water was a muddy brown and busy with boats, the width of it narrower than he would have expected. A light breeze carrying a whiff of low tide reached him, ruffling his hair, and though the heat covered his skin in a fine layer of sweat, he shivered as if a ghost were passing through his body. He leaned back, drawing his knees up to his chest, wondering when he would stop getting these chills. To reassure himself, he touched his thumbs and forefingers together, interlacing the rest of his fingers. He whispered the rhyme Ruth had taught him about the church and the steeple, and smiled. The Promin was working—he was getting better, though he still had a long way to go.

The sound of nearby laughter startled him. He got up and peered over the railing. Two boys and a girl, the same girl he'd seen between the oaks, were down in the tea garden, the sight of her sending a jolt of excitement into the pit of his stomach. She was wearing a yellow button-down shirt knotted over a pair of plaid shorts. His eyes lingered on the sliver of skin above her waistband as he imagined what it would feel like to touch her there. The three of them clustered together like friends, and he could hear them talking, but not what they were saying.

With the taller boy, who had a black pompadour haircut and dark olive skin, the girl's shoulders looked loose and relaxed as she smiled up at him, but with the other one, there was some kind of a charge. When she spoke to him, Victor noticed how she held her body stiff and straight, as if she were sucking in her stomach. He was shorter than the tall boy, but taller than the girl, and he had jet-black hair, too. When Victor caught a glimpse of his face, he thought he might be Chinese, a surprise especially given how the girl was acting with him.

Victor wasn't interested only in her, but in all of them. He wondered what it would be like to belong to this group. Images scrolled through his mind—the four of them eating their meals together, going to class, walking the grounds. He pictured himself in the garden with them, joking around. For a moment, he thought about calling down to them, but decided that would be too embarrassing. He didn't want to meet anyone until he was out of his bandages. Even though it was stupid, considering where they all were, he wanted to seem as normal to them as he could.

Victor had never really had a circle of friends. He hadn't fit into the cliques at school or in the neighborhood, where most of the kids were Italian, Jewish, or Puerto Rican, and he didn't like the two other Chinese kids he knew. Not the stuck-up boy whose father owned a restaurant or the timid girl who never said a word. And while he was sometimes included in the stickball games on his block, it was rare for him to get much closer to anyone than that. If he did make friends with someone, once he hung around with the rest of their group, it was only a matter of time before one of them would make a crack about eating dogs or ask him if his mother had bound feet. Then the kid he'd befriended would be put in the awkward spot of defending him or keeping quiet. Of course the kid always picked the latter, and while Victor was hurt, he would overlook it, figuring it was better to have one friend than none.

In fifth grade, there was a kid named Noah who seemed like a bit of a loner. For a while, he and Victor had tooled around together in the neighborhood, where, after a class trip to the Natural History Museum to see an archeology exhibit, they took to digging with sticks for bits of broken plates and old coins in the empty lot behind their school. When Noah's family moved in the middle of sixth grade, Victor started spending more time with Jackie, his Paper Brother, the boy who'd traveled with them from China, though he lived a subway ride away.

Victor imagined how things might be different with this group. Here at Carville, there were no parents, no families, and few other kids their age. With no one else to choose from, they would only have one another. Maybe that's what it took—to need and be needed—to be friends.

THE SUN STREAMED across Dr. Behr's desk. Victor watched him loosen his tie and mop his brow with a handkerchief.

"At this rate," he said, "you ought to be discharged to the colony in four, maybe five days and you can start the Diasone, barring any secondary infections."

Victor's sutures were gone now, his skin having knit back together. His bruises were fading, he was tolerating the Promin, and he could tell that his hands were getting better. At physical therapy last week, he'd made half fists, and yesterday, he'd managed to close them all the way. He was still tired and feverish sometimes, but everyone told him to be patient.

When Dr. Behr said he'd begin his monthly skin-scrape tests soon, Victor figured a negative result meant he could go home, just like a positive one had sent him here. He wasn't expecting the doctor to go on about detailed examinations once he got four negatives in a row, or to announce that after twelve, he'd appear before the parole board, as if it were the same as winning a prize.

"If they classify your case as arrested, that's as good as cured." Dr. Behr paused, a line forming between his brows when he saw Victor's face. "That means they'll send you home."

Victor couldn't quite make sense of what he was hearing. Heat crept up his neck as his heart began to pump hard. "What if I test negative for a while and then get a positive?"

"Then we might try a different drug and start the tests again," Dr. Behr said in a clipped tone.

Victor's body wanted to jump up and run screaming from the office, but he still had questions. Why did he need all those negative tests, and who was on this parole board? Whenever he'd asked how long it would take to be cured, the answers had been vague: "It depends on the case," and "We'll see how you get on with your drug regime." Even Herb had said he didn't know.

Now it seemed like the doctors at Bellevue had lied to get him to go to Carville after all. When they said it could take just a few months, they must have known it wasn't true. From what Dr. Behr was saying, even if he tested negative right away, it would be at least a year before he could leave since the tests were done once a month and twelve appeared to be the magic number. As it was, who knew how long it would take for him to get a single negative, let alone twelve in a row? And if he was positive on the eleventh test, he'd have to start all over again. It was just like Henry had said on the phone. They could keep telling him he was sick and he'd never get to go home.

Victor had been quiet for a little while, but Dr. Behr didn't seem to notice.

"You're lucky you don't have any lesions on your face." The doctor leaned in for a closer look, and Victor could smell the fried okra he'd eaten at lunch. "The microbes might have gotten to your nose cartilage a bit, but they haven't damaged your skin. A low nose bridge, like the epicanthic folds on your eyes, is common in Mongoloid features, so it's hard to say if the Hansen's is to blame."

"For what?" Victor wanted to say. To him, his nose looked fine, the same as it always had. But instead, he said, "What's a Mongoloid?"

"It's the scientific term for people from the Orient, like you." Dr. Behr reached for a fat red book on his shelf and flipped to a page of illustrated diagrams, rows of heads shown from different angles, reminding Victor of the medical pictures Sister Helen had taken. The doctor pointed at a head with long black hair braided in a queue, tiny slits for eyes, and a broad, flat nose. "You can borrow it."

Was that what Dr. Behr saw when he looked at him? Victor's face burned, but he took the book anyway, bending his fingers slowly around its thick spine.

Back in his room, when Herb greeted him, he responded with only a humming sound. He felt betrayed by everyone, including Herb, who could have easily told him the truth. Victor dropped the book on his bedside table.

"What have you got there?" Herb asked, reacting to the thud.

"Something about races. 'Physical Anthropology,'" Victor read from the cover, his voice low and cold. "Dr. Behr loaned it to me."

"Garbage," said Herb. "Eugenics, like the Nazis used to justify murdering not just Jews but homosexuals and people who were sick or handicapped, too." Victor knew all about this from Ruth, though he hadn't known what it was called.

"And they're not the only ones," Herb went on. "In Japan, they lock up people with Hansen's in places way worse than this. Places where they sterilize people and force pregnant women to get abortions."

"They don't do that here?"

"No. As a matter of fact, last year, a young lady not much older than you had a baby. She can't keep her on the inside, but her family pays a couple in the next town to take care of her. It's not perfect, but it beats the alternative."

Victor supposed that was true. It was better here than it could have been. Dr. Behr's book might be fake Nazi science, but maybe he didn't realize it, and what he said about Victor's skin was true, too. His face was smooth and unmarked, though the rest of him hadn't been spared. The surgery had left his arms with a set of dark, puckered tracks. Keloid scars, they were apparently called. He would have them for the rest of his life.

"So what else did Behr have to say?" said Herb.

Victor was quiet for a moment. "I found out about the twelve negatives. Why didn't you tell me?" He couldn't keep the bitterness out of his voice.

Herb sighed. "I didn't want to discourage you. I'm sorry."

No adult had ever apologized to Victor before. Not even Ruth, and certainly not Ba. It was so foreign that he wasn't sure how to react.

"At least they're letting me out of the infirmary in a few days," he said, changing the subject. He didn't want to think about how long he might be stuck here anymore.

Since he was starting school next week, Herb advised him to go to the supply office, where he could get new clothes for free, and asked about his physical therapy.

"You'll have to do more than squeeze a few tennis balls to get all those connections working again," said Herb. "You like music? I heard you whistling Prokofiev in the hall."

"Sure I do," said Victor. "But what's that got to do with therapy?"

"The piano would be good for building strength and flexibility. Or you could take typing classes, but wouldn't you rather learn how to make music?"

Victor had always heard the music in sounds, the calls of birds, the rhythms of things around him. For as long as he could remember, little tunes would come into his head out of nowhere and he'd hum them to himself as if they were real songs. Ma liked music, too, though there hadn't been much of it during the war years. At Ruth's, Victor was always allowed to listen to whatever he wanted from her record collection. She had classical, Broadway, big band, swing, and she had a soft spot for blues. If the record he picked had words, she'd sing along without an ounce of self-consciousness even though she was practically tone-deaf.

Once, at a subway station in Manhattan, on his way downtown with her and Ba, a man had been playing the saxophone, a sad, wistful tune with long drawn-out notes that made Victor think of oceans and broken hearts. He'd stood there listening, mesmerized. When the song was over, Ruth had opened her pocketbook and handed Victor some change. Ba had tried to stop him from giving it to the man, saying he was just a bum, but Victor gave it to him anyway. To him, he was a musician no matter where he was playing. But it had never occurred to Victor that he could learn an instrument, too.

"I don't know if I can play with my hands like this," he said. "And I'm almost sixteen. What if I'm too old?"

"Nah. A few years ago, a kid your age took lessons at Union Chapel. That's the Protestant church."

"But I'm not a Christian."

"I'll put in a good word for you."

Victor bent and flexed his fingers, his teeth clenched against the discomfort. He closed his eyes and tried to imagine his hands working again.

FIVE

In the middle of the courtyard, a weeping willow hung over a scraggly patch of grass surrounded by an iron fence. As they passed it, Sister Laura made the sign of the cross and Victor caught a glimpse of some low stone markers on the ground.

"That's the old graveyard," she said. "The new cemetery's near the pecan grove." The wet grass darkened the hem of her skirts as they continued to walk. "We have seventeen dormitories, each with thirty individual rooms. And here we are."

She stopped in front of a two-story building that was identical to all the others in the quad apart from a raised bed bursting with vegetables. Looking more closely, Victor could see that the borders were made from green Coca-Cola bottles stuck into the ground neck down, and to his surprise, he recognized Chinese long beans, bok choy, and the winding vines of winter melons.

"Number 29," said Sister Laura, "the Chinese House. This is where most of our Oriental gentlemen live. We thought you'd be more comfortable here."

Victor wasn't sure who she meant by "we," but nobody had asked him where he wanted to live. He'd assumed they'd put him somewhere with other young people, maybe those boys he'd seen in the tea garden who'd be in school with him. But he didn't say anything.

Instead, he looked up at the white building with its screened porches, peaked roof, and porthole-like window surrounded by decorations— two baskets shaped like upside-down horns spilling over with fruit.

He followed Sister Laura up the stairs as she pointed out the common parlors and shared bathrooms. "This is it," she said, opening the door to a small but airy room. "Home sweet home."

Brushing his fingers against the back of a chair, Victor found it cool to the touch and he wondered if his hands were misreading temperatures.

"It's metal," said Sister Laura, "for fire safety, like all the furniture in the dorms."

There was nothing warm or soft besides the bedding, but Victor had never had a room of his own before. Opening a drawer, he found the new clothes he'd ordered from the supply office folded beside the ones he'd brought from home. Someone must have unpacked his suitcase and put it in the closet, where he also found his backpack.

The walls were blank, and the only decoration was on top of the dresser, the family portrait he'd taken with Ma, Ba, Henry, and Grandmother at a photography studio in Toisan City shortly before he left. Seeing it now, he remembered how the camera had been made of wood, with a midsection that stretched out like an accordion. Ba had brought them new Western clothes all the way from New York City—suits for him and Henry, dresses for Ma and Grandmother—and everyone had worn them for the picture. How difficult it had been to hold still in that stuffy wool suit for what had seemed like forever, struggling to withstand an itch on his nose and the unfamiliar weight of Ba's hand on his shoulder. He'd been surprised to find the photo, which Ba had stashed in a drawer at the laundry, in his suitcase and wondered if sending it to Carville with him had been Ba's idea or Ruth's.

On the bedside table, there was a letter from Henry and another care package from Ruth on the floor beside it. Running his hand over the brown paper, he pictured her cutting it from the big roll in the laundry, wrapping it around the box, and securing it with twine.

At the window, past the branches of a tall magnolia tree, Victor saw the softball diamond, where some guys were playing catch so close to the fence that one of them was leaning against it.

The sound of turning wheels and squeaking pedals approached the room, and Mr. Wang poked his head through the door. A lit cigarette dangled from his lower lip.

"A room with a view of the hole," he said in English before switching to Toisanese. "Make yourself at home."

"Thank you, Uncle," Victor said by reflex, in the way he'd been taught to address older men, even though he felt funny about speaking Chinese in front of Sister Laura.

Mr. Wang raised a gnarled hand in reply, put it back on the pedal, and cranked himself down the hall, leaving a puff of smoke behind him.

"What's he talking about?"

"You mean the hole?" Sister Laura walked over to the window and pointed to a shady spot beyond the softball field, right by the River Road. "It's in the fence over there. Some of the patients made it years ago."

"What for?"

Sister Laura kept her eyes on the fence without replying. After a moment, she turned to Victor and smiled. "If you'd like extra things for your room, you might find some at the novelty shop in the Carville Mall. That's in House 24. What they don't have, you can buy from a catalog. Or, if you're feeling creative, you can try your hand at making something in occupational therapy." She pulled out a bottle of pills from her pocket. "Mustn't forget these. First dose is tomorrow."

Victor took the Diasone and nodded.

IN THE BATHROOM, after Sister Laura left, Victor stood washing his hands, avoiding his reflection in the mirror above the sink. He'd started doing this at home when his symptoms began to show in his face, afraid of what he might see, but now he braced himself and lifted his gaze. He looked almost normal, almost like himself, apart from the dark circles under his eyes. The puffiness was gone.

He went back to his room and shut the door behind him, not wanting to meet any more of his housemates. Not yet, maybe not until tomorrow. With the penknife he found in the front pocket of his backpack, he opened Ruth's care package and pulled out the sesame candies she'd sent. He stuffed three pieces in his mouth and crunched down on the hard praline. Ignoring the poke and scratch of the rough shards of sugar, he sat down with Henry's letter at the metal desk.

There'd never been a reason for them to write to each other before. When he tore open the envelope, the sound of the ripping paper filled the air in the nearly empty room. A piece of heavy off-white stationery Henry must have gotten from Mr. Lee's print shop protected what was folded inside—a letter on wafer-thin airmail paper, covered on both sides with Ma's elegant characters. Out of habit, Victor rubbed the crinkly paper between his fingertips and brought it up to his nose, trying to catch the scent of home as he imagined the letter traveling backward on its journey, like a piece of film rewinding, up to New York and across the ocean to Ma's hands.

But he couldn't bring himself to read it yet. First he skimmed the note Henry had added. A warning not to let the cat out of the bag when he wrote to Ma. A reminder to hurry up and send it back to him on the blank piece of airmail paper he'd included. Victor understood the logic behind this, but it was hard enough to write without Henry reading and judging his every word.

Henry didn't have much to say about Carville, not like he had on the phone. Just a bit at the end when he said, "I hope you're feeling better. Remember, you can come home any time you want. I meant it when I said I'd help."

For all his brother's faults, he'd always looked out for him, for as long as he could remember—when he had asthma attacks and there was no medicine, when soldiers marched through the village, when they said goodbye to Ma and Grandmother, when there was a storm at sea and the pitch and roll of the ship made him so sick and scared he thought he would die before they got to America.

Victor had just picked up Ma's letter when a knock on the door made him freeze. If he stayed quiet, maybe whoever it was would go away. But then came another knock, this one louder than the last.

"I'm resting," Victor called out, trying to sound sleepy.

The knocking stopped and Victor returned to the letter. Ma sounded like her usual self, making him laugh with a story about how the chickens had escaped in the middle of the night and scared Grandmother on her way to the outhouse. And because she knew he never bothered to look, she reminded him that his Chinese birthday was coming up on the lunar calendar right before the Mid-Autumn Festival. For the holiday, she was making extra mooncakes, she said, for him and Henry like she did every year. It made her feel like they weren't quite so far away. As part of her pact with Victor, so they could be together in their imaginations, she described the scene at home.

"Yesterday, I made twenty cakes, the ones with lotus-seed paste, and the flour got everywhere, on the table and chairs, and all over my face. Grandmother said I was as scary as a ghost, but I don't know what she's talking about. She's just jealous because it made me look like an opera star."

In return, she invited Victor to tell her all about his classes and friends, remembering that the new school year was about to begin. And before signing off, she asked if he was feeling better because in his last letter, he'd mentioned having a fever.

Victor sat at the desk for a moment with his head in his hands, his forehead feeling hot, as it so often did. From his backpack, he took out a pen, smoothed the creases on the blank piece of paper, and tried to think. Minutes passed, and all he had on the page was "Dear Ma." The pen dangled in the air as his fingers cramped, refusing to touch the paper again. He couldn't tell her where he was. He couldn't tell her who he'd met. He couldn't even tell her the fever had gone away. There wasn't a single thing he could say that was true, not even "I am well."

He pictured his mother writing to him, worrying about his fever as if it were just a cold or flu. His insides burned with shame as he imagined his first lie splitting and multiplying as soon as it hit the page into all the others he'd have to tell. Ma always said that lies were like mice, with one giving birth to ten, and each of those ten going on to produce ten more. If their pact had been an anchor, he was now unmoored, drifting further away from her than ever before.

His heart stuttered as his breath came shallow and fast. He'd lost Ma once and now he was losing her again. Henry had said she would die of grief if she knew he had leprosy, but by making him keep this secret, his brother had left him to carry the weight of the truth—and the burden of lying—all by himself. He laid his head on the desk, his cheek against the cool metal. He'd never felt so alone in his entire life. And with a flash of awareness, he realized this was what it meant to be a leper.

The feeling went off like a grenade, its shock waves radiating through him. Hansen's had forced him to leave his home and his family again, landing him here, wounded but still walking. He thought of what Henry had said on the phone, that they—the doctors, the government—had tricked him into coming with the promise of free treatment. They'd said he could be cured in just a few months when the truth was far bleaker. He wouldn't be allowed to leave without twelve negatives in a row, and there was no telling how long that would take. Who'd made up that rule anyway? And how would he know if the test results were real? They could tell him whatever they wanted. He couldn't trust anyone here. Not Dr. Behr, with his experiments and Nazi science book. Not the nurses and sisters, who did whatever the doctors said. Not even Herb, who hadn't warned him about the twelve negatives. All Victor knew for sure was that he was sick.

He could feel himself getting hot, not from fever this time but from his blood pumping faster, outward from his heart, down his legs and into his arms, where he could feel his scars throbbing. Sweat slickened the palms of his hands. Wiping them on his pants, he stood up and stalked across the room. He had to get out, to get some air at least, or he'd jump out of his skin. The window was open and he stuck his head outside with his eyes closed, inhaling the scent of the blossoms on the magnolia tree. He thought of the patients Herb had known who'd killed themselves instead of accepting their life sentence at Carville. If they felt anything like how Victor was feeling now, he could understand why. Staying would have been like giving in without a fight and suicide was the only way they could truly escape.

He opened his eyes. The softball diamond was quiet, the game of catch over. If he didn't do something now, he thought he might explode. It was just that he felt so trapped, not only by the institution and the disease, but by all the hiding and the lying as well. He'd had his operation and his first round of drugs, so the hardest part was done, and now he had a full bottle of Diasone pills. What if he went home like Henry wanted?

Victor squinted at the spot in the fence Sister Laura had pointed out, thinking about why she'd changed the subject so abruptly. Maybe she was afraid he'd use it to escape. The hole was right there, practically in front of him. It wouldn't be too hard to get away. If he snuck out before dawn, he'd have the best chance, even though he'd have to find his way in the dark. He could walk to town, hitch a ride to the nearest train station, and buy a one-way ticket back to New York. His face wasn't swollen anymore, and if he kept his sleeves rolled down, no one would suspect a thing. When he got to the city, he could go to Henry's. His brother would help him figure out what to do next.

Dusk was falling, the shadows beginning to rise up the walls like a silent tide, spilling darkness into the room. A wave of fatigue rolled through him. He sat on the bed and doubts started to form in his mind. If he got caught, what would they do to him? Lock him in the Carville jail and stop him from going to school? Experiment on him? Give him drugs that didn't work and operations he didn't need so he'd never get well? They could do some of those things to him anyway, even if he didn't try to run away. His family was always telling him to stop being so impulsive, to look before he leaped. Maybe he should give Henry some warning, write to him first, or maybe call to make a plan. On the other hand, if he didn't go now, he might just lose his nerve.

Victor grabbed his backpack and dumped its contents into an empty drawer before refilling it with some clothes, his family's portrait, the cash Ba had given him at the train station, and the bottle of pills. He felt bad about leaving behind the rest of his things, especially the money in his account, but it couldn't be helped. Leaning the backpack against the foot of the bed, he put his Dodgers cap on top of it, ready for when he would need them in the early hours of the morning.

After ignoring another knock on his door and the call for bread and milk, Victor changed into a pair of old pajamas, worn and soft from washing. It was the first time he'd been able to wear them since he was admitted, and the smell of the soap Ba used at the laundry still clung to the fabric. He stretched out on the bed. The springs creaked as he flipped to his stomach, hugging the thin pillow.

With his body still, he tuned in to the sounds coming through the window—the soft waft of the wind through the leaves, the insects chirping—the dense country quiet. The idea of having his own room had been exciting, but it meant he'd be sleeping alone. It wasn't that he was scared. He'd simply never done it before. Not in China, where he'd shared a room with Henry. Not in the Bronx, where his cot was on the other side of the room from Ba's. Not at the infirmary, where Herb's gentle snores had reassured him in the night. There had always been the presence of a familiar body nearby, and even though there was someone on the other side of the wall now, he didn't know who they were and he didn't want to. Sweat broke out from his pores as the nighttime rush of fever came over him again.

Carefully, as he'd done in the long, painful nights right after the surgery, he scanned his body. With his eyes closed, he imagined that he could see himself from overhead in his too-short pajamas on the narrow bed, with the image of the muscular system from Dr. Behr's examination room shining on him as if there were a slide projector on the ceiling. In his mind, he matched bone to bone, muscle to muscle, vein to vein, checking that everything was working right. He tried to feel it all happening—his blood traveling through its network, below the surface of the skin on his arms and hands where the nerves were learning to make new connections. He wiggled his fingers and toes, hoping, against his own animal instinct, to feel, instead of numbness, the pain of healing.

VICTOR WOKE UP shivering, with the scratchy wool blanket kicked to the foot of the bed. He squinted into the dark, wondering how long he'd been asleep. With his heart pounding, he rummaged in the drawer for his old Dick Tracy watch, a prized possession he'd saved up for when he was ten. It was too dark to see its face, but the fading stars outside told him that dawn was coming. In the blue shadows, he changed into an old button-down shirt and a pair of worn dungarees, struggling with the buttons before pulling on his Dodgers cap. He stuffed his tennis shoes into the side pockets of his backpack and cracked open the door. It creaked and, cringing, he stuck his head out into the hall. He couldn't see or hear anyone. No flushing or signs of waking.

He tiptoed out and made a right, expecting to see the staircase but ending up at the entrance to the back porch instead. Now he had to retrace his steps. Swearing under his breath, he made his way back down the hall again. In the room next to his, someone coughed, a wet, phlegmy sound, and he jumped as if a shot had been fired. Should he go back to his room and abandon the plan? He stood there for a moment, listening to the bedsprings squeak. They stopped, and after a bit of rustling, the dorm was silent again. Victor slunk down the stairs, past the parlor and the front porch, until, finally, he made it outside.

The sky was lightening, though it was still dark enough to give him some cover, and the cool, predawn air was fragrant with flowers, baking bread, leaf rot, and mulch. A breeze from the river reached its fingers out to him. He shivered, feeling wide awake, the adrenaline racing through his body also blunting his pain. He'd barely been outside since his arrival, and when he scrunched his toes in the dew-damp grass, the feeling of it reminded him of the summers he and Henry had spent barefoot when they were younger. Freedom, with good, clean dirt under his feet. He looked up at the horizon, where a cone of light was beginning to form, a hazy pyramid. It was beautiful, not orange, like true daybreak, but an eerie milky white.

Suddenly, there was a noise behind him, a distinct, metallic click. Then the clomp of heavy feet in the covered walkway, followed by the sounds of hawking and spitting. It must have been one of the watchmen patrolling the grounds. Victor crouched down in the shadow of the porch and made himself small, with his arms wrapped around his knees. When the footsteps faded, he got up and, sticking close to the side of the building, made his way to the softball diamond.

Fog lay thick along the marshy land, smelling like the river, fresh with a faint undertone of sewage and gasoline. In the white murk, the fence was hidden. He thought of the fairy tales where heroes stepped into the mist and emerged in another time or place. He thought of the people who'd been here before, who'd walked this same patch of land. The patients and, before them, the men, women, and children who'd been enslaved. Henry's voice whispered in his ear. This place might have been beautiful, but it had always been a prison.

Now he was in the open, at risk of being seen, but he stiffened his spine and trotted across the field to the fence. Following it with his fingertips, he walked in the direction of town, scanning the ground for the hole. In his head, he'd pictured a big circle cut in the middle of the fence, but what he found was just a spot where the wire had been pulled up a couple of feet. As he crawled through it, Victor could tell that someone had bent back all the sharp edges and dug out enough dirt for a person to pass comfortably underneath.

On the other side, he crossed the road, leaving footprints in the soft ground as he headed for the riverbank. There, he scrambled to the top of the levee and sat panting, covered in sweat. Even though it was September, the air was thick as pancake batter, and his shirt was sticking to him like a second skin. The sky was a medium blue now, the day beginning to break, but it was still early and he was so tired. He figured he could afford to rest here for a bit before walking to town. Catching his breath, he smelled the sweetness of mown grass and turned earth. Beneath him, the stones were damp with the memory of last night's rain. An egret croaked, taking wing from a neighboring rock, tucking its stick legs into itself during liftoff, an awkward single-passenger plane.

The fog was already dissolving, burned off by the rising sun, uncovering the rocks, the River Road, the fence, and the fields. As Victor craned his neck toward the institution, the outlines of the trees and buildings were more defined and the sleep-shuttered windows of the Big House stared back at him with black, disapproving eyes. Soon the workers who didn't live on-site—the maintenance men, groundskeepers, orderlies, and cooks from town—would come clattering in by the carload, and the sisters would begin their morning rounds. If he was going, it was now or never. The sun was above the horizon. He put on his shoes, slung on his backpack, and took off.

At the River Road, there was a flicker of movement. Victor caught a flash of color—hot pink—out of the corner of his eye. He turned and found himself face-to-face with a girl, no, a young woman. Her dark, wavy hair was all messed up, as if she'd just woken up, though she was dressed for a night on the town. Aside from the sleeveless pink top she wore, the rest of her outfit was black, her skirt so tight from her hips to her knees that Victor couldn't understand how she could walk in it, let alone climb through the hole in the fence. She looked like she was about to do just that with her high-heeled shoes in one hand, her bare feet dirty, with flecks of mud up to her ankles. Otherwise, he never would have guessed that she was a patient.

They seemed to be at a standoff, neither one of them making a move, and Victor didn't know what to do. What if she screamed and the night watchman heard? He tried to think of a good excuse for being outside the fence, something trivial and innocent, but maybe she couldn't tell he was a patient anyway.

Finally, the girl relaxed her wide, red lipsticked mouth into a cat-like smile. No one had ever smiled at him like that before. Fascinated, he watched her put a single red-nailed finger to her mouth in a shush before twisting an imaginary key to lock her lips shut, a silent plea and promise to keep their meeting a secret. He nodded, and the gears in his body shifted from wariness to desire. Turning away with a wink, the girl treated him to a magnificent view of her heart-shaped behind as she climbed through the hole in the fence.

The sun had risen, and up the dirt road, Victor could hear a car coming—the day staff on their way. Maybe he could wait at the levee for the morning rush to pass and then walk to town, but it was too risky to hang around here now. He didn't know how many people to expect or when they were supposed to arrive. And what if the girl, in spite of their unspoken pact, decided to tell on him? It was no use. He'd missed his chance. All he could do was follow her back through the hole in the fence and sneak into his dorm before anyone noticed he was gone. Next time, he promised himself, he'd leave earlier, when it was still dark.

SIX

Victor threw his bag to the floor when he made it to his room. The bottle of Diasone pills flew out of the front pocket and rolled under the bed. With a sigh, he got down on his stomach and groped under the springs until his fingers grasped its cool contours. He figured he might as well take his first dose now.

An hour later, he was throwing up into his wastepaper basket. Instead of going to the cafeteria with his new housemates for breakfast, he had to go right back to the infirmary.

"It's just a reaction," said Dr. Behr.

Victor fought through another wave of nausea, barely stopping himself from throwing up again. Maybe it was lucky that he hadn't managed to run away after all. He didn't exactly trust Dr. Behr, but in his current state, it was easier to do what the doctor said until he was stronger, or at least until his body got used to the Diasone like it had to the Promin. Of course he'd have to find out how to get more medicine once he escaped, but he tried not to worry about it now. When the time came, Henry could probably help him somehow.

Instead of going back to his room after his appointment, Victor slipped through the hole in the fence again to think things over on the levee, too sick and disappointed to care if he was seen. It wasn't even noon and the heat was already unbearable, the air soupy and stifling. He'd missed breakfast, but was too nauseated to eat. Sweat stung his eyes. Wiping them with his shirt, he lay down in the grass, his limbs as heavy as lead, his mind drifting back to home. Not to the Bronx but to China, to the threshold of his old house, where he saw himself as he'd once been, a small boy carrying a handful of thumb-sized blackberries in his shirt as carefully as he would have cradled a baby bird. He took his prize straight to the kitchen, but Ma wasn't there. Searching first in her bedroom, then the living room, he finally found her in the courtyard, bent over a bucket of water.

"Ah-Ma?" he whispered, offering her the berries.

She turned and smiled, her face bathed in a sweetness only he and Henry could bring out. Mirroring her, he smiled back, his cheeks warm with the pleasure of pleasing her.

The sudden three-chime blasts of a circus boat rang out, jolting Victor back to the present. He blinked as the sound of its steam whistle softened and faded, carried down the river by the breeze.

"Hey," said a teenage boy from out of nowhere, his high forehead, full mouth, and shock of black hair framed by the blue of the sky. Victor recognized him immediately as the Chinese-looking boy he'd seen in the tea garden with the girl. "What are you doing here?"

From his accent, Victor thought he might be from New York and might even have been born there. The other boy from that day was with him, too, the tall one with the grasshopper-thin frame and the pompadour rising above an olive-skinned face whose brow Victor could now see had the stain of a recently healed lesion. The noise of the steamboat must have kept him from hearing them approach.

"Nothing," said Victor, matching the first boy's hostile tone. "Who are you, anyway?" The boy's broad shoulders and air of superiority reminded him of Henry, but looking more closely, he saw there was something wrong with one of his legs. His right foot dragged as he took a couple of steps and stood with his arms crossed in a wide-legged stance.

"We're in the same house," he said. "I saw you this morning."

A pinprick of alarm poked Victor in the gut. Had the boy seen him trying to run away, or had he just seen him going to the infirmary?

"You're not supposed to go outside the fence," added his friend. He sounded like he was from New York, too.

"If I'm not, then neither are you." Victor kept a poker face. "Do people run away a lot or something?" he asked, trying to get a read on what they knew.

"Not really," said the taller boy. "Some of us just want to get out for a bit, blow off some steam at the river or the bar." He jerked his chin in the direction of town, and Victor guessed the girl from this morning must have come from there.

"Don't you get in trouble?"

"Not if we're smart. Sometimes people do, though. Some of the staff and the sisters let it slide, but not always. And Dr. Morton's cracking down. You don't want to get caught going through Harry."

"Harry?" Victor said, relaxing. It didn't seem like they knew about his earlier attempt.

"You know, like in *The Great Escape*," the Chinese-looking boy said, making a face as if Victor didn't know what water was.

"Is that a movie?"

The other boy shook his head. "It's a book about English pilots in a German POW camp. They dig these tunnels to escape and give them all code names, so we named the hole in the fence after one of them."

Victor blinked. Depending on what he said now, they would either be enemies or friends. "Well, I won't say anything if you don't."

"Deal," said the olive-skinned boy. "You going to school on Tuesday?"

"Yeah."

"What grade are you in?"

"Eleventh. You?"

"Same." The boy stuck out his hand and Victor took it. "I'm Manny. And this is Donny." He indicated the Chinese-looking boy. "Guess there's going to be four of us now."

Victor turned his gaze to Donny, prepared to shake his hand, too, but neither of them moved. They eyed each other for a long moment until finally Donny gave him a small, barely visible nod.

THE NEXT DAY, feeling less queasy on his lowered dose, Victor went out to Lake Albrechtson. He'd been doing hydrotherapy with Miss Abigail, sitting in a chair between two troughs, with his arms submerged in warm water that whirled around and soothed the pain in his nerves. It felt so good that he thought he might try swimming on his own. There was a pool, but it was only for staff, and the lake reminded him of the pond in his village.

Leaving his things on the grass, he lowered himself into the water and did a slow breaststroke to the dock, floating on his back every once in a while when he needed a rest. The leaves were already turning, beginning to fall and litter the surface of the lake, which, though the air was warm, was cool enough to give him goose bumps. He closed his eyes and let his head loll back, enjoying the relief from the relentless itch of his fresh scars.

"Swim all the way from China or something?" said a girlish voice.

"What?" Victor said to its owner, who was rising from the water like a teenage siren in a white bathing suit.

It was her. The girl he'd seen between the trees, the one with Donny and Manny in the tea garden. He watched as she popped onto the dock with barely any effort, her movements natural and athletic. It was like a scene from a movie where the boy meets the girl, but it was all wrong.

"What?" he repeated, struggling to get on the dock.

Of course he'd come across this kind of casual joke before, but he was usually more prepared. He hadn't expected it from anyone just now, much less this girl, and his face must have given him away.

"I didn't mean anything by that, you know," she said with a small smile.

Victor looked at her without saying anything. It wasn't quite an apology, but it was something.

"You're new, right?"

He nodded, with his eyebrow raised, but he sat down beside her.

"Me, too." She must have been the other young arrival he'd overheard those women talking about at the infirmary. "I'm Judith, by the way. But you can call me Judy."

"Victor," he finally said.

"Nice to meet you." She stuck out her hand and smiled in a nervous kind of way that made him want to forgive her. As they shook, her eyes traveled up his arm to the scar running along it like tire tracks on sand, and he felt self-conscious again. His scars were healed, but raised and shiny, and several shades darker than the rest of his skin. He could feel them tugging a bit and burning after scrambling on the dock. "They cut you open, huh?" she said.

"Yeah, ulnar nerve surgery. But I'm better now." He wiggled his fingers and Judy nodded.

"Scars look cool," she said. "On boys, anyway."

Victor raised one shoulder in a little shrug, unsure of what to make of that. Was she teasing or flirting with him? She seemed like the kind of girl who knew how to do both.

"I saw you," he said, his stomach tightening, "from the infirmary, once by yourself and another time with Donny and Manny." He gauged her reaction, worried that he'd said too much, but she seemed to take it in stride, as if she was used to guys noticing her.

"You know them?" she asked. They must not have told her about running into him on the river.

"I just met them yesterday."

She turned her attention to the shore. "Donny said they might come by." She slid into the water, and gestured for Victor to follow.

On the lawn, everything seemed sharper, more in focus—the smell of the lake on their skin, the individual blades of grass, green with yellow tips, the sound of the water sloshing against the wooden dock, the warbling song of the birds piercing the hum of other people's conversations. The tiny hairs on Judy's arms and legs were turning gold as they dried in the sun. Victor's fingers twitched, and he wondered if they would feel soft like down or bristly. As far as he could tell, she was perfect, without a single visible lesion, and he wondered why and how she was even diagnosed. She pulled out a bottle of suntan lotion and spread it on her chest, filling the air with a strong coconut smell.

"Mind putting some on my back?" she asked, to his surprise.

He shook his head and knelt behind her. The bottle was almost empty, and he had to shake it hard to get more lotion out, making his hand and wrist throb. He waited a moment for the ache to subside, not wanting her to notice he was in pain or how nervous he was to touch her. Steadying his hand, he tried to rub the lotion into her shoulders and upper back in a brisk, casual way, as if he'd done this a million times with thousands of girls before.

"Make sure you get my neck, okay? I always burn there," she said, gathering up the tail of her wet hair in one hand. It was such a simple thing, a twist of her wrist, but something about it felt special.

"Sure." Victor lifted the thick, white strap of her halter top where it was knotted at the base of her neck and spread lotion along the strip of pale skin crossing her dark tan.

When he was done, Judy heaved a dramatic sigh and turned to look at him.

"I hate it here," she said. He wondered if it would impress her to know that he'd just tried to run away. "Everyone in Philadelphia thinks I'm at boarding school. My mom was afraid we'd get kicked out of our synagogue, so she lied, even to the rabbi. What a riot, right?" She snorted, and Victor took her lead, laughing along even though it wasn't really funny. "What about your folks?"

"Oh, I don't know what my dad tells people, but my mom has no idea where I am," said Victor, and instantly regretted it.

"What?"

"She's in China," he said, trying to be as blunt and brief as possible.

"Wow. When's the last time you saw her?" Judy tucked a strand of wet hair behind her ear and leaned in a bit closer.

"When I was eight."

Her eyes widened with sympathy. He knew he'd caught her interest, but he didn't want to talk about Ma. At a nearby picnic blanket, a couple of girls were plucking the petals off the little white daisies that grew around the lake, their voices chanting, "He loves me, he loves me not." After a moment, Judy changed the subject back to herself.

"I keep thinking about what I'd be doing if I hadn't gotten sick— dates and dances and parties."

"I'm not sure my social calendar was as full as yours," Victor said, mimicking her teasing tone from before. "How much longer do you think you'll be here, anyway?" She looked so healthy, she was probably testing negative already.

Judy gave him a funny look and shrugged. "My friends at home are pretty clueless. All they care about is boys and clothes, and where they're going on vacation. Do I seem that way?" She cocked her head and frowned as if she really wanted to know.

"I haven't met a lot of girls like that in New York," he answered carefully, knowing that people from other places thought the city was exciting, "but I don't think so."

"My grandparents live there." She gave him a tiny smile that faded almost as soon as it appeared. "I was on the swim team and I was pretty good—came first in the state championship last season. This year, I was supposed to get serious. My dad says it makes you stand out to colleges. But now . . ." Judy shook her head, seeming to expect him to respond, maybe with something personal, something of equal weight, but he didn't know what he could offer her. He couldn't relate to swim teams or colleges. In the silence, Judy looked away.

"They're here," she said as Donny and Manny appeared at the edge of the clearing. Donny was in shorts and a T-shirt, and Manny was wearing a pair of bathing trunks, with a towel around his neck.

As they approached, Judy's mood seemed to shift. She sat up a little straighter and put her hands in her lap before moving them to her knees, and then back again. The boys walked slowly across the grass, weaving their way through the blankets and lawn chairs, saying hello to the people they knew. Manny sat down with the girls who were playing the daisy game, but Donny stayed standing, looking from the lake to the shore.

"They seem popular," said Victor.

"Yeah, they've been here awhile," said Judy.

When Donny spotted her, he gave a cool little wave.

Watching him walk toward them, Victor could see the drag of Donny's right foot even more clearly than he could yesterday, but in spite of it, the way he held himself reminded Victor of the athletes at his old school. Boys who'd shot up in height early and had the muscular lines of men, giving them a certain confidence that separated them from boys like Victor.

"Hey," said Donny, plunking himself down on the blanket. A lock of hair fell across his forehead.

Judy responded, her voice higher and a little breathy. Victor couldn't see her face, but a blush was creeping from the back of her neck to her ears.

"Going swimming?" he said to Donny.

"Nope."

"Well, I'm going back in," said Judy.

She adjusted her bathing suit, jumped to her feet, and ran quick as a colt to the lake. A couple of other girls were swimming, too, but Victor's eyes stayed glued to Judy. As she floated on her back, he studied her, watching her arms and legs move as if she were making a snow angel in the water, her hair spreading out like a fan.

It was hot that night. Victor had opened the window wide at bedtime in a useless attempt to catch a breeze, but now he woke up shivering, wet from the rain that had fallen and soaked his blanket after he'd gone to sleep. He slammed the window shut, changed into dry pajamas, and went into the hall in search of new bedding.

"What are you doing?" Donny whispered from his doorway, awake even though it must have been past midnight.

"Looking for a blanket."

"I have an extra one." Donny gestured for him to come inside.

Donny's room was next door and identical in layout to his own, but when the light switched on, Victor could see all the ways it was different. A blue plaid bedspread made the wrought iron bed look cozier than his. Dodgers pennants lined the wall above it, a transistor radio sat on the desk, and clusters of photographs in fancy frames were crowded on the dresser and bedside table.

"Here." Donny handed him an unused blanket from the top of his closet, the same scratchy wool one the supply office issued for every room. "You can keep it."

"Thanks," Victor said, wrapping it around his shoulders. Even in dry clothes, he couldn't shake the chill of waking up wet and cold.

"Sit down if you want." Donny indicated the metal chair decorated with an embroidered throw pillow and lowered himself into the one by his desk, favoring his bad leg. Victor wondered if it hurt, but he didn't feel like he could ask.

"Nice room," he said instead.

Donny shrugged. "My mom wanted it to look like home."

"How long have you been at Carville?"

"Since last winter. Manny got here a few months before me."

Victor thought for a moment. "So have you guys tested negative yet?"

"We don't talk about that," said Donny.

"Sorry," said Victor, looking away.

He went over to the dresser and started to inspect the pictures on it. There was one of Donny and his parents smiling in front of a white wooden house, with a front yard and a white picket fence. Donny's father in a suit and tie was square-jawed and tall like his son. His mother was pretty and petite in a checkered dress, with her hair curled and her lips tinted bright red.

"Nice house. Your folks own a restaurant or something?" Victor asked.

"No, my dad's an engineer. He came over for college and stayed."

Victor turned down the corners of his lips, impressed. Apart from Dr. Wu, he didn't think he knew anyone Chinese who'd gone to college at all, let alone in America.

"My mom doesn't work unless you count worrying about me." Donny rolled his eyes as if having a mother who cared about him was a real pain. "She's always knitting me sweaters as if it wasn't a hundred degrees in winter here, and she sends all these gross things from Chinatown. What's wrong with cash?" From underneath the bed, he pulled out a box. "Look at this. Preserved plums, melon seeds, dried cuttlefish."

"Oh, I like that stuff," said Victor.

"Are you serious?" Donny made a fake vomit sound and nudged the box toward Victor with his foot. "It's all yours. I usually give it to the old guys for their mahjong games. They don't care if they stink like rotten fish." Victor wasn't sure if that was meant as a dig. He decided to ignore it and kept looking at the pictures.

Next to the family photo was one of a much younger Donny in a striped Little League uniform, posing with a bat. Victor loved baseball, but had never been to an actual game. He'd listened to them on the little Emerson radio he'd bought himself with his delivery tips, entering the world of the game whenever he switched it on. Those cheerful voices painting pictures of play-by-plays with funny terms like "knuckleballs," "homers," "popups," and "cans of corn."

"You play ball?" Victor asked.

"I used to," said Donny, "but not anymore. Not with this leg. Manny does. He's the youngest guy on the team, but ever since he joined, we've been the River League champs. Home field advantage, I guess."

"You mean other teams come here? From outside?"

"Yeah. They can come in, but we can't go out. Not even if a ball goes over the fence."

Victor supposed this was another example of the rules Herb said had been made because people were afraid of Hansen's patients, not because of science. This one was not only unfair but stupid, and he wondered if it had anything to do with why the hole in the fence had been cut by the softball field in the first place. He looked again at the photo of Donny in uniform and tried to imagine what it would be like to have a life like that, only to have it taken away.

"You know," Donny went on, "my parents told everyone I have polio. Guess they think that's better than the package. They're big on the whole land-of-opportunity thing: I can do anything I set my mind to, be whatever I want to be. More like be whatever *they* want me to be. I'm not smart like my dad, not at school, anyway. I was good at baseball, but not good enough to go pro, no matter what my mom says. I don't know why I even keep that picture around. Give it to me, will you?"

Victor handed over the frame and listened to the uneven shuffle of Donny's slippers as he walked across the room. He put the picture facedown in the drawer of his bedside table, and for the first time, Victor felt sorry for him.

"Did you get surgery on your leg?" Victor asked.

"Yeah, but it didn't work. They said the nerves were too far gone.

My eyelid operation went fine, though. Now they can close all the way again, plus I got double eyelids."

Victor blinked, confused.

"You know, this right here." Donny pointed at the delicate fold across one of his upper lids. "Makes my eyes look bigger, less chinky, don't you think?"

A trickle of disquiet collected, pooling in Victor's belly. He could sense that Donny already felt superior to him, but did he think his new eyes made him even better?

Since they were the only Chinese high schoolers at Carville, Victor knew he and Donny would be compared to each other, and he'd come up short. It had happened before. In fourth grade, when Victor still had an accent, the only other Chinese kid in his class had been Benny Lum, an American-born boy whose father owned the Chinese takeout place on Allerton Avenue. The white kids pulled the corners of their eyes into slits on the lunch line and taunted them both with ching-chong noises in the schoolyard, but instead of opting to stick together, Benny had turned on him, now that he finally had someone else to pick on. He smacked books out of Victor's hands and kneed him in line so that his legs would buckle, making the other kids laugh.

The last straw was in the lunchroom one day when Benny tripped him. Victor fell flat on his face, his tray crashing to the polished concrete floor. Oddly, he felt no physical pain, but his body filled with a red-hot rage, ears rushing and eyes glazing over.

It was only when the lunch lady was hauling him up by the arms that he came back to himself. He was straddling Benny's chest, squeezing his throat tight between his hands.

"What? Speak up, Benny! I can't understand you!"

After that day, Benny left him alone, and the other kids stopped picking on him, too. He'd proven that when push came to shove, he wouldn't back down.

But Victor wasn't in the fourth grade anymore. This couldn't be solved with a fight. And it wasn't about the other kids at Carville either. This was between him and Donny. From the confident set of his shoulders to the easy way he had with people, Donny was the type of boy that girls seemed to like and the type of son that Ba probably would have preferred. A big, strong athletic boy who didn't show his feelings or talk too much. A boy like Henry, tough and handsome, and used to getting what he wanted. One of life's winners, like Victor's name was supposed to mean. Donny was so lucky, with so much going for him except for his leg and, of course, the fact of being here, of having the disease. Maybe Herb was right when he said they were all in the same boat. What good was Donny's luck at a place like Carville?

SEVEN

The crowded cafeteria was loud with the sounds of excited voices and the clashing of plates and cutlery. Victor took in the two long rows of four-person tables in the dining room, each with a light hanging overhead. His eyes snagged on the profile of a young woman, an impression of dark brown waves, bright red lipstick, and a pink sleeveless top. She gave a little toss of her head, flipping back her hair, and with a sharp intake of breath, he realized this was the girl he'd bumped into the other morning when he was trying to run away. He dropped his eyes to the floor, his face getting hot, praying she wouldn't notice him as he trailed after his new friends to the food line.

On the way there, from the far corner of the room, a group of teens waved, trying to call them over, the girls stealing shy looks at Donny and the boys joking around with Manny. Victor assumed they'd be joining them, but after they got their trays, Judy went off to a different spot by the window, and the three boys followed her.

Victor's jitters didn't stop him from wolfing down most of his food, his stomach responding to the smell of bacon and eggs fried in butter. Untouched, a pale puddle of grits lay next to them, spreading slowly across his plate.

"They're okay with sugar," said Manny, nudging the little bowl in the middle of the table.

Victor dumped some on the grits and shoved a spoonful in his mouth before using the same spoon on his eggs. As the Diasone killed more and more of the Hansen's bacteria in his body, his appetite began to return, and he'd been enjoying the larger variety of foods the cafeteria offered. As he'd told Ruth in his last letter home, it was like getting to eat at a restaurant every day, with three different options per meal posted on a placard by the door, plus side dishes, salads, soups, and desserts. He could choose pancakes for breakfast, roast chicken for lunch, and beef stew for dinner, with as many helpings of tapioca pudding, chocolate cake, or apple pie as he wanted. Donny and Manny's trays were piled with as much food as his, but Judy only had half a grapefruit, a soft-boiled egg, and a cup of black coffee.

Donny was eating not just with a fork, but with a knife, too, putting it down between bites in a fancy way. Victor felt himself blush, but there was nothing he could do about his table manners right now. With his hands the way they were, he wouldn't be able to eat like Donny if he tried.

By the time they finished breakfast, the other kids had left the cafeteria. As they rushed to school, a cluster of low black clouds sparked and a thunderbolt zapped the sky, leaving its bright imprint in Victor's eyes like a flashbulb. He counted to twenty-four before the answering rumble sounded, telling him the coming storm was still a few miles away.

The school Quonset hut stood by the recreation center like a giant bread box made of tin, which Manny said had been surplus from the nearby Army base. It was so different from Christopher Columbus High, where Victor had been going for the past two years, a hulking brick building swarming with more than two thousand students, seven hundred in his grade alone. When he heard they had a one-room schoolhouse here, he'd expected something old-fashioned, but the classroom looked like it could have been from the future, with rounded, corrugated metal walls, metal desks and chairs, freestanding blackboards, and pictures of the thirty-four presidents on the walls.

The teacher was busy organizing books and papers. A tall man in black horn-rimmed glasses and a striped jersey, with a head of thick, dark hair, he looked like he might have played college basketball not so long ago. Donny and Manny had said at breakfast that he was from an old Southern family, but believed in integration, and rumor had it that he'd dated a Creole girl when he was at LSU.

Besides Victor and his friends, there were a handful of other students, the younger brown-skinned girl Manny had talked to at the lake, three white girls about her age, and a couple of scrawny white boys. Judging from their long, fox-like faces, Victor thought they were probably brothers, though one of them didn't have any visible signs of disease, and the other one had hands cramped with the kind of nerve damage that his operation was supposed to correct. He wondered if the boy had had the surgery and if it had failed, but he knew by now not to ask questions like that, at least not off the bat.

"Good morning," the teacher called the class to attention. The thunder cracked loudly overhead, and the clouds finally let go, their falling drops pelting the tin roof. "Welcome to the Fall 1954 term of Carville High School. My name is Mr. Harland." He wrote it on the chalkboard with a flourish at the tail of the *D*. "I teach English along with history and occupational therapy in the Quonset hut next door. Our educational program will fulfill the requirements of St. Gabriel High. That's the school a few miles up the road. They'll be issuing your diplomas if you happen to graduate while you're here. But I'm of the opinion that it never hurts to spice things up a bit, so I've made a few additions to their curriculum that I think you might find interesting." Mr. Harland winked, and Victor thought he saw Judy blush.

"As a reminder, if you have a medical appointment, you will be excused, but please let me know at the beginning of class so we can avoid unnecessary disruptions." Holding up a battered copy of *Animal Farm*, Mr. Harland continued, "Those of you who were here last year can get a start on chapter one. I expect a two-paragraph summary when you're done."

As one of the girls handed out the books, Mr. Harland showed Victor and Judy to a couple of desks at the front of the classroom. "I've received your school records, but I prefer to do my own evaluation, just to see where you are in your studies. Wouldn't want you to be bored in my class."

Victor sat down in front of a copy of a Louisiana state standardized test and cringed. In the Bronx, with Ruth's help, he'd managed to stay in the right grade for his age, but not without the constant threat of getting left back, especially in those first couple of years after immigrating. The tests they gave at the end of spring term were what decided his fate, and even after he caught up and started to make decent grades, his stomach clenched whenever he had to take one. He'd told Donny and Manny he was going into the eleventh grade with them, and he didn't think he could handle the shame of repeating tenth grade if he bombed this test.

The rain continued to rattle overhead as he glanced at Judy, who gave him a tiny smile.

"Just do what you can and leave the rest," said Mr. Harland.

Victor wrote his name at the top of the first page, the pencil awkward in his hand, his letters big and clumsy. Miss Abigail had said some discomfort was okay while doing normal activities, but he should stop when it hurt. It didn't, at least not yet, but it was hard to keep his grip on such a slender thing.

Having already begun the test, Judy was chewing the tip of her eraser. Victor flipped through the booklet and decided to tackle reading comprehension first, the section he dreaded the most. Though he was a good reader now, the memory of being mocked when he struggled left a bad taste in his mouth. As he read, he started to twiddle his pencil between his fingers, a habit he'd picked up from Henry, and before he realized what he was doing, it slipped and fell to the floor. Someone snickered behind him. On the other side of the room, Donny elbowed Manny with a smirk.

"Sorry," whispered Victor. "My hands."

"Of course," said Mr. Harland in a quiet voice. "Would you like a hand cuff?"

"A what?"

Mr. Harland took a small leather sheath out of his desk and slipped it over a pen, showing Victor how the cuff made it easier to grasp. "We ought to come up with a better name for these. Or if you'd prefer to take the test orally, we could schedule a time after school."

"No, it's okay. I can do it as long as you don't mind my penmanship. And I've got a piano lesson this afternoon," he said a little louder than necessary.

"Wouldn't want to miss that," said Mr. Harland.

Judy had picked up Victor's pencil from the floor and was holding it out to him. When he reached for it, one of his fingertips grazed her hand.

"Thanks," he whispered, shocked to feel all the nerves in that finger firing at the touch of her soft, warm skin.

When she turned back to her test, he couldn't resist taking a quick peek across the room, to where Donny and Manny were sitting. Sure enough, Donny was watching them. And the moment he met his eye, Donny's face shifted from a scowl to a blank stare so fast that Victor thought he might have imagined it.

THE LEAVES AND mossy beards of the live oaks, heavy with the morning's rain, dripped cold, ticklish drops onto Victor's scalp as he headed to the Protestant church after school. Unlike the Catholic church's brick facade, Union Chapel's simple white exterior blended in with the surrounding dorms. At the door, he could hear the music floating out from the piano, stopping him in his tracks as a cascade of emotions rushed over him, one after the next—loneliness, hope, excitement. He didn't know if the song was putting them in his head or if it was drawing out what had already been there, building throughout the day as the time got closer to his first piano lesson.

A few years ago, he had discovered that the way he experienced music might not be the same as it was for other people. Henry had walked in on him listening to "How High the Moon" on his cot with his eyes half closed and his fingers fluttering in the air. He'd been lost in the story it was telling him of the moon and separated lovers, his head awash in a sea of aquamarine, his chest thrumming with the beat of the song.

"What are you doing?" Henry had demanded.

"Nothing," he'd said, sitting up. And when he'd tried to explain what was happening inside him, his brother had given him a funny look, with his face scrunched up, as if he thought there was something wrong with him.

Victor slipped through the door of the church now, where the cramped entryway opened out into a big, airy room with a high, peaked ceiling and white wooden beams. The afternoon light turned everything golden as it shone through the stained glass windows, yellow and many-paned like honeycomb. He'd imagined the church as a cold, dark place, but it was warm and bright, and in the front, at the end of a long row of pews and hanging lights, a woman sat playing the piano. She looked like she might have been about Ruth's age, and seemed made entirely of different shades of beige and brown, from her dirty-blond hair to her tortoiseshell glasses and her chocolate-colored dress dotted with little tan flowers.

When she noticed him, the woman looked up for a moment, but didn't stop playing. He walked down the aisle to the piano and stood there, watching her hands move over the keys and her foot in its brown loafer pump one of the three pedals underneath. At the end of the song, her hands stayed still, holding down the keys until the sound disappeared. He waited for her to lift them up before he started clapping.

"You must be Victor. My name is Mrs. Thorne," the woman introduced herself. Her voice was higher, more girlish than he'd thought it would be, and had the same soft vowels as Dr. Behr's. "I'm here to teach you sight reading and composition and, of course, how to play. I understand you're a beginner, so we'll be meeting for one hour, three times a week. Sound good?"

Victor nodded, looking beyond his new teacher at the piano. It was an intimidating thing, with dozens of black and white keys repeating themselves in groups of twos and threes. He understood already that from left to right, the sound went from low to high, but beyond that, he didn't know a thing.

"Have you ever seen a piano before?"

"Not up close."

"Well, let's take a good look, then." She opened the lid and showed him what was inside—rows of strings with hammers, pins, and levers put together in a complicated but tidy way.

"The piano is a stringed instrument called a chordophone, like a harp or a lyre." Mrs. Thorne played a single note, and Victor watched a hammer hit the string in front of it, making it vibrate. "But as you can see, it's also a percussion instrument like a drum."

She hadn't pressed hard, but the high, clear sound seemed to zip through the air like a boomerang, bouncing off the hard surfaces of the empty church, the pews, the windows, the walls, and the ceiling, until it circled back around to Victor's ears. After closing the piano's lid, she invited him to sit beside her on the bench, setting a copy of *The Blue Book for Beginners* on the music stand. At the top of the first lesson was a short bit of music, ten lines divided in half, with what he recognized as notes, following a couple of symbols that looked like an ampersand and an oversized comma.

"The top is the treble clef—you play it with your right hand—and the bottom is the bass played by the left. Now, this right here, between the treble and the bass"—Mrs. Thorne pointed at a blank space on the page—"is middle C." She held up her hand and pressed the key at the center of the piano, releasing a round, mellow note. "Now, you try."

"The same one?"

"If you like, but any one will do. I just want you to get a feel for the keys."

With his forefinger, Victor struck a black key way down on the left-hand side of the keyboard. It registered long and low in his ears like the hum of a colony of bees.

"That's E-flat," said Mrs. Thorne.

So sheet music was a code telling your hands what to do, a language made of sounds, not words. The lines on the page seemed directly related to the strings inside the piano, and this appealed to Victor's sense of order.

For the next half hour, he did the sight-reading drills in the book, learning the difference between whole and half notes and the names of the treble notes with ease. He didn't make any mistakes, and every now and then, Mrs. Thorne glanced at him with her eyebrows lifted over the rim of her glasses. When he said each note as she pointed to it on the page, he had no trouble staying on the beat, but when it was time for him to play them, the signals his brain sent to his hand arrived too late again and again. No matter how much he tried to make his fingers obey, they were slow, reluctant to move. A sudden zing went through his thumb like an electric shock. His hand jerked back as if the piano were hot.

Neuritis, Dr. Behr called it, and said it would gradually go away as his nerves healed. Lately, on top of the hydrotherapy, he'd been getting paraffin wax treatments, dipping his hands and arms in baths of purified petroleum, the warmth of it soothing his skin and joints, relieving the swelling and stiffness for hours at a time.

Victor exhaled through his nose with frustration. He'd thought he was doing better than this. He'd thought the pain had improved, but maybe his reaction to the Diasone had caused a setback.

"Need a break?" Mrs. Thorne looked at him with concern.

"No." Victor flexed and rubbed his thumb. "I just don't know if I can do this."

"Of course you can. But it's important not to strain yourself, especially so soon after surgery. Let's take it from the top, adagio. That means slowly in Italian." Mrs. Thorne turned back to the piano. "Rome wasn't built in a day, you know."

She counted out a slow, steady tempo, and following it, Victor got through the exercise without a mistake.

"Let's switch over to the bass," said Mrs. Thorne, turning to him with a smile. "We always want to work both hands equally."

At the end of the lesson, she gave Victor his homework, reminding him to begin with his drills every time, like the book said, and to practice only half an hour a day, for now. He could build up slowly, in fifteen-minute increments every week, and he had permission to use the piano whenever the church was free.

There was the simple pleasure of making sounds, the symmetry of the exercises and scales. After the first week, he was playing real songs. The ones in the book were easy, written for kids, but once he got their principles down, he found he could work out the melodies of other songs he knew or heard, "Mr. Sandman," "Earth Angel," adding two- and three-fingered chords with his left hand. Repeating them over and over, he stayed in the empty church long after he was supposed to stop.

EIGHT

Henry shoved his hands in the pockets of his thin trench coat as he walked from the subway to his building after work, wishing he'd worn his wool peacoat instead. Though the sun was still up, a wisp of last night's harvest moon hung in the sky, threadbare and pale, a shadow of its former self. Whenever he saw it, he thought of how, at four, Victor had stared at the morning sky and cried, not believing the moon would come back at night until Ma showed him its faint outline in the afternoon. It had been there the whole time, she'd said, and was just hidden by the brightness of the sun.

For the Mid-Autumn Festival, Henry had gone over to Ba's to eat the mooncakes he bought from Mei Li Wah Bakery on Bayard Street, but he hadn't felt much like celebrating. This was his first holiday without Victor and he'd been thinking of him eating the cakes Ruth had sent all by himself, or maybe with Donny, the Chinese boy he'd mentioned in his last letter.

On the corner, by the drugstore, Henry noticed a couple of teenage girls he recognized from Victor's school. The one with the pretty, round face was holding a cigarette to her lips while the skinny one tried to light it with matches that kept on going out. They followed him with their eyes as he came down the street, slowing his gait to a stroll and digging a lighter out of his pocket.

"Ladies," he said. "Need a light?"

Startled like a pair of pigeons, they fluttered, looking at each other before the pretty girl nodded. Her fingers shook a bit when he lit her cigarette with his hand cupped around the flame.

"Thanks," she murmured, wide-eyed and apple-cheeked, puffing the smoke without inhaling.

"Don't mention it." Henry inclined his head and kept on walking. As he rounded the corner, he heard the girls whispering about him.

"Victor's brother," one of them said. "How old do you think he is?"

"Too old for you," said the other, with a breathless little laugh.

Henry smiled to himself. If they only knew that his lover, Winnie, was an older woman.

At the entrance of his rundown building, he made a left into the mail room, where he opened his postbox with a tiny silver key. He stood sorting the contents: a bunch of bills, a letter from Victor, and one from Ma. Skirting a cluster of garbage cans the super hadn't bothered to take outside, he held his breath as he mounted the stairs to the third floor, where an Eddie Fisher song blared from his neighbor's radio.

His room was a shabby little box around the corner from Ba's laundry with a few pieces of beat-up furniture: a twin bed with a saggy mattress, a chair, and a small rickety desk. It wasn't much, but it was all his. With his first paycheck from the print shop, he'd bought himself an icebox and a hot plate. Victor had helped him cover up the peeling paint with collages of pictures he'd cut out from old magazines. His brother was creative that way, always making things and thinking up songs. When he was small, he would leave Henry little gifts in his pockets—lucky pebbles, abandoned snail shells, magic feathers.

As soon as Henry shut the door, he began to sweat. The landlord had just switched on the radiators for fall. They seemed to have only two settings: piping hot and stone cold. Henry tossed the mail on his desk and hung up his coat. He unlaced his brown wingtips and lined them up against the wall before stripping down to his boxers to do the Army exercises Ba had taught him, the routine of squat jumps, sit-ups, pull-ups, and push-ups they did in basic training. At the closet, where he'd installed a pull-up bar in the doorway, he suddenly felt exhausted and collapsed on the bed. He grabbed his packet of smokes and balanced an overflowing ashtray on one knee, fanning himself with Ma's letter before slipping his thumb beneath the edge of the envelope.

For as long as Henry could remember, letters had been at the center of his family's life. He pictured himself as a little boy, racing to the kitchen with a precious piece of paper covered in American stamps. How Ma's face would wash over with relief as she put it on the mantel to read out loud after dinner. How Victor would laugh and clap to see it there even though he'd been so young when Ba left that he couldn't possibly remember him. How his own excitement would make him eat too fast and wriggle with impatience in his seat, not because of the money Ba sent or the stories he told, but because his words were proof that he still existed. But when he'd introduced Ruth, Henry had realized the letters his family had cherished so much had been written by a traitor's hand.

In that moment and in many moments since then, he'd thought about telling on his father. But what could Ma do about it? She couldn't come to America unless Ba arranged it, and maybe she wouldn't even want to. Ma was a proud woman. Henry could see how knowing about Ruth could make her decide to turn her back on the marriage and stay in China forever. He'd also considered threatening to tell Ma unless Ba stopped seeing Ruth, but what if he got so mad that he disowned him, divorced Ma, or stopped sending her money?

His father had all the power and his mother had none; Henry's hands were tied. In the end, he concluded that it was better for her not to know. Sometimes he wished he'd stayed in China and sometimes he fantasized about what it would be like to leave New York and go home to Ma. But of course he couldn't have sent Victor across the world by himself and he couldn't leave him either, especially now.

A few weeks ago, Victor had called to say his operation was a success, but Henry was convinced they were not only experimenting on him but also keeping him there on false pretenses, dangling the hope of a cure that would never come. The longer Victor was at Carville, the harder it would be to keep it a secret from Ma. Henry was only five years older than his brother, but ever since Ba left, he'd done his best to fill his shoes.

Henry would never forget the day, almost fifteen years ago, when Ba had left for America for the second time. How Henry had sobbed and clung to his leg, the unfamiliar wool of Ba's Western-style traveling suit scratching his face, begging him to stay just a little longer—one more week, one more day.

"For shame, a big boy like you carrying on like a baby," Grandmother hissed, narrowing her eyes. "You will give your father bad luck. Is that what you want?"

"No," he managed to choke out, still crying, but biting his lip to make himself stop.

Ba was patient at first, trying to quiet him with promises of postcards and special American toys, but in the end, he threw up his hands and met Ma's eye, shaking his head.

"Ah-Mei," he said, his voice trailing off.

"It's all right," said Ma, with a tired smile, shifting Victor from one hip to the other so she could put her hand on Henry's shoulder. "You should go."

Ba nodded, pulled the brim of his fedora down over his brow, and strode out the front gate with his bags.

"Ah-Ba," Henry wailed, calling after him, but his father didn't turn around. When he couldn't see him anymore, he buried his face in his mother's shirt.

"My heart," she said, crouching down with Victor balanced on her thigh. "Ba will come back, but not for a long time. Do you know what that means?"

Henry shook his head, swiping the backs of his hands across his eyes.

"You are the man of the house now and I will need your help, especially with your baby brother."

Ma held the baby out to him, and he gathered his brother's heavy, round body in his arms. How soft and squashy he was, with fine tufts of hair sticking straight out from the crown of his head like a baby chick. And how good he smelled—sticky, salty, and milky sweet.

"Don't worry, Big Brother is here," Henry whispered into the seashell of the baby's ear, with his nose pressed against his warm, fat cheek. "I will take care of you always, even after Ba comes back."

"That's my brave little man," Ma praised him softly so that Grandmother, who was eyeing them from the kitchen, wouldn't hear.

Who would take care of Victor now at that horrible place? Ba could have found a doctor in New York to heal him, someone in Chinatown, for instance, who could keep his mouth shut. There was the cost of the surgery and the difficulty of treatment, but he could have taken out a loan. In the end, Ba had done what Ruth wanted, just like he always did, and she'd brainwashed Victor into agreeing. Either she wanted to get rid of him so she and Ba could finally live together, or she just had no clue, neither about how people with leprosy nor people from China were treated. Because of her, Victor was locked up far away, maybe for the rest of his life.

Of course they couldn't tell Ma about any of this.

"Everything will be better in America," he wrote to her over and over again. "Everything will be better when you're here."

Recently, Victor's letters had gotten pretty good at making things in Carville sound like they were in New York. New friends there became new friends here. Fields turned into city parks, and the Mississippi, the Hudson. They weren't exactly lying, Henry had told his brother. They were just holding back some facts and changing a few others so Ma wouldn't be upset.

In return, she wrote cheerful anecdotes filled with bright details of familiar things and happy memories. Sometimes Henry wondered if she was cherry-picking, too, though this letter did say that Grandmother had slipped on the stones in the courtyard and was having trouble walking now. Henry frowned, taking a long drag of his cigarette before continuing to read.

"Old age comes for us all," Ma went on, "even a woman as stubborn as Grandmother. Everything else is fine. The vegetable garden is more abundant than ever, and Cousin Kun comes over to help with the heavy work you used to do for me. Just last week, he picked all the rocks out of the field behind the house, the one that nobody's used since Grandfather Chin was young. Isn't that wonderful? I never could convince your father or Grandmother to farm it. Now we will have twice as much rice, maybe enough to sell by next harvest. To thank him, I cooked your favorite dish—steamed perch in black bean sauce—and now he says it's his favorite, too."

Why was Cousin Kun over at the house so much, and why did Ma seem so taken with him? Henry could see him now, sitting at her table as she scooped his rice, round and white as a snowball, into one of her blue-patterned bowls. What Henry wouldn't give to be sitting there instead, waiting for his mother to serve him his favorite dish. If he closed his eyes, he could smell it—the salty black beans, the ginger and garlic, the perfectly flaky fish pulled out of the steamer the second it was cooked through.

Ba was a decent cook, but he made only the simple, quick things he could manage on a hot plate after a long day's work. And Ruth could barely cook at all, not that Henry would've ever wanted to eat anything she made.

When someone in the family had a birthday, Ma would always kill a chicken and cook it for dinner in their honor. Henry could still picture her at the butcher block, mincing garlic with a cleaver while the chicken poached in a pot until it was tender enough to fall off the bone. When it was ready, she would serve it with a spicy raw sauce of scallions, ginger, and garlic mixed with salt and oil, a bowl of seasoned rice, and the rich, clear broth of the poaching liquid on the side.

Since he was small, Henry had loved to watch his mother cook. Instead of playing outside with the other children, he'd sit in the kitchen while she made dinner, fascinated by the way her hands moved, the way she'd add a pinch of salt to the butcher block before mashing ingredients together with the flat of her cleaver, seesawing the blade back and forth. It was how she made the bases for all her sauces and soups, and the minced meat and vegetable fillings for her dumplings.

On the afternoon of his thirteenth birthday, his last before leaving home, instead of smoking the pack of stale cigarettes his friends had found in the village square, he'd sat on a stool in the kitchen, snapping the long beans Victor had gathered specially for him because they were his favorite.

"Ah-Yat-ah," said Ma with a smile in her voice, "run outside and get me some more garlic."

Henry obeyed but lingered, feeling the dirt under his hands, knowing he might never dig in his mother's garden again, or at least not for a very long time. The garlic bed was next to a patch of the big white daikon radishes they ate both fresh and preserved, and the bumper crops Ma grew of bitter melon, bok choy, snow peas, and long beans. Beyond the vegetable patch was a cluster of magnolia trees whose blossoms released a scent so heavy that it perfumed the whole house whenever they were in bloom.

Ma was cutting up a chunk of preserved daikon to season the broth when he came back with a head of garlic the size of a cat's paw. He watched as she twisted off the sprouting green top and minced four cloves with a thumb of ginger before transferring the mixture with a scrape and flick of her cleaver into the hot peanut oil. A delicious savory smell surrounded them. She tossed two cups of rice into the pot to toast, and Henry's stomach growled like a wild animal.

"Patience." Ma laughed. "The birthday boy gets a whole drumstick, and on Gold Mountain, you'll have all the chicken you can eat."

A few weeks later, Ba arrived with the papers to take him and Victor to New York, and though part of him was excited for the trip, in his heart of hearts, it felt like a death. For his entire childhood, he'd been taught to look forward to this, and he had. The return of the father he so idolized came with the chance to make something of himself abroad, to earn and provide in a way he never could in China. In his family and his village, this was what it meant to be a man. But as the reality of leaving Ma and everything he knew set in, dread crept over him like a cold, dark mist. How shameful, how cowardly.

"Be strong, my heart," Ma whispered in his ear when she hugged him goodbye, "for your brother and for me."

He tried. When he was taking care of Victor, it was easier because he didn't have to think about himself. As Victor's sobs turned to silent grief when they boarded the ship in Kowloon Bay, Henry did his best to make him snap out of it. He praised their Paper Brother, Jackie, who was only seven, for how uncomplaining he was, to see if jealousy would make Victor less sad. He held the bucket for him when he was seasick and hoisted him up so he could look out the porthole as Ba pointed out interesting things—a school of flying fish leaping from the water in threes and fours in the East China Sea, the fins of sharks and pods of whales, and the locations of sunken pirate ships.

In San Francisco, when they were separated from Ba at Immigration and crammed in a holding pen with some of the other passengers, keeping Victor and Jackie calm kept Henry's own fears from overwhelming him. Ba was staying at a Chinatown lodging house. He'd prepared the boys for the interrogations on board, assuring them that their entry would be quicker and easier than his own. The rules of the Chinese Exclusion Act had relaxed, and Angel Island, the detention center where Ba had been held, was closed, but Jackie wasn't their real brother, and if one of them was caught lying, they might all be deported.

The morning of the interrogation, Henry woke up early in his bunk above Victor's. His eyes traced the seam between the ceiling and the wall where, halfway up the beam, a fly was perched. Immobile, its wings were spread, ready for flight. Watching it, he counted as ten seconds passed, then twenty, then a full minute, then five, but the fly never moved. Half an hour later, as the day fully dawned, it was still there, frozen like a statue, and Henry realized it was dead. The room began to rouse, and Victor's mattress squeaked underneath him.

Soon a monstrously tall guard, who looked like a strange version of a door god with his blotchy red skin and bright, fiery hair, came to take them one by one for questioning. Jackie was the first to go, and by the time Henry was called, he hadn't come back. Flashing a small smile at Victor, whose eyes were wild with fear, he followed the guard down a long hallway to a windowless room. With a large, hairy hand, the guard indicated a seat in front of a scarred wooden desk and shut the door behind him. Henry sat facing two empty chairs, waiting in the crown of light from the single desk lamp. After a moment, a man with yellow hair came in with a Chinese man in a dark blue suit. They hung their fedoras on hooks and took their seats.

"Are you thirsty?" the Chinese man asked in Toisanese, with a twang that told Henry he was from the city. The lamp cast shadows across the planes of his face, making it impossible to tell if he was twenty-five or fifty.

"I'm fine." Henry began to sweat despite the chill in the room.

The other man ignored them, shuffling papers in a file before making an impatient, circular gesture with his hand.

"This man is from the US government," said the Chinese man. "He's going to ask you some questions in English and I'm going to repeat them in Chinese. You must answer them as thoroughly as possible. If something is unclear, you can tell me and I will explain it. Everything you say will be written down. Do you understand what I've said so far?"

For a moment, Henry's parched lips were stuck together. He licked them and whispered, "Yes."

Henry couldn't remember all the questions and answers. He mostly remembered little things, like the scratching of the interrogator's pen and the way he avoided his face, moving his eyes from the paper to the interpreter and back as if Henry weren't even there. For an hour and a half, it went on, the odd, unnatural rhythm of the three-sided conversation building on itself, first with the rumbling gibberish of the interrogator's questions followed by the interpreter's translations, then Henry's answers, and finally the translations back into English before beginning again, round and round in a limping dance.

"How many houses in the village?"

"Seven brick houses," said Henry, and as the interrogator wrote what the interpreter translated, he added, "We were the first one on the right next to the school."

"Describe the house and where people sleep in it."

"The kitchen, the dining room, and the sitting room are on the first floor. There are two wings on the second, one with bedrooms, another with a storage room. My brothers and I slept upstairs, and my mother and grandmother sleep downstairs."

"Who did you share a room with?"

"My brothers."

"What kind of animals do you have?"

"Some chickens in the yard and a dog and cat as pets."

"What color is the dog?"

"Yellow."

"What color is the cat?"

"White."

When the interrogation was over, the guard brought him back to the holding pen where Victor and Jackie were waiting, huddled together on a bunk. Henry sat down between them, taking each of their small hands in his own. Victor's was icy cold. Ba had warned them on the ship not to talk to one another too much because the government might plant spies in their room. They stayed quiet, not daring to compare what they'd been asked or what they'd said, in case they gave themselves away.

After a sleepless night of worrying if their answers matched, the guard led them to an office where the interpreter and interrogator Henry had seen yesterday sat facing Ba. Even from behind, Henry could tell from the tight set of his father's shoulders that something was wrong.

"Mr. Chin," the interpreter said in a cold, formal voice, "there is a discrepancy. Your older and middle sons both testified that your family cat was white, but your younger son said the cat was black. How do you explain this?"

The interrogator sat back, with his hands folded on the table.

After a beat, Ba took a breath to reply, but before he could make a sound, Henry blurted out, "The cat had a litter of kittens and one of them was black. We kept that one, but it ran away."

Ba went rigid while the interpreter, with his eyebrows raised, translated what Henry had said. The interrogator scribbled for several long moments on his papers, then motioned for them to leave without even looking up.

"The paperwork will be ready tomorrow morning, Mr. Chin." The interpreter sniffed. "You can pick it up along with your sons then."

In the hallway, Ba said nothing, but gave Henry an appraising look, and nodded. He put on his gray fedora and left the building.

Victor butted his head against Henry's arm like a baby goat and looked up at him with admiring eyes shaped just like Ma's. Examining his face, Henry noticed a new hollowness to his cheeks and dark shadows under his eyes from lack of sleep. He squared his shoulders and ruffled Victor's soft hair.

When they were released the next morning, Ba met them in the lobby and took them to Chinatown for breakfast. Henry had expected it to look like a miniature version of Canton or Hong Kong, but the buildings were odd, with dragon gates, pagodas, and lanterns everywhere, and seemed too colorful, too loud, as if they were built as a set for a play. On the streets, white and brown people were walking among the bustle of Chinese shopkeepers and deliverymen. Henry couldn't help but stare.

At the restaurant, Ba ordered them all hot bowls of jook and savory, deep-fried youtiao to dip into it. Henry ate his fill, the tightness in his stomach relaxing for the first time in weeks, and was glad to see Victor finish his bowl, too. He'd lost so much weight since they'd left home.

Outside, the sun turned the cool, foggy morning into a fine September day, the only time of year, Ba said, when San Francisco was truly warm. Comforted by the familiar food, they took the trolley to Golden Gate Park. The little boys swung around the poles and knelt up on the benches to look out the windows. They pointed as the trolley climbed up and cascaded down hill after hill of streets so steep that the buildings had to lean way over to stop themselves from falling. Looking up, Henry saw rows of multicolored homes stacked on top of one another like books laid on their sides, and he couldn't decide if living like that would be magical or scary.

Finally there was the strait, with a magnificent red bridge straddling it. Above, the sky was filled with seagulls. All at once, the water reminded Henry of the ocean they'd just crossed and how far it had taken them away from Ma. Clenching his jaw, he glanced over at Victor. He and Jackie were hanging off the straps, waiting for Ba to tell them when they could jump out the back.

At the park, Ba flicked ash from his cigarette in the direction of a group of young people lying on blankets in the grass.

"Lazy good-for-nothings," he complained. "It isn't even a holiday."

They walked for a long while, passing flower gardens where ladies in big hats strolled, great pools of water where children and adults alike sailed toy boats, a meadow filled with grazing sheep, and a patch of green where old men wearing bushy white mustaches played a game with large metal balls. From there, the piercing sound of organ music reached Henry's ears, its cheerful high-pitched whistles rising and falling, growing louder as Victor and Jackie took off like shots toward its source.

On the path next to the playground, a circular stone building housed a weathered carousel, a menagerie of painted animals—a dragon, a camel, and a goat alongside frogs, dogs, roosters, pigs, and horses. Little children shrieked and squealed, flinging out their arms and legs. Their mothers and nannies waved and warned them to hold on. Leaning against the fence that separated them from the steps leading to the domed pavilion, the four of them watched the whirling beasts and happy children revolving between the columns.

"I wish Ma were here," Henry said to Victor. "Remember the puppet shows she took us to? She'd love these animals, don't you think? And the music, too."

Victor nodded, his chin quivering for a moment before he bit his lip and turned back to the carousel. Henry regretted mentioning Ma just then, but glancing over at Ba, he saw a a flicker of discomfort in his face, a slight pucker of his chin and a hardening of his eyes as he stared straight ahead.

The day after they were released from detention, they boarded the transcontinental railroad. When they got to New York three days later, it didn't take long for Henry to notice that something was off. Their very first night in the laundry, he woke up to use the bathroom and found Ba's cot empty. Peeking behind the curtain that separated the living area from the shop, he couldn't see him there either. He told himself Ba was probably putting out the garbage or fixing something outside, and managed to go back to sleep. In the morning, his father was back, acting as if nothing had happened, and Henry would have let it go, except for the fact that over the next few days, he kept disappearing, claiming to be making deliveries. What kind of laundry delivered at night? Henry was thirteen years old and hardly a fool. He knew his father was hiding something, or someone.

A few days later, at dinnertime, a white woman came to the laundry.

"This is Ruth," Ba said, simple as that.

He might as well have said, "This is your new mother."

At the table, he pulled out her chair and served her first, ignoring Victor's stares and Henry's stony silence.

For years, when Henry had longed for Ba to come back, he daydreamed about what it would be like with him in America. How he'd be Ba's right-hand man, working alongside him at the business and helping him in every way, as only a firstborn son could. Maybe Ba would even change the name of the laundry from Barker Avenue Hand Laundry to Chin & Son, and then they'd be partners. Those fantasies had kept Henry from facing what it would really be like—the struggle, the grueling work, the homesickness.

But Ba seemed to have already found a partner in this woman, and it was clear from the way he hung on her every word that this was no passing fling. Henry hadn't expected him to live a monk's life. He knew most men in America didn't. Grandfather Chin was rumored to have had a woman in New York, and he'd hidden her with no fuss, so why couldn't Ba be discreet? It must have been because he loved her, and that was what hurt the most. By loving Ruth, Henry thought, Ba was betraying not only Ma, but him and Victor, too.

Henry could have hated his father for this, but instead, he laid all the blame on Ruth, and the more she tried to win him and Victor over, the more he resented her. She was always buying them things they didn't ask for and offering to help with their homework. While Victor lapped up her attention, Henry couldn't bear it. She should have known that. She should have stopped, but Victor encouraged it. He needed a mother so badly that any mother would do.

If Henry could have avoided Ruth, he would have, but it was impossible with her living right across the street. He had to move out of the laundry. As soon as he turned sixteen, he got a job at Mr. Lee's print shop, dropped out of school, and rented a room in a building around the corner. Ba didn't fight it, Henry supposed, because he was sick of the tension with Ruth. In fact, he seemed less upset about him leaving school than about the money he was spending on a place so close to home. But it was worth it to Henry to get some space and still be nearby for Victor.

No matter how old he was, Victor would always be the baby of the family and Henry would always feel responsible for him. Even before he got sick, he had a way of looking for trouble and finding it, like the time he stayed out all night and the things he got up to with that little delinquent Jackie. He did whatever he felt like in the moment and never thought about the consequences until it was too late.

Even now, in her letter, Ma was saying, "Please keep a closer eye on your brother. He's at the age where boys start keeping secrets."

"Shit," muttered Henry, stubbing out his cigarette.

Ma couldn't possibly know, but she had an eerie sixth sense about things, especially when it came to her sons. When Henry was little, she could take one look at him and guess what he'd been doing with alarming accuracy. He'd had a horror then of disappointing her even in the smallest way, and now he was afraid that if she discovered the things he'd been keeping from her, she'd decide to stay in China once and for all.

"Someday we'll be together again," he read, reaching for another cigarette. Ma said some version of this in all her letters. "But I am so proud that the two of you have become real American boys. Please don't worry about me so much and don't let your father get you down. He's not an easy man, but it's not his fault. He has suffered a great deal. And he must have his own life in America just like I do here. Life is filled with so much pain, we should take what small joys the gods see fit to give us."

Henry read the paragraph over again. What was Ma hinting at here? Did she know something about Ruth after all? Ma was neither stupid nor naive. Maybe Ba had already told her the truth, or maybe they had an understanding. And was she saying she had someone in China, too? Cousin Kun came up in her letters far too often, and he'd been hanging around the house for years, since before Henry and Victor left.

Scratching an itch on his bare stomach, Henry opened the desk drawer and pulled out a fresh piece of paper. He should send Victor a note warning him that Ma was onto something, but he felt much too antsy to sit and write. Tucking the unlit cigarette behind his ear, he jumped off the bed, got on the floor, and started his push-ups.

NINE

They were hanging around the ferry platform, catching a breeze on the levee after class, the four of them, always the four of them now. Every day, they'd meet in the cafeteria for meals, sitting at their table by the window. After school, they'd check for mail before doing their homework together at the library, and if the weather was nice, they'd head to the lake or sneak out to the levee. And on Saturday evenings, they'd go to the theater by the recreation center to watch the second-run movies the entertainment committee had been able to get. *Roman Holiday, Shane, From Here to Eternity, Gentlemen Prefer Blondes.*

Besides the chapel and Herb's cottage, the only place Victor didn't go with his friends was the infirmary, not even to pick up meds. His first skin smear test had come back positive and he would have liked to compare notes, but he couldn't. Though Hansen's was the reason they were all here, none of them dared to break the unspoken rule against talking about their tests or anything else that could expose the medical differences between them. If one of them was excused from class for physical therapy or paraffin wax treatments, the rest would avert their eyes.

Manny had taken off his shirt to catch some sun, the smoothness of the skin on his chest interrupted by the pinks and browns of new and healing lesions. The Mississippi shimmered, the late-afternoon light turning its muddy water into gold as the sky began to blush, edging toward dusk. From someone's radio, the stray notes of "That's All Right" floated up the river.

"You like this song?" Judy asked Donny over her shoulder.

Victor watched as she tipped back her head, exposing the length of her neck, and crossed one bare ankle over the other. She was wearing a blue-and-white-striped shirt like a sailor's, cut wide to show her collarbones, and a pair of white pedal pushers.

"It's okay," said Donny, without bothering to look at her.

"Come on, man. Elvis is the king!" Manny leaped up and swiveled his narrow hips, with an expression of fake seriousness on his face. He was just clowning around, but when his body was in motion, it seemed to know what to do without trying, moving through space with a kind of ease Victor never felt.

Donny glanced at Manny and snorted before turning his attention back to the stones he was skimming with Victor. Choosing a flat, kidney-shaped one from the pile he'd gathered on the shore, he crouched down low, drew back his arm, and whipped his body around, letting it go with a flick of his wrist. The stone skipped eight times before sinking into the river. What a show-off. The most Victor had managed so far was three skips.

"You've got to follow through with your shoulder," Donny said, "and don't throw it so hard."

Victor picked up a stone, rolling his eyes at Judy behind Donny's back, but she seemed to look right through him. She got up and started to dance with Manny, mimicking his silly moves, twisting and turning her head so that her hair flew across her face. Victor thought she looked uncomfortable, like she was performing instead of having fun. He saw her eyes flit over to Donny, as if to check whether or not he was watching her. When she saw that he wasn't, her face fell for a moment before she pasted on a smile so big and bright that Victor could tell it was fake.

Henry always said the way to get a girl to fall for you was to give her some attention, then take it away, just like feeding and then ignoring a stray dog would make it follow you forever. Victor hadn't believed him, but here Judy was spinning and gyrating, whipping her hair around, trying to get Donny to notice her.

The chorus began, and on impulse, Victor sang along in a pitch-perfect impression of Elvis's voice. Everyone froze and stared at him.

"Whoa!" said Judy. "I didn't know you could sing like that." She sounded genuinely impressed.

Victor ducked his head.

"I thought you were just getting piano lessons," said Donny.

"You should start a band," said Manny.

"Yeah, we could be your backup singers," Judy said, swaying back and forth while snapping her fingers, "except I couldn't sing to save my life."

"Me neither. How about Victor and the Flat-Tones?" Manny swept his hand across the air as if he were reading from a marquee.

Everybody laughed. The song changed to "Shake, Rattle and Roll" and Judy invited Victor to dance with her and Manny. He would have liked to take her hand and spin her into his arms like he'd seen Ba do to Ruth once at the laundry, but he didn't dare, and besides, it was a fast song. He saw her eyes slide over to Donny again, his face dark against the sun. This time, he looked back, but when she motioned for him to join them, he shook his head. She laughed it off, turning to Victor and Manny, and kept dancing with that stiff, fake smile on her face. It occurred to Victor that Donny might have refused because of his leg, and he smirked to himself, feeling only a tiny pinch of shame for having such a mean thought.

"Hey," said Judy, tapping Victor suddenly on the chest, "your shirt's buttoned up wrong."

"Oh," he said, blinking.

It was only a casual touch, but she'd done it in front of everyone. Was she interested in him, or was she just trying to make Donny jealous? Victor began to fix his shirt, but stopped, annoyed at himself. He wasn't about to act like a puppy and obey her commands, especially when he didn't care about how he looked. Donny had the right kind of clothes, shirts and blue jeans that were perfectly worn in, not new and stiff like the ones Victor got from the supply office, and his haircut was like James Dean's, cool without trying. Victor wasn't that kind of guy.

Henry always said he was a slob, and compared to his brother, he probably was. He hadn't inherited Ba's eye for fine clothing, and he didn't know how to make himself look sharp. Most people thought being good-looking was like having an ace in your hand, but it didn't stop people from hassling Henry and Ba for being Chinese. In fact, it seemed to make matters worse, as if it rubbed white men the wrong way.

When Victor started high school and was worried about being on the shorter end of his class, Ruth had told him a good personality was what counted the most, especially when it came to girls. Victor wasn't sure if she was telling the truth or just trying to make him feel better, but he hoped she was right. He hoped his personality was enough to compete with Donny's looks.

LATER THAT EVENING, Donny poked his head into Victor's room before lights-out. Ever since the night they talked, Donny had been friendlier, inviting him to play cards sometimes before bed, with snacks they shared from their care packages.

"Hey, can you do me a favor?"

"What is it?" Victor put down the latest issue of *Green Lantern* he'd bought from the magazine shop at the Carville Mall.

"Think you could get a note to Judy for me?"

Victor's spine stiffened at the mention of her name. "Now?" he hedged, willing himself to play it cool.

"I want to put it in her room."

"We're not allowed in the girls' dorms." Victor felt sick to his stomach, listening to himself give such a lame excuse, but if he said no like he wanted to, he'd have to admit his feelings for Judy out loud. He could easily imagine Donny laughing at him for thinking he had a chance with a girl like her.

"You can climb up the side of her building and slip it in her window," said Donny. "It's always open. She's on the second floor, second room from the right. You don't even have to go inside. Believe me, I'd rather do it myself, but I can't." He looked down at his leg. "Think you can swing it?"

On the one hand, Victor didn't want to let Donny use him as an errand boy. On the other hand, if he didn't go, Donny would give her the note himself. "I guess so," he said.

"Thanks." Donny handed Victor a folded piece of paper torn out of his composition book. "I owe you one."

As soon as he was alone, Victor read the message.

"Your smile is more beautiful than the sun. Every day, I look forward to seeing it," Donny wrote in his looping, carefree handwriting, the penciled script slanting upward, going slightly outside the lines on the page.

The muscles in Victor's stomach squeezed tight as a fist, and before he knew what he was doing, he'd ripped the note until it was nothing but tiny shreds of paper. He thought of the way Donny had treated Judy today, ignoring her on purpose, toying with her. And now this?

Victor pictured Judy, her hazel eyes flecked with gold in the sun, the admiration he saw in them when she'd complimented his voice. He thought of how on the day they met, she rose out of the water like a mermaid. How she made him feel like his scars weren't anything to be ashamed of. How something about her triggered a hunger he'd never felt before, for her skin, her touch. That was special, wasn't it? That was real. How could Donny's feelings be anything compared to his?

Victor buried the remains of the note at the bottom of his wastepaper basket and took off. He crossed the quad instead of using the covered walkway, steering clear of the porch lights so he wouldn't be seen. As he approached Judy's dorm from the shadows, the night felt full of possibility.

On the second floor, her window was open like Donny had said it would be, her ponytailed silhouette moving faintly behind the thin curtain. For a moment, he stood there, nervously squeezing the physical therapy ball he kept in his pocket. He only had forty minutes until curfew, so he'd better make them count.

"Judy," he whispered through his cupped hands.

She didn't hear him, but he couldn't risk being any louder. He looked down at the base of a nearby oak where there were pebbles just the right size for throwing. He picked one up and tossed it overhand, meaning to hit the window frame, but he missed. It sailed through the curtains and landed inside Judy's room with a thud.

"What the hell?" he heard her say in an angry voice as she thrust her head out the window. She was wiping her face with her hands.

Though he couldn't see too clearly, Victor thought she might have been crying.

"Sorry," he whispered, but at the sound of his voice, her body relaxed and she gave a little wave. "I just wanted to see you."

"You did?" She cocked her head to the side.

"Of course. Want me to come up?"

"Nah." She went back in, and he was afraid that he'd blown it, but after a moment, a long, bare leg shot out the window. Climbing onto the ledge, she shimmied down the gutter spout in a sure-footed way that made Victor suspect this wasn't her first time sneaking out.

"Teenager by day, cat burglar by night," he joked. He was watching her every move, admiring her lightly muscled limbs. When she landed, he said, with a little bow, "Where to, milady?"

Judy rewarded him with a laugh and said, in the same jokey tone, "To the lake, kind sir."

The moon was up, half full and halfway across the sky, making her skin shine in the dark as they walked behind the quads. As they made their way in silence to Lake Albrechtson, the grass smelled of rain and night. The scent of the late-blooming flowers hung thick in the air around the ornamental gardens by the infirmary. When they got to the lake, they kicked off their tennis shoes and sat dangling their feet in the slippery, dark water. Somewhere to their left, a frog croaked and leaped, plopping into the wet. Judy sniffled, wiping her nose on her sleeve.

"You okay?" Victor asked, rubbing his eyes. They'd been itching all day.

"Yeah." She hesitated. "No. I don't know." She sniffled again and slapped at a mosquito on her leg.

"Did something happen?"

"I got a letter from my grandma. My dad moved out. She didn't say so, but I know it was because of me. Because I'm here."

"I'm sorry."

"Don't tell anyone, okay? She said he wasn't going to divorce my mom, but still." Judy gave a long, shuddery sigh.

Victor wanted to say something to make her feel better, something wise and helpful, but he couldn't come up with anything. Instead, he reached over and touched her wrist, the skin there cool and slightly damp. She put her hand over his for a moment and then took it away.

"Want to know a secret?" he said, putting his hand back in his lap.

"Sure." She turned toward him.

"You know how I said my mom stayed in China? Well, my dad has a girlfriend in New York."

"Wow."

"Yeah. My brother hates her. But she's nice to me. I feel like I'm supposed to hate her, too, but I don't. And sometimes I feel bad about that. Stupid, right?"

"It's not stupid at all. Is she Chinese?"

"Ruth? No, she's Jewish, but she's not religious or anything."

"Well, I gathered that." Judy laughed and Victor felt his face get hot.

He didn't know why what he'd said was funny to her, or what she'd meant. Was it that a religious woman wouldn't be involved with a Chinese man or a married man, or both? And did that mean Judy wouldn't be involved with him since she'd mentioned going to synagogue?

Sometimes Victor was sure she was flirting with him, but other times, she'd pull away or say something kind of mean or weird, like the joke she'd made about him swimming from China. She didn't send clear signals and, of course, she flirted with Donny, too. Sometimes, like when she'd touched his shirt earlier today, he thought she was using him to make Donny jealous, or, if Donny was ignoring her, as a backup. It didn't feel good, but somehow it didn't make him want her any less.

Victor stayed quiet, preferring to say nothing than to say something wrong. His ears homed in on the shushing sound of a sudden breeze in the trees and the soft, lapping slosh of the water against the wooden dock. From his pocket, he dug out his physical therapy ball and kneaded it with his left hand. Working with it had gone from an uncomfortable chore to a nervous habit, and he was progressing quickly as a result, moving from the soft tennis balls Miss Abigail had first given him to smaller, less flexible rubber ones. Still, his hands and fingers felt maddeningly slow at the piano, though he pushed himself hard, to the point of pain.

"Does it help?" Judy asked.

"Yeah. I can practice for longer now."

"Will you play for me sometime?"

He was taken aback. If he said no, she might lose interest, but if he said yes, he might make a fool of himself. "I'm not very good," he hedged. "Singing's not the same as playing the piano."

He looked up at the sky scattered with its confetti of stars burning so much closer and brighter than they did in the city, as close and bright as they had burned in China. When he was little, Henry had taught him some of the names of the constellations and the seasons when they were visible, but groping for them now, he found he could only think of a few—the Cowherd; the Weaver Girl; the Celestial Gate; the Silver River, known as the Milky Way in English. Come to think of it, Victor couldn't remember a lot of the things he'd known back in China, things he'd learned in Chinese, and he wondered if they were really lost or if they'd just been put in a box in his mind and stored away.

Earlier, at lunch, Judy had been carrying an astronomy book. When Victor flipped through it, he'd found the star maps and their names as beautiful on the page as they were difficult to pronounce. Orion, he'd recognized. That was the White Tiger of the West. Then there'd been Cassiopeia, Ursa Major, Ursa Minor, and Pleiades. What language was that? Greek? Latin? He would have asked, but he hadn't wanted to sound stupid, not in front of Donny, even though he was pretty sure he didn't know either. Judy was the only one of them whose parents spoke perfect English, though she said her family also spoke Yiddish at home. Even so, it set her apart from the rest of them, along with being white and, of course, being a girl. She was both like them and not, one of them and not.

"Do you know the names of the fall stars?" Victor pointed up at a constellation. "What's that one called?"

"Which?" Judy scooted closer to him and leaned in to see exactly where he meant. "I think that's Pegasus. See how it looks like a flying horse?"

"Kind of. But that part of the sky is called the Black Tortoise in Chinese." He traced its outline with his finger as a light breeze blew the ends of her ponytail in his direction, tickling his neck. He didn't dare to move. It was a warm night, but his skin erupted in goose bumps as he breathed in the scent of her strawberry shampoo.

"I think part of Pisces might be inside the Black Tortoise, then. It's right next to Pegasus." Judy pointed again and sat back down a couple of inches away. "Do Chinese constellations have astrological signs, too?"

"You mean the zodiac animals? No. How do you know about those?"

"The back of the menu at the Chinese restaurant we go to has the chart. I'm a tiger."

"Oh no, I'm a rabbit," said Victor, playfully leaning away. "Should I be worried?"

Judy leaned back on her elbows and said in a low voice, "I guess you'll just have to wait and see."

"On the Levee" was the last song in *The Blue Book for Beginners*, a simple tune somehow managing to mimic the sounds Victor heard around the river, the steam whistles and calliopes, the bits of zydeco and snippets of Creole and Cajun music coming from the porches and dorms. The other day, after he'd mastered playing it straight, first slow, then fast, he took a phrase from the bass and let his right hand do whatever it wanted, ignoring the treble, finding new notes all on its own. It was a fun game, not unlike changing the lyrics of a song and singing it to himself. He was just messing around, but he found the tinkering so satisfying that he started doing it with other songs, too.

When he finished what he was supposed to practice, he'd take apart a tune and let one hand or the other float free from the way it had been written, for ten, fifteen minutes at first, a phrase here and there. Soon he was improvising over whole songs for an hour at a time, playing new made-up variations, pleasing himself until he exhausted their possibilities.

Today, Victor had been playing not to be heard and not just for practice, but for the feeling of the notes moving through him and the joy of setting them free. Now he was nervous, even a bit dizzy, knowing that Judy was going to show up at any moment. He'd finished *The Blue Book*, but it didn't have anything he wanted to play for her, not even "On the Levee." The songs were little more than technical exercises written for children that were silly and embarrassing sometimes, like the one called "Wun Long Pan" that was supposed to be Chinese.

"I thought you'd like this one," Mrs. Thorne had said after he tapped out the melody, but the piece sounded to Victor like the score of a Charlie Chan movie. "Isn't it fun?"

"Sure," he'd said, because it was easier than telling the truth.

But she'd read his expression and given him a skeptical look.

"It's not exactly authentic," he'd admitted, his face burning with the awkwardness of having to explain his discomfort.

In the end, he picked Minuet in G Major from the new Bach book he was working on. After getting through his assigned pieces and practicing the Bach a few times, he was in the middle of fiddling with a passage from "Am I Blue?" when Judy finally came in, the sound of the door silencing his hands.

"Oh, I know that song," she said, humming the end of the phrase he'd just been playing. She sat down at the front pew and unknotted the white cardigan tied around her waist. "My dad plays the piano, too. When I was a kid, he used to let me lie down underneath it while he played. It made me feel safe."

"Nothing's stopping you now." Victor laughed, half joking, not thinking she'd take him seriously.

"Really?"

"Be my guest," he said, and watched as she got down on the floor by his bench and crawled under the piano.

He watched her all the time, noticing all kinds of little things about her. The slightly higher arch of her left eyebrow. The triangle of freckles on her right forearm, just above her wrist. The soft patch of hair at the back of her neck, shorter and finer than the rest, exposed only when she put her hair up in a ponytail. He imagined touching it with his fingers, his lips. Did she have any idea? She must. He couldn't take his eyes off her, so much so that it hurt to tear them away.

Judy was stretching out under his feet, on her back, with her head toward him and her legs sticking out the other side. It was thrilling to see her there, and all the more because it was probably sacrilegious to lie down in a church. He touched the keys, his heart beating in his hands, and played a single chord with the soft pedal down, worried about Judy's ears.

"Too loud?"

"No, it's fine. You don't have to make it quieter."

He lifted his foot and tried a soft set of arpeggios. "Is this okay?" Judy nodded.

He was putting the Bach he'd prepared on the music stand, smoothing down the page, when she said in an airy, theatrical voice, "Play it again, Sam," quoting *Casablanca*, a movie Ruth loved.

He laughed. "Play what again?"

"What you were playing before, when I came in, 'Am I Blue?' And sing it, too, okay?"

He took a deep breath, hoping he wouldn't embarrass himself. After the first few bars, he opened his mouth and let the sound come out, melding with the piano's in the air. His voice was a bit thin and his fingers unsure, fumbling a chord or two, but with every note, he fell deeper into the song until he forgot his body. Until the world faded from color to black and white, and all that existed was the music and the job of making it. What he couldn't say with words, he could say in a song. He sang it once all the way through, and then he began to riff. His hands danced, improvising, nothing too complicated, but running up and down the scale, trilling, showing off and enjoying it. He could hear Judy humming along, and when he peeked under the piano, she had her eyes closed and her hair spread loose on the floor, with one foot crossed over her knee, jiggling it to the beat. The notes flowed into one another, turning, in the end, into liquid sound, completing the loop of the song.

When he was finished, he held the final chord and lifted his hands, releasing the breath he hadn't realized he'd been holding as Judy burst into applause. She crawled out and knelt by him at the bench, staring up at him with the light falling through the yellow stained glass window, the flood of gold setting the bits of red in her hair on fire. Her hands were folded loosely in her lap, her lips slightly parted in a dazed sort of smile before a change overtook her face.

"How do you do that?" she said, her eyes round with awe.

"I just try to make it sound like it does in my head," he said honestly, a sudden, uncomplicated happiness washing over him.

Her reaction felt so good that he was instantly self-conscious. Was he grinning like a fool? She was looking right at him in that straightforward way she had, and he forced his face into a normal expression, not wanting her to see how hungry he was for compliments, especially from her. If she did, she'd know the power she had over him.

Judy said she had homework to finish and left him at the piano, elated and sweaty with the heat of performing. As he tugged at the collar of his shirt to get some air on his skin, his eyes began to blur. As his field of vision narrowed, the keyboard lost its breadth and his stomach churned with nausea. He'd thought the dizziness was just nerves before, but here they were again, the symptoms the drugs were supposed to have taken care of. Gripping the edge of the piano seat, he closed his eyes, trying to slow his breath, his beating heart, and just as quickly as they'd come on, the symptoms drained away, leaving him limp and shaken.

Victor shoved his books in the backpack he'd left by the pew where Judy had taken off her cardigan and forgotten it. Up close, he realized it wasn't actually white, but the color of fresh cream, thin and soft, with a tiny hole at one sleeve where a moth must have nibbled on it. Pressing his face into the wool, he took in the smell of lavender soap and underneath it, Judy's own delicious scent.

TEN

It was October, but still summer-warm, with sparks of fall in the air touching the leaves and the light, the sun, the slow gold of honey. Victor had gotten his second set of test results. Positive again. By the cottages, he passed the husk of an old hunter green De Soto blooming with rust on his way to Herb's to help him with his correspondence. Reading to Herb out loud reminded him of cozy afternoons he'd spent with Ruth when he was little, with library books she'd taken out for him, *Grimms' Fairy Tales* and *Curious George*, his mouth learning the strange new shapes of the English language.

Next to the car, a woman was doing her laundry in an old-fashioned washtub. Herb said she and her husband had children on the outside, taken care of by nearby relatives. They snuck out of the hole in the fence every couple of weeks to have picnics with them on the levee, under the willow trees. Lifting her head, the woman waved at Victor with a gently clawed hand and went back to cranking the lever. The rolling pins on the tub's wringer squeezed the water out of the bedsheet she was washing in a rhythm of repetitive squeaks and squishes. Victor wasn't paying particular attention to the noise, but beneath his awareness, he must have been registering the beat, because after a few rounds of the pattern, he started to hear a melody.

On top of this, with more notes and pauses and a few extra beats, a sequence of harmonies took shape inside his brain, too.

The variations kept on going even after Herb's neighbor stopped turning the lever to hang her sheets on the clothesline. A song had formed in Victor's head that hadn't existed in the world before, and he realized he'd been doing this for years without knowing it. Somewhere inside him, music came out of something like a radio station whose frequency faded in and out of tune. Before, he could never control whether it was staticky or clear, but now, if he concentrated, he was able to twist the dial until the sound got sharp. Since his piano lessons had started, the channel was switching on more and more often, triggered by everything around him—the trilling calls and answers of the birds, the patter of the rain, the turning of a bicycle wheel in the covered walkway, the whistles of the steamboats and the churning of their paddles as they passed on the river.

In the front window of Herb's place, paper ghosts and pumpkins had been put up for Halloween. The cottages were supposed to be for married couples, but Herb had somehow gotten one for himself, arguing that it made managing his disabilities easier. The blindness that was almost complete now and the atrophy of his limbs made it impossible to walk without a cane. There were three dorms for blind patients with extra orderlies, but he preferred his cottage, where he lived with a younger man named Fernando, who, like Herb, came from a small town in Texas. An amateur mechanic, Fernando had been working on the De Soto for the past few months, and though the neighbors said it made the place look like a junkyard, Herb refused to let anyone take it away. Victor figured the homemade Halloween decorations in the window were Fernando's, too. Smooth-cheeked and compact like a matador, he was known as Herb's caregiver, but the two of them weren't much different from the married couples who lived around them.

Once, when Victor lost track of time at the piano and skipped lunch, Fernando had whipped up a couple of plates of chicken salad, sliced tomatoes, and potato chips in the little kitchen. When he set their food on the table, Victor had seen his hand rest for a brief moment on Herb's shoulder before taking off like a hummingbird, so fast and light, it would have been easy to miss. But Victor hadn't missed it, and he noticed, too, the gentle way Fernando would loosen Herb's tie to tuck a white linen napkin into the starched collar of his shirt before meals. A slight smile would play at the corners of Herb's lips at these little gestures, and his head always seemed to tilt like the tip of a compass toward the sound of Fernando's footsteps.

"So when's your Carnegie Hall debut?" said Herb, recrossing his legs in a floral armchair. On the side table next to him was the stack of mail he wanted Victor to read.

"Never." Victor gave a short, sharp laugh, surprising himself at how bitter it sounded. "I'm so behind, I don't know if I'll ever be able to really play, at least not the way I want."

"You might if you stick to it." Herb readjusted his dark glasses, perching them higher on the bridge of his misshapen nose, and ran a hand over his sparse hair. Being blind didn't seem to stop him from caring about the way he looked. Apart from the hospital gown he'd worn at the infirmary, Victor had only ever seen him in a shirt and sport coat like he was wearing today, or a suit if he was going to have an editorial meeting at the *STAR* office.

"When I was a young man," Herb went on, "I wanted to be a journalist, but my father was a pharmacist, so I wound up becoming one, too. I left all that behind, of course, but now I have my own magazine. If you turn your attention to what you can do instead of what you can't, you might be surprised at what you accomplish. Especially here. Do you understand what I'm trying to say?"

"I think so," said Victor, though he didn't really understand.

Was Herb trying to tell him that his life was better now than it was before he came here? How could that be true when he'd lost so much, practically everything? Or was this his way of warning him to make the best of things because he might end up losing everything, too? In any case, Victor didn't think his music compared to what Herb did at *The STAR*. He enjoyed his lessons and loved how it felt to play, but the more he learned, the more he realized what he didn't know and what he couldn't do, whether or not his hands got better.

Victor rubbed his eyes. No matter how much he rinsed them out with saline solution, he felt like there was grit in them.

"At first, *The STAR* was just a little gossip rag. It took years of practice to make it what it is today." Herb leaned forward in his chair and paused. "Listen," he said, dropping his voice, "Mrs. Thorne says you're gifted. You have perfect pitch, and you're learning way faster than she expected, even with your nerve transplant."

Victor was quiet, but in his heart, a dangerous hope was swelling with Herb's words. It should be enough that the piano was helping his hands to heal and that he enjoyed playing it. It was better not to expect too much. The grandfather clock chimed.

"We should get to those letters. Your appointment with Behr is at four, right? Nando," Herb called into the kitchen, where Fernando was puttering around, "better get the tea now. Victor has to go early today."

Victor was nervous about the appointment. Something was off with him lately. He'd feel fine for a few days and then, out of nowhere, get hit with the familiar fevers, along with sweating, chills, nausea, dizziness, and a fatigue that made him have to go to his room and lie down. Sometimes the episodes came and went in a flash, like the one in the chapel, and once in a while, he'd get a sensation like an electric shock through his hands. Though Miss Abigail said it was normal since his nerves were still healing and he might have brought it on himself with too much exercise, it made him worry that his surgery hadn't worked after all, or that he was relapsing. When he couldn't finish his homework, he'd tell his teachers he was unwell or his hands hurt too much to write, but no matter how bad he felt, he never skipped piano lessons or practice.

"Cream if we're out of milk, and don't be stingy with the sugar," said Herb as he shuffled over to the row of records on the alphabetized shelf where he'd asked Fernando to take out *Show Boat*.

"You know you're not supposed to have that," said Fernando with a click of his tongue.

"It's not for me, it's for our guest." Herb flashed Victor a sly little smile behind Fernando's back. He slipped the seventy-eight album out of its sleeve and set it carefully on the turntable for later.

The first piece of mail had a Hollywood address and the letters "PMP" stamped on the envelope.

"'Per manu propria,'" Herb explained when Victor asked what it meant. "That's Latin for 'delivered by hand.'"

"So it's important?"

"Probably not. Tallulah just has a flair for the dramatic, but you can start there."

As *The STAR* grew from a hospital newsletter to a monthly publication with articles on research, treatment, and patients' rights, Herb had somehow become pen pals with the Hollywood actress Tallulah Bankhead. She got all her famous friends to subscribe to the magazine, and now it even had an international circulation. Victor liked the idea of helping out with something that could make a difference. Something that could, as Herb said, shine a light on their condition and show the world that people with Hansen's weren't the "lepers" they imagined them to be. Maybe that was why everyone treated Herb like he was special. He had power. The power to say what he wanted about this place and the power to make people listen.

Victor tried to get through the letters quickly. Apart from Ms. Bankhead's, they were all about *The STAR*. The one from the American Legion pledged continued support for the magazine and asked how many veterans were currently living in Carville. A letter to the editor from a doctor in the Philippines praised the work they were doing around the world, to lift the stigma that prevented people from seeking treatment. The rest were requests to renew or cancel subscriptions, or place ads in upcoming issues.

Fernando came in holding a silver tray with a teapot and matching rose-patterned cups and saucers. Victor inspected his cup, turning it over to find a stamp saying "Made in England" underneath. Most things in Carville were government-issued and plain, but Herb's cottage was filled with little luxuries, from several different tea sets to real wooden furniture, comfortable armchairs, and lamps with fringe dangling from their shades.

Herb poured a good glug of cream into his cup, mixing it in before Fernando could stop him. The silver spoon etched with leaves tinkled against the china, reminding Victor of the sound of Ruth stirring her coffee. Maybe she was drinking some right now, alone at her kitchen table, and he wondered if, in moments like that, she thought about him, too. Like Ruth, Herb had no children of his own, and Victor thought it was a shame, because they would have made good parents. He missed Ruth almost as much as he missed Ma, and he missed Henry, too, but he realized with only a touch of guilt that he didn't particularly miss Ba.

Victor couldn't remember a time when his father had shown him much affection, not even when he was small. He was barely a year old when Ba had left, and all he knew about him was what Ma, Henry, and Grandmother told him. On the day of his departure, the story went, when their father spat into their palms for remembrance, Henry had cried, but Victor had wrinkled his brow and wiped his hand on his pants, a poor sign. The sea he crossed later with this unknown man he was supposed to call Ba separated one life from another, and in the years since the voyage, his memories of China had become a jumbled mix of images—berry picking, swimming in the village pond, boiling grass and bark when there was nothing else to eat, running to the hills during the war.

The older he got, the more he avoided his father, who seemed happy to leave him to his own devices so he could see Ruth or socialize with other Chinese business owners downtown. Victor didn't mind much. He could explore the city by himself, riding the subway to see Jackie in midtown or to Chinatown where he could wander around as he pleased.

He could still hear the clack-clack-ping of the tiles popping and echoing, drowning out the roar of the gamblers' voices the last time he'd opened the door to the basement mahjong parlor on Mott Street where Ba sometimes played. Recognizing him, the doorman had shooed him away. The door slammed shut as Victor spun on his heel and did a little step-ball-change like he'd seen Gene Kelly do in *An American in Paris*. Trading the stale tobacco air of the mahjong parlor for the fish and rotten-vegetable stink of the street, he pretended to be Jerry Mulligan, zigzagging up the grimy steps to the sidewalk, his arms outstretched like a seagull coasting on a gust of wind.

With a handful of coins from his delivery tips jangling in his pocket, he was going to get a lo mai gai—warm and meaty, and fragrant with the scent of the lotus leaves wrapped around the pearls of sticky rice like a gift. At the dim sum joint on Doyers Street where they sold their morning leftovers for half price if you went at the right time, he paid and took his meal to Columbus Park on Mulberry Street. There, on a worn wooden bench surrounded by old men playing chess and little kids piling on the teeter-totters, he picked open the knot of red-and-white thread. Unfolding the steam-darkened leaves, he dug in to the rice to find pieces of soy sauce chicken, lengths of lap cheong sausage, a single shiitake mushroom, some char siu pork, and half a hard-boiled egg.

What he wouldn't give for a lo mai gai now, or any Chinese food, for that matter, especially Ma's. He thought of the homemade joong she always made for the Dragon Boat Festival—sticky rice packets bound in bamboo leaves. Sometimes they had peanuts mixed in, and inside, there would be mushrooms and pork belly, a salty preserved egg yolk, and a sprinkling of dried shrimp. The joong were supposed to celebrate the poet Qu Yuan, who'd committed suicide to protest the government's corruption by drowning himself in a river. Because his friends couldn't find his corpse, they made joong as an offering to the fish so they wouldn't eat his body.

Victor had helped Ma and Grandmother make hundreds of them in his old kitchen on the other side of the world, unspooling and cutting the twine for tying them up. He'd give anything right now to be home with them instead of here, even for a single day. If only he could tell Ma the truth about where he was. The worst part was the pretending, but as Henry said, what good would it do to tell? He'd still be here and she'd still be there.

He was sinking into the sadness of his thoughts and he tried to talk himself out of it, like he always did. What was there to grieve for? Ma hadn't died. She was still there, with Grandmother in the house, where she'd always been. If he closed his eyes, he could see her. Ma laughing and clapping when he brought her a string of fish from the pond. Ma stuffing valuables into tins and jars, and burying them in the kitchen garden. Ma rubbing a piece of jade over his chest late at night, releasing the heat in his body when he couldn't breathe. He hadn't lost her. But no matter what he told himself, sorrow still rushed over him from time to time, like summer monsoons, flooding his heart. He tried with all his might to make it stop. If he let himself swim too long in those dark waters, he might go under and never make it out again.

Lifting his teacup as the opening strains of *Show Boat*'s overture played, Victor concentrated on the music, doing his best to push his feelings away.

He'd seen the Hollywood version a few times at the Chatham Square movie theater where, sitting alone at the matinee, he'd stood and clapped every time William Warfield sang "Ol' Man River." But now Paul Robeson's voice swirling in his eardrums stirred up something he couldn't name, and at the song's crescendo, it spilled over into two fat tears he was glad Herb couldn't see.

"That ought to do it for now," said Herb, lifting up the needle. "The record's four hours long."

"Can I borrow it?" Victor asked. He wanted to listen to the whole thing on his own, and Donny had a record player he let him borrow sometimes.

"I don't think that's a good idea."

Robeson had been accused, Herb explained, of being a Communist by Senator McCarthy and was blacklisted. Since Carville was a government institution and Herb was a freethinker and Jewish to boot, he had to be careful.

"Wouldn't want anyone to think I was a bad influence on you," he said. "Robeson is a man of humble origins and look what he's become. A singer, actor, athlete, and activist, too. A man of substance and ideas."

Victor made a noncommittal noise. He knew that Herb meant well, but it gave him a funny feeling, a tightness across his shoulders when Herb said these kinds of things. Maybe he didn't understand Victor as much as he thought he did. Herb might have had it tough in small-town Texas, but if he and his father were pharmacists, it meant they'd gone to college. And it meant they had money. What did he know about coming from a family like Victor's? Henry never even finished high school and Ba was okay with it because he had a job lined up at Mr. Lee's print shop. Before Victor got sick, Ba had expected him to work at the laundry full-time after graduation. Now he didn't know if he'd ever get to go home, let alone get a job. He knew Herb was trying to encourage him to think big, but what was he supposed to do? Wave a magic wand? How could he become a man of substance and ideas when he was stuck here at Carville?

VICTOR'S PUPILS CONTRACTED as Dr. Behr shone a penlight into his irises, one after the other. The light was irritating, making his eyes water uncontrollably. Focusing on the doctor's hand, he fixed his gaze on the black bristles of hair sprouting out of his knuckles.

"Hansen's bacteria often attacks the eyes," said Dr. Behr.

"Is that what happened to Herb?" Victor's brows snapped together with alarm.

"Relax your face, please. I really shouldn't discuss Mr. Klein's case, but yes."

Usually, during his appointments, Victor studied the diagram on the wall of the human body with lines labeling all its parts, but today, he found that couldn't read the names. He couldn't even make out the big letters spelling "Tulane" on Dr. Behr's medical school diploma.

"Is that what's happening to me?"

"No." Dr. Behr clicked off the penlight and put it back in his breast pocket. "This is just entropion. Very common. Your eyelids are inverting, and your lashes are rubbing against your corneas."

Victor frowned again. "I thought the drugs were working."

"You couldn't tolerate the Diasone, so we had to reduce your dose. The bacteria must have gained back some ground."

"Is that why I'm getting fevers again?" The fatigue, nausea, and dizziness were back, too, but he didn't mention them or the zaps of pain in his hands either.

"It's possible."

Victor had been afraid of that. How much time would this setback cost him? His chances of getting a negative test anytime soon were certainly shot.

The doctor glanced at his chart. "You're on a decent dose now. And a simple operation should take care of your eyes. We'll inform your father, of course, but the paperwork's already in place."

"Another operation?" Victor's shoulders tensed. "You said I just needed the nerve surgery."

Dr. Behr looked up, seeming surprised at the note of accusation in Victor's voice. "These things happen." He sat down and put his fingertips together, making a pyramid with his hands. "I'll tell you what, though. Since it's your upper lids we have to treat for the entropion, we can correct your epicanthic folds while we're at it."

"Is something wrong with them, too?"

"Not medically, but I can create an upper eyelid with a crease. It'll make your eyes look bigger and rounder, less slanted." Dr. Behr opened his eyes wide as if to demonstrate. "The surgery's all the rage in Asia right now. I have a colleague over in Korea, Dr. Millard. We served together in the Pacific theater. Fascinating place, as you know. The culture, the women." Dr. Behr laughed in a way that seemed to invite Victor to laugh along.

"Millard pioneered an operation to help Korean war brides feel more comfortable by making their features a bit more American so they'd fit in when they came over. You know what they say—when you look good, you feel good."

As Dr. Behr made a note in Victor's chart, whistling "Happy Talk" from *South Pacific*, it dawned on him that this was the eye operation Donny must have been talking about in his room. On the one hand, it made him less suspicious of the entropion surgery, but as far as the extra procedure went, he didn't like the idea of doing something— especially something that would permanently change his face—just because Donny had done it. But on the other hand, what if it really did make him better-looking? Maybe it would level the playing field or even tip the balance in his favor with Judy.

"So, what do you say? If you're worried about Dr. Morton, we won't have to tell him about the extra procedure. Doctor-patient privilege."

"I don't know," said Victor.

Dr. Behr folded his arms. The sleeves of his white coat rode up, exposing his hairy wrists. "I'll need your decision by tomorrow."

As bicycles passed him on his way to dinner, the eyelid surgery wasn't the only thing on Victor's mind. Even though his early attempt to escape had failed and he hadn't tried again, he hadn't consciously decided to stay. Somehow reasons to wait just kept on coming up—first his bad reaction to the Diasone and now the entropion, not to mention the alarming flare-up of his other symptoms. Henry would have said they were making things up to keep him in quarantine, but he could feel the truth in his body. They were monitoring him closely at the infirmary, but he was also monitoring himself, and despite Henry's suspicious voice in the back of his mind, he had proof that Dr. Behr had been straight with him. Victor didn't trust him completely, but the operation on his nerves had gone the way he'd said, and his explanation about the entropion made sense, too.

His medical progress wasn't the only reason Victor had put off running away. The longer he stayed, the more he found himself getting attached to things and people he'd lose if he left—school, piano lessons, practice, Herb, and his friends, especially Judy. Even the daily routine at Carville—the predictability of mealtimes, classes, lessons, practice, appointments, and curfew—was soothing, in a way. In New York, besides school, he hadn't had much of a schedule and never knew when things would happen, not doing homework, making deliveries, having dinner, or going to bed. The rhythms of the laundry business were erratic, with something always coming up that had to be taken care of no matter the time or day. And as far as music was concerned, Ba never would have been able to afford piano lessons, let alone a piano to practice on, not that he would have dreamed of asking for either one if he hadn't come here. When he'd tried to leave a few weeks ago, on his first night in the dorms, he thought he'd be escaping a prison, but in reality, his life on the outside, without music, without school, without his friends, would be a pale shadow of what it was now.

"Don't let perfect be the enemy of good," Mrs. Thorne liked to say, and maybe she was right.

Maybe being here was good, or good enough, and he shouldn't give it up. And since he needed another operation Ba could scarcely afford, he didn't see how he could possibly go home anyway. He had no choice, and something about the finality of that, of knowing he wasn't responsible for choosing, was a relief. Henry couldn't blame him for staying anymore, and he couldn't blame himself.

As for the eye surgery itself and whether to get the extra procedure, Victor didn't know what he wanted to do. He wished he could talk to Henry, but there was no time to write, and the patients' phone in the canteen was always booked out by at least a week. Maybe he could get Herb to ask Sister Helen if he could use her phone again, but she'd said it was only a onetime thing. What if he snuck into the lab after curfew and made a quick call? He didn't think he'd get caught. After exploring it during his stay, he knew the infirmary like the back of his hand, and he knew how to avoid the watchmen from when he'd tried to run away. It didn't seem too risky, and if he could pull it off, it'd be worth it.

THAT NIGHT, AFTER dinner, piano practice, and a half-hearted attempt at his algebra homework, after the bridge games on the porches and the drawn-out good-nights, the bread-and-milk cart, and the flushing and washing before lights-out, Victor propped open his window with a tall stack of textbooks. Listening with his eyes closed, he peeled back the layers of the night's sounds, separating the crickets from the nocturnal birds, the fitful snores from the peaceful breaths of deep sleep. When he was sure the coast was clear, he ducked his head and leaned out into the dark.

He gasped as something brushed against his brow bone, something damp and wafting and paper-thin—a wing or a leaf. With a shiver, he braced himself against a rush of vertigo, a sick, swimming feeling.

He gathered his nerve and slid out further on his stomach, balancing his slim hip bones on the ledge. Reaching out his arms, he grasped the nearest solid thing, a branch of the magnolia tree. The earthy smell of mulch drifted up to him, and the yellow leaves on the branch were slimy, making his fingers slip on the bark as he grabbed it with both hands. With his body almost horizontal, he scrambled for a moment, then pushed off with his feet and managed to wrap his legs around the thicker base of the branch. From there, he found the trunk and shimmied down to the ground, where a bed of fallen leaves softened his landing. The magnolia tree loomed even larger than usual tonight, with the black mass of its limbs just visible against the slightly lighter sky where the moon was hiding behind some clouds.

A barn owl shrieked, streaking through the air, swooping so close that he felt the wake of its wings in his hair.

"Slow down," Victor whispered to himself, "slow down."

He fished in his pocket for his Medihaler, put it to his lips, and squirted the medicine into his lungs, counting one Mississippi, two Mississippi, all the way to ten, waiting for the iron band around his ribs to let go. After a moment, relieved, he puffed out his cheeks and took off again into the shadows, knowing he only had ten minutes before Jay the night watchman would reach his dorm.

When he got close to the infirmary, he ran the last few feet as silently as possible. Getting caught there was probably a bigger deal than getting caught on the grounds, especially if he was seen using the phone. He wondered what kind of punishment Dr. Morton would give him for that, since it was technically stealing.

With his back pressed against the wall, he crept to the side entrance, crouching below the windows of the examination rooms even though the lights were out and no one was there. Feeling for the door, he found it unlocked and opened it slowly as the eye-watering smell of disinfectant hit him hard. He held his breath and sidled into the hall, tracing the walls with his fingertips in the dark—cool, smooth, slightly damp paint, a bulletin board, a door, a stretch of wall, a poster, another bulletin board. His heart was pounding in his ears. He'd never been on the ground floor of the infirmary at night before, and without the usual bustle of people, he was suddenly much more aware of the morgue in the basement, just beneath his feet.

The lab was the second room on the left, just as he remembered. The doorknob turned with barely a squeak as he opened and closed the door behind him. Through the windows, a clear yellow light poured in as the moon, nearly full, came out from cloud cover, and he could see the room more clearly—the rack of lab coats, the line of long wooden tables and stools, the shelves stocked with glass bottles and Bunsen burners, the big black telephone on the desk. He crept over to the phone, picked up the receiver, and dialed 1–1–0.

"Hello, long distance," said a woman in a sleepy Southern voice.

"Hello, operator," said Victor, trying to sound older so she wouldn't question why he was making a phone call in the middle of the night.

He was relieved to have remembered the numbers and what to say, though he knew he might have to wait awhile since he was calling the shared telephone in the hall of Henry's building, which was on a party line. Hopefully, it wouldn't take too long since it was so late. The longer the call, the more likely it was that someone would notice the extra charge on the telephone bill. Of course they might notice it anyway, but Victor was hoping the bills got paid automatically by some government administrator who didn't care enough to check every item.

Victor was getting more and more nervous as the wall clock counted off the seconds. The ticks seemed to get louder with each passing minute. Should he hang up? He looked toward the door and his breath caught in his throat. There was an animal behind the glass of an unfamiliar display case, crouching on four tiny claws as if suspended in mid-pounce. Covered from head to toe in beaded armor, it looked like a pangolin, though he'd never seen one in real life, or a cross between a piglet and a roly-poly bug. It must have been hidden behind the open door the last time he was here, but what was it doing in the infirmary in the first place?

The animal seemed so lonely, so out of place, but thinking about the morgue again, he imagined it could be an animal spirit sent to protect the people from the death below them. Maybe, like Zhu Bajie the Monk Pig in *Journey to the West*, the creature was a minor god who'd misbehaved, and his punishment was to be frozen in a glass cage here, in the middle of nowhere, Louisiana, in a leprosarium.

"I have Henry Chin on the line," said the operator in Victor's ear.

"What's wrong?" said Henry, sounding gruff and alarmed.

"Were you asleep?"

"It's two in the morning." Henry cleared his throat. "Where the hell are you?"

"In one of the labs, so I have to be quick. I'm getting another operation."

"It didn't work? I told you—"

"My hands are fine," Victor interrupted. "It's my eyes. They're going to fix them, but they said I could get an extra thing at the same time, and then I'd have double eyelids."

"What does that mean?"

"They're doing it in Korea for women getting married to US soldiers, so they'll feel more American or something."

"So it's plastic surgery. Why would you want to do a thing like that?"

"I don't know," said Victor. He stared at the animal in the glass case, and it stared back, its black eyes shining in the dark, judging him. "Donny, the guy I told you about, did it a while ago."

"Wasn't he born here?" said Henry, his tone turning smug. "He doesn't know who he is."

Victor had heard people say things like that about American-born Chinese kids before. He thought of how Donny seemed so embarrassed of the things his mother sent in the mail and how he answered in English when people in their dorm spoke to him in Chinese.

"Letting some quack cut your eyelids won't make you look any more American. You know that, right?" Victor could hear the faint rasp of his stubble as Henry scratched his cheek. "You're Chinese and there's nothing you can do about it. Besides, you have Ma's eyes."

Victor didn't know if Henry had meant to shame him, but it worked. He felt pathetic and more than a little ridiculous now. How could he have thought that an operation would help him compete with Donny? The shape of his eyes was the least of his problems.

A WEEK AFTER the surgery, Victor examined his face in the bathroom mirror—beady-eyed, puffed up, and plum-colored—as he got ready for school. It had been, as Dr. Behr promised, simple and a success. No more itching, no more blurry vision, and no double eyelids. People got surgery at Carville all the time, and once they could get around, they didn't have to stay in the infirmary. Bandages and bruises were such a common sight that Victor didn't look at them twice, but he felt self-conscious about what Judy would think when she saw him.

"You look like a boxer," she told him when he showed up at breakfast.

"You should see the other guy," he wisecracked, mimicking the voice Ruth used for jokes. Judy laughed and he felt a flicker of pride.

That night, antsy and unable to sleep, he snuck out to get another look at the creature in the glass case. An armadillo, Sister Laura had told him after he described it to her at the library. Retracing the steps he'd taken on the night he called Henry, he climbed out his window and made his way to the infirmary, back to Sister Helen's lab.

Getting away with it once had made him feel bold, and without the pressure of having to figure out the phone, being out in the night air filled him with a sense of adventure. Sometimes, in China, Henry would wake him up when Ma and Grandmother were asleep, and they'd go off to the fields to play follow-the-leader and hide-and-seek, or to the pond to hunt for frogs, their lanterns stunning them into stillness. Ma must have known what they'd been up to since they'd leave her their catch to make for dinner the next day, but she'd never ask too many questions, not wanting to spoil their fun. Maybe that's what had given him a taste for breaking the rules because later, in New York, he and Jackie cooked up dozens of little schemes.

Once, when they were about twelve, they'd come up with a plan to loot the penny gum machine in the 5th Avenue and 53rd Street subway station near Jackie's grandfather's laundry. Getting off the train a few minutes late, Victor had scanned the length of the platform on the Brooklyn-bound side, where they were supposed to meet, but Jackie was nowhere to be found. His eyes darted from the two rats scrabbling down on the tracks to the overflowing trash can by the stairs, and then he heard the patter of Jackie's tennis shoes on the steps.

"What happened?"

"The usual," Jackie said, his shirt untucked, his hair a mess, his eyes red and swollen.

He must have just gotten a beating since he almost never cried. An angry drunk, his grandfather had once worked him over so badly with a belt that he'd had to stay home from school for three days.

"You sure you're up for this?"

"Definitely." Jackie shoved his hands in his pockets and flashed him a mischievous smile.

They tiptoed up the stairs to where the penny gum machine was just far enough from the attendant's booth to be out of sight. Jackie held up his hand, signaling Victor to wait, and squatted down next to the machine. Victor did the same, leaning his back against the cool white tiles, his senses on high alert. Every noise, from the clanging of the attendant making change to the grinding of the turnstiles, made him jump. He was sure that anyone—the attendant or a cop or a passenger—who saw them would know they were up to no good. But a man in a business suit and two old ladies walked past without seeming to notice they were there.

"See?" Jackie mouthed. Maybe he was right when he said nobody ever paid attention to kids like them.

Even before Victor could hear the train, he felt its vibrations. As it got closer, he realized they were in luck. It was coming in on the Bronx-bound side, away from them. When the screeching on the tracks got good and loud, Jackie met Victor's eye and, quick as a mouse, he slipped his hand into the coin slot. Victor held his backpack open, ready to catch the pennies, but nothing happened. Undaunted, Jackie squeezed his eyes shut and kept wiggling his fingers. The station got quieter as the train pulled in and the doors opened, letting out passengers who were about to come up the stairs.

"Come on," said Victor, tugging at his sleeve.

Jackie ignored him and gave the slot one last shove. The springs released with a click. Victor caught the flood of pennies in his bag and the two of them flew down the stairs just in time to jump on the departing train.

Victor didn't know why breaking the rules had always felt so good, especially when everything else in his life felt bad. Tonight, he moved around the infirmary with confidence.

He'd just walked into the lab when he heard footsteps—loud, echoing in the hall—a brisk, purposeful tread. All the hairs stood up on his arms as options fanned out in his mind like a hand of cards. He could creep out of the room and steal away in the opposite direction, but the footsteps were too loud, already too close. He could hide behind the door, but what would happen if the person closed it behind him? Scanning the room, he decided his best bet was to try to get out through the window.

The light switched on, exposing every surface of the lab with its merciless glare, and there was Sister Helen, holding a notebook to her chest as Victor struggled to push up the window sash with all his might.

"What do you think you're doing?" she demanded. Even at this late hour, she was wearing her heavy woolen habit and cornette, but not her lab coat.

Victor squared his shoulders as if he were facing a firing squad. "I didn't touch anything, I swear."

Sister Helen's eyes swept over the table, the instruments, the beakers, and bottles, as if accounting for them. "Are you here to use my telephone again?"

"What do you mean?"

"The bill shows a charge for a long-distance call to New York City at 2:05 a.m. last week." Sister Helen cocked her head to the side. "Don't insult my intelligence by pretending it wasn't you."

Victor's eyes dropped to the floor. "I had to talk to my brother about my surgery, and there wasn't time to wait for the phone in the canteen."

She took a closer look at Victor's bruises and nodded. "Why didn't you ask? I let you use the phone before."

"I thought that was just a onetime thing, as a favor to Herb."

"You thought I'd say no, so you took it upon yourself to go behind my back?"

"I'm sorry." Heat flooded Victor's face.

"At least it was off-peak." Sister Helen put the notebook she was carrying on the table, under the shelf lined with identical ones.

Victor thought he could hear a touch of amusement in her voice, but her face didn't give anything away. "I'll pay you back," he said. At least then, he wouldn't be guilty of stealing, just breaking and entering. "Am I going to jail?" He figured they'd have to let him out for medical appointments and school, but what about his piano lessons and practice?

"Wanting to speak to your brother about your surgery is understandable," said Sister Helen, crossing her arms, "so I won't tell Dr. Morton this time. But if it happens again, I most certainly will. Is that clear?"

"Yes, Sister," he managed to whisper.

"So, did you come to use the phone again?"

"No, I came to see the armadillo." Victor pointed at the display case. "Why is it here?"

Sister Helen gave a surprised laugh. "For inspiration."

She had a hunch, she explained, that armadillos could contract Hansen's, too, and if she was right, they'd be important for research. Scientists could find out, for instance, if armadillos passed down the gene for getting Hansen's like people did.

"All we'd have to do is infect a female like the one in that case, breed her—they always give birth to four pups at a time—and then we could see how many of her offspring get the disease. I was in the middle of working something out, an idea for a series of experiments." She tapped the notebook. "But I needed to check something in my other notes."

Victor didn't like the idea of mothers and babies being experimented on or locked up in cages, even if it was for the sake of research. "What happens when they get sick?" He swallowed hard, trying to push down the nausea rising from the pit of his stomach, not knowing if it was from what they were talking about or his lingering symptoms.

"We'd do biopsies, cutting out pieces of their nerves to test." Sister Helen took off her glasses, cleaned the lenses, and put them back on.

"While they were alive?"

"Well, yes, that would be the best way. Same as the biopsies you get."

Victor shuddered, exhaling through his nose like a horse, unable to stop himself from thinking about how his own nerves had been cut.

"Time for you to get to bed," said Sister Helen, glancing up at the wall clock with a shake of her head.

"Okay," said Victor, expecting to be dismissed, but Sister Helen was gazing at the armadillo, her brow furrowed in a thoughtful expression. After a moment, he said, "I'm sorry for what I did. I won't do it again, I promise. Thank you for not telling on me."

Sister Helen turned to him. "I take it that you're a Buddhist. Is that right?"

"Sort of," said Victor with a frown, not knowing where this was going. "My mother and grandmother are. How did you know?"

"I've known many Chinese patients in my time here, plus I grew up in San Francisco," she said with a wave of her hand. "It's said that even an apology given by the Buddha himself is not complete unless the recipient forgives him. But in *my* faith, forgiveness is for God to give. When you do something wrong, you must make up for it."

"You mean make up for the call? I can pay you back, like I said."

"A penance is more of what I had in mind. An act of service. I've been gathering research on armadillos for the past few years." She pointed at some cardboard boxes with the toe of her flat black shoe. "Photographs, articles, notes. Everything needs to be filed by year, author, and type. I haven't had a chance to do it myself, but since you've shown some interest, you could help me organize these boxes."

Victor gave a tentative nod.

"I'll see you tomorrow, then," Sister Helen said. She held his gaze for a long, uncomfortable moment before gesturing toward the door.

Over the next couple of weeks, Victor worked hard to organize the boxes of armadillo research. Filing each item in alphabetical order, he ignored the long, boring articles, but Sister Helen's notes—her observations and ideas—caught his attention, and he even jotted some of them down.

"What are you writing?" she asked, noticing one afternoon.

"'The exterior scales of an armadillo are bone and horn but do not constitute an exoskeleton,'" Victor read out loud. "'The armadillo therefore has an armor that is protective but capable of being breached.'"

Sister Helen made a humming sound. "No matter how you slice it," she said, with a faraway look in her eyes, "every living thing is vulnerable. Human or armadillo, the price of life is suffering."

It was a horrifying thought, but the photographs in the boxes seemed to confirm what she said, with their close-ups of dissected armadillo parts, sinew and nerve beneath their protective shells. Victor would have preferred to leave those gruesome images in the lab, but on some nights, they came to him in his room, in dreams, the female in the glass cage alive again, with four offspring, all infected with Hansen's disease. The sick mother and her babies would curl up and barrel like armored bowling balls down the dark lanes of his sleep, rolling toward him over and over, as in the dreams he would become a single pin left standing. Once they got close, instead of knocking him down, the family would unfurl to reveal their soft, vulnerable parts, battered paws worn into raw stumps, tender snouts covered in lesions as they crowded around his legs. He'd crouch, letting them push their rough little muzzles into his hands, and the mother armadillo would open her mouth as if to speak, but he covered his ears. Even in his sleep, he knew it would be too terrible to bear.

ELEVEN

The air was damp with a nip of cold when Victor met his friends in the field behind the dorms at 11:20 one night in late fall. They were safe for a while since Jay the night watchman always took his break at 11:15. Donny had heard Victor come in on the night he got caught by Sister Helen a couple of weeks ago, and when he told the others, Judy had seized on the idea that they should all sneak out for a nighttime concert at the chapel.

"Forget it," Donny told Judy when Victor hesitated. "Maybe he isn't any good."

"He is," she insisted. "I could hardly believe it when I heard him."

"Come on," Manny said, elbowing Victor in the ribs. "It's just us."

The truth was, Victor didn't feel ready to play for anyone besides Mrs. Thorne or Judy, and with his penance freshly paid, he wasn't really up for sneaking out either. But how could he say no? Now here he was, creeping around in the dark, telling himself that he wasn't breaking any promises to Sister Helen. After all, they weren't going to the infirmary, and he'd never said anything about the chapel.

That afternoon, he'd been distracted at his lesson. Instead of listening to Mrs. Thorne explain solfège since they'd added singing to his studies, his head had been filled with Judy's voice and the look of awe on her face when she'd listened to him play. It was like the sun coming out on a cold, cloudy day, and he wanted more than anything to feel that warmth again.

Afterward, he'd had a hard time practicing his scales with the new method Mrs. Thorne had suggested. Keeping his hands and wrists still, he was supposed to move one finger after the next individually, marching them up and down like the legs of toy soldiers. He'd gotten through only fifteen minutes of this when his hands began to cramp and he had to rub them until the muscles flexed and finally relaxed. Whenever that happened, he worried he was having another relapse, but with his Diasone dose at the maximum now, the flare-up of symptoms he'd had before the eye surgery—the fevers, dizziness, nausea, and fatigue—had calmed down. He'd shaken out his hands and gone right back to his scales, playing doggedly through the pain. Then he'd gone over the piece he'd picked for tonight, "On the Sunny Side of the Street."

The looseness of that kind of jazzy music was less exhausting for him than the precision demanded by the classical pieces Mrs. Thorne assigned. While his speed was improving at a steady pace as his nerves continued to heal, unless the song was slow, he still often played a fraction of a second behind the beat. As frustrating as this was when he was working on his Mozart or Bach, it was less of an issue with jazz or blues, which were somehow able to absorb the delay without ruining the music. In fact, the slight withholding of a note made his ear anticipate the sound, so that when it came, it was all the more satisfying for the wait.

Now, overhead, the moon was bloated in a field of stars as they walked in silent pairs, Victor with Manny, and Judy with Donny in front of them, the tread of their feet across the soft, muddy earth the only sound. Manny was in a restless mood, bouncing around like he was on springs, swinging on a low branch of a live oak one moment and rubbing Victor's head with his knuckles the next. He didn't do it very hard, and Victor knew he was just being playful, but he shoved him away with a burst of real anger, thinking he wouldn't have the guts to do that to Donny.

If it weren't for Donny, they'd be going faster, but because of his leg, they all had to wait while he picked his way around the surface roots of the old trees. Passing beneath them, the powdery, green, and musky-sweet scents of the Spanish moss and decaying leaves were strong. Victor kicked at a leaf pile the groundskeepers had raked together earlier in the day, thinking how good it felt to be outside, with the grass and dirt under his feet. Not the filth of the city littered with garbage and dog shit, with nowhere to go to get away from people and their mess.

Donny tripped, and in the moonlight, Victor could just make out Judy's hand reaching to steady him. It was only a reflex, an automatic gesture, and she let go of Donny's arm as soon as he found his feet, but it made Victor's stomach tighten to see it.

When they got to the chapel, they switched on their flashlights and lit the path down the aisle to the altar like movie theater ushers, careful not to let the beams escape through the windows.

"You can't hear anything until you get right up to the door," said Victor, shining his flashlight on the steps leading up to the piano. "We should have time for a song before we have to leave."

Judy was settling herself at the front pew in between Donny and Manny. "Make it a good one," she said.

"That's the idea." Victor sat down at the bench. "Can I get a little more light up here?"

"Sorry," said Manny. He directed the beam at the legs of the piano, and the others did the same, creating a trio of low footlights.

Victor could see the keyboard but not the music stand. Good thing he'd memorized the piece, he thought, lifting the piano lid, but maybe this was a mistake. Not sneaking out, but opening himself to judgment. Donny was probably waiting for him to make a fool of himself, but seeing the look on his face when Judy praised him had been priceless.

With a shaky breath, he tried to unclench, to stop himself from straining not just in his body but his mind as well, telling himself as he laid his hands on the keys to just let go and let himself feel. His ears opened, and in the next breath, the music started almost as if someone else were playing. From the pew, he heard Judy murmur something, probably recognizing the old tune she'd mentioned her father playing for her when she was younger. He smiled to himself, and everything but the instrument disappeared—the chapel, his friends, his body, his sense of self. Giving the intro a medium tempo, light and easy, like he'd practiced it, he opened his mouth and his voice poured out, sliding in and out of the notes.

Closing his eyes at the bridge, he began to improvise, the tightness inside him released, his hands running over the length of the keys as an image of Judy under the piano popped into his head, of her hair spread out on the floor. The song flowed as it wanted to, willing Victor to follow its lead. It didn't even throw him when he missed a few notes. He was both there and not, inside himself and somewhere else entirely. The frequency was open, and all he had to do was give himself over to it and channel what he heard through his hands.

A noise broke into Victor's consciousness, a small, choked sound. He dropped his hands from the keys and shone his flashlight on the pews. Judy was crying, her face pressed against Donny's shoulder. Donny had his arm around her, but the light startled him into taking it away as she lifted her head. Victor stared at them, confused. Why was she crying? What had he missed? He thought of the day—a day that seemed like a long time ago now—he'd seen Judy, Donny, and Manny in the tea garden from the roof of the infirmary. Judy and Donny had kept their distance from each other as if they'd been resisting a powerful pull. Now, somehow, the resistance had broken and they were colliding like magnets. A sick rush of jealousy rose from the pit of Victor's stomach into his throat, burning all the way, mixing with an anger directed not only at Donny but at Judy, too.

How could she do this to him when he'd chosen and played that song especially for her? This was supposed to be his big moment, and it had been going so well.

"What's wrong?" he asked, searching all three of their faces.

Manny shrugged and Donny looked away.

"Nothing," said Judy, wiping her nose on her sleeve. "It's stupid. I was just thinking about my dad. You didn't have to stop."

"I'm sorry," he said, shaking his head, angry at himself now, too.

What a mistake to pick that song. He thought it would show her how closely he listened and cared about the things she told him. But it had upset her and, even worse, it had given Donny the chance to comfort her, to touch her. Victor couldn't have miscalculated any worse if he'd tried.

"Don't be sorry," she said. "That was beautiful. I'm sorry I ruined it."

"It doesn't matter," said Victor.

"It really was amazing," said Manny. He turned to look at Donny, who made a grudging positive sound.

"Anyway," said Victor, "we'd better go."

The four of them left, clicking off their flashlights and easing the door shut behind them. No one said a word as they made their way back until Victor heard a rustling noise up ahead, somewhere near the hole in the fence. He put his finger to his lips and pointed in the direction of the sound.

"Is it Jay?" Judy whispered.

"No," said Victor. A familiar figure stepped into the open space of the softball field, a woman, young and shapely in a tight dress, juggling a handbag and high-heeled shoes. She was weaving as she walked. "I've seen her before."

His heart beat fast, remembering her from the cafeteria and, before that, from the morning he'd almost run away, how she'd drawn her fingers across her wide, sexy lips, making a secret between them.

"It's Crazy Ava," said Donny as the woman stumbled. "She looks drunk."

"Don't call her that," Manny snapped. "She's my cousin, okay?"

"But she's white," said Victor.

"Nah, she's just light, like our grandpa. But she changed her name when she got here and told me not to say anything when I showed up."

"What do you think she's doing out here?" said Judy.

"Probably picking someone up at the Red Rooster," said Donny in a suggestive tone.

"Shut up." Manny shoved him, not hard but enough to make him lose his balance a bit.

"Hey," said Donny. "Well, she did have a baby by herself."

"Nobody can have a baby by herself," said Judy, sounding annoyed. "Not unless she's the Virgin Mary."

"The guy promised to marry her," Manny said, "but he disappeared the second he was discharged. And when the baby came, they wouldn't let Ava keep her."

"How come she doesn't just go out with another patient?" Donny asked.

"After the way everyone's been treating her? Calling her names like you just did? Forget it."

"She's gone," said Judy when Ava was out of sight, and she strode off toward the dorms.

Victor had just started going after her when Donny grabbed him by the arm.

"I know what you're up to," he said in a harsh whisper.

"What are you talking about?" Victor jerked his arm out of Donny's grasp.

"I know you never gave her that note. Maybe you think you have a shot with her or something, but this is happening—me and her—whether you like it or not."

Victor's fists clenched hard, his nails digging into the palms of his hands with the effort of controlling the urge to hit or shove. Without a word, he took off in a run back to his room, leaving Donny and Manny behind in the field.

THE NEXT MORNING, Victor woke up in his underwear, facedown on his bed, his clothes scattered on the floor beside it. For a moment, he hoped what happened last night had been a bad dream, but squinting against the light, he knew it was real. The blue of the shadows meant it was still early. His stomach was growling as he rolled out of bed and threw on a clean set of clothes, but he couldn't face Donny or Judy. He'd rather starve than sit down at breakfast with them as if everything were fine. It was a quiet Saturday, with nothing on his to-do list besides occupational therapy, a paraffin wax treatment, and piano practice, so he decided to go to Herb's instead. He and Fernando never seemed to mind when he dropped by and were always happy to feed him.

"What a nice surprise!" Herb stood at the threshold wearing a paisley silk bathrobe over a pair of striped pajamas. "Come in!"

"Is that Victor?" called Fernando from the other room.

"Yes," said Herb, closing the door.

"Want some eggs?" Fernando asked.

Herb sat at the head of the dining table, hands folded on the white lace tablecloth as Fernando laid three plates of soft scrambled eggs and hot, buttered toast beside their matching blue-gray cups. The smell of the food and strong chicory coffee made Victor's mouth water, but following Herb's lead, he didn't touch anything until Fernando took his seat. Mimicking them, he shook out the cloth napkin to the left of his plate and laid it in his lap.

He was shoveling a large forkful of the rich, creamy eggs into his mouth when he caught Fernando's glance and realized he was being ill-mannered. The temperature in the room seemed to shoot up by ten degrees. He must have been eating like that at the cafeteria, embarrassing himself in front of everyone, in front of Judy and Donny, without even knowing it. With his eyes downcast, he swallowed and chased the bite with a sip of coffee. Its bitterness surprised him. Hiding a grimace, he reached for the sugar bowl and poured half-and-half into his cup until the coffee was the color of his own skin.

"It's a treat to have you here for breakfast," said Herb, taking a delicate bite of toast, "but wouldn't you rather be with your friends?"

"No," said Victor. "Not today."

"Did you guys have an argument?" said Herb.

Victor didn't want to get into it, and even if he did, it was too humiliating to say.

"Maybe it's girl trouble," Fernando teased.

"Don't be silly," said Herb. "Victor's a catch. You know girls can't resist us sensitive, artistic types."

"Not just girls," said Fernando in the same teasing tone.

Herb flapped his hand in a dismissive gesture, but Victor could see his lips struggling to hide a smile.

After they ate, Victor helped clear the plates, and with a couple of hours left before occupational therapy, he and Herb moved to the living room to listen to some records.

"So what's it gonna be? More musicals?"

"Sure," said Victor.

"Since you liked *Show Boat* so much, how about we keep going with Kern and Hammerstein?" Herb told Victor to fetch him *Very Warm for May* from the shelf. "Not their best musical, but it has one of their best songs." He skipped a few tracks until "All the Things You Are" came on, which Victor recognized from a Tony Martin album he'd heard at Ruth's.

He hadn't liked that version much. The sappy swell of the strings and the drama in Martin's voice had made him cringe, especially when Ruth's eyes welled up and he figured she was probably crying because of Ba. This version was plain and straightforward, and there was something to be said for that.

"So what do you think?"

"I've heard it before," said Victor.

"I'm sure you have. It's been recorded many times, in many different styles."

"Do you have any others?" Victor was curious now and wanted to compare.

First, they played Tommy Dorsey's rendition. The sentimental sound of the big band orchestra and his voice failed to appeal to Victor. But what did intrigue him was the trombone, how it dominated the song, the instrument saying far more than the lyrics.

"Now, here's a jazz version on the saxophone, one of my favorites." Herb put on a Charlie Parker album, and from the jarring, repetitive notes of the intro, Victor felt like he'd been knocked over, by the sadness of it, the longing and yearning.

He could hear the saxophone expanding the melody, taking it apart and running it in different directions, to turn it into a whole new song. His appetite whetted, he was hungry for more.

"Have you got any jazz versions with the piano?"

"Coming right up," said Herb. "Let's try some Thelonious Monk."

At first, it seemed like a more upbeat and subtle version of the song than Parker's, with the original melody still clear, but soon the rhythms began to tilt, quick and offbeat, turning askew as Monk's hands hit notes that sounded almost like mistakes, playful and childish. But then he brought the tune back around in a full, perfect circle.

Victor had never heard anything like it before. Moving his fingers to the beat, he found himself listening with his whole body, seeing colors, floods of purples and greens, feeling the music reach in and connect him to something outside himself. Tender and swelling, a perfect chord struck an internal vibration that wouldn't stop. Something inside him had awoken.

When the track was over, Victor asked to listen to it two more times, and he began to hear how Monk was exploring the song, flirting with its boundaries, as if he were trying to map them. It reminded him of how, years ago, he'd repeated new words in English to himself, feeling them out in his mouth.

When Monk played the same section again and again, it was clear that he wasn't wrestling with it this way because he didn't understand it. Instead, he was mastering it note by note, transforming it, repetition by repetition, into something of his own. Victor was painfully aware of the fact that most musicians began their training as small children, but Monk's method spoke to him as something he could do, too, to catch up on the years he'd missed. And it occurred to him that maybe he was already doing this without knowing it, when he thought he'd just been fooling around with other people's songs, and it gave him hope.

"This is amazing," said Victor.

"You've got good taste," Herb said. "Musicals and jazz are a lot more alike than most people think. They both have their roots in classical music, and if you ask me, musicals are American opera. Did you know that Kern was the child of immigrants and Hammerstein's an immigrant himself? Imagine that. A couple of foreigners writing the most popular songs in America."

Victor rolled his eyes. Herb was always trying to inspire him with these kinds of stories and observations, as if dreaming big were enough to make things happen. It was typical Carville talk, normal for people here, but nothing he'd ever heard before, not in New York or China, and it made him wonder if Herb would have said things like that if they were on the outside.

When Victor first moved to the Bronx, he'd drag his scooter up what seemed like an enormous hill that took what felt like an eternity to climb. At the top, before losing his nerve, he'd hop on, set his jaw, and let go. Holding on to the handles for dear life, he'd glide down the street with the wind in his ears, his eyes a jumble of sky and asphalt, trees and parked cars. How free he'd feel. How fearless to fly from such a dizzying height. But every year, the hill grew smaller and smaller, until finally, by the time he was in high school, it had shrunk down to a little slope. Victor didn't want to lie to himself. He wanted to know what was real.

When he had to leave for his paraffin wax treatment, Fernando handed him a brown paper bag with a ham-and-cheese sandwich and an orange.

"So you won't starve while you're lying low," he said.

Victor ate his lunch outside the occupational therapy hut, where he was whittling a wooden starling for Ruth. Afterward, he went straight to the chapel for practice.

The air smelled like vinegar and furniture polish as he walked down the light-drenched aisle, passing the pew where his friends had been sitting last night. His mind flashed back to the image of Judy's head on Donny's shoulder, and he could barely resist the urge to kick it. He clenched his jaw, his body remembering the feeling not only of seeing them but of being torn away from the music, the violence of the interruption.

Sitting at the piano, he smoothed the crease of his Schumann book, going over it so hard with his thumbnail that the paper tore a bit at the edge. The sun streamed softly through the windows, casting its golden beams across the comments Mrs. Thorne had written on the piece he was supposed to work on today, "The Happy Farmer." She was a big believer in what she called the fundamentals, focusing on classical and church music, with some popular songs and show tunes thrown in for fun. But Victor's heart wasn't in it, and he sat there for a while, his mind drifting to dark thoughts.

"Keep your chin up, young man," Mrs. Thorne had said at his last lesson when he got frustrated over his left hand stiffening up on an octave. "God smiles on those with a cheerful outlook. My own mother was a difficult woman, God bless her, with a sour disposition. And wouldn't you know, she got cancer and died within a year of finding out. Goes to show, disease is a test. And with any test, a positive attitude is key."

Victor hadn't said anything at the time, but he wondered how his attitude had anything to do with getting or recovering from Hansen's. Nobody, not even the doctors, knew how anyone got it, but everyone here seemed to have a theory.

Miss Iantha, an elderly woman he saw sometimes at the hydrotherapy clinic, insisted that leprosy came from sin, and in her case, from the sins of her father, a Scottish businessman who'd come to Jamaica and gone back ten years later, leaving his nine children and their three mothers without a single penny. When Miss Iantha was diagnosed with Hansen's as a young woman and the doctors told her she could either go to Carville quietly or be taken there by force, she knew she would never see her family again. As one of the older patients who didn't get the sulfone drugs until it was too late, she had leonine facies from the bacteria thickening and cracking the skin on her forehead and earlobes, making her eyebrows fall out. Victor had been afraid to look at her at first, but after a while, he realized she was just a nice old lady who liked to bake.

"It is for God to judge and for Man to suffer," said Miss Iantha, struggling to hand Victor a slice of her famous black cake after one of their hydrotherapy sessions.

"What did your neighbors think when you left?" asked Victor, his mouth sticky with chocolate and rum-soaked fruit.

"My mother told everyone I died. And maybe I did, in some kind of way," she said, passing a slice of cake to Miss Abigail.

And then there was Mr. Wang, who told just about anyone who would listen that he'd gotten Hansen's from living through the Great San Francisco Earthquake when he was a boy.

"It was seeing all those awful things that did it," he said when he found Victor trying to do his homework on the porch one day. "My father, my brother, my uncle, the street opened and swallowed them up. Nothing I could do but watch. I just lay there on the ground with all those arms and legs and heads covered with rubble and dust around me. My house, my street, all of Chinatown, nothing left. You could hear people trapped under buildings, still alive and screaming for help. You could see others, just bodies, quiet. When I got up, I ran to Golden Gate Park to get away from the fire. They already had food and water, and tents set up there. From the park, we watched the city burn with the ground still shaking. And then came the looting and the hunger and sickness. No more food. No clean water. Everybody getting dysentery. A lot more people died, especially kids with nobody to take care of them." Mr. Wang plucked a wad of tobacco from the bag on his lap and packed it loosely in his pipe, tamping it down with his thumb.

"You were just a kid, too," said Victor, picturing the big, pretty park he'd gone to filled with people who'd just survived a disaster.

"I could take care of myself," said Mr. Wang, winking his one good eye. "Funny thing. After the sickness, when we started to build again, the city fathers, you know, the guys in charge, they want to get rid of us. They want to push Chinatown out of the city, but not all the way, just to the edge of the county, to the mud flats, because they still want our tax money, you see? So greedy. But we say, if you make us go, we go to a different city, pay our taxes there. How 'bout that? So they say, okay, and we stayed in San Francisco." Sticking his pipe between his teeth, he struck a match with surprising ease and lit it, puffing his cheeks as smoke curled up to the ceiling like wispy clouds.

Mr. Wang went on to tell Victor how, since all the city's birth records had been destroyed in the fires along with the city hall, he and a large number of other foreign-born Chinese claimed American citizenship and were then able to bring their families over from China. Of course, when the authorities found out, they opened the Angel Island detention center, a place known to all families with Gold Mountain men as a hellish camp where, at the whim of the officials and the luhk-yi, the policemen in charge, anyone coming from Asia could be sent back or, worse, imprisoned there for years without knowing when or how they might ever be released. As the poems left on the walls by some of the immigrants described, suicide wasn't an uncommon way for people to escape the unbearable wait.

"Surviving," said Mr. Wang, "uses up too much qi, so diseases like cancer, like leprosy, they sneak in. I'm no doctor, but if you ask me, leprosy is a special kind of ghost that comes in through the eyes when you see too many bad things. And that ghost, he is hungry. Look at me. Once he made himself at home, he didn't want to leave."

Then Mr. Wang laughed—at what, Victor didn't know. At the horror of it all, maybe, and his laughter made him feel like he had to laugh along, too.

Victor couldn't figure out when or how he'd contracted Hansen's, especially since, as he learned from Dr. Behr, the symptoms could take a very long time to come out. The average was five years, but cases of twenty had also been reported. It could have happened back in China during the war or in the hungry times after. It could have happened on the ship to America when he'd felt the sea sinking into his pores, the water so dark at night that it made a mirror for the moon. At first, he'd found the sight of it soothing, but then he thought of all the dead things and predators underneath. That something so pretty could hide so many horrors was proof that he couldn't trust his eyes because nothing was as it seemed.

It was so long ago, half his life now, that the details of the journey had grown hazy and scattered, but he did remember Henry taking care of him and being afraid of Ba. And his seasickness, how it mixed with his longing for Ma and pooled into a bottomless well of grief. After that conversation with Mr. Wang on the porch, he thought it was probably the grief that had done it.

The path of the sunbeam had moved from the music stand to the other side of the piano. Victor didn't want to think anymore, not about Judy and Donny, not about Hansen's, not about anything. He just wanted to play until he forgot himself, where he was, and why he was there.

He started with his scales. Then, instead of working on the Schumann, he launched into his favorite classical piece, Debussy's "Clair de Lune." After playing it through a couple of times, he decided to try taking it apart and putting it back together like Monk did with "All the Things You Are." He played it over and over until his ears were stuffed so full of that hopeful little tune that nothing, no more words, no more thoughts or feelings outside the music could get in.

BY THE TIME Victor became aware of his surroundings again, the sun had set and he was late for dinner. He'd wanted to get to the cafeteria early to avoid Judy and Donny, but that would be impossible now, not unless he skipped the meal altogether. He stood up and winced, his left foot full of pins and needles. Was it happening again? He rotated his ankle for a few anxious seconds, grunting as the blood began to rush back into its vessels, a burning but normal kind of pain. When he could walk on it again, he gathered his music books and rushed out of the chapel, letting the door slam behind him.

By the cafeteria, a bicycle bell dinged, followed by the sound of wheels as a couple of his classmates passed by, waving. Maybe he should go back to Herb's for dinner, or maybe he could hold out for the bread-and-milk cart, but he was already here, and he was starving.

Keeping his head down, he went inside and slid his tray down the line, nodding thanks to the cafeteria ladies who filled it with Salisbury steak, peas and carrots, and a cup of gumbo. He chose an apple from the fruit basket, a Red Delicious, perfect and unblemished, its skin cool against his palm. He was expecting a crisp, juicy bite, but when his teeth sank into its flesh, it was floury and bland, a disappointment. Putting the apple down on his tray, he went over to the drinks station, where he found Ava standing in front of the milk pitcher, chatting with another woman.

He stood there, waiting, and after a while, he cleared his throat, finally catching her attention, but she still wouldn't move. With a quick sideways glance, she blew him a kiss, and went right back to her conversation, talking with her hands and her face as much as her voice. His eyes traveled down the column of her throat, round and soft above the neckline of a tight red sweater. She laughed with her head tipped back, as if she didn't care where she was or who was watching her.

The other woman picked up her tray and left, but Ava lingered, serving herself a scoop of vanilla ice cream as Victor poured milk into a glass.

"How come you're not with your friends?" she said, sidling over to him, her voice throaty, with a hint of the same New York accent Manny had.

She was standing so close that he could smell her skin beneath the strong floral scent of her perfume. Dipping her spoon into the ice cream, she licked it and smiled as if they were sharing a secret, just like she had on the day they met by the hole in the fence. He smiled back, trying to ignore the mortifying throb in his pants.

"I dunno."

"Lovers' spat, huh?" she said, with a knowing look.

"What are you talking about?"

"The girl you're always with. Judy. You like her, don't you?"

"She's just a friend." Victor tried to arrange his face in a cool expression.

"Right." Ava raised an eyebrow and glanced at the table by the window where Judy was sitting with Donny and Manny. "Well, she's looking over here right now. How about we give her something to think about, huh?" She leaned in and whispered, her mouth so close to Victor's ear that he thought she might leave a lipstick stain on it, "Sometimes you've got to play hard to get. Make her a little jealous. Say something to me now."

"Like what?" he whispered back.

Ava threw her head back and gave a loud, convincing laugh, slapping him on the arm as if he'd just made a hilarious, off-color joke. Everyone in the cafeteria was looking at them now, and out of the corner of his eye, Victor could see that Judy was looking, too.

"Go get her, tiger," said Ava under her breath, looking pleased with herself. She dug out another spoonful of ice cream and put it in her mouth upside down. "You're welcome, by the way."

"Thanks," Victor muttered without meaning it. There was nothing he could do now but go over to the table.

His friends were watching as he approached. Manny's lips formed a skeptical twist while Donny gave him a wary look, but Judy's face was tense, the color high in her cheeks. When Victor got to his seat, her eyes fell to her plate. Nobody spoke, and for a moment, he just stood there, holding his tray. Finally, Judy looked up at him with a lopsided half smile. It struck him as both shy and apologetic, and he felt his anger start to drain away.

"Long time no see," he said in a wry tone as he sat down.

Manny laughed, and everyone at the table let out the breath they'd been holding. The awkwardness was still there, unspoken, but it was as if they'd decided to let the tension blow over as suddenly as it had blown up last night.

"Where have you been all day?" said Judy.

"Nowhere. I just needed some space." He hadn't meant for it to sound pointed, but when he looked her in the eye, she blushed again.

Laughter from a nearby table pierced the air, the sound of it bouncing off the high ceilings. Ava was sitting on Hank the canteen man's lap, tussling with him over a forkful of pie, trying to make him eat it. Seeming not to notice the shushing of the sisters or the disapproving looks of the ladies at the next table, she kept on laughing as she slid off his lap, took a seat beside him, and slowly crossed her legs.

Judy pursed her lips and wiped them with a napkin before dropping it on her unfinished dessert. "Lost my appetite," she said.

Victor ate quickly. The others were almost finished, and he wanted to grab some dessert, too, but just as he was about to get up for it, Ava sauntered over to their table.

"Hey, Manu," she said, sounding as if she talked to her cousin all the time instead of pretending not to know him. "Grandma sent me something for you by mistake. Why don't you come by after dinner to get it?"

Manny stared up at her in silence, with a stunned look on his face. She cocked her head to the side and widened her eyes at him.

"Sure," he said finally.

Ava gave her cousin a nod and wiggled her manicured nails at the rest of them, saying, "Bye, kids," in a singsong voice before turning to Victor. "Good thing you decided to stick around, huh?" She didn't wait for a reply.

Victor watched her walk away, mesmerized by the rhythmic swing of her hips in a pair of tight plaid pedal pushers.

Judy was watching her, too, shooting daggers at her back. "What was all that about?"

"Yeah." Donny looked at Victor and said in a tone of disbelief, "How do you even know her?"

"She must have gotten me mixed up with someone else." Victor shrugged, barely managing to hide a self-satisfied smile. He turned to Manny. "I thought you weren't supposed to talk to her."

"Me, too," Manny said.

The dining room was nearly empty, and they quickly bused their trays, the strain between them seeming to have been smoothed over by the intrigue. But outside, when Judy got her bike, instead of walking it beside them like she usually did, she hopped on and pedaled away.

It was still warm enough that some wildflowers, snow white and purple, were blooming in the underbrush at the bottoms of the trees. In New York, Ruth had written to say, they'd already had their first snow. On the way to breakfast, Victor, Donny, and Judy surrounded Manny, prodding him about what Ava wanted. After a good deal of cajoling and swearing on their mothers' lives not to tell, Manny gave in.

"She met someone," he said in a low voice, checking to make sure no one else could hear. "He's not from inside. And he doesn't know about her. Not the Hansen's or the baby or her real name."

Donny whistled. "How come she told you?"

"He proposed, and she wants to run off to Texas with him. Says his father's in the oil business. And when I'm discharged, she'll send for me, too." Manny told them in a dreamy voice about his plans to work maintenance on an oil rig, driving around checking the pumps. And later, since he knew Spanish, he could become a landman, convincing people to rent their property to the oil companies. Victor wondered how many negatives Manny had gotten and if he was close enough to his twelve to make this a real possibility. Ava said she'd help him if he helped her, too. All she needed was a driver's license with her Carville name, Ava Martin, and Manny knew of a guy in town who could make it.

"I hope you know what you're getting into," said Judy.

Manny sucked his teeth and looked at the other boys as if they were the only ones who could understand.

"She's right," said Victor. "You could get in a lot of trouble."

"Not if nobody snitches," said Manny.

Judy shook her head. "I don't get it. She acts like you don't exist, and then the second she needs a favor—one that involves committing a crime, I might add—you hop to it."

"She's blood. That's how family works."

"Hang on," said Victor. "If this guy thinks she's white, then how's she going to explain about you? You really think she'll stick her neck out like that?"

The honking of a flock of geese burst into Victor's ears. He looked up beyond the lacy canopy of the oaks and caught the passage of the birds' elegant arrow pointing south, passing them in a low, slow arc across the sky.

"Once they're married, they're married, right? Besides, our grandpa came from Spain," said Manny.

"So?" said Judy.

"So we're part white. Ava more than me, because her mom's light, too. She can just say her aunt married a Cuban guy, like Lucy and Desi. No big deal." Manny sniffed and jutted out his chin. "What do you have against my cousin, anyway?"

"Nothing. It just seems risky," said Judy. "For both of you, I mean. And what about her baby? Is she just going to leave her behind?"

"Get real," Manny scoffed. "What kind of life is she going to have with her mama locked up in the Leper Home? Better for her to get adopted by a nice family. Or maybe my aunt and uncle will send for her if they can get the money together."

"Wow." Judy shook her head.

"Hey, you don't know what it's like. You might be Jewish, but you're still white. You've got plenty of money, and you didn't have a baby with somebody who ran out on you. Ava's got a shot at a better life now. Maybe it's not the way you would do it, but she's not like you."

"Who says?" Judy put her hands on her hips. "I have relatives who were killed by the Nazis, you know, and there are a lot of country clubs where I come from that don't let in Jews."

Manny gave a scornful laugh. "Do you even hear yourself? I wish my family only had to worry about which country clubs to join."

Judy looked down at her shoes and then at Victor and Donny. Victor could tell she wanted them to back her up, but Manny's words rang true, and neither he nor Donny was about to disagree. At Carville, everything was more or less the same for everyone, but once in a while, Judy would say something to remind Victor that on the outside, she belonged to a completely different world. A world of private schools, fancy clothes, and vacations to Miami. And she probably couldn't imagine what it was like to be him, or Manny, or even Donny.

"I knew I shouldn't have told you. It's her life and her kid, okay? Believe me, it's not easy for her. But she's made her choice and I'm going to help. All you have to do is keep your mouths shut, okay?" Manny turned his head, spat on a patch of grass, and stalked back to his dorm, leaving the rest of them to eat breakfast by themselves.

THE INVITATION FROM Judy had been a surprise, whispered into Victor's ear awkwardly as they were leaving dinner that night.

"We should talk," she'd said.

"Okay, when?"

"After lights-out. My room."

He'd nodded in response, though he realized now that it had been more of a command than a question. What was so important for her to say, and why did she only want to tell him in private? He didn't particularly want to talk about what happened in the chapel, but maybe she was going to apologize. Or maybe she was mad at him for not defending her to Manny, but there was no reason she couldn't tell him off about that in public. Was it possible that she was actually jealous of Ava? He'd seen the look on her face when Ava was pretending to flirt with him in the cafeteria. But maybe she just wanted to know what Ava was talking about when she alluded to his failed attempt at running away.

Whatever Judy's reason was for asking, he wanted to go to her room. Of course he did, even if she didn't want anyone else to know about it. If he closed his eyes, he could still feel the heat and tickle of her breath on his skin, caramel-sweet from the crème brûlée she'd eaten for dessert, and it was easy for him to imagine her whispering other, more romantic things.

When he reached her dorm, he went around to the side of the building and scaled the gutter's downspout to the second-floor balcony. The glow of the lamp in her room gave him just enough light to keep his footing on the ledge.

"Hey," Judy whispered, sticking her head out the window. "Get in here before you break your neck."

She opened it all the way, and Victor climbed in, pleased at the thought of her waiting for him.

She plopped herself cross-legged in the middle of the bed and patted the spot beside her. He perched politely on the edge of the mattress, moved by the sight of her in a pair of pink polka-dot pajamas. Even though he'd seen her wearing far less at the lake, this felt more intimate. And now he was in bed with her, well, on the bed with her, and that thought aroused him as much as her closeness. He swallowed painfully, and his Adam's apple bobbed, a sensation he wasn't quite used to yet. His hand rose to touch his throat, but he stopped it midway, running it over her blue-and-lavender quilt instead.

"My bubbe made it for me," said Judy in a quiet voice.

Victor nodded, remembering that it meant grandmother in Yiddish. He'd never been in a girl's bedroom before. Judy's room was similar to his—the same bed, the same chair, desk, chest of drawers, and lamp—but on the wall she'd hung a poster of Grace Kelly cut out of *Photoplay* magazine and on the dresser was a cluster of knickknacks: a porcelain rabbit, a small blue vase holding a single red paper rose, and a wooden music box painted with a scene of old-fashioned ladies with umbrellas.

Now that he'd decided to stay, Victor was finally decorating his room, too, putting the three photos he had from home—the one of Ma wearing a smart wool suit Ba had sent her; the studio portrait of Ma, Ba, Grandmother, Henry, and himself taken shortly before they left for America; and a snapshot of Henry, Jackie, and Ba standing on the street in front of the laundry. On the walls, he'd put up a charcoal drawing he'd done of the armadillo in the infirmary, a macaroni collage of the Brooklyn Bridge, and a watercolor of Lake Albrechtson he'd painted in occupational therapy, sending the rest of the things he made to Ruth. He was used to having his own room now, though he still couldn't fall asleep until he'd done his hand exercises and body scan, checking for numbness or pain, or the telltale prickles of pins and needles.

He went over to Judy's desk, turning his back on her to hide his nerves. Rapping it lightly with his knuckles, he acted like he was fascinated by the mess of things on its surface—pots and tubes of makeup and creams, a bottle of strawberry shampoo he hadn't seen for sale at the Carville store, a jumble of hair clips, ribbons, and bobby pins, a silver handheld mirror and a matching brush with a snarl of brown hair stuck in its bristles. A marble notebook pushed to the side of the desk caught his eye. It was open to a page where Judy had listed the months from June to November, next to a bunch of X's and checkmarks.

"What's this?" he asked.

A flicker of annoyance crossed her face. "Nothing."

"Sorry." He took a step back and put up his hands in playful sur-render. "I didn't mean to snoop."

Her face cracked a little smile. "It's okay. It's my calendar." Victor gave her a puzzled look. She raised her eyebrow and repeated, "My *calendar*. You know, for the tests."

"Oh." He glanced at the page again, and when she nodded her permission, he examined it more closely. "Are the checkmarks posi-tives or negatives?"

"Negatives."

"You know that's kind of backward, right?"

She let out a nervous laugh and clapped her hand over her mouth. July, August, and September were checked, but October and Novem-ber were crossed out.

"What was it like?" He touched the X beside October with his fingertip.

"The pits. I'd even told my brother I might be going home soon. I'm never doing that again. Not unless it's a sure thing."

"Don't feel bad," he said. "I haven't gotten any negatives at all. But it's weird, you don't really have symptoms, right?" He frowned.

If Judy was still testing positive with hardly anything wrong with her, what chance did he have?

"I had a few lesions, but now there's just this one spot on my leg." She smacked her inner thigh. "The doctors at home told my parents I'd be out of here in a few months, but it just won't budge. It's so disgusting."

"Nothing about you is disgusting," he blurted out, without thinking.

"Hardly," she scoffed, then lowered her eyes and blushed.

"What about the others?" he said, changing the subject.

"We don't talk about it. All I know is Donny got here about a year ago, a few months after Manny, so your guess is as good as mine."

Judy's face changed, an unreadable expression moving across it, and Victor kept quiet, not wanting to put his foot in his mouth. He picked up the dark blue pen lying next to the notebook, smooth and heavy, with a gold-tipped cap. Twisting it open, he touched its golden nib. It was shaped like a bird's beak and left a dot of black ink on the pad of his finger, where it bled into the tiny loops.

"How come you didn't say anything when Manny bit my head off? I thought you were on my side."

Victor tried to think of something to say that at least felt true even if it wasn't. "Sorry." He rubbed his fingers together, smearing the ink with his thumb.

"You don't think it's a good idea, do you?"

"Not really, but I get why he's doing it. Family is family, right?"

"I don't trust her, though. Speaking of which, are you going to tell me what that was all about in the cafeteria yesterday?" Victor could hear a hint of jealousy in Judy's voice. Maybe Ava had been right.

"What do you mean?" he hedged, fighting the impulse to smile.

"Come on." She rolled her eyes. "And what did she mean about you sticking around? Spill."

"Fine," he said, rolling his eyes back at her. "I was going to run away right after they discharged me from the infirmary and she saw me outside the fence." He paused, and Judy motioned for him to sit next to her on the bed again, leaning forward with interest. He told her about the encounter on the River Road, and how he and Ava had silently agreed not to snitch.

"So, are you going to try again?" She kept her voice light, but her expression was uneasy.

"I don't think so. For a while, I was still planning to," he said, "but then I guess I found a few reasons to stay." He let the corners of his lips lift with a touch of flirtation.

"I'm glad." The smile she gave him was soft, and he smiled back, thinking how beautiful she looked in that moment, with her face half in shadow and the light from her bedside lamp skimming the curve of her other cheek. "So there's really nothing going on between you?" She placed her hand gently over his.

"Who, me and Ava? God, no," he said. He was far more focused on her hand than on what they were saying. When she didn't take it away, he flipped his palm to meet hers.

"I have to tell you something." She hesitated, looking down at their joined hands. Here it was, the thing she'd invited him to her room to say. He gave her hand a quick, encouraging squeeze. "It's about Donny. We're seeing each other."

Victor's stomach lurched and he let her go. Donny. Big and handsome, with features that might have been too pretty were it not for his square jaw and tough-guy act. He wasn't even nice to her, but that clearly didn't matter.

"Are you upset?" She searched his face.

Of course he was, but how could he say it? He turned away, eyes fixed on a glass figurine, a ballerina standing like a stork on one pointed toe, in an effort to stay calm.

"So you like him," he said, a sick feeling traveling up his throat.

Judy shrugged. "He makes me feel special."

"Really?" he said, trying to keep his face expressionless, a trick of Henry's and Ba's, but he couldn't. He felt his brows pinch together, betraying him. "I haven't seen him do that. Looks to me like he mostly ignores you."

"Not when we're alone." Judy's face was turning red.

"Don't you think there's something wrong with that?"

"That's just what boys are like."

"That's not what I'm like." The words hung in the air between them, and Victor realized it had been a vulnerable thing to say, maybe the most vulnerable thing he'd ever said to anyone in his life, but he didn't regret it.

"I know," said Judy, reaching for his hand again.

The heady combination of her touch and her words had a chemical effect on him, shooting his heart up to the sky, and the rush of it pushed him toward her on the bed. As he leaned in to kiss her, he could sense her moving toward him, too. When their lips touched, it was nothing like the kisses he'd shared with the girls in the Bronx who'd announced that he was their boyfriend one day and spent the next few weeks holding his hand in the school cafeteria. This was completely new and unexpected—that she wanted to kiss him back, that she was putting her hand on the back of his neck to pull him closer. All of him was concentrating on her now, on the feel of her soft mouth against his, the faint taste of peppermint lingering from her toothpaste, and the strawberry smell of her hair falling loose over her pajamas.

The kiss broke off after what could have been a second or an hour. Victor had lost all sense of time.

"The first time I saw you, you were walking through the trees and I thought . . ." He hesitated. "I thought you were the prettiest girl I'd ever seen."

"You did?" she said, sounding dazed. Her face was still, but Victor could see the thoughts darting like minnows behind her eyes.

He nodded. His heart was racing, and he was breathing fast, his lungs only able to take small sips of air. He wondered if he should kiss her again and tilted his head in a silent question, but in that moment of hesitation, the energy seemed to shift. Judy swung her legs off the bed and set her feet on the floor, without a word. She turned away, her lower lip caught between her teeth.

"You okay?" he asked, wanting to reach for her, to reassure her—and himself.

"Yeah," she said, but she didn't really sound okay. Had he done something wrong? Had he misread her?

"Do you want me to go?" he croaked, his throat bone-dry.

As he waited for her to answer, his mind floated up and watched the scene from above, his own cracked voice, her fingers fiddling with the edge of the quilt. He mopped his sweaty hands on his pants and stood up. That seemed to snap her out of it. She looked at him and blinked.

"No," she said, her voice hollow and expressionless, "but you probably should."

Victor stared at her, the chirring of the crickets suddenly loud in his ears. Trying to understand what had happened and failing, he couldn't do anything but leave.

TWELVE

Victor had learned in class that the Mississippi River was a watershed, where the clams and mussels produced pearls. At one time, the button industry was a big business in the region until the fashions changed. Abandoned now, the shells littered the shore, though they were once highly prized. Blister pearls attached to clams in which a free pearl would sometimes grow. Pink pearls produced by washboard mussels. Wartybacks, muckets, and sand shells. Mr. Harland said that once, a man across the river had found a bright blue pearl inside a three-ridge mussel and sold it for so much money that he bought a cattle ranch in Texas. Now that it was the middle of November, the salt in the water meant the fall trout run was starting. In the daytime, Victor liked to watch the anglers stacking up to catch them on the opposite shore.

The levee felt different at night, the river restless and aloof without the songs of the boats and the birds, its dank, eggy smell more pungent in the dark. The cold breath of the water smacked the back of Victor's head. With a shiver, he hunched his shoulders as he and his friends picked their way through the trees. They'd gone straight from Harry across the River Road to the safety of the wooded area in between, avoiding the shore so they wouldn't be seen coming from the direction of the institution. The sounds of teenage laughter and revving car engines told Victor they were close before he could see a thing. One of the older kids in their class had told them that the St. Gabriel high schoolers were having a party on the river and warned them to stay away, but Victor convinced them to go. Manny had been here the longest and acted like he knew all the ins and outs of the place, but why should he be the only one deciding which risks to take?

They stopped, peering through the branches at the ferry platform, where a roaring bonfire lit up the faces of the townie boys in letterman jackets and the girls in poufy skirts standing around it, the cherries of their cigarettes glowing like fireflies.

"There they are," Victor whispered.

"Double, double, toil and trouble," muttered Manny. "I don't know about this."

"Yeah," said Judy. "You really think we can just waltz in without an invitation?"

"What's the matter? Chicken?" Victor said with acid in his voice.

"No," she snapped. "But what if they ask?"

Victor scoffed, "It's a bonfire, not a ball."

"We're already here. Might as well get some free booze," said Donny.

They trickled out from the trees one by one to avoid suspicion, staying away from the light as they approached some kids hanging around the edge of the fire, the smoke from the driftwood they were burning billowing up into the night sky. For some reason, it hadn't occurred to Victor that they would all be white. There'd be no way for him or Donny or Manny to blend in. Though he knew that schools were segregated here, he'd thought it'd be fine because none of them were Black.

He glanced over at his friends, but he couldn't see their faces. He was getting that feeling he sometimes got in New York, a tingle at the back of his neck alerting him to danger, telling him to cross the street or change subway cars. Henry said he should always listen to that feeling because even if he was wrong, it was better to be safe than sorry. Victor had the urge to tell his friends to leave now before anyone noticed them, but he didn't want to admit to being scared, not after goading Judy. Maybe it would be okay if they just stayed in the dark.

The townies looked like they were mostly upperclassmen, seventeen or eighteen years old, and some of the guys were pretty big, like they might be on the football team. A girl with short hair and horn-rimmed glasses handed Judy a big brown medicine bottle as she walked away from the fire with a boy. Judy sniffed it, took a careful sip, and coughed before giving it to Donny. He took a big gulp and passed the bottle to Manny, who drank and then passed it on to Victor.

He brought the bottle to his lips, and as the fumes from the moonshine burned his nostrils, he hesitated. After his initial reaction to the Diasone, he was worried the alcohol might mix with it badly and make him sick again. And drinking wasn't really his thing. It made him talk too loud and too much about things he'd rather keep to himself. Once, when Jackie had stolen half a bottle of Southern Comfort from his grandfather, they got to reminiscing about their old village, and before he knew it, Victor was blubbering about Ma and throwing up on somebody's stoop. He thought about tilting the bottle and pretending to drink without swallowing any, but then again, maybe getting a little tipsy would help him forget.

Yesterday morning, with the taste of Judy's kiss still on his lips, unsure of how things stood between them, Victor had left his room early to wait outside her dorm so they could talk in private before breakfast.

"So, last night—" he began.

"Don't worry about it," Judy interrupted. "We can just pretend it didn't happen."

"What do you mean?" said Victor.

"We're friends. And we don't ever have to talk about it again, okay?" She said this as if she were giving him something he wanted or letting him off the hook.

"Okay," he said. But it wasn't remotely okay. He walked with her to the cafeteria, feeling like he might throw up even though his stomach was empty.

That afternoon, Judy disappeared for a few hours, and when she came back, she was different. At dinner, she and Donny walked in holding hands as if to announce that they were a couple. Victor felt like his heart had been torn out of his chest. So why shouldn't he have a drink now?

He tipped back his head and swallowed deeply, holding his breath while the burning liquid slid down his throat. It tasted like how he imagined paint stripper might, spicy and oddly sweet, smelling vaguely like corn.

"Should we go?" said Manny in his ear.

"One more drink," Victor whispered. He took another swig and passed the bottle on.

Digging his heels into the layer of shells littering the shore, he listened to the vicious crunching sound they made as he broke them. He could hear the water, but he couldn't see it. The alcohol had been a bad idea. It was dulling his senses, making everything go fuzzy around the edges as he stared into the burning yellows and reds.

Without realizing it, while they were drinking, he and his friends had edged closer to the bonfire. As soon as Judy stepped into its circle of light, the townies took notice. A short, pug-faced blonde with an oversized letterman jacket draped over her shoulders squinted in Judy's direction.

"Who are you?" she demanded, putting a hand on her blond boyfriend's meaty shoulder as if to mark her territory.

"Why, it must be Miss Scarlett O'Hara," said a beetle-browed boy, looking Judy up and down. "Fashionably late to the party, I see." He was long and tall, with dark hair and the face of a handsome ferret.

The beefy blond boy pointed at the rest of them and hollered, "These your servants, Miss Scarlett?" His girlfriend giggled and slapped his arm. "Nobody invited them."

A shiver darted up Victor's spine, telling his body to get out of there as fast as it could, but he forced himself to stay still. While they were talking, the group of boys had formed a loose circle around them, and they were tightening it now.

"They're with me," said Judy in a voice that Victor didn't recognize. She sounded calm and composed, like a high-class lady who was used to having her way.

The ferret-faced boy gave the blond one a nudge. "It's okay."

Victor thought of the warnings Henry had given him that he'd dismissed about lynchings in the South. The river slapped against the posts underneath the ferry platform, and he thought of how easily they could be drowned. Judy and Manny had been right. It was a mistake to come.

He cut his eyes at Manny, wondering if it was too late to turn and run. But in which direction? And what about Donny's leg? He'd get caught, for sure. Plus, if they ran toward Carville, the townies would know they were patients right away. What would happen then? Would they be afraid to touch them, or would they follow them inside? If they made it back far enough, Victor could yell and the night watchmen would come, but then they'd get in trouble. Real trouble.

"I don't think I've seen you at school or I would have noticed," said the dark-haired boy, flashing Judy a toothy grin. "What's your name?"

Victor could feel Donny stiffening by his side.

"Judy. I'm just visiting. My father's a doctor," she said in that voice again, waving vaguely toward Carville.

"What about them?" The girl jerked her head toward Victor, Manny, and Donny.

"Their fathers work for my dad."

This didn't quite add up, but the group had been drinking for a while and seemed to accept it. Victor was surprised by how easily Judy had come up with that story.

"Where are you from, Yankee Doodle Judy?" said the dark-haired boy, continuing to flirt.

"Philadelphia."

"You sure your name's not Tracy?" he teased in a bad imitation of Cary Grant's accent in *The Philadelphia Story*. "Because mine could be Dexter, if you want it to be."

He bowed, took Judy's hand, and kissed it, making the crowd burst out in catcalls and laughter. Victor could see Donny's hands clench into fists. For a moment, he thought Donny might tackle the boy, but while everyone was still laughing, he stepped into the shadows. Victor glanced around the fire at the faces lit up like cartoon devils and wondered if he could slip out, too. He and Manny exchanged a look, and then, much more easily than he would have thought, he backed away into the darkness of the trees. The farther he went, the quieter the sounds of the bonfire—the voices, the laughter, the water—became as the crunch of the leaves and twigs under his feet filled his ears instead.

Nobody seemed to notice when he left. It was like that time in the subway station with Jackie where they were virtually invisible to the white people there. Or maybe the townies were just too drunk and too focused on Judy to care. But where the hell was Donny? Victor had expected to find him waiting in the trees, but there wasn't any trace of him.

The dark-haired boy was all over Judy, flattering and teasing, and Victor pictured himself marching over there and punching him in his arrogant face. Of course he knew that would probably get him killed, but he wondered what it was like to be the kind of boy, rough and cocksure, who couldn't imagine losing a fight. Maybe if he were like that, Judy would have picked him instead. He kept his eyes on her, afraid to let her out of his sight. He had to get her out of there, but how?

The circle around the bonfire broke as the couples went off together and Manny made his way toward Victor in the cluster of trees.

"Hey," whispered Victor. "We'd better go."

"No shit," Manny whispered back, his breath stinking of booze. "It's like a Klan rally out there. Where's Donny?"

"No idea. Can you signal?"

Manny cupped his hands around his mouth and released a series of high-pitched trills that sounded exactly like a screech owl's. There was still no sign of Donny, but Judy reacted to the call, jerking her head in their direction.

"I'll go get her," he said. "You find Donny, okay? We'll all meet back at Harry."

They separated, with Manny making his way toward the River Road. When Victor neared the fire, he realized Judy must have been waiting for rescue. As the drunken ferret-faced boy swayed over her, she kept on turning toward the trees whenever his attention wavered. Once she caught sight of Victor, he motioned in the direction of the fence.

"Listen," she said, interrupting the boy's monologue, "it's been great, but I have to get back before my father finds out I'm gone."

"Hey, wait!" the boy called as she dashed into the dark. He stumbled after her for a few steps and stopped.

Tripping over the tree roots, Judy nearly crashed into Victor. "Where are the others?" she whispered.

"By Harry."

She grabbed his hand and yanked. It was the first time she'd touched him since their kiss, since everything between them changed, and he knew it didn't mean anything, but holding her hand made his body feel weightless. The fact that she still had this effect on him made him furious, not only at her but at himself.

"He wouldn't dare come after us," he blustered, looking back toward the bonfire.

"Are you drunk?"

"No," he said, but maybe he was tipsier than he thought. "I'm not afraid of him, that's all."

"You should be. If you're not drunk, then you're stupid."

Victor felt stung and suddenly much more sober as she dropped his hand and kept walking.

Over by Harry, Manny was waiting with Donny, and Judy marched right up to him.

"Why did you just leave me there?" Her voice rang with accusation.

"You seemed like you were having a fine time without me," said Donny, sounding cold. "I had no idea you were such a good actress. Your dad's a doctor? Our families work for yours?" His voice was angry now.

"I was trying to protect you guys. What else was I supposed to do?"

Donny didn't answer, but turned away, pulling out a bottle of the townies' crude corn liquor from the waistband of his pants.

"Where did you get that?" asked Victor.

"Fell off the back of a truck." Donny took a swig. "I got a few."

Manny clapped him on the back and took a sip, too, before handing the bottle to Victor. Only Judy refused. She turned to leave, and one after the other, they followed her, climbing back through Harry to the hospital grounds, to safety. There, the Big House loomed, a great, familiar shadow in the distance, feeling for the first time like a refuge from the night.

THE NEXT MORNING, his mouth desert-dry and his head pounding, Victor dragged himself over to Herb's for their Saturday reading appointment.

"Not sure we're going to get to this today," said Herb, straightening the stack of mail against the side table, the sound of each tap feeling like a hammer against Victor's skull. "What on earth have you been up to?"

"Nothing," Victor said, his tongue feeling huge in his mouth.

"You smell like a hillbilly distillery." Herb fanned the air beneath his nose.

"Sorry," said Victor, suppressing an acidic burp, too nauseated to keep last night a secret, not that Herb would tell. "Bonfire on the river."

"I'll get you some aspirin and an Alka-Seltzer." Herb pushed himself upright and reached for his cane. Fernando was outside working on the De Soto. "Did you and your friends sneak that moonshine back through the hole in the fence, or did you drink it all at the event?" He was already halfway to the kitchen, so Victor figured he could get away with not answering that.

Everyone knew about Harry, of course. For one thing, it was right there, plain as day, by the softball field, and nobody lifted a finger to fix it. Herb said Dr. Al had even ordered it to be cut bigger than the original hole so that patients wouldn't get hurt when they went through. Most people used it to go shopping in New Orleans or Baton Rouge, fishing on the river, or drinking at the Red Rooster, but patients with children on the outside, like Herb's neighbor and Ava, would sneak out to see them if they lived nearby.

Not long ago, Victor had spotted Ava crawling through the hole with a picnic basket to meet a car pulling up along the side of the road. At first, seeing her from behind, Victor had mistaken her for Judy—they were about the same size, with the same shoulder-length brown hair, and proud, straight backs. He'd been about to call out to her when a middle-aged woman came out of the car with a baby bundled in pink. Seeing her drop the picnic basket to cover the child in kisses, Victor had realized it was Ava and watched as she carried her baby across the River Road, to the levee.

Herb hovered as he swallowed his aspirin and drank the fizzy, salty water. "That was a St. Gabriel High party, am I right?"

"Yes," Victor admitted.

"You're from up North, so maybe you don't quite understand what things are like down here," Herb said in a voice he'd never used with Victor before, somewhere between angry and grave. "Carville may be integrated, but we're in the Deep South. White folks around here don't like to see race mixing." He rubbed his right temple as if his head hurt, too.

"I know about all that," said Victor.

"Then you ought to know that inside the fence, you can be the four musketeers, but outside, if you see a bunch of white boys driving up in a pickup truck, you'd better grab your friends and run. Understand? And I wouldn't be crashing any more of those parties if I were you."

THIRTEEN

Henry never meant to get involved with a married woman. It was the last thing he thought he would ever do after what Ba had done to Ma. And Mr. Lee was more than just a boss. He was like a second father to him. A small, neat man with an easy smile, he'd taken Henry under his wing and was teaching him all the tricks of the trade, printing restaurant menus, business cards, calendars, and invitations for weddings and babies' full moon parties gilded in the traditional way, by hand. It hadn't been discussed, but since Mr. Lee had no sons, everyone assumed he was training Henry to take over when he retired. Henry would never have done anything to hurt him, but he just couldn't help himself when it came to Winnie.

She was five years older than Henry and Mr. Lee had married her three years ago, shortly after the first Mrs. Lee died of cancer. He'd taken six months off to bury her in Hong Kong, and when he came back, he brought along a brand-new bride who was young enough to be his daughter. No one thought much of it. A Gold Mountain man of means had his pick of women of any age, but in Chinatown, where men outnumbered women ten to one, his wife made Mr. Lee a source of envy.

The trouble started when Winnie had reached a level in her English classes at the Chinese Mission Church where she wanted to practice her conversational skills. Mr. Lee himself suggested that since Henry knew how to speak proper American English, he could make some extra cash as Winnie's conversation partner.

When Winnie opened the door for their first session, Henry felt like a character in one of those silly cartoons, with his eyes bugging out of his head and steam pouring out of his ears. Her beauty wasn't flawless, but even her flaws seemed charming to him, from the stubborn pucker of her chin to the broadness of her slightly flat nose. And the intoxicating way she smelled when he brushed past her in the narrow entryway—not the scent of her sandalwood soap or her rose perfume, but the smell of her body—made him feel weak in the knees. He could tell she was attracted to him, too, from the way her eyes flitted over the planes of his face and the nervous way she served him tea, blushing when she spilled some on the tablecloth. Even so, it took almost a year of lingering looks and meaningful pauses before they gave in to anything physical.

Henry had been talking about his mother when Winnie said in her soft, halting English, "I have no mother," as a single tear made a slow journey from the corner of her eye down the curve of her cheek.

"I'm sorry," he said, and without thinking, he reached out to trace the path of the tear with his finger. "I'm sorry," he repeated, this time for touching her.

He was shocked to have done it and even more shocked that she hadn't stopped him. Instead, she placed her own fingers in the palm of his open hand with a look of such pure hunger that he stood up, pulled her to him, and crushed his lips against hers.

After that day, their English conversation lessons were conducted as pillow talk, and though they had to be careful, they turned those hours into an oasis of stolen time. Before Henry left the apartment, they took turns washing off the evidence of their lovemaking in the small bathroom and rebuttoned each other's clothes in a ritual that ended with each of them drawing a hand over the other's face as if it, too, could be wiped clean of the evidence of their feelings.

Henry had had girlfriends before, some of whom he'd gone to bed with, but he'd never fallen in love with any of them. The closest he'd come to that was with Angelica, the lovely Puerto Rican girl he dated in high school, whose English at the time was as rough as his own. Their relationship ended when he dropped out and her father forbade her from seeing him anymore. Then there was a string of girls in Chinatown, cocktail waitresses who, though fun both in and out of bed, never quite got under his skin.

Winnie wasn't a girl but a woman who was, in Henry's eyes, achingly beautiful, ambitious, pragmatic, and remarkably sad. In 1949, she'd gotten herself out of Canton City by sheer force of will just as the Kuomintang fell to Mao. Showing up at the border and insisting to the immigration officials that her grandmother was "just over there" she'd pointed toward the crowd of people waiting on the other side. But there was no grandmother, neither in Hong Kong nor in Canton. Winnie had lost her entire family during the war, and with no connections, the only work she could get in Hong Kong was as a receptionist at a funeral home, a bad-luck job nobody else wanted.

But her luck soon turned. At the first Mrs. Lee's wake, Winnie had been the one to usher Mr. Lee to the back office, offering him privacy and a handkerchief when he cried. From that small act of kindness, dim sum, a movie, and a marriage proposal followed. Henry could picture her as she must have been then, painfully young with her hair in two long braids instead of the fashionably short curls she now wore, and the same kittenish face with bright, snapping eyes and a plump, little mouth, alone and afraid, but determined. Though fragile and petite, she was in possession of an iron will. She was a survivor, just like Ma, and Henry was head over heels in love with her.

It didn't even feel like he was betraying anyone exactly. Mr. Lee was thirty years older than she was and acted more like a kindly uncle toward her than a husband. What he'd wanted was a companion, she said, not a lover but someone to take care of him, though Henry supposed they must have sex at least once in a while. The image disgusted him, so he tried not to think about it.

He would have liked to confide in someone about Winnie, but who could he possibly tell? It was a scandal too juicy to keep quiet—a young man biting the hand that fed him, a young woman cuckolding her savior, and three lives ruined in the process. Maybe he could have told Ba, but he didn't want to be judged by him or relieve him of his guilt. If Ba knew about Winnie, Henry wouldn't have a leg to stand on when it came to Ruth.

He'd been whistling along to "Sleigh Ride" on the radio, looking forward to seeing Winnie at lunch, when they got a last-minute rush order on a set of Christmas cards written in Chinese. Now he'd be stuck at work until they were done. He imagined her waiting, getting more and more disappointed in him with each passing hour, and he couldn't even call to let her know why he hadn't come.

The customer picked up the order at 5:45 and Mr. Lee left Henry to close up the shop. Mr. Lee's apartment was a couple of blocks away and it took him at least five minutes to walk home. Henry was about to call Winnie to explain when the door swung open with a strong gust of wind and in came Ruth, the last person he wanted or expected to see.

"What are you doing here?" he said, worried that something might have happened to Ba. Ruth had never come to the print shop before.

"I was just in the neighborhood, picking up some things for your father," she said, brushing a light dusting of snow off the shoulders of her blue wool coat.

Henry glowered as it melted on the floor, creating a puddle he'd have to clean up later.

"What a lovely shop," she continued, looking around. "I was wondering if you might want to chip in on a Christmas present for Victor." She paused, untying the scarf that covered her hair, and when he didn't answer, she kept on talking. "We could send him enough money for a bike, a secondhand one, at least. He said people ride them to get around Carville."

Henry eyed Ruth with suspicion. It had been weeks since he'd seen her at the laundry, and she hadn't spoken to him then. After years of trying to get him to accept her as a kind of stepmother, she seemed to have finally given up and had been leaving him alone for quite some time. So why would she come here to ask him about Victor's present when Ba could have easily done it?

"I think he gets around just fine," Henry finally said. "We didn't even know about Christmas before we came here, so it's not like he expects much. Why make such a big deal?"

"His friends must get gifts from their families, and I don't want him to feel left out, especially since we can't visit."

Henry was in the middle of saying something about how Victor was sixteen and she should stop treating him like a child when the door opened again. This time, it was Winnie, flushed and flustered from running in the cold.

"Ah-Yat-ah," she said breathlessly, addressing him informally by his first name since the only other person in the shop was Ruth. "Why didn't you come? Did something happen?"

Even though she'd spoken in Cantonese, a wave of worry surged up Henry's spine. After all these years with Ba, he thought Ruth might understand more Chinese than she let on, and even if she couldn't make out the words, she could probably read Winnie's tone and body language. Ruth was a lot of things, but stupid wasn't one of them.

Henry cleared his throat and said in English, "I apologize, Mrs. Lee. We got a last-minute order. Your husband should have told you. Has he not come home yet?"

Winnie's brow furrowed for a moment and then her face froze as she caught on.

"No," she said, trying to match his formality in her slow, careful English, "he has not. But I expect he will be back soon. Sorry to bother you, Mr. Chin."

"It's no bother at all." Henry inclined his head politely and glanced at Ruth, trying to keep his expression bland, but she wasn't paying attention to him at all.

Instead, she was looking Winnie up and down, and when she turned back to him, she gave him a slow, knowing nod as if she understood everything now.

"Well," she said, with a little smile, "I can see you've got your hands full here. If you want to put something in Victor's Christmas package, just leave it at the laundry. I'm mailing it out on Monday."

After Ruth left, Henry brooded over that smile for a long time, unable to decide what it meant. It had been shrewd, but not smug or self-righteous. In fact, there'd been something wistful, even a bit sad in her eyes, as if she felt sorry for him, and that bothered him more than anything, more than even the thought of her telling Ba about Winnie.

FOURTEEN

Seven months had passed since Victor's arrival, and so far, every single one of his skin smear tests had been positive, seven in a row, though the results from some lesion sites were starting to come back as "rare," meaning the infections there were getting less active. It was a warm, damp spring, and the Southern pollen was triggering such severe asthma symptoms that the bellows of his lungs heaved like a punctured accordion and his eyes itched so badly that he rubbed them raw. He was afraid it could be a sign of another regression, the Hansen's bacteria attacking his lungs or his eyes again, but Dr. Behr said it really was just allergies this time.

Having learned not to torture himself with false hope, Victor went in for his March test with especially low expectations, feeling worse than he had since fall. It came as a complete shock when, for the first time, his results were negative.

"Congratulations," said Dr. Behr, clapping him on the back. "Quite a milestone."

Victor gave him a skeptical look. "Maybe it's just a fluke." His lesions had been showing a reduction in bacteria for a while now, but it was hard for him to trust good news.

"I think we can be cautiously optimistic."

"Are you sure? Sometimes my hands still hurt," Victor confessed, "especially at night."

"That's not uncommon." Dr. Behr shrugged his thick shoulders and left him with a handful of prescriptions for his Diasone, inhaler, and allergy pills.

At physical therapy, Miss Abigail said the strength and overall coordination in his hands were nearly normal now. This wasn't as surprising as his negative skin smear test since he could not only see and feel the truth of it, but the road to getting there had been straight. As he carried on doing his physical therapy exercises and practicing the piano every day, he'd been able to track his own progress. Now the teachers at school expected him to do all his homework and show up at occupational therapy with no more excuses about his hands. He could have taken these things as signs that he really was getting better, but a part of him still couldn't believe it.

He was growing fast, gaining weight and muscle, his body stretching so quickly that his arms and shins often hurt. Telling Miss Abigail about the pain, he was afraid she might say his neuritis was coming back, but instead, she said it was just a normal growth spurt.

"Normal normal or Carville normal?" Victor asked, making her laugh, but he wasn't joking. "Normal" was a charged word on the inside because nothing about having Hansen's or being here was.

The first person he wanted to tell about his negative result was Judy, but it was the afternoon and he wasn't quite sure where to find her. She was always going off with Donny these days, disappearing for hours at a time to the thicket between the lake and the golf course, or the wooded area on the levee. She hadn't told him whether she'd added a check or an X to her calendar since the winter.

Things had gotten chilly between them when she and Donny started going steady, but thawed around the holidays, their first away from home, though they weren't as close as they'd been. He wondered if she ever told Donny about their kiss and if her attraction to him was still there. At one point, he'd felt it, and sometimes, even now, there were moments when they'd share a private smile and her lips would twist in a particular way or a look would last a second or two too long.

The things he liked about her hadn't changed. The way she looked him straight in the eye. The way she talked, dropping Yiddish words here and there like Ruth, though she wasn't quite as funny. The way she made him feel like his secrets were safe with her, not just about his tests but about his family as well. Come to think of it, that reminded him of Ruth, too.

Once, not long after they met, Ruth had caught him climbing a tree in the park after Ba had forbidden him from doing it. He'd been so sure that she'd rat him out that when she didn't, she won his trust completely.

As for Judy, what made him think he could trust her anymore? She was Donny's girl now, and he didn't think there was anything he could do about that. He'd been in love with her, and maybe a part of him still was, but the more he fell in love with music, the more the intensity of his feelings for her dimmed.

When he was done at the infirmary, Victor went straight to Herb's to share his news. Fernando had just brought in the afternoon mail, including a large package from Tallulah Bankhead.

"One down and eleven to go. This is cause for celebration," Herb said. "Want to do the honors?" He gestured at the package.

Fernando handed Victor a box cutter. Ever since he got turned on to jazz, Herb had started ordering new releases for him, and if he couldn't get them by mail order, he asked his show business friends to send them specially. Opening the box, Victor found two ten-inch albums of Charles Mingus's Massey Hall concert in Toronto with the Quintet, featuring Dizzy Gillespie, Bud Powell, Max Roach, and Charlie Parker, his idol, who'd just died in March. Herb said it had been released by Mingus's own label, Debut Records.

"This is why America is great." Herb paused, winding up for what Victor thought of as one of his "Only in America" speeches. "A Chinese-Negro achieving all that, against the odds. All you have to do is put your back into your work and pull yourself up by the boot-straps, no matter the circumstances. Only in America."

As a joke, Tallulah had also sent a copy of Mingus's how-to guide *The Charles Mingus CAT-alog for Toilet Training Your Cat*, a de-tailed, step-by-step primer for teaching a cat to use a human toilet, complete with a photograph of a black-and-white feline, probably his own, assuming the position.

Victor read it out loud in a deadpan voice, making Herb's whole body shake with silent laughter and tears stream down his face. Victor imagined himself reading it out loud to Judy, too, and making her laugh like Herb, but maybe he shouldn't. Maybe she'd think it was juvenile and stupid.

"Regrettably," said Herb, "I'm not an artist myself, but Mingus is an example of how art tears down the wall between the sacred and the profane."

Listening with his eyes closed, Victor could hear the strains of church music in the repetitions that were almost like devotions, as if the melody itself were bowing its head to the idea of endless practice. He could hear it in the phrasing, in the way Mingus would repeat a set of notes over and over, with slight variations each time. It was fascinating because Victor often felt the same impulse himself. He imagined Mingus working so hard for a mastery he knew was unachievable because the moment each new rung of understanding was reached, the next one would be revealed. It was like the illustration of Jack climbing the beanstalk in a book he'd been given his first year of American school. Since the beanstalk was covered in a thick fog, Jack couldn't see how far he had to go, so he just kept on climbing. When he reached the top, Jack found a giant, but what was at the top for Victor? Certainly not a giant or even a god. The simple answer, the humble answer, would have been the full use of his hands, but if he was honest with himself, what he really wanted was to use them in a way that most people couldn't. What he wanted was to make art.

On one of the albums, Victor discovered the Quintet's own version of "All the Things You Are" where they took apart the tune piece by piece, examining and reassembling it into something new. There were the high-wire acrobatics of Parker's saxophone and Gillespie's trumpet, and the low heartbeat of Mingus's bass, but it was Powell's piano that Victor's ears homed in on. All those magnificent runs. Could he ever do that? The fingers of Powell's right hand flew over the keys while his left fell on the anchor chords, the final notes nearly dissonant, with a sound that seemed almost to poke fun at itself.

Later, at practice, Victor tried to reproduce what he'd heard, taking apart and putting back together the tune, finding pockets for his own flourishes and expressions, finding space for his feelings to come out of his hands. After listening to those records today, something clicked in his brain, and he realized what he'd already been tinkering with for months, though clumsy and clunky and full of missteps, could maybe, with enough work, resemble what he'd heard.

Mrs. Thorne said his hands were ideal for the piano, and looking down at them as he played, at the delicate fingers that were long in proportion to his palms, he had to agree. In any case, he didn't think they were good for much else. Every day, before he touched the keys, he did his flexibility exercises, bending his fingers to make his hands into claws and stretching them into stars, one followed by the other, knowing he was getting strong. When he played a note, he now had a feel for the precise pressure it would take to get a specific sound, an expression of more than just volume, but of tone and meaning. He knew he was gaining control of what he wanted to say and how to say it in that wordless sea of sound, and as he lost himself like he always did when the music swept him away, he was finding something at the same time.

For most of his life, it had been useful for Victor to separate his mind from his body. During the war, he'd learned to hide inside his head so he wouldn't feel his fear or hunger. During his bouts of asthma, he'd drifted off inside his thoughts, waiting, pretending not to feel until feeling became a distant thing. And when he left China, the pain hadn't been so much in his body, but he learned how to push that away, too. When the Hansen's symptoms started, he already knew how to avoid what was happening to his body by going into his mind. Now, for the first time in many years, he was feeling both parts at the same time as music moved between them, pulling them back together, reawakening what he'd trained himself to make numb.

It was late, and Victor still had some homework to do, thirty pages of *The Catcher in the Rye* to read before tomorrow. Yawning, he rubbed a hand over his face, scratching the slight rasp above his upper lip. He gathered his things and stepped outside, where a musty, wet mushroom smell was rising from the earth after the rain. Breathing it in, he realized the air was lighter, gentler on his lungs than it had been when he arrived at the church, the clouds of yellow pollen washed away, at least for now. A crescent moon was peeking out over the tops of the oaks, but the sky was too overcast to see the stars. He liked going to the chapel while it was still light out and leaving after dark. The shift from day to night seemed to mark his hours of practice and how they were changing him.

FIFTEEN

After pulling some strings and paying only a little extra, the entertainment committee got their hands on a copy of *The Seven Year Itch* ahead of its June 3 general release, and now, for the first time, Carville was going to screen a new movie on its opening night, just like regular theaters on the outside. As Manny had predicted, the turnout was huge, a lucky thing since, after months of preparation, tonight was the night that Ava was planning to escape and Victor had promised to help. The theater was packed, with almost every seat taken by patients and even some of the watchmen. They just had to worry about the sisters, the doctors, and the orderlies who were working late.

Fresh from getting his fourth negative, Victor had agreed to be the lookout, ready to run interference at the theater, and though the job had sounded easy when he volunteered, now his heart was pounding like he'd just raced up six flights of stairs. This wasn't like the rule-breaking he'd done before. It was a crime with serious consequences, not just for Ava but for anyone who helped her.

The curtains parted, and the image of the American flag projected on the screen broke into a Tom and Jerry cartoon featuring Esther Williams in an underwater ballet, followed by a newsreel—Winston Churchill resigned, West Germany became a country, Albert Einstein died, and the Soviets signed the Warsaw Pact. By the time the movie started, Victor's nerves had settled enough for him to pay attention to the story.

The tinkling music of the title sequence signaled a comedy, but the subject of adultery was anything but a joke to Victor, and he couldn't help thinking about Ba. Had he even waited seven years before taking up with Ruth? The thought sounded so much like something Henry would say that he was surprised at himself. After all, the leading man was only away from his family for the summer whereas Ba had been away for years before straying, at least in any serious way. But then he thought of how things were between Ba and Ruth, and wondered what difference time and distance really made. If you picked the wrong person, even if you got married and became "one flesh," as he'd heard Miss Iantha say, you could still be very much alone.

When Marilyn Monroe, whose character didn't even have a name, was introduced as the object of the hero's desire, the audience saw her only in silhouette, the outlines of her body moving to the romantic string music in the background. When she walked through the door, her white halter-neck dress reminded Victor of the bathing suit Judy had been wearing at the lake when they met. Marilyn's animal magnetism was more like Ava's, but her girlishness had echoes of Judy's, along with her character's wardrobe of white. A couple of rows in front of Victor, Judy was wearing a white cotton blouse.

That wasn't the only thing that reminded him of her. The fantasy sequence where the hero seduced Marilyn by playing the piano for her made him squirm in his seat. How many times had he fantasized about the day Judy had come to hear him play at the chapel, when she'd listened while lying under the piano at his feet? Afterward, her praise had made him feel like he'd just sprouted wings. How often had he thought, if only he could have another shot, he might win her over this time?

Victor knew the scene was supposed to be ridiculous, the pathetic daydream of a pathetic man lusting after a woman way out of his league. What if he was like that, too? From the smirk Donny flashed him over his shoulder, he clearly thought so.

Taking his eyes off the screen, Victor squinted anxiously at his watch. If everything was going to plan, Manny would be meeting Ava right now by her dorm to give her the fake ID, help her get her luggage through Harry, and see her off in the taxi she'd ordered on the phone at the Red Rooster so she wouldn't be overheard in the canteen. The taxi would take her to Baton Rouge to meet TJ, and from there, she'd be free to start a new life as a Texas housewife. No one, not even her husband, would know her real name or race, or that she was a Hansen's patient and a mother. Victor was supposed to make sure nobody left the theater and to help Manny slip in unnoticed once Ava was safely gone.

Scanning the audience for anyone who might be getting up, Victor's eyes landed on Judy. She seemed to be concentrating on the movie, but even from two rows back, he could see her hand wandering up Donny's thigh. A rustling sound over to the right caught his attention. It was Herb searching in his breast pocket for his cigarettes while fumbling around for his cane.

Fernando put it in his hand and whispered, "Don't take too long."

Herb might have been blind, but his hearing was excellent, and if Manny happened to show up while he was still outside, it might raise his suspicions. Victor was going to have to stop him. Sliding out from his aisle seat as fast as he could, he scrambled to the door.

"Hey, you're missing the good part," he whispered, blocking Herb's way.

"Oh, it's you," said Herb. "Be right back." He gave his pack of cigarettes a little shake.

"You can smoke in here if you want."

Someone turned around and shushed them. They were drawing too much attention. Victor opened the door for Herb and followed him outside.

"What are you up to?" said Herb. A bead of sweat ran from his sparse hairline down to his temple. He patted it dry with his handkerchief.

"Nothing."

"A likely story. Why'd you try to stop me from leaving the theater?" Herb put a cigarette to his lips and lit it, rolling the flint of his silver monogrammed Zippo against his leg.

Victor shuffled his feet, trying to think of what he could possibly say. He didn't like having to lie to Herb. Torn between loyalty and the impulse to tell, he hesitated. Manny had sworn him and the others to secrecy, and he'd be furious if anyone broke their word, but Herb wasn't like the other adults. Maybe he'd help if something went wrong. Manny thought he knew what he was doing, but what if he was in over his head? If he got caught, Victor was sure he'd get in trouble, too.

Straightening his spine, he was about to confess that he'd gotten into something he couldn't talk about when he spotted Manny creeping up the walkway of the recreation center. His sweat-slicked face was shining in the outdoor lights. As soon as he saw Victor and Herb, Manny froze, but it was too late.

"Who's there?" said Herb.

Manny's eyes darted from Victor to the path behind him, as if he were trying to decide whether to make a run for it. Victor did a quick calculation. Herb already knew something was up. If he felt like he was in on it, he'd probably be less likely to tell. Victor gestured for Manny to come over.

"Hi, Mr. Klein. It's Manny," he said, managing to make his voice sound nonchalant while shooting Victor a desperate, wild-eyed look.

"Oh," said Herb. "What are you doing—" He interrupted himself and held up one hand. "Never mind. I don't want to know."

He took a deep drag of his cigarette, dropped it to the ground, and, with astonishing accuracy, stubbed it out with the end of his cane.

It wasn't until sometime the next day when Ava failed to show up for a doctor's appointment that anyone realized she was missing. At first, the administration wasn't particularly concerned since she'd gone off before and had come back on her own within a few days, but after a week, Dr. Morton got antsy. One by one, he called in anyone he thought might have information about Ava's disappearance— her housemates, all the men she'd dated, and, of course, Manny. After hours of interrogation, all he could get out of them was the name of the man who'd made her fake ID. Herb said Dr. Morton would probably keep the investigation "internal" if he could, because he didn't want people on the outside to think he couldn't keep the patients in line. After another week, however, he had no choice but to call in the local police.

Like most people in town, the police preferred to avoid the institution. None of the officers wanted to come in to question the patients, and the precinct certainly didn't want any patients there. In the end, they made do with the information Dr. Morton was able to provide from his own questioning. Manny was terrified that the man who made the ID would rat him out, but fortunately, he kept his mouth shut when the police brought him in. It would have been bad for business if word got out that he'd snitched on a client, even if the client was someone from the Leper Home.

For weeks, no one at Carville could talk about anything else, and their speculations ranged from wild to uncomfortably close to the mark. Miss Iantha's theory was that Ava had found God and run off to become a missionary, while Herb and Fernando figured a man was involved, though they guessed it was an old boyfriend from New York. All the while, Manny kept an eye out for news from Ava. Victor and he were both on constant alert, waiting for the axe to fall, but the summer dragged on and nothing happened. No letter, no postcard, but also no arrest.

School was on summer break and Victor had been helping out at the *STAR* office since the accident with the July issue. According to the rules, the magazine along with all the rest of the mail had to be sterilized before leaving the institution. It wasn't usually a problem, but this time, someone at the lab had turned on the heat and forgotten to turn it off, burning hundreds of copies of *The STAR* to a crisp. Herb and his staff had to print them all over again, and Victor pitched in. After that, he kept on going to the office a few days a week to run errands, mark Herb's edits on articles, and describe layouts and cover designs to him. He liked it there, the bustle of people, the rat-a-tat-tat of the typewriters. The smell of the ink and the noise of the printing press the Forty and Eight veterans organization had donated reminded him of Mr. Lee's shop.

"My brother's a printer," Victor said one afternoon, a sudden pang of homesickness taking him by surprise.

Herb seemed to hear it in his voice. "I remember you saying that. Maybe you can go home for a visit this summer."

"But didn't you say Dr. Morton was strict about that?" Victor moved a stack of paper over to the mimeograph machine.

"Wouldn't hurt to ask." Herb shrugged. "After all, I went on leave with only four negatives. Tallulah and I had a whale of a time in New York City. We must have seen a dozen plays. And you just got your fifth negative. Why don't you ask Dr. Behr what he thinks?"

At the end of his next appointment at the infirmary, Victor stared at the palm tree outside Dr. Behr's office, noticing for the first time how much its bark looked like an armadillo's shell.

Dr. Behr cleared his throat. "Is there anything else?"

Victor shook his head, but changed his mind and said, "Actually, I was wondering if I could maybe go home for a few days."

"Well, that's not up to me. Dr. Morton decides if patients can go on leave."

"But do you think I could?"

Dr. Behr leaned back in his chair. "Medically speaking, I don't see why not. Your treatment's going well, and you've had five negatives now. It's just a question of policy."

After almost a year at Carville, Victor had learned that there were often exceptions to policies or ways to get around them. "What if you asked Dr. Morton for me?"

Dr. Behr picked up his pen and drummed it on his desk for a moment. "I suppose I could write him a memo."

A feeling of excitement began to bubble up from the pit of Victor's stomach to his head at the thought of seeing Ba and Ruth and Henry again, and maybe even Jackie, of sleeping in his own bed and eating all the foods he'd missed. He pictured getting on the train and going back to the city, imagining what it would be like to see the familiar skyline and hear the rumble of the El on Allerton Avenue. He hadn't thought he'd even get this far with Dr. Behr. Maybe he had a real chance. He was both hopeful and afraid to hope, both excited at the possibility

of leaving Carville and afraid of leaving, especially since it would only
be for a short time.

A couple of days later, Dr. Behr received a reply.

"Bad news, I'm afraid," he said, tapping an envelope on his desk.
Two lines formed between his black brows.

"Can I read it?" Victor felt numb, his insides cold.

"Suit yourself."

Victor took the letter, the hospital's thick off-white stationery
trembling between his fingers.

Dear Dr. Behr,

This is regarding your inquiry into the possibility of
patient #2276 returning to his father's home at 2708 Barker
Avenue, Bronx, New York, for a short vacation. The patient's
records show that a home visit was made by the New York
City Department of Health to the residence at the time of his
diagnosis and revealed that while there were no small children
under the age of twelve occupying the household, the living space
is located in a single room at the back of a Chinese hand laundry
operated by the family.

Because of these crowded and unsanitary living conditions, it
does not seem desirable that the patient be permitted to visit the
Chin residence at this time. Furthermore, the patient would be
utilizing multiple forms of public transportation on his journey
back and forth from Carville, thus exposing a considerably larger
group than that represented by his family alone.

Most importantly, the patient has not yet completed the full
course of his treatment. Since he was admitted last August, he
has progressed from a very active lepromatous case to his present
status, which, though his recent negative skin scrapings are
noted, still remains active and therefore contagious. In short, the
patient does not meet the criteria for breaking quarantine.

While I understand that my predecessor allowed a number of
patients to leave the facility before they were medically qualified

for discharge, I believe this policy to have been haphazard and ill-advised. To allow such a visit would undermine our mission to carry out measures for the protection of public health and set a precedent that, as evidenced by the recent abscondence of patient #2038, may be misused by other patients who lack the cooperative attitude of #2276.

Sincerely yours,
I. Morton, Medical Director
Medical Officer in Charge

Victor stared at the letter for a long time, his eyes going over the words, disappointment and shame swirling in a spiral, tightening and closing in on him. Was that how others saw his home, his family? Now Dr. Morton and Dr. Behr saw them that way, too. Why had he let himself get his hopes up? A flash of anger tore through him, at Dr. Morton, at Herb, but mostly at himself. Then he thought, maybe it was better this way. If he went home, how could he be who they thought he was when he wasn't that person anymore? And how could he tear himself away? Or maybe that was just sour grapes.

"I'm sorry it didn't work out," said Dr. Behr.

Victor looked up. He'd been gripping the piece of paper so tightly that it had crumpled. "Thank you for trying," he said, and handed back the letter, avoiding the doctor's gaze.

Leaving the office, he felt like he was moving in slow motion. Outside the infirmary, in the tea garden, it was hot, but the cold was spreading inside him. He stopped and leaned against a palm tree, the one outside Dr. Behr's window, letting the rough, prickly bark press into his back until it hurt.

SIXTEEN

On her lunch break at the big public library next to Bryant Park, Ruth sat by one of the stone lions, eating a wax-paper-wrapped sandwich, chicken salad on rye, with her feet in their sensible black pumps swinging back and forth like a girl's. It was Rosh Hashanah, and she planned to leave work early so she could go down to Katz's in her old neighborhood to pick up a brisket and the potato knishes Sam liked, along with some extra honey cake to send to Victor. She might also stop at the electronics shop on Essex Street where they knew her aunt and uncle and would give her a good deal on a record player for him.

She couldn't believe he'd been gone for a year now. They wrote to each other every week, and she could cry from relief that he seemed to be doing so well now, getting through his surgeries, taking up music, and making friends. He'd mentioned a girl named Judy on a couple of occasions, piquing her curiosity, but she knew better than to pry. If this girl was special to him, he'd tell her in his own time.

When Victor first left, she hadn't been sure how often she should send him care packages, wanting him to receive them enough to make him feel loved, but not so much as to make him feel smothered or like she was overstepping. Henry often implied that she was trying to supplant their mother, but their mother wasn't here. She was. And she was doing the best she could.

In the end, she settled on a package every couple of weeks. Just little things, treats and comics and magazines she thought he'd enjoy, some family photos for his room when he mentioned his friends having them. She encouraged Sam to write a few lines in the letters she sent and to at least sign the cards. She wished they could go down on the train to see him, but when she spoke to Sam about it, he said that after the medical bills from Bellevue, he couldn't afford to close the laundry and pay for the trip. Plus, it was dangerous to travel as a couple in the South, where miscegenation was not only illegal but could get them killed.

The months since Victor's departure hadn't been easy for the two of them. They'd thought the silver lining would be time and a kind of togetherness they'd never had before, but without Victor to worry about, the facsimile of a family they'd made seemed suddenly flimsy and unreal. In its absence, Ruth could see how much was missing from her life. No real marriage, no real family, nothing she could count on. The only thing left was to worry about Victor.

It pained her especially to think of him spending holidays alone. To try to make up for it, she sent him festive things, foods he might miss and gifts, money for a bicycle last Christmas, and now a record player so he could listen to music in his own room. But none of it was enough, not enough to atone—for what, she didn't even know. She hadn't made him sick, and she'd done the right thing by getting him treatment, even if it meant sending him away. Maybe she was trying to make up for the pain his departure had caused the people who blamed her, Henry and Sam, even though he said he hadn't meant it. Maybe she just wanted to be beyond reproach, but that was impossible. Life was a series of choices, and all of them had consequences.

A gust of wind whipped down Fifth Avenue as she ate, sweeping the wide street clean of the fallen leaves and the tree pollen gathered there, a mercy in this fetid Indian summer. She was hot all the time these days, as if the furnace had been turned up inside her, and even though she was wearing only a crepe dress and her thin summer stockings, the wind barely cooled her down. Still, it felt good to be outside, and if it weren't for the way the wind was messing up her hair, she might have stayed a few minutes longer. She checked her watch. Only half an hour left. She popped the last bite of bread in her mouth, crumpled up the waxed paper, and headed for the stacks.

She did this often, visiting the library at lunch. Since grade school, she'd been a voracious reader, a self-starter, an autodidact. Well, maybe more like a dilettante, but who cared, anyway? And who was *she* to care? She was just a woman from the Lower East Side, sparsely educated, barely out of poverty. What good had all that reading done except show her all the things she couldn't have or be or achieve, and introduce her to all the places she couldn't go? She was a secretary. Wasn't that good enough?

All of a sudden, Ruth recognized the voice inside her head, speaking to her with such condescension. It was her uncle's. As if to get him out of there, she shook her head so hard that one of the bobby pins holding her chignon in place fell from its snood.

If Uncle Boris had had his way, she'd have ten children with some Orthodox shopkeeper by now, a good Jewish woman producing good Jewish children. It had been almost twenty years since she'd seen his face, since she left the Lower East Side behind and her beloved aunt along with it. But as hard as it had been for her to make her way alone, she told herself time and again that she'd rather be dead than go from one controlling man's house to another's. And she hadn't. She'd kept her promise to herself, and for that, she was grateful.

How ironic that Uncle Boris had spent so many years warning her not to get pregnant out of wedlock. Up until now, she'd done exactly as he'd said—no pregnancy, no wedding—but even a stopped clock was right twice a day.

Assessing herself naked in the bathroom mirror before work that morning, Ruth had imagined her baby curled like a comma inside her, a body within a body. She'd always wanted to be a mother and figured she would get around to it someday, but for one reason or another, it never happened. When her first love, the man she thought she'd marry, died in the war, a part of her had seemed to die with him. Going through the motions of dating other men, she'd been sure she'd never feel that way about anyone again. But then along came Sam.

Nothing about loving him was straightforward or without complication. She knew all that going in. But with him, every hardship had its reason, and every sacrifice was tempered by something that made it bearable. He was married, but his wife was so far away, it hardly seemed to matter. He couldn't give her a baby, but he had an eight-year-old boy who needed her and quickly came to fill the empty place in her heart. If she were a different kind of woman, she might have tried to get pregnant on purpose to force Sam's hand, but what kind of life would she have after doing something like that? So the years went by, and eventually, she came to accept that she would never be a mother, after all.

At first, she thought her pregnancy symptoms were the change of life, starting a little early, perhaps, but that wasn't unheard of. Given her age, it was a reasonable thing to think. What a surprise, then, at almost forty, after assuming it could never be, to receive such a magnificent, everyday miracle.

Her body was changing, transforming on the outside at the rate she imagined the baby was growing inside her womb. Her hair was getting thicker, and her breasts were heavier, denser, their nipples and areolas darkening. She'd never had much of a bosom before, not that she minded, because her shape was pleasing enough overall. Sufficiently womanly, Sam liked to joke, especially in the hips. And her nerve endings were getting more sensitive by the day, as if they were rising closer to the surface of her skin. Yesterday, she'd climaxed twice in bed, which, though not unprecedented, was unusual for her.

How had this happened? She was careful about putting in her diaphragm every time she was with Sam. Maybe it had slipped when she was taking it out. Or maybe not. Nothing, after all, was foolproof.

In the biology section of the library, Ruth leafed through a medical textbook on gynecology and obstetrics.

"Statistics show that diaphragms are sixty percent effective when used correctly," she read.

Only sixty percent, and even less with any kind of mistake. What an ass that doctor had been when he told her not to worry and even asked if she wasn't ready, at her "advanced age," to start a family?

"Not too late to catch a husband that way," he'd suggested with a wink.

The audacity! Flipping the pages further to the pregnancy section of the book, she squinted at the diagrams showing human gestation, the baby inside the bisected woman, growing, replicating its cells. In those illustrations, human reproduction seemed like an awesome, impossible act, enacting the very stages of evolution itself.

"Amazing," she whispered, gently patting her stomach without caring how silly it was to talk to a fluttering tadpole of a creature that didn't even have ears.

Tonight, over brisket and knishes, she would tell Sam, and they would eat apples dipped in honey, for sweetness. For hope. For their blessing. A new life for a new year.

SEVENTEEN

Sam whistled the opening bars of "Luck Be a Lady," the song from *Guys and Dolls* they'd been playing constantly on the radio in anticipation of the movie coming out in November.

He crossed the street, heedless, for once, of the nosy neighbor ladies who sat spying all day at their windows. Who cared if they saw him going into Ruth's building? He was going to become a father again, and he was proud as a bull, though the idea had taken some getting used to.

During the war, the whores weren't the only women whose heads had been turned by Sam's good looks. He saw the way regular French women, from the finely dressed ladies to the shopgirls walking down the winding rues and broad avenues after work, followed him with their sloe-eyed gazes. Those attractions, which led to a number of fleeting encounters, became some of the small sparks of humanity carrying him through the gore and the friendlessness of the front line, keeping him from going completely numb. Only now that Ruth had told him she was having a baby did he wonder if he'd gotten any of the women he'd bedded there pregnant. It was disquieting, both the thought itself and the fact that it had never occurred to him before. What would a half-French, half-Chinese baby look like? What would such a child's life be like now in France?

It was foolish, perhaps, that he hadn't considered the possibility of a pregnancy with Ruth, but it had never come up in all these years, and at their age, it was something of a shock. What would this new baby be like? If it was a boy, would he look like his brothers? If it was a girl, would she look like Ruth or, oddly, like Mei Wan, whose father had purportedly been the son of a Canadian whore, conceived on her grandfather's long sojourn to Ontario and sent back for his wife to raise?

Long-lashed, long of thigh bone and clavicle, Mei Wan was a good inch taller than he, and, being a year older to boot, had made him feel less than manly when they were first married. He'd never even seen her before their wedding day—the matchmaker had made all the arrangements—and when she got out of the sedan her family had hired to carry her to the Chins' house, she was a pillar of fine red silk, her headdress making her look even taller than she was. After all, he'd been barely eighteen, just a boy, and even at nineteen, she had a rod of steel in her, cold and unbending when she wanted to be. Even so, when he lifted her veil, it had pleased him to see the peacock feathers he'd sent her for their engagement, and after the wedding, she'd gotten pregnant immediately despite their mutual distaste for those early, embarrassed fumblings. When their first child was born a boy—Henry, whom they named Yat Kun, Powerful Sun—the marriage was, contrary to their feelings, declared blessed.

Because Old Mr. Chin needed him back in New York to help manage the liquor store where he was a silent partner, Sam hadn't stayed long enough to see the effects of the pregnancy on Mei Wan, much less be present for the birth. With only a set of black-and-white studio photographs as evidence of the baby's existence, the fact of his being a father remained abstract from so far away. Squinting at the small, blurry face of the bundle swaddled in Mei Wan's lap, Sam didn't feel much of anything. But by the time he returned, that baby had grown into a garrulous, sturdy four-year-old. And although he was stubborn and utterly spoiled as the only male of the house, he worshipped his father as something of a hero, an American cowboy, perhaps, and Sam couldn't help but be charmed.

When Mei Wan fell quickly pregnant again on that second visit since their marriage, he was surprised to discover the pride he felt at seeing her belly ripen, swelling tight and hard as a gourd. Even Old Mrs. Chin, who was as stingy with praise as she was with money, remarked on how her skin glowed. His eyes began to track her movements more closely, and he had to agree she was growing as full and luminous as the moon. She was, undoubtedly, a lovely woman with a broad, smooth brow, wide-set eyes, and a cupid's bow of unusual depth and definition. Even when they were first married, Sam had noticed how the admiring eyes of other men alighted on her, especially those of some of his cousins. And seeing her like this now, so soft and vulnerable, and round with his child, touched him.

"Come inside," Mei Wan said in a soft voice one evening, resting her hand on Sam's shoulder as she passed by with a basketful of kindling. "Dinner is ready."

He was smoking in the courtyard with his cousin Kun and some of the other Chin village men while his son galloped around on a rake, pretending it was a horse. He saw the men take in this small public gesture of warmth that was more than just an act of perfunctory marital deference, and something between them shifted.

That night, instead of lying back-to-back with Mei Wan in their bed, Sam made a point of turning toward her and sleeping instead with the growing baby pressed against the palm of his hand. And although she pushed that hand away when he brought it up to her breast, he understood it was to protect the baby and didn't reproach her for it.

When the baby was born another boy, they named him Vee Kun, Powerful One, matching the second character with his older brother's according to custom. With the Red Egg party and the general approval of the village, Sam felt, if not love, then at least affection for Mei Wan, along with the comfort of being part of a family again. Holding the baby in his arms with his nose pressed against the soft tuft of hair at the crown of his perfectly round head, the primal, salty smell of him elicited a rush of fierce protectiveness. Not since he'd been separated from his parents had he allowed himself to feel such tender things, the ties of flesh and blood. Mei Wan had given him this—he couldn't deny it. But after the baby, who would be called Victor, had celebrated his first birthday, Old Mr. Chin summoned him to New York again, and then the war broke out. Everything changed, and the door that had briefly cracked open for their marriage slammed shut when Sam met Ruth.

Gods, why was he thinking about this now? Guilt washed over him as he spat into the dirt at the foot of a tree in Ruth's courtyard, willing himself to banish these useless thoughts. But as he tried not to think of them, other bad thoughts bubbled up and, cringing, he couldn't help but remember what he'd said to Ruth yesterday when she told him she was pregnant, and on the Jewish New Year, too.

"How? How did you do this?" he'd blurted.

"How did *I* do this?" Ruth had said, dangling the "I" in the air like it was the most awful curse in the world. "You think I did it on purpose?"

Later, on his own, after the shock had worn off, Sam took stock of the situation and realized there was nothing really stopping them from having a baby, not anymore. Victor was off their hands now. He was safe, or as safe as he could be. And Henry was grown. Of course he was loyal to his mother and had never accepted Ruth, but he had a job and a life of his own. A baby would be expensive, especially in America, but he ran the numbers, and if Ruth gave up her apartment and he opened the laundry on Sundays from ten to four, they'd manage, especially with Ruth's savings.

On the other hand, if he sold the laundry outright, they'd have enough for a fresh start somewhere else, somewhere like California. San Francisco, perhaps, but then he remembered Old Mr. Chin talking about his rich cousins and their businesses in Los Angeles, a young city with plenty of opportunity. Jackie's grandfather had mentioned wanting to expand his laundry business the last time they played mahjong. Maybe he'd be interested in opening another branch in the Bronx. And if everything worked out, Sam could even ask Henry to come along.

It would be an adjustment, but hadn't he adapted to new places and circumstances before? Change was, in a manner of speaking, the sole mainstay of his life. Laughing at himself for thinking such a Buddhist thought, he began to imagine how things might be when the baby came. In many ways, before Victor was sent away, they'd already been living like a family, if an unconventional one.

Ruth would be a wonderful mother, caring, thoughtful, and warm. Sam knew it from how good she was with Victor, and he knew it even now that it was just the two of them, from so many little things—how she fussed over him, refilling his plate with seconds and thirds when they ate; how she scrubbed her hands with soap the moment she got back from work before touching him.

"Subway hands," she explained when he quirked his eyebrow at her. "Germs."

"You think a little dirt can hurt me?"

"That's how diseases spread. My mother, you know."

"It's okay," said Sam, taking her small, long-fingered hands and kissing them hard on the knuckles. "I understand."

And he did understand. It was difficult for him to think of his own parents, too, not Old Mr. and Mrs. Chin but his real parents who had sold him at the age of ten to save them all from starvation.

Though not entirely deaf, his father had been a mute and supported his wife and son in Toisan City, begging and doing odd jobs when he could. Sam never once heard his father's voice, but he'd spoken vividly with his facial expressions, often tender and cheerful, saying what he couldn't say with words. Sam's mother had been an anxious, birdlike woman who seemed surprised every day to find herself living hand to mouth as the wife of a pauper. She was certainly surprised when she learned that her husband had arranged for their son to be sold for twice the price of a girl and adopted by a prominent local businessman with connections to America. Sam tried never to think of that day—the silent, shamefaced bowing of his father as he accepted payment from Mr. Chin or the muffled wailing of his mother, who stayed hidden inside their one-room shack, unable to bear the sight of her only child being taken away.

In the years that followed, Sam endured the scorn of Mrs. Chin and her daughters, who saw him only as an interloper and never missed a chance to remind him of it. No one would have described Mr. Chin as kind, but the fact remained that he gave Sam his last name and a

Gold Mountain ticket, a reversal of fortunes for a beggar's son that was unheard of, the stuff of novels and fairy tales. He was lucky. He should be grateful, he was told countless times over the decades of uneasy transformation into a rich man's son, swallowing his grief and pride. In their little village adjacent to the town of Duanfen, life was nearly unbearable because everyone knew he was a fraud, but when he went to New York with Mr. Chin at the age of sixteen to help him set up shop, no one seemed to care who he was or where he'd come from.

On that first journey to America in 1931, after a jam-packed ferry ride from Canton City to Hong Kong, Sam and Mr. Chin had sailed together as father and son on a junk ship to San Francisco, where they were held for three weeks on Angel Island. That evil place had been shut down since 1940, but it was surely still full of ghosts. Even those who'd been lucky enough to pass through its wrought iron gates did so at the price of enduring the prodding of the interrogators, not with white hot pokers but with questions, seemingly endless rounds of them, designed to catch lies. In nightmares, Sam sometimes revisited the weeks he'd spent there, languishing in a room full of boys and men stacked on top of one another in narrow bunks where rats, lice, and disease spread like wildfire.

In the end, he'd passed his interrogations with flying colors. Mr. Chin had prepared him well, drilling him relentlessly day in and day out on the traps the immigration officials were likely to set, rapping him on the forehead with his knuckles if he got an answer wrong. As much as he resented the man, his methods had worked. When it was his own turn to prepare his sons for getting through Immigration, he followed his adopted father's lead.

Stoic and hard-faced, with high, proud cheekbones and a strong jaw just like his own, Henry seemed a good deal older than his thirteen years when they made the trip from China to San Francisco. On the ship, Sam saw him steal up to the top deck sometimes to smoke cigarettes with the other adolescent boys. That was good. Friendship between men was important in America, where it was impossible to survive without the network of fellowship and favors, the ladder that generations of Chinese men had built rung by rung. This was something Americans didn't understand, or didn't want to, as the papers seemed to relish portraying Chinatown's Benevolent Associations as mafia groups.

"Every man for himself," the saying went in the story told by the lone cowboy on the plains and the pioneer trekking solo in the wilderness. Any newcomer knew this was nonsense. Sam was grateful to Old Mr. Chin for teaching him these truths, as well as giving him the seed money to open his own laundry. He was comforted by the thought that his firstborn son had the makings of a survivor.

Victor, however, was another story. Seasick from the moment they claimed their hammocks belowdecks, the boy vomited and vomited, and when he wasn't vomiting, he was coughing until tears rolled down his cheeks, after which he kept on crying. Even Jackie, Sam's new Paper Son, had mostly stopped whimpering back in Hong Kong, proving himself to be tougher of mind and body than his own child. What was there to cry about, anyway? They weren't in chains. They weren't being tortured. It was true that steerage was by no means luxurious, with everyone cocooned in hammocks like silkworms. And the sailing wasn't easy either, the waves tossing them at gravity's unkind mercy with each sway and fall of the ship. But they all had three meals a day and were allowed to eat them in the dining room like human beings, not confined to their sleeping quarters like livestock, as they were on his first voyage.

Over the last eight years, from the moment he'd been thrown into the deep end of fatherhood to the moment Victor had been sent away, Sam had to admit that he'd been hard on his sons, Victor especially, but what choice did he have? How else could such a sensitive boy learn to cope with the brutalities of life? Most of the time, Sam convinced himself that his toughening was the reason Victor was not only surviving but doing well at Carville. But other times, he wondered if he'd done it all wrong.

Sam thought of the day when Victor was thirteen and a delivery van had hit him in the street, knocking him off his scooter. Hearing the crash from inside the laundry, Sam ran out to the sight of splinters of wood and wheels scattered across Barker Avenue, and Victor lying there, flat on his back, in the middle of the street. When he rolled over and sat up, Sam released the breath he'd been holding, and the spurt of fear that had propelled him out the door trickled back down his spine, turning into anger as it pooled in his gut. He grabbed his son by the arms, hauled him to his feet, and shook him hard.

"How could you be so stupid?" he shouted, pulling him out of the street.

Inside, Sam made him take off his clothes, and checked him over. He was fine apart from a few scrapes and bruises. They'd been lucky this time, but what about the next?

"What were you thinking?" Sam kept repeating, without expecting an answer.

Victor sat on a chair, staring at the floor, stone-faced and silent, seeming neither sorry nor afraid, and Sam thought he'd better do something, anything, to knock some sense into him. He whisked the bamboo feather duster off its hook and thrashed him with it, thwacking him on the calves and thighs. Nowhere important and not too hard, but hard enough, he hoped, to get through to him. Victor made no move to run away or defend himself. He just sat there, taking it without a peep. And as Sam hit him, instead of relief or release, he felt the opposite—a rushing tide of rage, not at the boy but at the world, at its danger, its unfairness. He threw the feather duster to the floor.

"Get dressed," he said, striding out to the storefront. He rested his elbows on the countertop and squeezed his temples hard between his hands.

After a moment, Victor emerged and, without acknowledging him, slipped out the front door. Sam let him go, telling himself that once he'd had time to cool off, he'd come back with a better attitude.

By nightfall, he was still nowhere to be found. Sam locked up, flipped the sign to CLOSED, and went in to make dinner. Ruth was out with some girlfriends, so he ate alone, the minutes ticking by as every sudden sound—the scuttling of the rats in the alley, the splashing of the cars hitting the puddle in a pothole on the street—made him jerk his head with anticipation toward the door. His state of high alert reminded him of being on night watch in France, and as if his body remembered, too, he spent the rest of the evening unable to concentrate, smoking one cigarette after another, reading the same passage in *The Odyssey* twice without taking it in.

Sometime after midnight, long after the food had grown cold, Sam put the leftovers away and lay down on his cot. Through the small window above it, he watched the moon move slowly across the sky as his dinner sat like a brick in his gut.

The sound of the garbage truck woke him the next morning. In the ugly light, the stale, tobacco-filled air appeared gray, and pinpricks of fear amassed in his body as he realized Victor was still missing. Dressing quickly, he unlocked the shop door, telling himself not to give the boy the satisfaction of being afraid, but as morning passed into afternoon, he couldn't ignore it anymore.

At six o'clock, Sam shoved the BACK IN FIFTEEN MINUTES sign in the window and ran over to Henry's building, but Victor wasn't there. When he got back, Ruth was waiting for him. Filling her in while gathering change from the cash register, he left her at the laundry and stomped down the block to use the pay phone at the drugstore.

"Laundry," barked Jackie's grandfather, answering on the first ring.

"Uncle Chin-ah," Sam said in Toisanese.

"Sammy-ah." The old man switched his language and tone, greeting him by the nickname he despised. "How's business?"

"Bad, of course. But I'm calling on a personal matter. Have you seen my ungrateful son? Is he with your grandson?"

"Maybe, but I haven't seen that little bastard either," said Uncle Chin with a chesty cough. "Not for two, maybe three days. I've been at my girlfriend's place uptown. New one. You know, they have a saying here," he said, quoting in English. "'The darker the berry, the sweeter the juice.' And I like them sweet." He chuckled and asked, "How is your girlfriend? Long time, same one, am I right?"

"Yes, yes. I must be going. Good business to you." Sam hung up. "What a waste of a nickel," he muttered to himself.

With shaky hands, he pocketed the rest of his coins and trudged back down the street, wondering if he should call the police. Would they even care about a missing Chinese boy? Would it be better if Ruth called? He hated asking her to do things like that, but maybe it was worth it this time.

Opening the door of the laundry, Sam stopped dead. Victor was back, standing behind the counter, looking tired and disheveled but no worse for wear, with Ruth, who was speaking to him with her hands on both his shoulders.

Like Sam, Ruth had been raised without her parents, but somehow she knew all the right things to do with a child, things that eluded him. She was going to be an excellent mother, and with her by his side, he would do his best to be a good father, a better one this time.

Outside Ruth's apartment building, the air was as thick as soup and the ground was littered with the yellowed fan-shaped leaves and fruits of the ginkgo trees planted in the courtyard. In his rush to get there, Sam stepped on a few and had to stop to scrape their stinky guts off his shoes before bounding up the six flights to Ruth's apartment, taking the steps two at a time.

"Ruthie," he said, out of breath, dripping with sweat at her door, "I know what to do. We cannot stay here."

"And we should go where?" Ruth gestured for him to come in. "To the kitchen? To Timbuktu?"

"Los Angeles," he said with a decisive nod. He mopped his brow with his handkerchief.

"It's a bit late for my big break, don't you think?" she deadpanned, making the corners of his mouth twitch.

"Now is not the time for joking."

She sat down on the sofa and put up her hands in mock surrender.

"I know some people there. Old Mr. Chin's cousin Mr. Yee." Sam sat down next to her and explained how long ago, Mr. Yee, who, incidentally, had an American wife, had opened an import-export business. It became so prosperous that the family was now renting Chinese antiques to movie sets and running restaurants and nightclubs all over LA. "I could sell the laundry and maybe buy into a partnership with them."

Ruth shook her head a bit. "But why?"

"Nobody knows us there. We can start over." He took her hand and gave it a gentle squeeze. "We can get married. Maybe not right away, but once I settle things with Mei Wan. Henry is grown up and Victor is doing okay down there. You said so yourself."

"New wife, new life, huh?" Her words were innocuous enough, but there was something odd in her voice. "That seems to be where all the men go."

He recognized her sarcasm now, and while he was used to her joking that way, it was a mode of English he found confusing, especially in serious conversations. He would have let it drop, but it seemed important to get everything on the table now. "What men? Tell me what you mean."

"My father went to LA when my mother died. And he never came back."

So it was to do with her childhood, her parents. "And do I look like your father?" he asked, drawing her close and raising his eyebrow in the way that always made her laugh. "I am not leaving anyone behind."

Ruth nodded. "Is this really what you want?"

"Why not?"

"'Why not?' the man says to me. 'Why not?'" Ruth put her hands on her head, rubbing her scalp as if she had a headache. Her loose bun unknotted as curls spilled out over her shoulders. She gathered her hair back up and straightened her spine. "Well, you must be eligible for some benefits from the GI Bill. Maybe we could take out a loan. I can help you with the forms."

Sam kissed her. "So that is a yes?"

"Why not?"

It wasn't the most romantic proposal in the world, but he was determined to make her happy.

"On Sunday, we will go to 47th Street."

Ruth's forehead crinkled in a puzzled expression.

"They sell diamonds in the Diamond District, am I right?" Sam grinned as her eyes opened wide.

"Sam, really?"

"Of course," he said, scooping her up in his arms, bridal style. "We will make it official. I am not a Rockefeller, but I want everyone to know you are engaged."

"Put me down," Ruth laughed, smacking him on the shoulder.

"Never," said Sam. And he held on.

EIGHTEEN

Later that night, as she was getting ready for bed, Ruth wondered why she hadn't told Sam the whole story about her father, that when her mother, Tsilya, had died of the Spanish flu, her grief-stricken father, Yakov, had run off and left her, his only child, with his brother and sister-in-law so he could start a new life. She barely remembered him—she'd only been three years old—and for the rest of her childhood, he'd send a card on her birthday with a bit of cash enclosed, but she never saw him again.

All she had of her parents were photographs. Papa, sober in his black suit, and Mama, so young, so beautiful in her good dress and diamond earrings on their wedding day. Papa holding Ruth as a baby on his lap, her eyes screwed shut and mouth wide open in a squall that the photographer couldn't stop no matter how many toys he waved in her face. Papa squinting in the strong California sunlight, young and slim as a scholar, leaning against a convertible, so different from Uncle Boris that they scarcely looked like brothers.

Ruth had been longing all her life for a man who, unlike her father, wouldn't leave and wouldn't stay only for the sake of obligation. She thought she'd found him when she met her first love, who'd seemed as different from her father as a man could be. He'd been a six-foot-tall Irish Catholic accountant from her firm, and she never even got to meet his parents before he enlisted, so who knew what would have happened if he'd lived?

On the outside, Sam seemed perfectly stable, never going anywhere, opening and closing the laundry like clockwork, day after day. But on the inside, he was unsteady, prone to allowing circumstances to decide things for him as randomly as the toss of a coin. Maybe this, his intelligence and sex appeal aside, was what had drawn her to him, like a fish to a hook. How could she not have seen it before? Papa had allowed his choices to be made by his circumstances, too, her mother's death and his own grief making him choose to abandon her. But now, with the baby and Sam's proposal, she had a chance to make it right, to prove once and for all that she was good enough to make a man stay.

Of course there were a thousand things that endeared Sam to her, things that through the years hadn't lost their sweetness. The precise inclination of his head bent over the books as his long, nimble fingers organized the unruly numbers, flicking the heaven and earth beads on his abacus. The way the light from her bedside lamp made the jet black of his hair and the few white strands at his temples gleam. The feeling of his solid, sinewy muscles under her cheek when she turned her face into the warmth of his shoulder. The scent of his skin beneath the fresh smells of laundry soap and crisp shirt starch. The meticulous way he dressed in French cuffs and three-piece suits, wearing them not in a dandyish way but as an act of defiance, as if to say he was far more than what people might think. The way he looked at her—with surprise, followed by gratitude—when she smoothed his hair back from his brow if it happened to fall. He was so impeccably neat, it made her heart squeeze to see him in rare moments of disarray, when he let himself be vulnerable, and it felt like a privilege to witness it.

She had so many of these small, dear moments clinging to her memory, refusing to let go, even when she was angry. Sam could be gruff and taciturn like most men of their generation, men who'd survived war and seen unspeakable things, but with her, he was tender and gentle, and even romantic sometimes. After disappointing her at first, he seemed delighted to be having a child with her now.

"Hello, California baby," he'd said in a whimsical mood to her belly a couple of hours ago. "This is your father speaking. Are you behaving for your mother?" He'd pressed his ear to her recently protruded navel and listened intently as if the baby could respond.

The California baby. Ruth swore to herself that this child would never be treated with resentment or reluctance. This child would want for nothing. Unlike Victor and Henry, her baby would never know the hot breath of the iron, the piercing hiss followed by searing clouds of steam. Her baby would never fall asleep to the stuttering piston of the needle on the Singer sewing machine whirring late into the night. This child would have a different life, a healthy life of sunshine and sea breeze, of new beginnings with a mother and a father who loved each other, something neither she nor Sam nor either of his sons ever had. Thinking of this new family she was going to create, this dream of a new home and future, she thought about the power of names, their practical magic, for making things come true.

"If you want your son to grow up strong," Sam once told her, "you have to give him a name that means strength. Like Vee Kun, Victor's name. For Chinese people, naming is like making a wish."

Though she was curious, Ruth knew better than to ask what Sam's own Chinese name, Guy Wen, meant. Once, when she'd made the mistake of asking why he didn't just go by Guy, its anglicized form, he told her it was the name his real parents had given him and was therefore too unlucky to use. Hearing it reminded him of his loss, and the pain in his voice was enough to stop her from ever mentioning it again.

"Jewish people, on the other hand, name their children after relatives who have passed away," she said. "Morbid, right?"

Ruth had laughed at Sam's appalled face. It was because they wanted their children to remember the past, she'd explained, to never forget. In a way, this was wishful thinking, too, because forgetting was a natural human inclination. How else could people survive tragedy and move on? How else could they live? "Forgive and forget," they said. The saying existed for a reason.

Spreading a thick layer of Pond's Cold Cream on her face, Ruth massaged it into a thick white mask to dissolve her makeup and wiped it all off with tissues. Then she dug her fingers into the jar a second time and rubbed more cream on her face, as the directions suggested on the back, to clean out hidden grime and seal in moisture. She was beginning to see some signs of aging around her eyes, and that wouldn't do for a new bride, now would it?

NINETEEN

In November, the temperature at Carville dropped and with the arrival of a true fall, the thick green shucks on the pecan trees split open, revealing the nuts inside. Victor went to work gathering them on his hands and knees, checking for bugs before stuffing them into a burlap sack. Every so often, he ate one, the chewy texture and intense flavor so different from the dry, crunchy pecans he'd had before. Beside him, Judy was kneeling in the grove, too, shoving pecans into her sack at breakneck pace.

"Trying for *The Guinness Book of World Records*? Some of those might be bad, you know."

"My dad moved *again*," she said, "to Brooklyn this time, so I have to send extra for my grandparents there. You getting those for your dad and Ruth?"

Victor nodded. "She told me she was craving them because of the baby."

Judy stopped and stared with her eyebrows halfway up her forehead. He pretended not to notice and continued gathering pecans as he told her the news like it was no big deal, but the truth was, Ruth's letter had knocked the wind right out of him.

A new sibling, while unexpected, wasn't the worst thing in the world, but California was a whole other story. Ruth and Ba weren't just moving. They were going all the way across the country, as far as they could possibly get, leaving him and Henry behind just like Ba had left them in China all those years ago. Not to mention the fact that Ba was giving up the laundry, so he was losing his home. Again.

Why hadn't Ba told him? Why hadn't Henry? When he called, Henry said he didn't want to do Ba's dirty work anymore and launched into such a long, vicious rant about Ruth that Victor could hardly say a word. And what about Ma? Was somebody going to tell her?

In her letter, Ruth kept going on about what a good big brother he'd be and how he'd come to live with them in Los Angeles when he got well, maybe in a house by the beach. Victor knew she was trying to make him feel included, but he couldn't help thinking that it was only out of guilt. And no matter how much he told himself to stop being immature, he couldn't help feeling like he'd been replaced. Ba was going to have a new American kid now, maybe even a boy. A boy who wouldn't have anything wrong with him.

"Wow," said Judy. "You sound so calm. I'd be . . . I don't even know. Will you go to California when you're discharged? They have some good schools out there."

They were seniors now, due to graduate in June, and the counselor had been talking to them about their options since the start of the school year. Those who had a chance of getting discharged soon were encouraged to apply for college or, depending on their skills and level of disability, jobs from the national list the institution kept of Hansen's-friendly places on the outside. Graduates who had to stay for treatment could take continuing education classes with Mr. Harland unless they just wanted to work. There were jobs available at the infirmary and other parts of the institution, and at some of the small businesses in the Carville Mall. Two of the kids who graduated last year were working at the canteen.

Judy and Donny came from families that expected them to go to college, and had no trouble paying for it, but nobody would have mentioned it to Victor or Manny if they hadn't been sent to Carville. Ba always said a high school diploma was enough, and Henry didn't even get his before starting his job at the print shop. Manny was up front about having to go to work as soon as he could. Like Ba, his father sent part of his paycheck as an elevator operator back to relatives in Cuba, and with two younger children at home, their finances were always tight. Victor knew college graduates could have careers that earned more money, not to mention respect, but aside from the cost, the whole process was a mystery—what school to pick, how to get in, what to study, how to study, what to do when you were finished.

It had never been Victor's intention to lie or pretend to be better off than he was, but Judy had a way of assuming that they were all the same, and he found himself going along with it. Early on, when the four of them were talking about what their fathers did, and the others had given their answers—dentist, engineer, elevator man—he said Ba was a businessman. It wasn't exactly untrue. He did own the laundry, after all, and though Victor felt a twinge of guilt about twisting the facts, once he said it, he couldn't go back. He couldn't let Donny have something else to feel superior about.

In the Bronx, everyone knew he was the kid from the Chinese hand laundry, and while he wasn't ashamed of what Ba did or even of being poor, Carville had given him a blank slate. Here, he was free from who he'd been and who his family was, and he had to admit that it felt good to be treated like everyone else for once.

When Mrs. Thorne would talk about continuing his musical education after he was discharged, he'd agree without having to worry about how, because going home didn't seem real. But now that it was a possibility, he was going to have to figure it out. With Ba and Ruth leaving New York, he'd have to go with them or fend for himself, and in either case, he didn't know how he'd pay for piano lessons, let alone music school. He promised himself he'd find a way to at least keep practicing, but he didn't like to think about it.

Victor shrugged. "I've got nine negatives now, but who knows?"

Judy's eyes opened wide. "In a row?"

Nodding, he waited for her to tell him how many negatives she'd racked up, too, like she used to before she and Donny had gotten together, but she didn't, and he instantly regretted volunteering. "No use in counting chickens."

Overhead, a flock of starlings swarmed, hundreds of them whipping back and forth like a black shark in the sky. Mr. Harland said they were an invasive species, introduced in the 1890s by a group who wanted America to have all the birds that Shakespeare had ever mentioned. The starlings reminded Victor of the mobs of pigeons in New York that would churn in tight circles between the buildings. Ruth thought they were disgusting. Flying rats, she called them. But Ma said seeing so many pigeons around was a sign of prosperity since people would eat them when times were lean.

"Damn it," Judy muttered, struggling to crack open a pecan.

Victor moved closer to her, so close that their legs were touching. "Here, let me show you."

He took the pecan she was holding, added another to it, and demonstrated how to push at their seams with the palms of her hands until they popped. He could feel her eyes on him and every millimeter of her leg against his, and though it hadn't happened in a year, he could swear there was an energy between them now, like there was on the night she'd invited him to her room.

He used to think about it all the time. The blissful rush of sitting on her bed, the intimacy of it, the kiss. The confusion of her kissing him back and then pretending it never happened had made him go over every moment again and again, like a record skipping, wondering if he could have done something different, or if it had even been real. As time passed, he'd thought about it less and less, that is, until now.

"This is the best way," he said. "Just pry open the shell and get it out in one piece. See?"

Victor passed her two more pecans. Trying to copy him, she pressed too hard and they flew from her hands. She laughed at herself, big and loud, reminding him of Ruth.

"Looks like you'll have to show me again," she said, peering at him from beneath her lashes.

He reached over, held her hands together, and squeezed with just enough pressure for the pecan shells to pop.

She put one in her mouth and, offering him the other, said, "I like your hair that way."

Flustered but trying to hide it, he dropped his gaze as he said, "Thanks." He'd just gotten it cut at the barbershop in the Carville

Mall where they'd convinced him to try a new style, short back and sides, with longer hair on top instead of the crew cut he'd always gotten before.

Judy reached out and smoothed down his cowlick. "It's so soft," she said, as if to herself.

What was she doing? She still flirted with him from time to time, but not like this. Or maybe he was reading her wrong. With a playfulness he hoped would mask his uncertainty, he mirrored her, touching her hair, too, for the first time, he realized. He'd been imagining what it would be like to run his hands through it ever since the day they met, and he might have found out when they were kissing in her room if things hadn't gone south so fast.

Now that he was finally holding a tendril of that thick brown mane, he was surprised by how coarse it felt between his fingertips. "Yours isn't," he teased.

She smiled and leaned in, the pecan scent on her breath making Victor anticipate the taste of her mouth. He stayed still, letting her close the distance to make sure there was no mistake. Not this time. He closed his eyes, feeling his skin grow warm as her lips, dry and a little chapped, grazed his. The sticks and stones in the grass were beginning to hurt his knees, but he didn't care. He was too busy imagining the layers of sediment, their different colors and depths, stacked beneath the two of them, like the picture in their earth science textbook. He thought of how the bones of ancient animals and dinosaurs became fossilized in stone, and how, deeper still, the earth's molten core burned. If he and Judy were to die right then and there, they would become a part of it, this connection, not just to this place but to everything.

A blackbird shrilled, squawking at them from a branch just above their heads. Judy's body jerked backward, away from his.

"Sorry," she said, with a little shiver.

Victor leaned forward again, but she didn't move. He wanted to go back to where they were just a moment ago. He wanted more. He wanted to say so, but he couldn't. Though they were sitting in a patch of sun, there was a chill in the air, and she was wearing only a thin white cardigan and old dungarees wet at the knees from kneeling in the grass. It was the same sweater she'd worn that day in the chapel when she went to hear him play.

"What's wrong," he said. "Is it Donny?"

She shook her head and crossed her arms.

Looking up, Victor silently cursed the blackbird staring down at them, though the presence of birds in a recent dream made him wonder if its sudden appearance might mean something.

In the dream, he was performing Chopin's Polonaise in A Major in front of an audience of white-haired men dressed in black tuxedos. He was wearing one, too. Sweeping the tails of his coat behind him on the piano bench, he raised his hands in the air and struck the keys, making them ring. He could feel the vibration of the chords as he played a song he could no longer remember. When he was done, the audience rose to its feet and burst into applause.

Turning from the broad body of the grand piano, he faced the sea of sober suits whose claps gave way to cheers of "Bravo! Bravissimo!" before transforming into birdsong. The men were gone and in their place was a flock of black birds whose species he couldn't identify. Then the riot of their chuck-chuck voices pierced the skin of the dream and woke him.

What if the blackbird had been sent to interrupt this kiss for a reason? What if it was telling him that to be a musical success, he'd have to forget about Judy?

By the time they got to the cafeteria for dinner, Donny and Manny were already eating. Manny gave them a little wave when he saw them weaving through the dining room, but Donny kept his eyes on his plate, lifting his chin in brief acknowledgment only when they sat down. When Donny acted cold like that, Judy usually tried to coax him out of it by cracking a joke or touching his hand. This time, she ignored him and started to eat like nothing was wrong.

Victor tried to make conversation, telling everyone about his dream.

"My mom told me a story about blackbirds once," Donny said. "A husband gets separated from his wife, so they make a bridge in the sky for them to meet every day."

"Magpies, not blackbirds. And they only do it once a year," Victor corrected him. "You're such a jook-sing."

"What's that?" said Judy.

"A bamboo pole or something," said Donny. "Just a stupid Chinese saying."

"It's what people call you if you're Chinese, but you were born in America," said Victor. Bamboo was hollow, he explained, but it had different sections inside, and if you poured water into one end, it couldn't come out the other. The saying meant American-born Chinese kids had both American and Chinese parts, but they'd always be at odds, unable to come together. It wasn't true for everyone, but Victor thought it was for Donny.

"Stupid, like I said." Donny opened his windbreaker, giving them a quick glimpse of the flask he'd tucked in its inside pocket. "You guys coming?"

Sometimes after dinner, they'd all go to the levee to watch the sunset, and more often than not, Donny would bring something to drink. Since his stash from the bonfire had run out, he'd talked one of his housemates into getting him a few more bottles of whatever he was buying, with an extra ten percent on top to keep his mouth shut.

Victor had to make up for the hours of piano practice he'd lost since he spent the afternoon with Judy. He shook his head, and Judy did, too, surprising him. Under the table, her knee touched his, and he felt a million soda bubbles fizz inside him. Regardless of the dream and the blackbird in the pecan grove, and whatever they might mean, she still had this effect on him. She caught his eye and flashed him a small, secret smile. Returning it, Victor imagined a glow rising around them as the spark from their kiss reignited.

OVER THE COURSE of the next week, Victor gathered more sacks of pecans, so many that he got ten dollars for them at the canteen, which sold what they couldn't use in pralines and pies to some of the grocers in the area. Hank, who ran the place, didn't question why the stores were willing to buy Carville's pecans when so many other companies were too scared to do business with them. The Coca-Cola trucks, for instance, refused to pick up their empty bottles, even though the factory always sterilized them before reuse. Over the years, there got to be so many left inside the fence that green glass bordered all the gardens as patients took matters into their own hands.

Along with the sack of pecans Victor sent to Ruth, he'd written her a note: "These are the best pick-ahns you'll ever eat, I do declare. Happy Thanksgiving from the Deep South!"

A week later, he received a package from her with a reply.

"Thank you for the pea-cans," she wrote. "What a treat! Your father, the baby, and I are enjoying them immensely. I'm sending you some of the rugelach you like. I hope they survive the journey. Is it warm there right now? Your painting of the Mississippi has been given pride of place in the kitchen, where I'm looking at it as I write. You seem to have a gift for art as well as music! Please remember to send me a list of the songs you're working on so I can get the albums, though I'd much rather hear you play them yourself. It's starting to get chilly here in the Big Apple. We miss you, our very own Huckleberry Finn."

Victor bit into a rugelach, the flaky dough and swirl of raisins and walnuts filling his mouth with sweetness. Ruth had introduced him to a lot of different foods over the years. Every time he went over to her place, she'd have a tall glass of milk and a plate of something—poppy seed bagels stuffed with cream cheese and chives; American cheese sandwiches on white bread, skillet-fried in butter and cut into triangles—waiting for him on the table. Sometimes Ruth would eat with him, too, but if she wasn't hungry, she'd sit down with a cup of coffee and a pack of Lucky Strikes, praising him when he remembered to light them for her "like a gentleman," cupping his hand around her mother-of-pearl lighter.

Once, a few years ago, Ruth had set a plate of hamantaschen cookies in front of him, a dozen triangles filled with jam. Encouraging him to try an apricot one, she'd stirred sugar into her coffee, the teaspoon clinking against her blue-and-white bone china cup.

"That's pretty," he said.

"It was my grandmother's, brought all the way from Russia. She liked things from China, too," Ruth said with a wink.

Victor smiled at first, thinking she was referring to him, but when he realized she meant his father, his smile faded and a deep mulberry flush climbed from the collar of his sweatshirt to his face. He tried not to think of her as Ba's mistress. Unlike Henry, he could barely remember seeing his parents in the same country, let alone in a marriage, so it wasn't hard for him to separate his life with just Ma from his life with Ba and Ruth. But her joke had broken down that wall, bringing Ma into the room, making him feel like he was betraying her.

As grateful as Victor was for Ruth, for all the ways she showed him how much she cared about him, the fact that he couldn't tell Ma any of the things he told her—about music and Carville, the most important things in his life—was filling him with guilt and resentment. Guilt toward Ma and resentment toward Henry and Ba and the whole situation, made worse now by the engagement, the baby, and the move to LA. If he was honest with himself, he had to admit that he resented Ruth, too.

Of course some of this was Ba's business and it wasn't his place to tell, but was it true that Ma wouldn't come to America if she knew he had Hansen's? Would she really be so devastated that she'd stay away? At first, when Henry had warned him against telling her about his condition or Carville, he'd taken his word for it, too afraid to question him. But over time, he started to wonder if Henry was mistaken. It was getting harder, too, to think of things to write to Ma without giving himself away. She was beginning to catch wind that something was wrong, and she wouldn't let it go.

"Son," she wrote, "I am very worried about you. I think you are not telling me something and your father and brother are hiding it, too. I am your mother. I love you more than anyone will ever love you in this world. Please tell me, no matter what it is."

"Everything is fine, Ma. I promise," Victor tried reassuring her, and when that didn't work, he started to avoid the subject.

When they were younger, he and Henry were convinced that Ma could see inside them, that she knew everything they thought and did just because she'd given birth to them, but as he got older, Victor learned that being known didn't just happen on its own. You had to be present with someone, close in a way that wasn't necessarily physical, like the ritual he and Ma used to have of meeting each other in their imaginations. He still had that feeling of closeness with Ruth, but with Ma, it was gone.

Victor had already been through so much without her knowing and finally, with his negative test results stacking up, he had a solid chance of recovery. How could he tell her now? How could he explain why he'd been lying for all this time? Plenty of people at Carville lied from the moment they arrived, disappearing inside other names, other identities. They made it seem normal, even noble, because they were doing it to protect their families, but Victor couldn't see how they didn't lose a part of themselves in the process. How could you get close to anyone if you were pretending to be someone else? It didn't matter that there were people around all the time. If you didn't let them really know you—the things you cared about, the things you'd been through—you'd be alone.

TWENTY

It was a slow Saturday afternoon and the postman had just come, leaving behind a trail of slushy footprints across the shop floor. Ruth watched Sam's spine go rigid and was about to pass him the mop when she spotted the red-and-blue border of a stained, stamp-covered airmail envelope in the stack of bills he was holding. She froze, reminded of the ones she'd received from Europe during the war, telling her the very worst news, and held her breath as he unfolded the translucent letter.

"It's Mei Wan," said Sam, not looking up. "Old Mrs. Chin is dead."

"Your mother?"

"She is *not* my mother," he snapped, making her flinch. He took a breath and softened his voice as he continued to translate. "Mei Wan says she has enough money for the burial, but then she wants to be reunited with her sons. She says she has done her duty as a daughter-in-law and now she is free."

"I see," said Ruth, though she didn't, really. Somehow she'd never considered the possibility that this would happen. Over time, with the lulling effect of distance, she'd begun to think of Mei Wan as existing on much the same plane as her own mother, long dead and unknown to her. But clearly China and death weren't the same at all.

"Her parents are gone and she has no relatives nearby. It has been hard for her. The war and now the revolution. It makes sense to leave." He refolded the letter and placed it carefully on the counter as if he were handling a grenade.

"So, what now?" she said, as much to herself as to Sam, the plans they'd made seeming suddenly fragile, capable of being undone by a single piece of paper.

After avoiding the subject of Sam's first wife for so long, the conversation felt utterly surreal. How could this woman on the other side of the world affect her life so profoundly? But here she was, discussing Mei Wan's wants and needs, wondering how she should negotiate them with her own. The situation was so absurd that she wasn't even angry, at least not right now. And even if she was, it wasn't Mei Wan's fault.

"I don't know. She has a sister in Hong Kong. Maybe I can pay for her to live there." He scratched at a pink patch of skin on his cheek, irritated from shaving with only soap at her place that morning. "But she wants to be with the boys. That was part of our bargain."

Ruth's throat burned as a wave of acid rose up from her knotted stomach.

"When I left with Henry and Victor, we agreed that she would stay to take care of Mrs. Chin, but I said I would bring her to America once the old woman was gone. War Brides Act." Sam's eyes refused to meet hers.

"I have to sit down," said Ruth.

He dragged out a stool from behind the cash register. When she sat on it, she closed her eyes, feeling a headache come on. It was one thing to accept that Mei Wan should be provided for—and even that wasn't exactly easy—but it was another thing entirely to find out that Sam had promised to bring her here. How could he have kept such a secret for all these years? How could he have spent these last few months making plans for their wedding, their baby, their new life in Los Angeles, and not say a word? Ruth felt dizzy, her mind reeling, trying frantically to catch up, to understand what was happening. Her life as she thought it was—as she thought it would be—had just been upended like a table and everything was crashing to the ground.

"Henry can take care of her since he is staying," said Sam, as if that would solve the problem. "I asked him to go to LA with us, but he said no."

"You did what?" Ruth's voice went up by an octave, loud and shrill in her own ears.

Assuming that Henry was still involved with his boss's wife, Ruth knew he wouldn't want to go to California with them, but that wasn't the point. It was the principle of the thing. When she saw Henry and that woman together at the print shop last winter, she couldn't believe it. What a hypocrite he was, judging her so harshly when he was doing something even worse. At least she wasn't taking Mei Wan's money and betraying her right under her nose. It wasn't even a betrayal as far as she was concerned.

On the subway ride home, she thought about telling Sam, imagining his expression, his eyebrows flying up with shock, and the deep satisfaction she would feel, the vindication. She was so sick of the way he was always propping Henry up, making excuses for him, especially when he'd been more disrespectful to her than ever. She'd thought it was because of Victor, because she'd been in favor of Carville, but somewhere between Times Square and Harlem, it dawned on her that the real reason might have been his affair. If that was the case, then telling Sam would not only make Henry hate her more, but it would drive a deeper wedge between father and son. Shame and guilt made people do terrible things, things that hurt themselves as much as others. No good would come of it, so she kept her mouth shut.

Ever since then, when Henry made her angry, she was tempted to let it slip, but she stopped herself, for Sam's sake. And knowing what it was like to love a married person—the isolation, the secrecy—she even found herself feeling sorry for Henry sometimes.

Maybe it was irrational, but a part of her expected something from Sam for this, more loyalty, perhaps, and certainly honesty about things that affected her. She was protecting him and his relationship with his son, so why wasn't he protecting her now?

"He has no other family here," said Sam. "What was I supposed to do? He is my son."

It was on the tip of her tongue to say Victor was his son, too, and he had no problem leaving him in Louisiana, but that was a sore spot she thought best to leave alone, for now.

"You were supposed to talk to me first. If I'm going to be your wife, then I should have had a say in this."

"I did not ask him to live with us in LA," Sam offered in the tone he used when he was trying to placate her.

"Well, thank heaven for small mercies. But we have to decide things together, okay?" She tried to tell herself he hadn't meant to cut her out; he just wasn't used to answering to anyone. But her mind went straight to what else he might be keeping from her, the worst possible things—unpaid debts, another woman, another child. Pregnancy was making her paranoid.

Sam nodded, holding up his palms in a gesture of assent and she decided to let it drop. There were bigger issues at hand, namely Mei Wan.

Ruth pictured her, the tall, unnervingly pretty woman from the sepia portraits she'd seen, the first wife of the man she loved, the mother of a boy she loved and a young man who hated her. She imagined the shop bell ringing one day and seeing her there, on the threshold of the laundry, worn out and rumpled from her journey, with a battered suitcase in her hand and a beatific smile on her face.

"Where are my boys?" she'd ask. And then what would she and Sam say?

"It's too bad she won't be able to see Victor right away. I wonder if she could visit him somehow," Ruth said now.

"She doesn't know about Carville," said Sam, setting his jaw. "I know what you're going to say, but what good would it do to tell her? You cannot solve every problem by talking about it. How was I supposed to know she would want to come now?"

Ruth shook her head, too stunned to answer him. Maybe she wasn't being paranoid after all. If Sam could lie to Mei Wan about something as important as her own child, then why wouldn't he lie to her about any number of things?

A blade of afternoon light caught the silver strands in Sam's hair as he squeezed his temples between the heels of his hands, her silence seeming to make him nervous. "If she comes, I will, of course, explain about Victor. And I will repay her no matter what. A man of honor always settles his debts."

"Are you kidding me?" Ruth rolled her eyes. "You think sending for her will make you honorable? Or make up for running off with me?" Sam raised his head and gave her a look. "Oh. Of course she has no idea about me."

"I know I am not an honorable man," he began in a conciliatory tone, "but who knows what she has been doing in China?"

"She's been taking care of your mother, that's what."

"I told you she is not my mother!" he snapped. "It is true, Mei Wan has been a good daughter-in-law, and I owe her for that. But I did not force her. When Mr. Chin died, she agreed to stay. This is not what you think. It is a matter of duty, hers and mine. She is the mother of my sons, and I am simply trying to do the right thing."

Ruth snorted. The right thing would have been to divorce her years ago, but Sam wouldn't see it that way.

"Okay. So maybe those are not the correct words." He cut his eyes at her. "Maybe there is no right thing. Maybe it is only possible to do the better thing."

"What does that even mean? You want us to all live together like one big happy family?"

"Let's stop talking about it now," said Sam, clearing his throat. "Please. It is bad for the baby."

Ruth sat up and squared her shoulders. She wasn't about to let him use the baby to get out of this. "If not now, then when? You didn't do anything when Henry dropped out of school. When Victor got lesions, you wouldn't have done anything then either if I hadn't stepped in." She picked at a bit of dry skin on her lip and went on. "Old Mr. Chin said go to America, so you went. Uncle Sam said go fight the Nazis, so you fought. You never want to make a choice. So why don't you just flip a coin? Me or her?" The piece of skin came off, and she tasted iron as her lip began to bleed. "Bet you thought this would be easy as long as it didn't cost you anything."

"I am not afraid of the cost," Sam barked. "I will pay for my child."

"That's not what I mean." She was on her feet now, pacing the shop floor like a cat. There were so many things she thought she knew about him, things she'd just assumed. Were any of them true? Maybe she'd just filled in the blanks with whatever she wanted to believe. Maybe he didn't even love her. She was just there, across the street, a convenience until now. She stopped and looked him dead in the eye. "If you only want me out of duty, then I don't want you."

"I can tell her to go to Hong Kong. Say it and I will not send for her." Sam reached out and grasped her hand.

"No." She yanked her hand away. "I won't let you make this my fault so you can blame me for it later, just like you blamed me for what happened to Victor. You would just end up hating me." She turned away, looking out the window where the midwinter sun was setting fast.

"Maybe there is another way," he said in a quiet voice. She had to admit he was good at thinking on his feet as he began to paint her a picture: Mei Wan would come to New York and they'd stay, too, keeping the laundry and moving into Ruth's apartment. "Everything will be the same. And I can find her another place if you don't want her here."

"Are you joking? Nothing will be the same. It makes no difference if she's across town or across the street. She'll be in our lives. And the baby will be here." Ruth put her hands on her belly, clutching it.

"I will take care of you," he said. "You can stay home with the baby."

"We can't afford that. And what about our plan? I mailed the loan application to the VA already and I gave notice at work."

"I don't know what you expect me to do." Sam shook his head.

"Well, you know what they say about expectations," said Ruth in her vaudeville-comedian voice. "If you keep 'em low, you'll never be disappointed." She gave a bitter laugh, but it caught in her throat.

Sam pulled her up to face him and held her hands between his. "Everything will be all right, because I love you," he said, tweaking the Dickens quote, "against hope, against happiness, against all discouragement that could be."

"So you like to read," she said, her lips quirking up at their well-worn joke.

Their eyes met, and Ruth felt the tension in her diaphragm release. Her shoulders began to shake and he opened his arms. She fell into them, planting her forehead on his shoulder, her hands over her mouth, so the neighbors wouldn't hear her cry.

"I will fix this," he whispered into her hair. "I promise you."

As she stood there, letting him hold her, she thought maybe it was over, this storm. Maybe, like their arguments in the past, they'd find their way back to each other in bed. The sun would rise the next day and things would feel normal again.

Outside, Ruth could hear the car horns honking and the El rumbling into the Allerton Avenue station. It was rush hour. Dusk had fallen, the bit of sunlight gracing the laundry long gone and, though Christmas was over, the neighbors' decorations were still blinking, on and off, on and off, in her building across the street.

Together, they made their way to the bed in the back room, where she tugged the thin chain on the lamp, the clink of it against the brass base breaking the silence in the room, the bulb casting a circle of golden light around them.

"I'm tired," she said, squinting against the glare as he held her from behind, with his hand on her belly, on the baby.

This time, there would be no lovemaking. Sam seemed tired, too, too tired to notice that behind her closed eyes, she was, in fact, far, far, away.

TWENTY-ONE

Shortly after the New Year, a wave of sudden warmth swept through the state of Louisiana, causing a fake spring that lasted more than a week. Confused, the winter-tight buds began to open on the trees and the early bulbs inched out of the ground, pushing toward the sun. One night, a storm came, freezing all those tender new leaves and burying the flowers under six inches of snow. Carville awoke to the unfamiliar music of icicles turned into wind chimes by the breeze coming off the Mississippi. Transparent spikes decorated the eaves of the buildings while tiny crystals frosted the beards of the Spanish moss on the oaks. Down by the lake, the weight of the ice dragged down the branches of the weeping willows, making them bow even lower to the water.

But after a single, glorious day of snowmen and snowball fights, the flakes that had been so perfect when they fell were ruined, first by sleet, then rain, and finally the piss of animals around the trunks of the trees where pockets of bare ground showed through, dark and muddy. It reminded Victor of how, after the big, magical blizzards in the Bronx, all that was left once the snow melted was dog shit, uncollected trash, and disappointment. Maybe that was how this time of year felt to everyone, after the holidays and the New Year had passed, after the presents had been opened and the celebrations were over and, with them, the expectations of the season. For Victor, though he didn't talk about it, the letdown seemed even worse this year, his second one separated from his family.

He thought of Ava on the outside and wondered if she'd gotten what she'd hoped for. Was she married yet? Was she living on a ranch? Would she keep her word and send for Manny? Something about Ava reminded Victor of Henry. They were both willing to do whatever it took to get what they wanted and were good at getting other people to help them. Victor only hoped that he and Manny wouldn't wind up paying for it. They kept waiting for news, for some kind of message or sign, either from Ava herself or Manny's family, but in the months since her escape, there hadn't been a peep.

It was the sixth of January, celebrated as Twelfth Night or Epiphany at Carville, a feast day twelve days after Christmas. The Catholic church bells were ringing and the winter birds responded to the Westminster chimes. Victor looked up at the trees as he walked to school, spotting two bright red cardinals and a raven joining their song. Today, they were performing the scenes Mr. Harland's class had been working on from Shakespeare's *Twelfth Night*. Victor didn't have too many lines, but his stomach was in knots.

The walls of the Quonset hut were still decorated with the New Year's posters from their school contest, which Manny had won with a collage of the Times Square ball drop, specks of bright confetti forming the year "1956" against a black-painted night sky. On the eve of 1954, the year he was diagnosed, Victor had finally been allowed to tag along with Henry and his friends to watch the ball drop, but standing around for hours in the cold, getting jostled by a crowd of drunks, wasn't his idea of fun. Manny was already at Carville by then, but Victor imagined what a good time they'd have had if they'd been there together instead.

The desks were arranged in a semicircle as an homage to the stage at Shakespeare's Globe Theatre. As the class settled into their seats, Mr. Harland handed back the term papers they'd written on *The Great Gatsby* worth twenty percent of their final grade in English. Glancing to either side of him, Victor wasn't unhappy with the B at the top of his paper compared to Manny's B-minus and the A-minus

Judy had. Donny was sitting two desks away, so Victor couldn't see what he got, but since he'd immediately stuffed his paper in his bag, he wouldn't have been able to anyway. Judy shot Donny a questioning look. He gave a tiny shake of his head and turned to face the teacher.

Mr. Harland was explaining that the church had based Epiphany on the ancient Roman festival of Saturnalia when everyone would get drunk and the masters would become slaves, and vice versa. The Christian feast day continued the tradition of reversals, with men dressing up as women and women as men. And so, Viola pretending to be Cesario, the male servant of her beloved Duke Orsino, was part of the holiday's theme of turning the everyday rules upside down. The spirit of Carnival, its parties, parades, and excess, spread along with Catholicism to many countries around the world. Here in Louisiana, with its melting pot of French, Spanish, African, and Creole cultures, Epiphany began the countdown to Mardi Gras, the biggest event of the year.

As seniors, Victor and his friends were now in the running for King and Queen of the Mardi Gras Ball, and were in charge of the high school's float in the Carville parade. After learning the papier-mâché technique for his Mardi Gras mask, Victor got the idea to build a giant armadillo for the float, convincing his friends that it should be Carville's mascot. They were the only animals besides humans that could contract Hansen's, Victor pointed out, and according to a Mexican legend he'd read about in Sister Helen's research papers, an armadillo had carried a handful of clay on its back to the god Teotl, who used it to make mankind. As a result, the armadillo represented the importance of life and the balance between humans and gods, war and peace, right and wrong, the earthly and the spiritual. What could be a more perfect choice for their Mardi Gras float? Donny shot down the proposal as soon as he heard it, saying they shouldn't have such an ugly thing for a mascot. Victor was sure there wouldn't have been a problem if anyone else had suggested it, but Donny didn't have a better plan and the others outvoted him.

For the ball, Victor had been practicing a musical number to perform with a barbershop quartet Fernando helped him put together, tapping a couple of guys from the Catholic church's choir. Last year, looking in on it all as an outsider, Victor had thought Mardi Gras was just about wearing a mask, like Halloween, but now he understood it was a chance to try on what it was like to be different, to be bold and self-assured, unafraid of making a fool of himself.

It was a day when the usual hierarchies could be reversed or mixed up, the pecking order from doctors to nuns, to staff and patients; from men to women; from white to yellow, to brown and black. Victor had never thought of himself as yellow before, but that was what his records said he was, so it must have been how most people saw him. On Mardi Gras, maybe he could be free of that, though just like the ending of *Twelfth Night*, everyone had to take off their masks the next day and go back to being themselves again, back to who they'd been.

"It's always like that here," said Victor, not bothering to raise his hand. Unlike the other teachers, Mr. Harland didn't have too many rules. "There are people who were a big deal on the outside and now they don't have anything. And there are people who didn't have anything before, but in Carville, they have the same as everyone else."

"That's true. And in the state of Louisiana, segregation is still the law, but look at our classroom." Mr. Harland gestured around the Quonset hut. "*We* are integrated."

"But the dorms aren't. Otherwise there wouldn't be Negro Houses or the Chinese House."

Mr. Harland gave him a thoughtful look and said it was time to do their monologues.

Victor went last, speaking Sir Toby Belch's lines while staggering around, pretending to be drunk with a pillow stuffed up his shirt: "Out o' tune, sir. You lie. Art any more / than a steward? Dost thou think, because thou art / virtuous, there shall be no more cakes and ale?"

"And with that," said Mr. Harland, after the class applauded, "we *shall* have cake, a king cake, to be exact. Bravo, everyone."

The king cake was a round twist of dough covered in yellow, purple, and green sugar crystals representing gold, justice, and faith. Victor had thought it tasted more like challah than cake when he'd tried it for the first time last year. According to tradition, Mr. Harland cut a wedge for each person and held up a paper crown. Whoever found the Baby Jesus would be the king or queen for the day and could pick a royal consort. Last year, the winner had been Donny.

Mr. Harland poured milk into paper cups to hand out with the cake. Judy ate hers quickly, and Victor was watching her lick the sugar off her fingers when he shoved his last bite in his mouth and bit down on something hard. He spat it out, thinking he might have chipped a tooth, but wiping off the gunk, he could see that it was the porcelain Baby Jesus.

"I got it," he crowed, holding it up.

"Le roi! Victor is the king," Mr. Harland declared.

Victor crowned himself as he climbed up on his desk.

"Speech," said Manny, through the bullhorn of his hands.

Standing there, looking around the classroom, Victor thought of Ruth and the story of how she'd given herself her name, how she'd taken a thing that had meant something bad and changed its meaning by claiming it, making it her own.

"I am King of the Armadillos," he announced, "All hail the king," as the class applauded and repeated after him.

"Who does the king choose as his royal consort?" said Mr. Harland.

"Judy, if she'll have me." Victor extended his hand toward her with a bow.

Laughing, her lips speckled with bright red sugar crystals, Judy took it and climbed up on the desk beside him.

"All hail the Queen of the Armadillos," said Victor, feeling triumphant but trying to carry it off like a joke.

"All hail the queen," the class chanted. "All hail the King and Queen of the Armadillos."

Riding his chair backward, Donny clapped along with the others, but his mouth was set in a thin, straight line. Victor glanced at Judy, who didn't seem to notice. She wasn't looking at Donny at all.

"Le roi boit," said Mr. Harland. "That means drink, Your Majesty."

Victor lifted the cup to his lips and downed its contents in a single gulp. Sliding his arm around Judy's waist, he drew her to him so that they stood hip to hip, and to his great satisfaction, she didn't move away. He cut his eyes at Donny and met his glare with a slow, smug smile.

VICTOR SAT AT the piano bench, cracking the spine of his Chopin book to make it lie flat on the music stand. Before practice, he'd picked up his mail and read the letters at a pew where they were stuffed in his backpack now. One of them was from Ma.

"Your father knows already," she'd written, "but in case he didn't mention it to you, I have some sad news. Grandmother has passed over. She had a long life and did not suffer in the end. It was her time. As they say, the end of one thing is the beginning of another. There is also happy news to share. I have asked your father to make the arrangements for me to come to New York. It may take some time. The paperwork, settling our affairs in the village, the land, the house. But it is finally going to happen. I will see your face again after these nine long years. You were my little boy then, and now you are practically a man."

Victor's body was in the chapel when he read Ma's words, but his mind had floated away, back to China, back in time. To Grandmother brewing him tea from the bitter herbs she gathered for his asthma. Grandmother hoisting him onto her skinny back. Grandmother slipping him extra slivers of fresh sugarcane. She was the first person in his immediate family to die, and though they hadn't been close, a heavy feeling spread inside him. Later he'd change into something white to show his respect. In China, when someone died, their family members mourned for forty-nine days, the time it took for a soul to be reborn within the six realms, but Victor only had one good white shirt, so however long it stayed clean would have to do.

When he thought of China, it comforted him to imagine his village exactly as it had been when he left, fixed in time, never changing, along with the people in it. A part of him had expected his grandmother to live forever, he realized, and now that comfort was gone. But at the same time, this meant that Ma was free. She was coming at last, and his heart leaped. They'd been separated for so long that the idea of reuniting with her was like a dream he'd gotten used to never coming true. Sometimes in his nightmares, she'd be on her way when some catastrophe would strike—a car accident, a plane crash, a ship sinking into the sea—and he'd wake up with his sheets twisted together in a sweaty mass at the foot of his bed.

But now that his dearest wish was becoming a reality, he was worried about what she would think of him after all these years. What if she was disappointed? He prayed that when he saw her again, things between them would be the same as they were before. Time could be oddly elastic, slow and stretched out, but capable of snapping back like a rubber band. He couldn't believe how long he'd been at Carville, for instance, seventeen months already.

Sometimes he thought that if he ever went home, he'd be totally out of sync with everyone there, even if no one else could see it. The person he'd been a year and a half ago was miles away from who he was now, and he'd been deceiving Ma this whole time, every lie, every unsaid truth increasing the distance between them. How could she possibly reach him? He wanted to tell her about himself, not just about the Hansen's but about the music as well. Not what Mrs. Thorne said about his abilities or even what he was working on. Ma wouldn't know or care about those things. What he really wanted to tell her was how it felt for him to play and how much it meant to him. If he could just make her understand that, it might be enough to bring them back together.

In the envelope with Ma's letter was a note from Henry. All it said was, "Tell her you can't wait to see her. Don't say anything yet. By the time she gets here, you might be out."

Victor wished Henry hadn't committed such a dangerous thought to paper. What if he was still stuck in quarantine when Ma arrived? At Carville, nobody would dream of tempting fate like that. Henry had better not have jinxed him. He'd gotten eleven negatives in a row now, but anything could happen between now and number twelve. Herb had told him how, years ago, he'd gotten twelve consecutive negatives, and while he was waiting for the parole board to clear him with one last round, a single lesion showing a small amount of bacterial activity disqualified him from discharge. Victor told himself he wouldn't worry about how to tell Ma until the time came, and when it did, maybe he'd leave it up to Henry. After all, not telling had been his idea.

The pain Victor felt about lying and severing his connection with Ma when he first got to Carville had faded, but it wasn't entirely gone. He was just used to it now, like he'd gotten used to missing her in the first place. If his grief were a sea, then the waves were crashing on the shore less often and with less force, having calmed over time to accept the loss, piece by piece. But now there was the potential for a whole new kind of hurt.

At the piano, he laid his hands on the keys and pressed them down so he could think of something else, so he could forget. Nocturne in E-flat Major, Opus 9, Number 2. On the top left of the first page, it said to begin it dolce, or sweet, and he did, seeing in his head the blue-black sky, the stars, the nearly full moon on the night he and Judy had gone out to the lake back when they first met. Wistful and dreamy, the piece haunted him.

After the soft opening, it launched into a yearning melody rising into a series of romantic crescendos. In some ways, it reminded Victor of a waltz, the architecture of the song, like the walls of a building, sturdy and essential. But then its sections became more complex with each repetition, and the broken chords of the left hand tested his octaves, stretching his hands.

Still, his mind wandered back to the letters. The other one he'd received was from Ruth.

"I'm so pleased you're getting some use out of the record player we sent for Christmas," she wrote. "I confess I don't know half the jazz musicians you've been listening to. I'll have to educate myself to keep up. Fortunately, I am already an Art Tatum fan. Did you know he was blind? I read somewhere that he learned to play at a church, too. How are things going with the barbershop quartet? I wish I could hear your performance. I'm curious about how you'll arrange the song. 'Sh-Boom' came on the radio the other day at the laundry and I turned the volume way up, annoying your father, of course, but it was worth it."

Victor wondered if Ruth knew that Ma was planning to come to New York. She must, unless Ba hadn't told her yet, though it didn't make sense to keep such big news from her. But why wouldn't she have mentioned it if she knew?

When the melody crested, it soared to a fortissimo that felt good to bang out, especially now, loud and strong. The ending felt so free, even instructing Victor to play it senza tempo, without tempo, an unusual thing, he thought, for a classical piece, so he could do whatever he wanted. When the song was over, he played it again, letting the notes wash over him like rain, and when the final pieces of the puzzle fell into place a second time, the sense of release in it was so satisfying that tears came to his eyes. And all at once, he was reminded of how it had felt to listen to music when he was younger, the purity of how it overtook him so completely.

He'd never been exposed to much religion. Though they had an altar in the kitchen when he was growing up, like there was in everyone else's house, Ma observed only the big Buddhist holidays and Ba didn't seem to believe in anything at all, but Victor thought there might be something spiritual about what music made him feel. Maybe that was what people meant when they said they felt the presence of God. A feeling of not being alone, a feeling of being safe. A feeling that there, in the temple of sound he visited when he listened or played, he could let go of what he'd been holding on to so tightly. His eyes darted from the music stand to his hands. When he sat in front of the piano, nothing mattered to him more. It would never change, never leave, never reject or fail him, its eighty-eight keys keeping him anchored to the world.

FOR THE PAST few weeks, Miss Abigail had been telling Victor that his hands were close to being fully rehabilitated, so close that soon he wouldn't need physical therapy anymore. This seemed like a good thing until Mrs. Thorne told him the budget committee had ruled that once there was no longer a therapeutic reason for his lessons, they would stop funding them.

"So you can't teach me anymore." Victor said this as a statement, not a question, as if ripping off the Band-Aid of bad news would make it easier. He looked up at Mrs. Thorne, who hadn't yet taken her seat on the piano bench next to him, bracing himself for what else she might say. He didn't think he could handle it if she acted guilty or sorry for him, which was even worse.

"Over my dead body," she said, with her hands on her hips and a vehemence that Victor wasn't expecting. "We can't stop your lessons now."

"But I don't have the money to pay you." His hands were sweaty with embarrassment. He never talked about his family with her, so she probably didn't understand. "I could keep practicing on my own."

Mrs. Thorne clucked her tongue. "We'll figure something out. With the kind of talent you have, I think you could try for a music scholarship at LSU in a year or two."

Victor's mouth went dry. "Really?" Was she offering him free lessons? Did a scholarship mean he wouldn't have to pay? This was the first time anyone had spoken to him seriously about college. LSU was supposed to be a good school, and it was close by, in Baton Rouge. Mr. Harland had gone there and Mrs. Thorne, too.

She nodded and sat down beside him.

"What if they discharge me? I've been getting negatives since March. Eleven now." How strange to consider staying when he'd spent the past year and a half dreaming about going home.

Mrs. Thorne didn't think it would be a problem since the government allowed patients to live at Carville indefinitely if they wished, regardless of their status and Dr. Morton's economic reforms. That must have been true since Mr. Wang had mentioned once that he was in remission and he seemed to have no intention of leaving, probably because he had nowhere else to go.

"You can move into the dorms in Baton Rouge if you get the scholarship. As long as we prepare your audition properly, I really think you might. My old teacher is on the committee, you see." Mrs. Thorne pushed her glasses up her nose and gave him a knowing smile.

Was that how it worked? Not talent or luck, but knowing the right people. How was that fair? But the fact that Mrs. Thorne thought he was good enough to study music at college and make it a career was beyond anything he'd ever imagined for himself. Victor glowed, letting himself dream for a moment about what his future as a musician might be like, performing at clubs and concert halls, maybe even his own compositions, alone or with a band, like his heroes—Monk, Mingus, Powell, Tatum—who spent all day, every day at their instruments. LSU could be his ticket to a life where he'd never have to work like Ba and Henry at a job he didn't care about.

But as soon as the fantasies played out in his head, a heavy sense of doubt clamped down around them. What was the use of having dreams like these when they so rarely came true for people like him? Ba had always warned him not to be indebted to anyone he couldn't pay back. If Mrs. Thorne was offering to teach him for free, then Ba wouldn't like it if he accepted, though he didn't have a choice unless he wanted to give up. And maybe he should.

He had no idea how he measured up against people his own age on the outside. What if he was only good for someone at Carville and he'd make a fool of himself at the audition? Or even worse, what if they treated him as a curiosity like those sideshow freaks at Coney Island? The piano-playing leper. How could he possibly compete with people who'd been studying since they were little kids? And if he did get the scholarship, he'd always wonder if it was out of charity.

"Let's get to work," said Mrs. Thorne.

Victor turned to Opus 35 of Brahms's Paganini Variations, a difficult piece he'd been wrestling for the past week. So what if it was charity that got his foot in the door? He knew how to work hard, so he would just work harder than anyone else. He would catch up and prove that he deserved his place. He would show them all, or at least he would try.

TWENTY-TWO

Victor was going over one of his audition pieces in his head, Gershwin's *Rhapsody in Blue*, his fingers working the imaginary keyboard on his lap as he waited on the chair outside Dr. Behr's office. He didn't think he was early. When Sister Helen walked by, he asked her for the time. Twenty to four. His appointment was supposed to be at 3:30, but the door was still shut, and he could hear voices inside, the doctor's and Judy's.

He couldn't make out much, but when the hallway was quiet, he thought he heard Dr. Behr say the word "Oriental." Was he talking about him because he was next in line, or was he talking about Donny? Victor leaned forward, straining to hear more, but Dr. Behr's voice had dropped to a low drone.

Judy was talking quietly, too, which made sense since she was probably getting a skin smear test like Victor was. Last month, in tears, she'd told him her latest test result for the first time in a year, a positive after ten negatives in a row. He'd hugged her, a part of him feeling genuinely sorry for her and another part thinking that if he got the scholarship and stayed, she'd be here, too, at least for a while. Who knew what might happen then?

Ever since the day at the pecan grove and especially over the last few weeks, Victor had noticed a change, not only in how she treated him, looking at him with the kind of attentiveness he would have killed for a year ago, but in how she and Donny were acting toward each other. Instead of being joined at the hip like they were when they first got together, Judy had started to play bridge some evenings with the girls in her dorm, leaving Donny to hang around with Manny, usually on the levee with a bottle, while Victor was at piano practice. And they were no longer holding hands everywhere they went; there was a new distance between them, a coolness that would have been normal for some couples after a while if Victor hadn't seen other signs of trouble. Last Tuesday, when he was leaving the post office with a package from Ruth, he saw the two of them emerge from the wooded area beyond the golf course, which wasn't unusual except for the fact that Judy was walking two feet ahead of Donny, with her arms crossed and head down, as if they'd just had a fight.

"Ava," Victor heard Judy say, clear as a bell. A prickle of apprehension made the hairs on the back of his neck itch. Why were they talking about her? He tried to listen some more, but all he heard was the word no.

After a few more minutes, the door opened and Judy came out, looking startled to see him.

"Oh, hi," she said. Her face was flushed. A light sheen of sweat glazed her upper lip. Maybe she'd gotten more bad news, or maybe the smear test had hurt. Even so, she was acting strange.

"Come on in," Dr. Behr called.

Victor stood up. "You okay?" He gave her a concerned look.

She nodded. "I'm gonna go work on the float for a while." They were constructing the armadillo in the rec room at Victor's dorm. "Good luck," she said as Victor opened the door.

DR. BEHR LOOKED pleased with himself as he secured a small bandage over the lesion on Victor's back, the final spot he'd scraped after running his scalpel across the ones on his chest, arms, legs, and earlobes. Trying not to listen to the ominous clinks of the instruments on the metal tray, Victor stared out the window at the palm tree, counting the rows of spikes on its bark.

"There goes number twelve," the doctor said. "If these results are good, we'll set a date with the board. A few more negative punch biopsies, and you'll be home free."

Victor's eyes leaped from the tree to Dr. Behr, and down to his left arm where the bandage had come loose. He lifted the corner of the adhesive with his fingernail, pulled it taut, and smoothed it back down over his skin.

"You are one lucky young man. Never would have thought you'd make so much progress so fast with the sorry state you were in." Dr. Behr shook his head, and turning to the door that connected the examination room to his office, he added, "You can get dressed now."

Victor sat for a moment on the table, listening to the paper crinkling beneath him. When he'd gotten his first negative a year ago, he couldn't believe he'd ever be where he was now, let alone so soon. With every negative result that followed, he'd been sure the next one would be positive, depositing him back at the start like a game of snakes and ladders. Each time had been a surprise, and afraid of jinxing it, especially after last summer's disappointment, he hadn't allowed himself too much hope, so he wasn't allowing it now.

Grabbing his shirt, he noticed that Dr. Behr had left behind a bunch of files in addition to his own. Maybe it was the way Judy had acted so startled at the sight of him, but he could sense that she was hiding something, and he felt compelled to find out what it was. With a quick glance at the door and only a tiny bit of guilt, he started riffling through the stack. At the bottom, he found Judy's and her latest test results were on the first page.

"Patient #2273. Name: Judith Claudia Katz. Age: 17 years. Race: Semitic. Height: 5 feet, 6 inches. Weight: 130 pounds. Mycobacterium Leprae: None Found."

And farther down, in the white space at the bottom, Dr. Behr had written by hand, "Consecutive Test No. 11."

Victor frowned at the piece of paper and read it one more time, checking the date again—this month. How could this be when Judy had told him she'd gotten a positive? They'd always told each other the truth about their results before, so why was she lying to him now? Did Donny know? Were they in on this together or was she lying to him, too?

Victor's hands seemed to belong to someone else as he closed the file and put it back where he'd found it, under the others, then buttoned his clothes, tied his shoes, and let himself out without waiting for Dr. Behr to return. Leaving the infirmary in a kind of trance, he was aware of passing Tony in the hall and waving when he spoke to him, but he didn't hear what he said. Outside, it was drizzling, though he couldn't feel the rain on his face or his feet on the ground, or the six spots on his body where Dr. Behr had scraped and bandaged his old lesions. All he noticed were the drops making tiny dark dots on the concrete steps.

Movement made his senses return. Overhead, he could hear the geese flying back north, honking at one another as he stalked across the grounds. It was still chilly, but the spring bulbs were flowering, blue and white, purple and yellow, like Easter eggs popping up from the earth. Hatching as they bloomed, they opened wide like the mouths of baby birds, with tiny yellow tongues. Last year, Sister Helen had told him what they were called—crocuses, snowdrops, aconite, fritillaria—such delicate names, so vulnerable that a single night of frost could kill them. He did his best to avoid trampling the flowers and when he arrived at his dorm, the music from Judy's red transistor radio floated out through the door of the rec room, Elvis crooning "Don't Be Cruel."

She was alone, the skeleton of the armadillo float in mid-construction, towering over her on a platform, nearly touching the ceiling. Clipping stray wires, she was getting the base ready for the layers of papier-mâché they'd add to it as a group that weekend. She looked up when Victor came in, and a shaft of light from the top of the window struck her cheekbone, bringing it into sharp relief.

"I need to talk to you," he said, keeping his face expressionless so he wouldn't lose his temper.

She tried to catch his gaze, but he avoided it, staring up at the armadillo. "What's wrong?" she asked, her voice going high and thin.

Instead of answering, he grabbed a broom to sweep up the bits of wire and trash on the floor. She was wearing only a cotton day dress, and out of the corner of his eye, he saw her wrap her arms around herself. Normally, he would have offered her his sweater, but not today.

"I saw your results," he said, turning to her now. He watched her eyes widen before falling to her feet. "Why did you lie to me?"

"I'm sorry." She hunched her shoulders. "I had to." It was Donny who was positive, she started to confess in a slow, quiet voice before the words built on themselves and tumbled out. Dr. Behr told her a couple of weeks ago, saying Donny was a drunk, a lost cause, and they should break up. He'd been hiding his results, pretending he was on track to be discharged soon, like her. She thought he was afraid she'd ditch him if she knew, and if she told him she was positive, too, he might come clean. Then she could tell him the truth. But he didn't come clean. He kept up the lie, even promising to stay at Carville to wait for her. "So now we're stuck." She nibbled a hangnail on her thumb, her eyes downcast.

"You could have told *me* the truth." Victor shook his head. "I thought we trusted each other."

"I know." She looked up at him, her chin quivering as if she might cry.

"Next up is Frankie Lymon and the Teenagers with their Top Forty hit, 'Why Do Fools Fall in Love,'" the disc jockey announced.

Victor strode over to the radio and switched it off. "What happens when you leave?"

"I'm not going to. Not until he does. We don't have to go home if we don't want to, right?"

"But that's crazy," said Victor. "Why would you do that?"

"I love him." She gave a little shrug. "That's what people do when they're in love. I'll tell my parents I'm positive, too."

Victor felt as if she'd slapped him in the face. If she really loved Donny so much, then what was going on between them? Had she just been toying with him these past few months? And what about her and Donny—the distance, the fights? He wanted to ask her all these questions. He wanted to demand that she explain exactly how she felt about him and why it wasn't enough to stop her from picking Donny. But all he managed to say was, "I can't believe you're throwing your life away."

"I don't think I am." She took a step toward him, close enough for him to smell the Elmer's Pecan Egg she must have eaten before he showed up. "Promise you won't tell Donny, okay?"

"Why should I?"

"Please," she said, her voice breaking as she touched his arm.

Victor would have shaken Judy off, but he couldn't move or speak, or even look at her anymore. All he could do was nod his head.

THE NEXT DAY, Victor trudged from the infirmary to Herb's cottage in the February gloom. Overcast and humid, the cold seeped through his jacket as he crossed the lawn, the grass yellow and patchy, with holes made by a mole that Herb had forbidden Fernando from trapping. It was blind like him, he said, and had just as much of a right to residence as he did.

In the living room, the Arts and Leisure section of *The New York Times* lay on the coffee table, quartered in a subway fold, giving Victor a little pinch of jealousy. Someone else from New York must be coming to read to Herb, too. Fernando had brought their tea, but Victor wasn't drinking his. He was too distracted, his brain bouncing from music to Ma, to Judy, to the news he'd just received.

"I said, Fernando tells me you're the star of the Mardi Gras number," Herb repeated himself, "but never mind about that. You're miles away. What's going on?"

Victor's eyes drifted up the wall, behind Herb's chair, where a collection of photographs in all different sizes and mismatched frames hung in clusters, Fernando had once explained, according to the Victorian style. There was Herb as a proud, young pharmacist, hair thick and black, eyes free of dark glasses, next to an older man with the same long nose, his father. His mother, plump, dignified in pearls and a big, broad-brimmed hat captured in mid-laugh. Herb and Tallulah Bankhead posing with the cast of a Broadway show. Herb and Fernando at a summer picnic by Lake Albrechtson, watermelon slices in their hands, their arms draped casually across each other's shoulders. Herb had a good life here.

"Well, I got my twelve," Victor said. The lab had processed his results overnight in anticipation of closing for Mardi Gras.

Herb hooted, smacking the armrests of his chair, making twin puffs of dust erupt from the fabric. "Talk about burying the lede. But you don't sound too happy."

He wasn't. Contrary to what he'd been wanting for the past two years, a small part of him had hoped for a positive so the decision would be taken out of his hands. That way, he'd have to stay and he could study music guilt-free, except for the problem of Mrs. Thorne.

He paused, trying to think of the right response. How could he explain without sounding ungrateful? "It's complicated. First of all, the board stopped paying for my lessons when I finished PT. Mrs. Thorne's been coming for free. I told her she didn't have to, but she wants me to try for a piano scholarship at LSU, so she says we have to keep working."

"She's right about that," Herb knitted his brow. "Must be Morton's doing. Damned reforms. I take it that you're staying here to prepare your audition. He may try to put a stop to that, too, but it'd be some time before any decision would pass at the board. Months, maybe even years, if I've got anything to do with it. The name of the game in politics is delay." Herb raised a forefinger in the air. "You should have told me about the lessons, you know. Maybe I could have—"

"You do enough for me already," Victor interrupted, embarrassed for being the cause of a problem.

"Listen," said Herb, "if the administration takes something from you, they're taking it from the rest of us, too." Victor remembered his very first day, when Herb had told him they were all in the same boat. "It's too late to get your funding back from the board, but there's something I can still do. I'll be taking care of your lessons from now on, no ifs, ands, or buts."

"What?" He already owed Herb so much. It was because of him that he'd gotten his lessons in the first place. How could he take his money, too? If Ba knew about this, he'd wring his neck before dying of shame. A ticklish feeling Victor couldn't quite recognize welled up in his chest. He shook his head, but of course Herb couldn't see that.

"I should have said no whats, too," said Herb. "I've got some money squirreled away. But this isn't charity, it's a scholarship, okay? The sooner you get used to accepting those, the better." Victor thought of the first time he'd played one of his own arrangements for Herb at the chapel, an homage to Monk's "'Round Midnight." Sitting in the pew where Judy had cried on Donny's shoulder, Herb had cried, too, silent tears of pride streaming down behind his dark glasses. He stuck out his hand now and said in a mock-formal voice, "Congratulations on being the first recipient of the Victor Chin Music Fund."

Victor laughed. He couldn't help himself. But at the same time, he began to tear up. From relief, from gratitude, from the shame of needing help. From wanting the lessons so badly that he had to say, "Thank you, Mr. Klein."

Herb's hand was like a very large C cupped around his, with long fingers and cool, dry skin. He imagined it could have once reached tenths or even elevenths on the piano with ease. Herb squeezed a bit before letting go and Victor fell silent again.

With the problem of his lessons solved, the most difficult choice was still in front of him, and he wasn't used to having many at all. Leaving Ma behind and sailing to New York hadn't been a choice. Not his, anyway. And going to Carville hadn't been much of one either. But now it was up to him to decide whether he should stay for his music or go home for Ma. The choice was his and his alone.

"There's something else," he said. "It's my mother. She doesn't know I'm here."

Herb looked confused. "Doesn't she send you all those nice care packages?"

"Those are from Ruth . . ." Victor hesitated, not sure what he should call her, before settling on "my father's fiancée."

Herb made a sound in his throat. Victor examined his face, and seeing no judgment there, he decided to tell him everything: that Ma was in China and didn't know about Ruth or his condition or Carville; that he'd been lying to her, not only since he got here, but since he first set foot in New York. He'd never put the full scope of the situation into words before, not even to Judy, who knew only bits and pieces. He'd been carrying his secrets for so long that he'd stopped noticing their weight.

"I can understand your discretion about Ruth," said Herb, "but why not tell your mother what's happening to you?"

"My brother made me promise not to, but I'm pretty sure she knows something's going on. Now she's coming to New York and he thinks I'll be discharged before she gets there, so there's no point. But I don't know what to do if I stay."

"When, not if," Herb corrected him. "No reason why you can't make a quick trip home before you get down to work here." He raised his teacup in a little salute as if the problem had been solved.

"What if she needs me?"

"First things first. Come clean and then you'll see what's what."

In Victor's mind, he'd composed hundreds of letters telling Ma everything. But there was a big difference between imagining something and doing it for real. Maybe there was no such thing as a good choice and the best he could do was pick the better choice out of two bad ones.

To VICTOR's SURPRISE, his letter came out all in one piece, the words finding their places on the page far more easily than anything he'd written to Ma since his arrival. Of course he told her about the diagnosis, the operations, the medications, and the cure, but it wasn't just unburdening himself from his medical secrets that felt so good. He could finally tell her about Carville itself without twisting the facts. He could tell her about his friends, his teachers, and, most of all, his music. What a pleasure to describe what it was like to play the piano and sing for hours each day. To explain how he might have the opportunity to study in college for free, if he worked hard enough, so he could become a real musician someday. He hoped it would soften the blow of not being in New York with her for a few years, though he promised to visit.

"There's a big magnolia tree outside my window," he wrote. "I'm looking at it right now. In the summertime, it smells just like the one at home. Maybe now you can picture where I am and meet me here in our imaginations."

Victor knew it was probably just in his head, but when he put down his pen, he could already feel something shift, not just lifting but clicking back into place as if the thread between him and Ma had reconnected. He only hoped that she'd understand, not just about the secrets but about his studies, too, and be happy for him. If she asked him to go back to New York when he was discharged, he didn't think he'd be able to say no.

It would probably be a few weeks before Henry discovered what he'd done, and even though he'd decided against telling Ma it was his brother's fault, Victor knew he'd be furious. But what was the worst that could happen? A nasty letter? An angry phone call? So what? It would be too late for Henry to do anything about it, and if Victor was staying in Louisiana, he wouldn't have to deal with him much anyway. Now that it was done, he wondered why it had taken him so long to realize this.

Before he lost his nerve, he folded the letter into thirds and stuffed it into an envelope, swallowing the bitterness of the glue as he licked the edges and pressed them down. He flipped it over, and for the first time since he got to Carville, he wrote Ma's name and his old address in both English and Chinese on the front. In the morning, he'd take the letter to the post office and send it directly to Ma.

He'd planned to finish his math homework tonight, but after writing the letter, he was full of nervous energy, palms sweaty, heart beating too fast, and he couldn't seem to calm down. Should he put a record on? It was too late for that. As he drummed his fingers on his desk, his eyes landed on the box of hamantaschen Ruth had sent for Purim. He grabbed it, and without letting himself think too much, he went next door to Donny's room.

Donny was sitting up in bed with a car magazine in his lap, face flushed and hair disheveled, looking like he'd just woken up or had been about to fall asleep even though it was only 9:30.

Victor had heard him come in early, and when the bread-and-milk cart came around, he hadn't opened the door. Maybe he was having a regression. The soft plaid quilt his mother had made lay in a crumpled heap on the matching rug. The night was damp and chilly, with a breeze blowing raindrops through the open window, speckling the pages of an English composition on his desk. It appeared to be a makeup assignment for the *Gatsby* paper he must have flunked. Victor closed the window.

Handing Donny the box of cookies, he was hit with the stench of alcohol. What a slob. Donny wasn't witty or fun like Manny when he drank. He just got sloppy and sullen, and sometimes angry. Victor imagined him a few years from now, still at Carville, drunk and bloated, face as red as a baboon's ass, a loser holding Judy back. Maybe he'd get her pregnant and they'd have to sneak out of Harry, stealing off in the night to get married. A disgusting thought.

"Go ahead," said Victor, urging him to try a cookie. "The black ones are poppy seed."

Donny scrunched up his nose like a picky child and took a raspberry one instead.

"You okay?"

"What's it to you?" said Donny. He bit into the ruby-red center of the cookie.

Victor wadded up the piece of waxed paper from the box and went to throw it away. In the wastepaper basket, the glossy cover of a brochure caught the light, and he could see the word "Cornell" across the top, the name of the school, he remembered Donny mentioning once, where his father worked. Or maybe it was where his father had gone to college himself. Donny was so spoiled. He wanted for nothing and didn't need to concern himself about anyone else. He wouldn't have to choose between going to school and getting a job. In fact, his father could probably get him in wherever he wanted to go. He'd been born with money and looks, and the confidence that came with them. Even with his limp, he was lucky. The Hansen's had left the rest of him unscathed, without a single scar that Victor could see when he came out of the shower in just a towel, which only someone who looked like him would do. He was lazy and had no real talents because he didn't need any. It made Victor sick. And Judy was just as spoiled. Neither of them had a clue about real life or what it was like to be someone like him.

"Listen, I know you're positive again. Judy told me," Victor said. He watched as Donny's jaw stopped mid-chew, and his forehead creased for a split second. "And here's the thing. She's got eleven negatives."

"That's not true."

"Ask her yourself. She just said she was positive so you'd admit the truth."

Donny stared as if Victor had been speaking in a language he couldn't quite understand. He had been drinking, after all. Victor held his gaze until his expression changed, closing in on itself, brows lowered, mouth pinched.

Victor knew he had him cornered now. For once, he had the upper hand. "I just thought you should know," he said.

"Fine," said Donny in a hollow voice. He'd regained his composure. His face was as unreadable as a marble statue's now, handsome but cold and hard. "So, now I know."

With nothing left to say, Victor picked up the box of cookies and went back to his room, the conversation ringing in his ears. He hadn't planned on confronting Donny tonight, but even if he had, he couldn't have anticipated his reaction. So quiet, so detached. Judy would be angry when she found out, maybe so angry that she wouldn't want to have anything to do with him anymore, let alone be with him, but he didn't care. Not after what she'd done. Not just lying to him, but stringing him along. He'd gotten over her once, and that had been hard enough.

There were times when, reflected in her eyes, he saw himself the way he wanted to be—talented, creative, interesting, and kind. Nobody had ever made him feel that way besides Ruth and Ma. Did Judy think he was a dog who'd stay loyal no matter how often she kicked him? At least he'd stood up for himself this time.

He wanted her to be sorry so he'd have a chance to forgive her. And maybe she'd even thank him one day for helping her when she was about to make a big mistake. How could she not see? What did Donny ever do to deserve her, not just her love but her willingness to stay? He was a liar, and love shouldn't be based on lies. If their relationship couldn't handle the truth, then they shouldn't be together.

TWENTY-THREE

M ardi Gras fell on Valentine's Day, and most of the floats had taken it as their theme—Cupid with a bow and arrow, the Queen of Hearts scene from *Alice in Wonderland*—apart from Carville High's armadillo, the Chinese House's dragon, and the Roughneck House's Zulu float, featuring a smoking cauldron filled with dry ice and a ham bone. A group of near-naked men danced around it in headdresses and grass skirts, with black paint on their faces and bodies.

The men were leaping up and down, beating their chests, chanting nonsense words on the slow parade to the ballroom. Victor was right behind them, pulling the armadillo float with Manny and a couple of other boys from school. He watched the men bask in cheers and hoots of laughter until they passed the women's Negro House, where Miss Iantha's stern expression matched her housemates' before lifting into a smile when she saw him. He waved and she waved back, standing up from her wheelchair. Behind her, Tony grinned and gave him a loud, sharp whistle with his fingers. A moment before, he'd been standing with his arms crossed, his face showing no emotion, as if he couldn't see the Zulu float at all.

Every Mardi Gras at five in the morning, Tony would join the Carville Skull and Bone Gang, a chapter of the Black Mardi Gras krewe from New Orleans's Sixth Ward, when they went to the graveyard in white face paint and skeleton costumes to welcome the dawn. As the sun rose, they'd proceed from the cemetery to the dorms as the captain beat his drum with an animal bone to honor the dead, inviting them back into the community for the day. Watching them from his window that morning when the drumming had woken him up, Victor thought of how Herb had said that in the old days, Hansen's was like a death before death.

When the parade ended in the ballroom, the guy dressed up as the Zulu chief jumped onto the stage, where Donny and Judy, the King and Queen of the Mardi Gras Ball, were sitting on a pair of thrones.

Grabbing Judy by the arm, he grunted, "Queen!"

"Get off me!" Judy growled and pushed him away while the crowd laughed as if it were the funniest prank in the world. Donny didn't exactly defend her, but he snatched a cloth napkin from a nearby table, whispered something in her ear, and dabbed at the marks of greasepaint on her arm.

Victor's whole body had been vibrating with nerves from the moment he set foot in the ballroom. When he got backstage, Fernando and the rest of the barbershop quartet were already in their costumes, Zorro masks and green satin suits donated by the Ladies Auxiliary in New Orleans. Waiting in the wings, his hands trembled as he zipped up his suit, but when he slipped on the armadillo mask, a calm fell over him. He was lead tenor of the group. The song and the stage belonged to him. He was King of the Armadillos now.

"And now, we have a special treat from Victor and the Dukes of the Royal Court," the master of ceremonies announced, "bringing you 'Sh-Boom' by the Chords."

Stepping into the spotlight, Victor snapped his fingers, swaying, and launched into the tune as Fernando and the other two singers took the harmony.

The ballroom erupted, cheers and wolf whistles nearly drowning out the music. Victor did a spin and looked out at the audience. Herb sat smiling at a nearby table, tapping his foot to the beat. On the dance floor, Judy was rotating in Donny's arms, wearing her crown and a strapless white dress.

Somehow Judy and Donny hadn't broken up, though the tension

between them was obvious. At meals, they were like a bitter old couple, barely speaking, and Donny had stopped carrying Judy's books after school. Victor was still angry at them both, and while neither of them mentioned the test results again, they were awkward with him in different ways. Donny treated him like he was invisible, averting his eyes and tuning him out whenever they were together. And though Victor had expected Judy to be furious with him for telling on her, she seemed intent on smoothing things over, acting extra sweet and attentive, almost as if she were a little afraid of him. Maybe it was because he'd stood up to her, or maybe she was just trying to make things up to him. He hadn't forgiven her either way, but in the last week or so, the edge of his anger had dulled.

It crossed his mind that Donny might not have said anything to her. Was he planning to keep up the lies and let her stay for him? If he was, then he was even more selfish than Victor had thought. In his heart of hearts, he knew that if Judy dumped Donny tomorrow and said she wanted to be with him, he'd probably say yes, but whatever happened, he was through with trying to compete for her.

In the middle of the number, as he and the guys had practiced, Victor stepped forward and sang directly to Judy, extending his hand to her in a dramatic gesture. She looked up at the stage, meeting his eye with a shy smile, before Donny twirled her away. When the quartet got to the closing chorus, a bunch of other couples joined in, including Manny with the girl he was dating from their class.

Victor did a spin and held on to the final note until he made a closing motion with his hand, silencing their four voices in unison. The crowd exploded with applause. Standing tall in the circle of light, Victor felt invincible, like the winner Ba had named him for, and after the bows, he left the stage in a shower of praise and pats on the back.

Parched and shaking with the adrenaline of the performance, he zeroed in on the bowl of bright red punch at the buffet table. He gulped down an entire cup, barely tasting the the sickly-sweet concoction of soda water, orange juice, and grenadine syrup. Just as he was picking up the ladle for seconds, Judy came up next to him and plucked a chocolate éclair from a tray.

"Your Majesty," she said, stuffing the pastry into her mouth, making them both laugh. "You were amazing."

He could have just said thanks and brushed her off, but he was so happy right now. He felt like he was flying and he didn't want to let anything spoil it. Singing her one last bar of the song, he removed his armadillo mask with a flourish.

Judy laughed again and clapped. "Really. You could be a star."

"I don't know about that, but Mrs. Thorne wants me to try for a music scholarship at LSU. If I get it, I should be able to go. I got my twelfth negative the other day."

Victor thought he saw a shadow cross her face, but she threw her arms around his neck and squeezed him hard. "That's incredible!"

His cheek was pressed against her hair, and he could smell her strawberry shampoo and the chocolate from her éclair. "So I guess I'll still be around, too."

"I'm glad," she said, looking up at him.

"You are?"

"Of course I am."

Strings of lights twinkled overhead between the cutout hearts hanging from the ceiling, catching the delicate silver chain around Judy's neck. It must have been new. He'd never seen it before. The little round pendant resting in the hollow of her throat sparkled.

"You look beautiful," he said in a quiet, serious voice.

She lifted her head and crossed her eyes at him. "How about now?"

He laughed and she laughed with him.

"What does this mean?" He pointed at the symbol stamped on her pendant that looked kind of like the Greek letter pi, though he knew it must have been something in Hebrew.

"It's 'chai,' the word for life. Like when you say 'l'chaim' for a toast."

"L'chaim," Victor repeated, lifting his cup of punch.

Judy laughed again. "Not bad."

"Dance with me?" he said, trying to sound like it wasn't a big deal.

She popped the last of the éclair in her mouth and wiped the chocolate off her lips with the back of her hand. "Follow me."

She led him to the dance floor, and since he didn't have much experience, she took his left hand in her right, and set his right hand on her waist. When Victor looked down at her face, the lightness in his body, in his heart, made him feel like anything could happen tonight.

The band started playing "Rock Around the Clock" and Judy swiveled this way and that, showing him how to do a simple swing. She was a great dancer, somehow able to communicate with a tiny push or pull how and when he should move. He tried his best to follow along and as he started to get the hang of it, his feet went faster and his moves loosened up. He was having fun with it now, and he could tell she was, too. They were dancing together like magic, like people in a movie. When he twirled her at the musical interlude, she whirled and shimmied back into his arms.

Holding her by the waist, he could feel the heat of her body. He let his fingers press into the curve, keeping hold of her, not wanting to let her go. He wanted this night, the dancing, the closeness, the laughter, to last forever.

"Happy Valentine's Day, by the way," he said.

That morning, he'd seen Donny slip a card into her bag, a red construction paper heart with a doily pasted on top and the words "Be Mine" written in his uneven, slanting script.

"Same to you," she said, smiling, her cheeks gently flushed.

Suddenly, Donny appeared, reeking of cigarettes and alcohol. He grabbed Judy's hand and yanked her toward him. Before he realized what he was doing, Victor shoved him hard. Donny staggered, letting go of Judy, but he didn't shove back. He just stood there, his eyes unfocused, a stain on the lapel of his white tuxedo.

"Where have you been?" Judy asked him.

"Out," he said.

Across the ballroom, Victor saw Manny sidle in through the side door.

"You should get him out of here before there's trouble," Victor said in Judy's ear. The three of them were standing stock-still in a crowd of dancing couples, and while nobody seemed to have noticed, that could change at any moment.

"Can you help me?" said Judy.

"Fine." He didn't want to, but she couldn't handle Donny alone. He raised his hand to call Manny over.

With Victor on one side and Manny on the other, propping him up, they half carried Donny to the door. Judy held it open, and they got him outside as fast as they could. Coming from the brightly lit ballroom, the night seemed pitch black, with a chill in the air.

"Better sober him up," said Victor. "Any way we can get some coffee?"

Before anyone could answer, the darkness was pierced by the flashing lights of a police car driving through the front gates with the siren turned off.

"What the hell?" said Manny.

They watched as two police officers removed a young woman from the car in handcuffs and led her into the Big House. The woman had her head down, but even in the dark, Victor knew who it was.

"They've got Ava," he said, glancing at his friends, their faces lit up by the police lights.

Judy looked odd, her eyes wide with an expression almost like fear, her white dress turning blue and red and blue again. Manny was staring at the police car, horror-struck. He turned to Victor, shook his head, and broke into a run.

AVA WAS SENTENCED to thirty days in the Carville jail, where the police and Dr. Morton interrogated her for five days straight. Victor worried that if the whole story came out, he'd be identified as an accessory, but he didn't mention it since Manny had much bigger problems. His parents had guessed what he'd done so easily that he was terrified his cousin would crack under pressure or let some detail slip, maybe about the ID, that would reveal his involvement. But none of that happened. With her marriage hastily annulled and her big chance ruined, Ava was so depressed that she would hardly eat or speak, or maybe that was because of the shots Dr. Behr was giving her for her nerves. Now, two weeks after the arrest, Victor felt like he and Manny had evaded a disaster, as if they'd run out of a burning building moments before it caved in.

The sky was a murky shade of purple, the sun having just sunk into the river where Victor and his friends were sitting around, the atmosphere between them thick and heavy as the fog that rolled in most mornings. Donny had headed there after dinner, stalking off to the levee in a silent huff. Judy went after him, of course, and Victor would have just gone to piano practice if Manny hadn't asked him to go with such a sad look on his face that he had to give in. Anyone could have seen them, but there was no point in waiting until lights-out. With all the commotion around Ava's big escape, the administrators had stopped caring about the usual comings and goings through the fence. As long as they stayed close by, nobody worried about getting caught off grounds anymore.

"Where's the other one?" Donny tilted back his head to catch the last drops of alcohol from the bottle he'd just finished.

"Aren't you pretty tight already?" Manny sighed. He'd just tried to see Ava again at the Carville jail, but she wouldn't even look at him.

"Not tight enough."

Manny handed him the other bottle. They'd been drinking more than ever since Ava got caught, going out to the levee or lake together almost every day, but tonight, it seemed like Donny had gotten a head start.

"What a lush," Victor muttered under his breath, annoyed to be wasting his practice time babysitting Donny again. He was struggling with Bach's Toccata in C Minor, not with his technique, but with his feeling. He just couldn't seem to tap into the heart of the piece, but Mrs. Thorne said it would round out his repertoire, an important consideration for the scholarship committee.

"Why don't you come here and say that to my face?"

"Leave him alone," said Judy. "What's wrong with you?"

"If you like him so much, you can have him." Donny staggered a bit, then righted himself, looking out at the water. The lights on the other side of the river blinked as the dusk turned dark. "I see the way you flirt. You're just a tease."

"That's not fair," said Judy, her voice quavering.

Victor stood up and took a step toward her.

"I know what you're up to." Donny got in his face and made a show of looking him up and down.

"Oh, please," Victor scoffed. "You could fill a book with what you don't know."

Manny stepped between them. "Hey, relax."

"Here." Donny shoved the bottle at him. "I'm going for a swim."

"Don't," said Judy. "Let's just head back."

"Go ahead," said Donny. "I'm staying."

"She's right, man. It's too cold," said Manny. "And what about your leg?"

Donny winced. None of them ever mentioned his leg to him. He kicked off his shoes and pulled his shirt over his head. The broad, clean V of his back gleamed as he strode off toward the water, and Judy started to go after him.

"Let him go," said Victor. "He's just doing it for the attention."

Judy ignored him and said to Donny, "Come on, let's forget about all this." She picked up his shirt and held it out to him.

Donny swatted it away. "Leave me alone. All of you."

"Fine," said Manny, gesturing for Judy to back off as Donny lumbered toward the water. "You need some space? You got it. Just go easy. Everybody cool off."

Donny waded in slowly at first, clumsy with his bad leg. The air was relatively warm for this time of year, but the burning cold of the Mississippi licked his body from his feet to his ankles and shins, making him shiver. As he got farther away from them, Manny and Judy exchanged a look. Victor thought the cold might sober him up and get him back to shore more quickly, but it didn't seem to be stopping him. Donny scowled, splashing and swearing under his breath, though he kept going as the water went over his knees and thighs, hips and stomach. When it came up to his chest, he dove in.

"Where is he?" said Judy.

"It's okay, I see him." Manny pointed to where he'd just surfaced a surprising distance away.

It must have been the current. Victor knew there was no way he could have swum underwater so far and fast on his own. He wasn't a good swimmer, not with the damage to his nerves. And now he was drunk, too.

"You're too far out!" yelled Judy.

"Come on!" Victor shouted. "Don't be such a jerk!"

Donny raised one arm and waved when suddenly, Victor saw him drop as if an invisible hand had yanked him by the ankle. At first, he disappeared for what felt like a long time. Then the river seemed to change its mind and loosen its grip, releasing him. Victor saw him bob to the surface again, but instead of shouting for help or waving, he was still.

"Should we go in?" said Judy.

"Nah, you know what he's like. It's just a tantrum," said Victor in a reasonable voice. "Let him tire himself out." Donny was clearly fine. The water had calmed, and soon he'd get out and be, if not sorry, then at least more sober. He'd probably give them the silent treatment for the next few days, but what else was new?

"Maybe you're right," said Manny.

"Look." Victor pointed. "He's on the other side now. It's shallower over there."

"I don't like this," said Judy, untying her shoes. "I'm going in."

But Victor put his hand on her arm. "If he needed help, wouldn't he be struggling? He'll come back if we stop bugging him."

"He did say to leave him alone," said Manny.

"I guess." Judy kept her eyes glued to Donny.

Donny's arms were frozen on the surface of the water, making him look relaxed, at least from a distance. He wasn't swimming, but he wasn't sinking either. Victor thought he might just float downriver, and he was about to suggest that they follow the current to meet him. But changing its mind again, the river grabbed Donny and pulled him under.

As they waited for him to surface, there was a moment of quiet, like the eye of a storm, noiseless in contrast to their three voices—Judy's, Manny's, and his own—screaming, "Donny, Donny, Donny," when they finally realized he was drowning in silence, so silent compared to the splashing and flailing of their bodies jumping in after him.

Judy dove down, blind, searching in the water with her arms

outstretched. Feeling for his presence, she held her breath as long as possible and plunged over and over around the spot where Donny had gone under. But every time, she surfaced empty-handed. The current had swept him away.

TWENTY-FOUR

Sam selected an album from Ruth's collection, an old favorite of hers, and put it on the record player. The orchestra blared as soon as he set the needle, and he fumbled with the knob to dial it down. She always put the volume up too high. He rolled his eyes, hoping the neighbors wouldn't complain as Fred Astaire began his slow opening to "The Way You Look Tonight."

Sam remembered watching Astaire perform the song in *Swing Time* in a scene where, after wandering from the bathroom to the living room, Ginger Rogers stood right behind him at the piano, with her white-blond hair covered in suds. The movie had intrigued him as much for its plot as for Astaire himself. His character, Lucky, was engaged to a girl, but after getting prewedding jitters, he went off to New York City to make his fortune with the idea of trying to win her back. But then he met Penny, a dance teacher played by Rogers, and fell head over heels in love with her. If the similarity to his own story weren't enough, there was also Astaire's appeal as an actor who, in spite of being neither handsome in a typically American way nor young, became a star and carried his slight frame and long, thin face with an air of elegance.

When he saw the movie, Sam had only been twenty-one, though a husband and father already, and he was inspired enough to teach

himself to fox-trot and waltz from instructional books he found at
the library, in hopes that dancing might ease his loneliness. But when
he went to the dance halls, the only girls who were willing to be his
partner were taxi dancers, and he couldn't afford more than a few
songs a night. Years later, when he found the record in Ruth's apartment, it had pleased him to think of them both watching the same
movie, perhaps even at the same theater, tied together by the flicker-
ing images on the screen, a thin yet significant thread.

Astaire was still singing when Ruth walked into the living room,
carrying two mugs of oolong tea from the kitchen, his favorite.

"Ruthie," Sam said, turning the volume on the record player all
the way down, "I want to talk to you."

She set the tea on the coffee table and took a seat on the narrow
couch.

"You want us to make decisions together, so that is what we are
going to do," said Sam. After going back to the drawing board, he felt
as if he'd solved a very long, very complicated mathematical problem,
and had figured out a way to make it come out even. "I think we
should stick to our plan and go to Los Angeles." He paused, waiting
for her reaction.

"Great." She reached for her mug, and Sam handed it to her, catching her eye. She nodded thanks, but didn't smile. Was that all she had
to say?

"So we move out there, find a place to live, and I go back to New
York to finish up business while you get ready for the baby. Then I
will come to you a little while later." He exhaled, glad to have gotten
it all out in one piece.

Ruth shook her head and frowned. "Finish up what business?"

Sam laid out his new plan. For them to get married, he and Mei
Wan would have to get a divorce. To sweeten the deal, he'd give her
half the laundry, selling the other half to Jackie's grandfather. That way,
she could stay and run it once he taught her how. She'd be so grateful
that he'd have no trouble getting her to sign the divorce papers, after
which he could meet Ruth in Reno. "No contest divorce there, just like
in the movies. Mei Wan does not even have to go. This way, we can
start our new life free and clear. Get married in style. Or maybe right

away in Las Vegas, if you want. Might as well. We will be in Nevada already."

Ruth took a sip from the steaming mug and swallowed even though it was scalding hot. "How long do you suppose this little detour of yours will take?"

"No more than a few months."

Ruth set the mug on the coffee table hard, spilling some tea on the wood. "You'd leave me alone with a newborn?"

Sam got a dishrag from the kitchen and mopped up the spill. Ruth's moods were like this sometimes, like slow lightning, where the streak of electricity in the sky came a while before the boom.

"I am sorry," he said, the words feeling awkward in his mouth. He wasn't used to apologizing. "Are you worried the baby will come before we are married?"

"No," said Ruth. "I'm worried you won't come back. What if you decide to stay with Mei Wan after all?"

"Impossible."

"Don't say that. I'd be out of sight, out of mind, just like she was. I bet ten years ago, you would have thought it was impossible to be in the situation you're in now."

"Ten years ago, I never thought I would be so lucky." Sam smiled.

It was true. From the moment they first met, Ruth had made him feel lucky, his passion for her turning his sense of self upside down with what the French called a coup de foudre, the shock of being suddenly, madly in love. But what shocked him most was how she seemed to love him back without reservations or qualms about letting him know it.

"I love you," she'd said in bed only two months into their affair. Back then, they met mostly at his place because he was afraid of what the neighbors might think if they saw him coming and going from her apartment. She'd paused for a beat to look him in the eye before repeating, "Sam, I love you."

The mattress springs creaked on his cheap little cot as she rolled onto her side, and he knew she was waiting for him to say it back, but something stopped him. He didn't know what it was, because surely he felt the same way. Earlier that morning, when he'd woken up before her, with his thighs fitting perfectly behind hers and her back cupped against his chest, he'd pressed his cheek against the soft riot of her hair, willing himself to keep his breath even so she could sleep for a few more minutes. Was that not love?

"You make me very happy, Ruth," he said, kissing her right where her jaw met her ear, where he knew she was sensitive.

"You should have been a lawyer," she said with a laugh in her voice, but he could hear a tinge of disappointment in it, too. "You're so careful with your words."

Sam didn't know what to say to that, but fortunately, Frank Sinatra's "It Had to Be You" came on the radio.

"Oh, I love that song," said Ruth, the awkward moment seeming to have passed. "Louder."

Sam padded barefoot across the room to turn up the volume. He'd always liked it, too, ever since *Casablanca*. Ruth's eyes roved over his naked body as he made his way back across the room, and when he got to the bed, he pulled her up by her hands, laughing, a jumble of limbs and loose, dark curls. After spinning her into his arms, he held her there for a moment, breathing in the scent of clean bed linens and sex, feeling her skin against his, the warm, smooth expanse of it, before leading her in a slow foxtrot.

She sang softly, off-key into his ear until the song was over, and Sam pulled her down on the bed again. Lying back, she pointed at the window of her apartment at the top of the building across the street whose exterior reminded him of English castles in the movies.

"Before I go to work, I like to watch you open up the shop," she said, her voice suddenly shy.

He smiled, letting his fingertips trace the wings of her shoulder blades.

The next morning, knowing she was watching, he produced a bunch of lilacs—her favorite flowers—from behind his back and displayed them in the window for all the world to see.

"They're beautiful," she said, hugging the bouquet to her chest and inhaling its heady fragrance when she claimed her gift at the end of the workday.

From then on, he would think of those days whenever things were hard and sad and unfair. Casting his eyes up at Ruth's apartment, he would picture her watching over him, imagining the glint of the sun on her window as the wink of her eye, telling him it was okay. And the thought of her, of their love, secret though it was, would go some way toward thawing the coldness of heart that came from carrying a lifetime of so much pain. Now that it was no longer a secret and he was about to get everything he'd ever wanted, he felt truly, for the first time in his life, like a lucky man.

Ruth was looking down at her mug of tea, holding it with both hands as if she were trying to read the leaves.

"Don't tell me you are jealous of her." Sam raised his eyebrow in the exaggerated way that usually made her laugh, but she still wouldn't look up.

The truth was, he'd never intended to take the boys away from Mei Wan for so many years. The thought of doing to her what his father had done to his mother was unbearable. And he didn't want to take away his sons' chance of reuniting with their mother either. Though he tried not to think of her, in his heart of hearts, he would have given anything to see his own mother again, even for a moment. But he didn't say any of this to Ruth now. What was the point?

"She is the mother of my sons and I am responsible for her," he said instead. "That is all."

"But what about our budget? You said you worked it all out. How can we afford to give her half the business? I don't have a lot of savings. And what about the loan? We're borrowing against the laundry."

"So we can cancel this application and get a smaller loan." Sam dismissed the problem with a little wave. "We will manage. Maybe rent instead of buy. And maybe, when the baby is bigger, you could go back to work. It won't make a big difference. Not in the long run."

"Look, the laundry is your business. You can do what you want with it. And I'm not saying it isn't fair, but this is a really big sacrifice for us. You see that, don't you?"

"You know," said Sam, looking Ruth in the eye, "my mother, my *real* mother, used to say if you want something big, you have to make a big sacrifice to get it."

Her face softened as he'd hoped it would, and even though it was clear to him that she wasn't entirely convinced, after weeks of fighting, they were both too worn out to carry on. He'd worked so hard to come up with these solutions, making a new plan that wasn't entirely disappointing or, in the end, that different from their original one. He was doing the right thing, wasn't he? Doing what she'd asked, talking things through with her, asking her before pulling the trigger. His plan was fair and practical for everyone involved. It would be a sacrifice, but in the end, he'd have a clear conscience. Victor would stay in Louisiana for a few more years, hopefully studying at LSU, but if not, his mother would have enough to provide for him in New York. And Henry would probably take over Mr. Lee's print shop someday, so he didn't have to worry about him either.

Once everything was settled in New York, he would join Ruth in California, and things would almost be like they were before, at the very beginning, when it was just the two of them, or even better now that they were going to be a real American family. They were lucky, weren't they, when all was said and done?

TWENTY-FIVE

Henry stared out the window as the subway broke out into the open, hurtling from tunnel to air toward the Bronx. The sky, heavy with clouds, was tinted with mauve, a sign of a late-winter storm on the horizon.

"Shit," he muttered, looking down at the new Italian loafers he'd chosen for work that morning. Hopefully, he'd make it back to his building before the snow began to fall.

A brown-skinned family was sitting across the aisle, a mother and two boys who looked about seven and twelve. The little one was kneeling up on his seat to look outside. As he fidgeted in his heavy winter coat, he slipped, bumping into his mother, who'd fallen asleep with her bags of groceries wedged between her feet. She didn't wake up, and Henry smiled to see the older brother shushing the younger one, thinking of himself and Victor and Ma.

He was overjoyed about her coming to New York, and it was only right for Ba to give her half the laundry. It was the least he could do, though it wasn't nearly enough to make up for what he'd done or what he was planning. Running away with Ruth and starting a whole new life as if his family had never existed was unbelievable. Shameless. A baby and an engagement with a ring, a diamond one, no less. When Henry first noticed it on Ruth's finger, he froze, his body going rigid. His eyes stared so hard that he found himself looking right through it and seeing instead the image of Ma sorting through her jewelry, her dowry, before she sold it.

That was after the war, during famine time when no one, not even an American Army veteran, could send anything to China. Victor was always sick then, wheezing with asthma, and every few weeks, Ma walked miles to catch the bus to Toisan City so she could trade their valuables, piece by piece, for food. Most of the time, she traveled with a group of other women from the village, and sometimes with Cousin Kun, but after a few months, there was nothing left in the house to trade.

"What will we do now?" Grandmother moaned. "Even the tree bark and the grass are gone."

"I will think of something," said Ma.

That night, Henry woke up to her shaking him gently by the arm and motioning for him to follow her outside, where, in the darkness of the kitchen garden, by the melon patch beneath the magnolia tree, she whispered, "Help me dig."

Holding the lantern Ma had brought, he fetched the basket of gardening tools from the shed and they began to turn over the soft, moist soil with trowels. He didn't know what they were digging for, and he didn't ask—it didn't matter. It was just so wonderful to be out here with Ma in the night, doing something mysterious and important.

"Ah," she said when, a foot or so down, she struck something hard. "Here it is."

She quickly unearthed an old almond cookie tin and, prizing it open with the tip of the trowel, checked its contents. As she unwrapped a number of old rags to reveal her wedding jewelry—jade bracelets, twenty-four-karat-gold necklaces, and a Western-looking diamond ring that Ba had brought her from America—it sparkled in the lantern light and Henry's eyes grew as round as coins. He'd never seen such precious things.

"Don't tell," said Ma, tucking the jewelry into her top. "Nobody must know I'm selling these. Grandmother wouldn't like it."

Henry nodded, not daring to question her, feeling somber but proud that she trusted him and him alone.

"Don't be sad," she said. "They are only things." She pushed the dirt back into place.

Early the next morning, Ma set off for Toisan City, alone this time. She came back late with rice, sugar, salted fish, and pickled vegetables like she always did, but something was different. Something was very wrong. She was tired like she usually was, but she barely spoke or looked at them, and she flinched when Victor tried to climb into her lap. Henry never did find out what had happened to her, and he'd been too afraid to ask.

When Ba told him about Ruth's baby, the engagement, and the move, and asked if he wanted to go with them to California, he'd been too shocked to know what to say or how to react. The invitation made him suspicious, as he often was, that Ruth had told Ba about him and Winnie, and this was Ba's way of trying to end the affair, but he didn't seem to know anything about it. Of course Henry didn't want to leave Winnie, so he gave his father a simple no, keeping his face from betraying any emotion though he felt like he was choking. Inside, he was hurting like the little boy he'd been when Ba left for America and stayed away for seven long years, abandoning his family through the war and the chaos after. And now it was happening all over again. Ba had no idea what they'd been through.

Once, during the war, the Japanese had come without warning. The sentinels sounded the alarm after seeing a few soldiers at the village gate, and the teachers rushed the children to the caves in the hills where everyone went to hide. Henry had been playing by himself in the wooded area behind the school and didn't hear the alarm until it was too late to get to safety. Not knowing where else to go, he ran back into the deserted school building.

Ma had already gone with Grandmother and Victor to the caves, but once she realized Henry wasn't with the other schoolchildren, she went right back to the village to get him, even though everyone told her to stay put. Certain that he knew better than to go home, she made her way to the school, where she found him hiding in a broom closet.

"Ah-Ma's here," she whispered. "Come." She motioned for him to get up and follow her outside.

Putting her finger to her lips, she took his small hand and led him to the ditch beyond the yard. It was full of mud and garbage, and smelled like piss, but it was too dangerous to try to go anywhere else now. Ma lowered him in and climbed down after him, covering them both with dried grass and leaves as well as she could. Soon they heard the sounds of boots and breaking glass. With Ma's weight crushing him, Henry tried his best to keep still, knowing that she was covering him with her own body in case the soldiers found them and decided to shoot. He squeezed his eyes shut, not daring to open them, while his ears took in every noise, every shout and gunshot, until finally his nostrils were seared by the smell of smoke as the soldiers set his school on fire.

He and Ma stayed in the ditch for what seemed like hours, even after it had grown quiet and the fire had burned itself out. At sundown, Ma decided it was safe enough to venture out. Their bodies were so numb with pins and needles that they could barely stand, let alone climb and walk. But together, holding on to each other, they made their way, mother and son, to the hills, where the others had stopped expecting them.

That was the way it was back then and that was the way it was going to be again when Ma came, just the two of them making the best of things without Ba, trying to keep their family safe. Victor had always been a dreamer, impractical and impulsive, thinking of no one but himself. But now he was going too far with this music-school plan. Henry was sick and tired of cleaning up Ba's messes, covering for him for all these years, and he could only imagine the explosion when Ma finally arrived. Did it ever cross Victor's mind that he could use some help? At the very least, didn't he want to be with Ma?

After Victor wrote to her behind his back, she sent Henry an angry letter.

"Your brother has finally told me the truth," she said. "Have you no shame? How could you lie to me, and for so long, about something so important? I would have come right away if I had known that either of you boys was ill. Do you not know your mother at all? I am not even going to bother to ask, because I know in my bones it was your father's idea to keep this a secret from me. He is a fool, and you are a bigger fool still to go along with his nonsense. To think of how your poor brother has suffered without his mother to comfort him. It makes me sick. In any case, I will be there soon.

"I am leaving the house and the land to be cared for by Cousin Kun. He will collect the rent from the tenants and handle everything for us, for which we owe him a debt we cannot repay. At first, we spoke about him going to America, too, but in the end, he decided to stay. It is for the best.

"I am overwhelmed with joy to be seeing you and your brother again, but I must confess it is bittersweet to leave China behind. I understand how you must have felt now. I called you my brave little man when you left, but you are truly a man now. It is difficult for me to stay angry. I have waited so long for the gods to grant my wish, for my family to be together again. There can be no sweeter happiness."

Henry would do whatever it took, he promised himself, to make Ma's wish come true. Outside, the snow clouds had opened and big, fluffy flakes were starting to fall. It was too late to save his shoes. Henry buttoned up his coat as the train approached Allerton Avenue and the screeching of the wheels woke the mother across the aisle. He watched her gather her groceries and children, readying them to get off the subway, and imagined her struggling on the slippery steps leading to the street. It was his stop, too.

"Excuse me," he said, standing up. He held out his arms to help her with the bags.

TWENTY-SIX

It was seven in the morning on a Tuesday and Ruth was brushing her teeth when she heard a knock at the door.

Spitting a mouthful of toothpaste into the sink, she yelled, "Be right there!" and threw on her robe.

She left the chain on the latch as she unbolted the door and cracked it open a few inches. "Henry. Is something wrong?" He'd never been to her apartment before, not in nine years.

"No," he said, his face impassive. "I just thought we should talk since you're leaving soon."

Ruth removed the latch and gestured toward the living room, running her tongue over her teeth, the taste of mint and baking soda sharp in her mouth. After he refused her offer for coffee, they both sat down, Ruth on the couch and Henry on a chair facing her. He put his hat on the coffee table, smoothing back his hair, and unbuttoned his gabardine trench coat. Sitting there ramrod straight, with the tension in his jaw the only indication of emotion, he looked exactly like Sam had when they first met.

His eyes rested on her belly. "I should say congratulations," he said, his tone polite but chilly.

"Thank you." She readjusted the lapels of her blue silk robe, pulling them up around her throat. "Of course this is your sibling, too."

"Half," he corrected her. "And congratulations on your engagement."

"You know," she said in a joking voice, "according to Emily Post, you're supposed to say best wishes to the bride and congratulations to the groom."

Henry didn't laugh. "I didn't know that," he said. Ruth twisted her engagement ring around her finger and watched his hawk eyes seize on it. "So Victor says he's coming home soon."

"Really? That's not what he told me. I thought he was staying so he could get that scholarship. He sounds very excited about it."

"Well, our mother's coming now," said Henry, putting his elbows on the armrests of the chair. "Of course he'd rather be with her."

She gave him a sideways glance, leaning back against the cushions and resting her arms on her bump. "I hope he doesn't give up his studies."

"He wouldn't have to if you weren't forcing our father to leave New York."

"I don't see what that has to do with it, and I'm not forcing your father to do anything," she said, shaking her head. "It was his idea in the first place, and he's going to set up your mother at the laundry before he joins me in California."

"I wouldn't be so sure about that if I were you."

Ruth sat up straight, one hand moving over her belly, where the baby wasn't quite kicking but fluttering its limbs. So this was why Henry had come.

"You really think he's going to stay with you in LA? You think he'll just drop everything for you? His wife? His family? His business?" Henry kept his voice steady, controlled, but his eyes were blazing.

"That's not what's happening here," she said, trying to sound calm. "Your father isn't abandoning anyone, including me."

"What makes you think you're so special?" he hissed.

Ruth flinched but managed to gather herself. "Nothing at all," she said. If she spoke plainly, she thought, maybe she'd get through to him. "We just love each other. You should understand that. I assume you decided to stay in New York because of Mrs. Lee. I know how you must feel . . ."

"What did you tell my father?" Henry cut her off, his voice dripping with acid, his eyes as hard as stones.

"I haven't said a word."

"I guess there's a first time for everything." The expressionless mask dropped over his face again as Ruth ignored the dig. "At least you won't have to worry about money out there. He'll pay. He always does. But with two extra mouths to feed, I don't see how he can afford to stop running the laundry. Do you?"

"You know, I don't think this is any of your business," said Ruth, with as much dignity as she could muster, but in her head, she kept hearing Sam's words.

"I will pay for my child," he'd shouted at her when they were fighting.

It had been in the heat of the moment, but he'd still said it. For the most part, she thought Henry was just trying to rattle her, to run her off, but might he also be telling the truth? After all, he'd seen how this pattern had played out with his mother. Ruth could imagine all too easily how Sam might have promised Mei Wan he'd come back as soon as he could, and then, as months stretched into years, and years into a decade, she'd have eventually accepted their so-called bargain. Ruth loved Sam, but she knew him, too, for better or worse.

"Believe what you want," said Henry, with a sour little smile, "but don't say I didn't tell you."

"I won't. And I don't believe what you said about Victor either."

"Look, you've been good to my brother. I'll give you that. But he's not your son and he never was."

"I think you should leave," said Ruth.

Henry stood up, grabbing his hat.

"Goodbye, Henry." Ruth opened the door for him. "Good luck. I mean it."

She could hear the rapid taps of his shoes on the stairs as she turned the lock with a decisive click and sank back on the sofa, feeling suddenly ill. Did she need to throw up? Maybe not, but maybe she should call in sick at work anyway. Then she could go over to the laundry and talk to Sam, confront him, tell him everything Henry had said and get it all out in the open. Or maybe that was a terrible idea. Whenever they talked about Henry, it blew up in her face. And what if he was right?

Up until now, Ruth had told herself that she was the understanding one, the patient one, the bigger person in all of this. What was her crime, after all? So she loved a man who was married, but to a woman who lived across the sea, whom he hadn't seen in years. She'd never begrudged Mei Wan the money Sam sent her, had she? And hadn't she tried her best to do right by her sons? She truly loved Victor as if he were her own child. And she'd tried to be warm with Henry. God knew she'd tried for years. And hadn't she come to terms with giving Mei Wan half of the business even though it would make things harder for them in California?

Ruth could tell herself all these things, and they would seem true in a certain light, but now she had to wonder if she'd been lying to herself. Hadn't there been a voice in her head whispering all these doubts already? Why hadn't she listened? She believed that Sam loved her, but she didn't trust him, not fully, and maybe he didn't trust her either. Maybe she was a fool and he really was trying to get rid of her. Maybe his plan was to string her along from a distance, so slowly that she wouldn't realize what was happening. And if he kept sending her money, he wouldn't even have to feel bad. Wasn't that exactly what he'd done to Mei Wan?

"A man of honor always settles his debts," he'd said.

On rare, uncomfortable occasions, Ruth would look at herself as others might, as Henry might, or Mei Wan. She wasn't much of a cook, but in their eyes, she'd been turning scraps into meals for years. Oh, how ashamed she'd be if she found out that she'd been telling herself fairy tales this whole time. Telling herself she was the heroine and Mei Wan was a distant obstacle when she had it backward. If that were true, then that would make her the real obstacle, the villain in the story of this family, trying to claim a man who was never hers to begin with, and never would be.

TWENTY-SEVEN

Five to two, the clock in the kitchen said. Sam went into Ruth's small green-tiled bathroom, used the toilet, and flushed. Washing his hands, he glanced at the array of bottles and little pots lined up around the sink—makeup, perfume, a tub of Pond's Cold Cream. How did that old ad go?

"She's engaged! She's lovely! She uses Pond's!"

Well, that was true enough. He smiled to himself and went back to the living room. Still not home. Where was she? The narrow Formica countertop was cluttered with bags of snacks, along with a note.

"Dear Victor," it said, "Here are some more peanuts and sesame candies. They were out of your favorite brands, but the man in the store said these were almost the same. I said this in my last letter and I'm probably embarrassing you now, but I'm just so proud of you, for everything you've accomplished. I have no doubt that you not only have the talent, but the persistence and grit to get that scholarship, and someday, I'll be listening to records with your name on them. Your teacher must believe in you almost as much as I do. Music isn't your only gift, Victor. Your curiosity is a gift, too. That, and your sense of joy. Don't ever lose them. Don't ever forget that you're smart and brave, and even if you don't know what to do, you'll know how to figure it out. I'm sure you will have a wonderful life. Love, Ruth."

So, she was sending him another care package. Sam dug some cash out of his pocket and laid it on the table next to the note for her to mail to Victor, too. He put the kettle on for some tea, and sitting at the kitchen table to wait for it to boil, he let his eyes wander across the room to the mishmash of bric-a-brac, milk glass vases, floral teacups, and other tchotchkes on the shelf next to the watercolor painting Victor had sent from the institution, a river scene. What a relief that he was well now, after all that worry. And what an unexpected source of pride he'd become, the first musician in the family and the first with a chance to go to college. Surely it meant their luck was turning. The kettle whistled and, smiling, he switched off the burner.

His good spirits couldn't even be dampened by the scathing letter Mei Wan had sent him after Victor told her his good news, revealing, in the process, everything they'd been keeping from her about his illness. It had been a mistake, perhaps, but his intentions had been good—he'd only wanted to spare her the anguish of knowing her youngest son's diagnosis, which was, for many in China, a fate worse than death. But what she'd said in her letter was right, if he was honest with himself—if she'd known, she would have insisted on being by her son's side. Mei Wan was that kind of mother. And maybe that was one of the reasons he'd kept it from her, too. But she was wrong when she'd accused him of forbidding Victor and Henry from telling her. Somehow the boys had decided to keep quiet all by themselves—he'd had nothing to do with it.

In the painting, the brownish hue Victor had given to the Mississippi reminded him of the Hudson, whose mud-colored waters were teeming with jellyfish and garbage.

A few summers ago, the three of them—Victor, Ruth, and himself—had taken the ferry to Staten Island. At the railing on the upper deck of a boat called *Miss New York*, they'd been standing shoulder to shoulder, with a picnic lunch and three empty Chock Full o' Nuts coffee cans.

"My aunt says she was the first person to greet her and my mother when they got to America," said Ruth as they sailed past the Statue of Liberty.

Sam rested his hand on the small of her back, ignoring the curious looks of the couple a few feet away.

"You docked in San Francisco, right?" asked Ruth.

"Yeah. We were greeted by Alcatraz," Victor quipped.

"Good one!" Ruth snorted and knocked her shoulder against his, making the couple look over at them again.

On Staten Island, they caught a bus to the wetlands where they could harvest clams and marsh snails at Wolfe's Pond Park, just as he and Old Mr. Chin had in the old days. It was low tide when they arrived. Victor went straight to work, plucking snails from the wet stones and dropping them into their cans while Ruth stood watching. Wrinkling her nose, she picked one up and turned it over, examining its slimy underside with distaste.

"Don't tell me you don't like escargot." Sam reached over and patted her on the hip.

"I guess you can still read my mind," she said, with a smile.

"Wait until you try my recipe before you decide."

Later, down the beach, Victor brought Ruth a purplish shell of some kind. Sam watched as she cradled it in her palm, her face animated with interest. He couldn't hear what she and Victor were saying, but to see her so happy, with her hair flying in salty swirls and her bare feet dusted with sand, made him smile. When it was time to go, she was still carrying the shell.

"I read that the Indians who used to live here gathered these to make into beads," Ruth said, holding it up. "They traded them as money. Wampum, they called it."

Sam nodded. "You know, the Indians and the Chinese, we come from the same people. They walked over to America from Asia on a land bridge many thousands of years ago."

"Really?" Victor looked over at Ruth for confirmation.

"I read that, too." Ruth nodded. "A land bridge at the Bering Strait. Your father is right."

Sam thought of that moment now, the way Ruth had backed him up, as a hopeful sign of their future together as parents. One day soon, they would be on a beach again, on a different coast, with a different child, who would ask them questions that they would also answer as a team.

Out the window, a flash of movement caught his eye—down on the pavement, across the street, Ruth was walking in the direction of Allerton Avenue, away from her building and Barker Avenue. Where on earth was she going?

It was unusual for him to see her from a distance, as other people did out in the world, accustomed as he was to being with her in private, confined spaces. He watched her T-strap heels tracking a brisk, straight line as if she were balancing on a tightrope spanned along the sidewalk. Though the window was closed, he thought he could hear the faint clicks of them on the concrete, determined and precise as typewriter keys. She was still close enough that when the wind blew against the voluminous fabric of her old blue swing coat, he could just about make out the swell of her belly. The child. His child. He rolled the words around in his mind.

As Ruth looked to the left and stepped off the curb, jaywalking across the street, Sam had an urge to call out to her, to warn her to be careful and look both ways. He wanted to tell her to always look both ways from now on, wherever she went. With his fingertips, he tapped on the windowpane and then rapped on it louder with his knuckles, as if she could hear him. But of course she couldn't. What was he thinking?

He just wanted to keep her safe. He wanted to protect her and the baby in all the ways he hadn't managed to protect Mei Wan and the boys, Victor especially. Now that he was about to become a husband and a father again, he understood why he'd failed his first family so badly. He'd been so busy preparing for the possibility of losing them that he hadn't let himself love them as fully as he should have.

Sam thought of the war, of the children he'd seen in France and the children in China whose parents had been slaughtered by the Japanese, legions of orphans. He thought of his own parents and tried to see their faces in the window, through his own ghostly reflection, shuffling his collection of ever-dimming memories of them. He would never let this happen to the new baby. Never again, as Ruth liked to say.

He was going to start over and make a real American family, American style, with hugs and kisses, and presents on birthdays, with pleases and thank-yous and I-love-yous. This time, he was going to do it right.

TWENTY-EIGHT

Victor preferred the Mississippi when it was cold. In the winter, the breeze swept away the low-tide smell, and the sunlight that shone through the mist tricked the eye into seeing the color of the water as gray instead of its true mud brown. A few rowboats were docked by the ferry, but otherwise, everything was quiet.

Watching them bob up and down, his gaze blurred and turned inward, seeing the river as it was the night Donny died, as if it were a scene in a movie. He could see the image of three boys and a girl on the levee. In his ears, he could hear the sound of their tennis shoes crunching the broken shells on the shore.

It was an accident. Of course it was. But an icy thorn of doubt pricked his heart as he thought of the night he told Donny about Judy's lie, and the things he said on the levee. A small, stale breeze ruffled the surface of the water. He couldn't look at it now without seeing the black mouth of the river, its undertow, its greedy, groping hands.

Beyond him, the whir of the grasshoppers might have been the distant sound of someone's breath forced into the folds of a pinwheel from the O of their lips. Funny how the ears and eyes could play tricks like that, making something out of nothing.

On the river, a barge was passing, and high above it, a pair of egrets sailed like paper cranes. Today would always be connected to those white wings and the exact blue of this sky. Heading back through Harry to check the mail, he felt so uncomfortable, ungainly, so unlike Donny with his natural ease. Victor hated how his words sounded one way in his head and another when he said them, how they stopped making sense as soon as they fell from his mouth. How his feet landed on the ground, one after the other, so awkwardly when he walked. How some spots on his body, on his back and thighs, were still numb even though the lesions had healed long ago.

The lady at the post office handed him an envelope from the parole board, the report on his final round of tests. Tearing it open right there at the window, he skimmed the page.

"Twelve negative routine skin smear tests performed by Dr. Hoffman Behr . . . Six punch biopsies were made in widely separated areas of atrophic lepromatous remnants on the skin . . . In all sites examined, no acid-fast bacilli were found . . . The Board determines failure to produce M. Leprae in this case to be consistent with procedure . . . Recommendation: Patient #2276's condition meets the criteria for the arrest of leprosy. Discharge granted. Patient's request to remain in residence: Granted."

"Bad news?" said the lady, reading the expression on his face.

Victor looked up and shook his head, feeling like he wasn't quite there, as if he'd floated away like a balloon. A voice inside him was saying, "You should be happy," but all he felt was numb. Finally, the patient behind him in line tapped his shoulder and he stepped aside.

In the afternoon, he was at piano practice when one of the guys who worked at the canteen came in to tell him he had a long-distance call from Henry. The telephone there was the old-fashioned type, mounted on the wall in the corner by the door. In the busy little restaurant, he had to practically yell to be heard.

"Hello," said Victor into the receiver. He held up the earpiece, resigned to the lecture he knew he was about to get for sending that letter to Ma.

"Have you heard?" Henry sounded cheerful, but Victor could detect a funny note in his voice. He didn't answer, waiting for him to go on. "Ruth's gone."

"What do you mean, gone?" Victor was almost shouting, and the two guys drinking coffee at the counter swiveled around in their seats to see what was going on. "I just got a package from her."

"The wedding's off. She must be on her way to California by now. I guess she'll have the baby there by herself."

"What happened?" Victor was getting that strange feeling of leaving his body again, but this time, he was sinking. He put his hand against the wall, as if he needed it to hold him up.

"How should I know?" Henry snapped.

"I can't believe it." Victor shook his head. He pictured Ba, alone and ashen-faced at the laundry. And Ruth, waiting in line at the airport with one hand on her suitcase and another on her big belly.

"Yeah, well, I can't say I'm sorry," said Henry. Victor listened to the sound of his lighter and the crackle of his cigarette as he drew on it. "Ba asked me to move back in, but I told him, no way."

"I get it." He didn't think Henry would ever forgive their father after everything that had happened.

"I was hoping you'd say that." Henry paused, taking another drag, and Victor could almost see the thin stream of smoke coming out of his mouth when he exhaled. "I know you have plans to stay down South for your music. Ma said she was proud of you."

Victor's body tensed, the muscles in his jaw tightening. "Are you mad?" He hated himself for asking. Henry had no right to keep him from telling Ma the truth, but in his whole life, he'd never broken such a big promise before.

"Not really. Not anymore. But listen, I need you to come home." In his most persuasive voice, Henry told him that when he was a baby, things had been good between their parents, and if he was living with them again, they might patch things up for his sake. At the very least, he'd stop them from getting a divorce. Henry said he understood how much his music meant to him and promised to help him pay for lessons in New York.

"You don't have to," said Victor. It would only give Henry another thing to hold over his head, and besides, he couldn't imagine studying with anyone other than Mrs. Thorne.

"Look, I thought about whether I should even bring this up, but things have been really bad with Ba and I could use your help. Haven't I always looked out for you?"

Victor thought he could hear a catch in his voice and he couldn't help but soften a bit. "Yeah." He sighed. Even though Henry was trying to make him feel guilty, what he'd said was true. "You have."

"You're almost a man now, and you know what Ba says." Henry paused. "Men have to live up to their responsibilities. When Ma comes, we'll be a real family again. Won't that be something?" Victor didn't think they'd ever stopped, but it wasn't worth arguing about.

After Henry hung up, Victor put the earpiece back on its hook, a chill spreading over his heart like a stain. He wanted to cry, but in the crowded canteen, with the guys at the counter watching, he couldn't.

There was nothing to cry about, he told himself. It had been almost two years since he'd seen Ruth, and even if she hadn't split up with Ba, she would have been going to California anyway. It wasn't like they'd have gone back to living across the street from each other. But now he might never see or hear from her again, and he might never know his baby brother or sister either. How could she just leave without saying goodbye? He knew Ba was the one she'd left, but a part of him felt like she was leaving him, too.

And then there was Henry, being his usual self, trying to force him to do things while making them seem like they were his own choice. What Henry was asking for wasn't fair, but Victor owed him a lot, and this would go some way toward repaying his debt. Maybe Ma really did need him. Maybe Henry did, too. And they had no way of knowing what he was really giving up, or what it would be like for him to leave Carville now.

Outside the canteen, the sky was dark with gathering clouds, the spring rain getting ready to fall again. Instead of going back to practice, Victor turned and ran to the cottages. When he got there, Herb was having his afternoon tea and invited him to join him in the living room.

"Go ahead and pour it in the sink if it's too sweet," said Herb, hearing him drop four lumps of sugar in his cup instead of his usual two. "We've got plenty of tea. Morton hasn't gone and put a tax on it yet."

"It's fine," said Victor, not wanting it anyway, and ignoring Herb's joke. "I just . . ." His voice broke off.

"I know how you feel," said Herb. "Death, unhappiness, suffering, they're just numbers on the price tag of living. But there's good stuff, too, if you let yourself have it. I know you're broken up about your friend, but you've got your whole life ahead of you. When you're in college, things will start to look different."

"That's just it, Herb. I don't know if I can go. My brother called. That's what I came to tell you."

Herb put his teacup on the saucer with a clink and recrossed his legs as Victor told him everything Henry had said. Outside, the vibration of the first clap of thunder shook the windowpane next to Herb's chair. The clouds broke, releasing their burden of rain.

"I'm sorry about your stepmother," said Herb, and hearing him call her that made Victor swallow hard. It was never official, but in all the ways that counted, Ruth had been his stepmother for years. She'd raised him, and now he'd lost her. "Do you agree with your brother?"

"I don't know." Victor slumped down in his chair.

It would be a big sacrifice to move back home, but Ma would need a lot of help. At her age, moving to another country wouldn't be easy. It had been hard enough for him when he was just a little kid. She'd have to learn English from scratch and how to get around, and figure out how things worked in America. As for what Henry had said about their parents' marriage, Victor was no fool. He knew his brother was playing him to get his own way, but if there was anything he could do to help Ma and Ba, then it was worth a try.

"Family's important," said Herb, "but when I say you'd be giving up the chance of a lifetime, I'm not exaggerating. Talent will only get you so far, and Mrs. Thorne's connections with the committee at LSU give you a leg up. You've got a real shot here, and a free ride for college is no small thing. Anywhere else, especially in New York, it'll be a lot harder."

"I know, but I'm going to get a job and maybe I could take lessons at night or on the weekends." Victor cleared his throat. "I'm really sorry. I know I'm disappointing you and Mrs. Thorne. And I'm sorry for wasting your money. At least you won't have to pay her anymore." He shifted in his seat.

"Nothing to be sorry about." Herb gave a dismissive wave, surprising him. "It's your choice and I don't blame you for it. But for your information, the Victor Chin Music Fund is nonrefundable. You won't just need lessons in New York, you know. You'll need a piano to practice on, too."

"I can't let you do that." Victor stared at Herb, at his kind, sad smile.

"Of course you can. And you will." Herb leaned forward, resting his gnarled hands on his knees, the skin over the knuckles hardened, like a shell. "It's wrong to waste a gift like yours. I'm telling you, I won't stand for it. My parents left me some money. I have no children of my own, and Fernando and I have everything we need. Who else would I give it to?" Herb straightened up and said, in a mock-formal voice, "Consider me a patron of the arts. It would be an honor for your music to be my legacy."

Victor's throat was so tight, he could barely choke out the words. "Thank you."

Herb waved him off again. "You know, when I was in New York with Tallulah, I met someone at a party. I think he said he taught at Manhattan School of Music. Or was it Mannes? Fernando," he called into the other room, "do you know where I left my Rolodex?"

On the wall behind Herb's head, a movie-star calendar was pinned on the bulletin board, the days marked with appointments and meetings in Fernando's neat handwriting, with Rita Hayworth holding a bouquet of flowers for the month of April. Victor thought of the calendar pages in newsreels and movies, how they would fly as if blown by the wind, flipping forward to show the passage of time or backward to show you something from the past. And without wanting to let them, the scenes that kept playing on an endless loop, intruding on his days—in the dorm, at practice, at school, at the cafeteria, in dreams—pushed themselves to the front of his mind, taking him back to the night when the river had opened up and swallowed Donny whole, sealing itself over his head like a secret.

Once, when Victor was ten, Ba took him and Henry to the Empire State Building, where, high above the city on the observation deck, he'd warned him not to drop his toy soldier over the edge.

"It could kill someone by the time it reached the street," Ba had said, explaining the physics of velocity, how it built up with the downward force of gravity to accelerate falling things.

Victor had shoved the soldier deep in his pocket and taken a step back, awed by the thought that such a small act could have such enormous consequences.

"I'm sorry," he wanted to say now, but there was no one to say it to. Donny was dead.

Since it happened, Victor had gone over it again and again, what he should have said, what he should have done. He should have taken the danger more seriously. He should have tried to stop him, like the others. He should have let Judy go when she wanted to jump in. He should have jumped in, too. Even if they hadn't been able to save him, at least they could have tried. Instead, Victor had convinced them all to stay put, and by the time they realized he was drowning, it was too late.

"It was me," Victor had said to Manny while Judy was talking to the police. "I said not to go in after him."

"No," said Manny, "you were right. He was so blitzed, he would have fought us."

"You don't know that for sure. He was drunk because of me." Victor thought about how much he'd hated Donny sometimes and how he'd told him about Judy's negatives not out of concern for her but out of spite, to break them up. A part of him wanted to come clean so that Manny could reassure him for real, but all he said was, "I didn't want him to die."

"Of course not." Manny put a hand on his arm and squeezed. "Is this because of Judy? Because you were jealous? You didn't make this happen with your mind, okay?"

"Okay," he said, but he didn't think it was true.

After the police and the fire department left, after all the patients and the nuns who'd stood around watching and praying had gone to bed, the three of them went back to their dorms. As they walked, Victor put his arm around Judy. Her head fell against his damp shoulder, but he felt nothing.

Later, when they found Donny's body washed up miles down

the river, the church bells rang, calling everyone to a special meeting in the ballroom, the only place that could hold the entire Carville community. When Dr. Morton announced Donny's death, a wave of shock rolled through the room, the women gasping, the sisters and most of the staff and patients making the sign of the cross. In the moment of silence that followed, Victor stared at a single spot on the floor in front of him, his hands and feet as cold as he imagined Donny's to be, his mind curiously blank, unable to look to either side of him, at Manny, who was wiping his face on his sleeve, or Judy, whose shoulders were shaking in quiet sobs. What was wrong with him? Shouldn't he be crying, too? Shouldn't he at least be feeling something?

Victor stayed that way, frozen, going about his regular routine—school, piano practice, meals—like a robot, and it wasn't until a few days later that he thawed. He was on his way to his room after piano practice when he noticed that Donny's bedroom door was open. Inside, a woman dressed all in white stood stripping the bed. Victor thought for a moment that she was a nurse, but instead of a cap, she was wearing a white chrysanthemum in her jet-black hair. She looked up and he recognized her from the pictures on Donny's dresser.

It was Mrs. Sung. Her eyes, swollen and rimmed with red, met his, and somehow his body remembered to bow, showing his respect. He searched her face. Did she know who he was? Had Donny ever mentioned him? He should have also remembered to say, as Ma had taught him at Second Great-Uncle's funeral, "May you restrain your grief and come to accept it." But the only thing that came to him was the urge to confess, to fall to his knees and beg for forgiveness.

He imagined himself telling her everything—about him and Donny and Judy, about their friendship and rivalry. Donny wouldn't have gone in the river that night if he hadn't meddled. If he'd never snooped in Judy's file in the first place, he wouldn't have discovered her secret and been tempted to tell. Why had he looked? Why hadn't he just left it alone?

Standing there, facing Donny's mother, he wanted to do the right thing, to be honest with her and make amends. But how could he? The truth was far too complicated to tell. How much did Mrs. Sung know about her son and his death? Did she know about Judy, or his test results, or his drinking? And how much did she want to know? Victor didn't speak, and neither did Mrs. Sung. After a moment, she gave him a small, formal nod and went back to folding Donny's sheets.

He should have offered to help, but he was afraid he might run into Donny's father, who was probably carrying his son's belongings to their car, and he wouldn't know what to say to him either. Instead, he slunk back to his own room, where he sat listening to Mr. and Mrs. Sung's hushed voices through the wall, not daring to move until they were gone.

Now, weeks later, Victor wondered what Donny had been thinking after he told him about Judy's betrayal and his mask went up. He hadn't expected him to hold it all in—how his positive test took him back to square one, how Judy's negative test set her free. How must it have felt for Donny to see her reach the finish line when he'd slid back to the start? It was so unfair.

Henry was right about one thing; he wasn't a kid anymore. His choices were his own, but their consequences would affect everyone around him. There was nothing he could do to change the past now. He couldn't bring Donny back to life. He couldn't make Judy love him. He couldn't make Ruth stay. But he could go home and help his family.

Victor glanced up at the grandfather clock in the corner of Herb's living room. It was time to meet Judy and Manny. Yesterday, on his way to the chapel, the echoes of laughter and wheels in the covered walkway had reached his ears. For a split second, he thought he could hear their voices, Manny's and Judy's and Donny's, as they'd been just a few short months ago, racing along the same stretch of concrete, dodging the older patients, the doctors, and the sisters, who were slow in their long, heavy robes. Judy on her shiny red Schwinn. Manny on a pair of metal roller skates strapped to his tennis shoes. And Donny on his bike with playing cards stuck in its spokes, snapping like distant gunfire as he pedaled.

Sometimes, when they used to walk together, he'd watch them from behind, Judy slowing down to match Donny's gait. In his mind's eye, he could see again how Manny's long blade-like limbs would pump and relax as he bounded up behind them, leaping onto Donny's broad, unsuspecting back. He could still hear the echo of their whooping laughter.

From a distance now, Victor realized that it wasn't Judy but Donny who'd been at the center of their circle of friends, with the rest of them spinning around him like planets around a sun. But the circle had broken, and now that time was gone.

TWENTY-NINE

Victor was alone in the chapel on his last day at Carville. He wanted to play there one more time, to say goodbye to this room where he'd learned how to make music. When he looked out from the piano bench, the empty, polished pews seemed to hold the memory of the people who'd sat there. Inside him, the familiar switch flipped as his fingertips brushed the keys, then pushed them down, making the tiny hammers pop up and hit the strings in a flurry of sound. The magic of this, no matter how many times he witnessed it, never failed to move him, and he was both there and not, wading in the sea of notes and dissolving into them at the same time. There was no numbness to be found, not in his hands, his body, or his heart. He was feeling it all, everything alive, the music and himself. He played his old favorites, the first pieces he'd felt proud to master—the Chopin Polonaise, "Für Elise," and the *Moonlight* Sonata—before riffing off "Autumn in New York," singing about crowds and clouds, in honor of going home.

When he'd told Mrs. Thorne he was going back to New York for good, she'd blinked and looked at him for a long moment.

"My mother needs me, you see."

"I understand," she'd said, giving his hand a gentle pat. "It's all right. I'll ask the department about teachers for you. I'm sure we have some graduates in New York. And you can count on me for a recommendation when you're ready to apply for a conservatory." Mrs. Thorne had taken off her glasses and was dabbing at the corners of her pale brown eyes with a tissue. "I wish I could keep teaching you myself, but we'll just have to maintain a positive outlook."

If he let it, his brain could keep on buzzing with all his missed notes, missed words, missed chances, but none of it mattered now. He was outside himself and inside the music, listening to its beating heart—or was it his own?—seeing the colors change and changing them, his hands an extension of his mind, his imagination, and his instrument.

Only when he realized that he'd sweated through his shirt did Victor fall back into his body to find Judy and Manny clapping at the pew, where they'd sat so long ago on the night they'd all snuck out to hear him play. When had they come in? In the brief, breathless moment between the final note and the applause, there had been suspended in the air the memory of the first time he'd played a note on this piano, E-flat, as if the present and the past were meeting like a pair of hands, touching their fingertips together. As they kept applauding, he felt his face crack into a bittersweet smile, his mouth a wound.

Afterward, Manny went to softball practice while Victor and Judy walked over to the lake, their place, where they sat side by side on the dock, close enough for their shoulders and legs to touch, close enough for him to smell the sweetness of her hair and the spice of her skin. Funny how people smelled of different things; Henry like a worn leather belt, Ba like tobacco and shirt starch, Ruth like typewriter ink and French perfume. And Ma? He closed his eyes and cast his memory back as a waterthrush chittered at its mate in a nearby tree. Ma smelled like ginger, sandalwood soap, and smoke from the old kitchen stove.

"I still can't believe you're leaving," said Judy, nudging his leg. Now that Donny was gone, she'd be leaving soon, too.

"I know." Victor sighed. "Things have changed at home."

Judy made a sound that Victor couldn't quite interpret, but before she said anything, the smell of rain filled the air. The low rumble of distant thunder announced itself from somewhere upriver and the sky opened up, pocking the surface of the lake. Fat, heavy drops pelted their heads and shoulders, but instead of running for shelter, they stayed, silent and stubborn together in the downpour, watching the rings ripple across the water.

Tipping back her head, Judy let the rain fall over her face. With her eyes closed and her hair slicked back from her broad, clear forehead, Victor thought, as he had since the moment he saw her walking through the trees, that she was the most beautiful girl he'd ever seen. He looked down at himself sitting next to her in the spot where they'd first met, thinking it could be a scene from a movie, a tragic romance, maybe. In that movie, the boy and the girl would kiss, but that didn't happen now. The wind picked up, and a streak of lightning crackling above the pecan trees was answered right away by the thunder's boom. Victor could feel the electricity in the atmosphere.

"Guess we'd better go in," she said, sticking out her tongue to catch the rain.

At their last dinner together, with their hair still damp from the storm, Victor and Judy sat with Manny at their table in the cafeteria, talking and telling the same old jokes, trying to act normal, but Donny's empty chair made it impossible. A sadness hung in the air like an icy hand gripping the nape of Victor's neck, refusing to let go.

Dr. Behr and Sister Laura had told him never to tell anyone on the outside about Carville so he could put it behind him, but why should he? For the rest of the day, he tried to fix every part of it in his mind, to remember how it really was. Springtime was here. Nubs of pale green on the trees. Clouds of gnats like dandelion fluff. Softball season again. Rain, rain, and more rain washing over the ground to expose what had been there all winter—cigarette butts on naked earth, broken bits of Coca-Cola bottles winking when the sun came out.

All day long, people were asking him to write down his address in their little black books—the kids in his class, Tony, Miss Iantha. He accepted the congratulations, the promises to keep in touch, and the parting gifts. Mr. Wang gave him a red envelope stuffed with a five-dollar bill. Herb gave him the Massey Hall concert albums he'd so admired, along with *The Charles Mingus CAT-alog for Toilet Training Your Cat*. Mrs. Thorne gave him several books of sheet music—Mozart, Chopin, Bach, and Scott Joplin.

Later, after curfew, when the three of them snuck back out to the lake with their flashlights, Manny presented him with his prized 1953 Mickey Mantle baseball card.

"Down payment," he insisted when Victor refused to take it. "Now you can't change your mind about getting a place together."

"Here," said Judy, dropping a tiny brass armadillo into the palm of his hand, "so you can take her with you, so you won't forget."

"How could I?" He shone his flashlight on the figurine, careful not to let it fall. "We haven't exchanged addresses yet, you know."

"I don't think we should," she said in a quiet voice.

Until that moment, they'd been avoiding the subject of Donny, tiptoeing around it so as not to spoil this last day together, but now here it was.

"Because you think it was my fault." Victor stared at the armadillo cradled in his hand, at its finely wrought features. He didn't want to look at Judy, but he forced himself.

"Sometimes. And sometimes I think it was my fault, too."

"I'm sorry," said Victor, his voice breaking.

"I know," said Judy. "Me, too."

Victor nodded, his fingers closing around the smooth bit of brass, feeling the warmth it still held from her touch. Then they sat together, the three of them, holding the silence that had fallen between them gently, as if inviting Donny, his absence, to sit with them one last time.

All day, people had been telling Victor they'd see him "out there" or "on the outside," but they didn't say goodbye and neither did he, not to the patients or the staff, and not to Judy and Manny now.

"See you," said Manny when they finally hugged outside their dorms. Victor clapped him hard on the back, echoing his words.

"Good night," he said when Judy moved into his arms. He inhaled the smell of rain and strawberry in her hair, and bit his lip so he wouldn't cry. When she let go, he turned and went inside so he wouldn't have to watch her walk away.

Afterward, he lay in bed, thinking of how he would never see her again and trying to accept it. In the weeks since Donny died, he'd given her space, but he thought if he waited long enough, she might come around. Though she didn't know he'd betrayed her secret to

Donny, he could still see why she blamed him—he certainly blamed himself—and he could understand why she'd want to move on without looking back.

With his itchy wool blanket pulled up to his chin, he watched the now familiar shadows moving across the room that would soon belong to someone else, maybe to someone just like him. Outside, a gust of wind smacked a branch of the magnolia tree against the window, and suddenly, he heard the sound of hail, the sky pelting the glass with tiny pebbles of ice. Groaning, he shoved his pillow over his head.

He thought of the night not long after he arrived when, woken by a heavy rain, he'd ventured out of his room for an extra blanket and Donny had invited him in. His room next door was empty now that his parents had taken all his things. By tomorrow, Victor's room would be empty, too, as if keeping Donny's company. Though his body had been cremated and sent home to be buried in the Sung family plot, in a way, Donny would never leave Carville.

The longer Victor had lived inside the fence, the more distant his life on the outside had begun to feel, like the hint of words on a blackboard after someone had erased them, or the vibration lingering in the air after the final notes of a song had been played. Instead of Technicolor memories, he was left with still images, smudged and blurry, like watercolor paintings left out in the rain. As time washed over them and they continued to fade, he'd gotten more and more afraid of how much he was forgetting, because of how much he'd changed. On the train to Carville, he'd been so worried about everyone in New York moving on without him, but he wasn't afraid of that anymore. He'd moved on as much as his family had, and they would just have to get to know one another again when he got home.

The hail had stopped, and the silence it left behind filled Victor's ears. Giving up on sleep, he pulled on his traveling clothes, a pair of worn dungarees and a well-washed shirt, and sat alone in the dark of predawn until an orderly came to carry his bags to the taxi. The driver was waiting at the entrance. On the way there, Victor could only just make out the shadows of the great live oaks on the avenue and the silhouette of the Big House overlooking it. He got in the taxi, and as it exited the iron gates, the headlights shone against the hexagons of the hurricane fence that had contained him these past two years.

Surely there should have been something more to mark this moment, some sign of turning from a leper back into a young man, from diseased to healthy, quarantined to free. But there was just this, the quiet return of the journey he'd taken to Carville as a very sick boy, witnessed by no one who cared. The taxi passed the hole in the fence and accelerated down the River Road, carrying Victor away.

In New Orleans, he bought his ticket and boarded the train. After getting to Tuscaloosa by lunch, it would arrive in Atlanta by evening, and then it would be all Pullman sleeper cars all the way to Grand Central. By the time he woke up the next morning, he'd be in New York again. At home, things would seem almost like they'd been when he left. Almost, but also not at all. The city would be the same, and the old neighborhood, and the laundry. Henry would be there, and so would Ba. But not Ruth. Victor knew now that the note she'd tucked in her last care package had been her way of saying goodbye. He couldn't say she'd lied to him, exactly, but she hadn't told the truth either.

Once, years ago, on a golden summer evening, during a stickball game with the boys on Barker Avenue, Victor had looked up at Ruth's apartment building, where she happened to be sitting at her window, watching him. She'd smiled and waved, then lifted her chin so that her face caught the light of the late sunset just as the street lamps switched on. The way she'd looked in that moment, all lit up, with that smile on her face gave him a feeling he couldn't put into words. All he knew was that he'd wanted it to last forever. Did Ruth remember seeing him that evening, and if she did, did she remember it in the same way?

He would have asked her when he got home, but she was gone, vanished into thin air, and for this, Victor felt an anger that was all the more terrible for its failure to cover up his sadness. He'd loved her, though he'd never said it, and he loved her still. He'd probably never stop. And he'd never stop feeling guilty for missing her so much and wanting her to come back. She'd been like a mother to him, but what was he supposed to do with that now that his real mother was on her way?

Ever since he left China, he'd been dreaming of being with Ma again, but he hadn't thought of what it would cost. Now that it was really happening, it seemed surreal. The truth was, he couldn't even imagine what it would be like to have Ma in the States. At this point, he'd lived without her longer than he'd lived with her. It would be a big change, but he'd managed change before, not once but twice. Like Ruth said in her note, he'd figure it out.

Now, on the northbound train, it occurred to him how strange it was to be seated in the main coach section with everyone else. How strange to be able to go to the dining car for meals with no one thinking anything of it. Rolling the little brass armadillo between his fingers, he felt the bumps of its scales and the points of its snout and tail. On the outside, he was the same as anyone else, but on the inside, he knew he was different, and nothing, not silence, not test results, not a clean bill of health, could take away the things that had happened to him.

Just before sunset, somewhere in South Carolina, between Clemson and Greenville, Victor stared out at the sky, remembering how the clouds had moved over the tree-covered mountains back home in China. How they'd cast shadows across the emerald green, making shade from the relentless southern sun. In the flatness of the Louisiana landscape, he'd longed for those hills, though his life in Toisan was a distant memory. The "-san" part of the name meant mountain, after all. He would never forget as long as he remembered where he came from. He came from those mountains as much as he came from the Bronx, and now he was from Carville, too. A part of it would always be inside him.

ACKNOWLEDGMENTS

For telling me his story and letting me tell mine:
  Walter Chin

For turning belief into reality:
  Jamie Carr
  Nadxieli Nieto
  Kukuwa Ashun
  Mary Beth Constant

For their invaluable research assistance:
  Elizabeth Schexnyder
  Richard W. Truman
  Anthony Sanchez, Jr.
  José Ramirez, Jr.
  Ryan Alexander-Tanner

For fanning the spark:
  Robin Jennings
  Jill DiDonato
  Melissa Febos

Eleanor Stafford
John Nathan

For their careful reading:
  Mark Davidov
  Cari Luna
  Rene Denfeld
  Lidia Yuknavitch
  Alex Segura
  Pam Fessler
  Erika Wurth
  Annie Cheng
  Elizabeth Harding Snodgrass

For being the ideal eye, ear, mirror, and "friend of mind":
  Veronica Davidov

For childcare and domestic support:
  Kam Fong Chin

For their patience and encouragement:
  Madeleine Chin-Tanner
  Lucille Chin-Tanner

For everything:
  Tyler Chin-Tanner

ABOUT THE AUTHOR

Wendy Chin-Tanner is the author of the poetry collections *Turn* and *Anyone Will Tell You,* coauthor of the graphic novel *American Terrorist,* editor of *Embodied: An Intersectional Feminist Comics Poetry Anthology,* and copublisher of A Wave Blue World, an independent publishing company for graphic novels. Born and raised in New York City, she lives in the Hudson Valley with her family. *King of the Armadillos* is her first novel.